The Perfect Fit

OTHER BOOKS AND AUDIO BOOKS
BY MICHELLE ASHMAN BELL:

A Candle in the Window

An Enduring Love

An Unexpected Love

Finding Paradise

A Forever Love

Latter-day Spies: Spyhunt

Love Lights the Way

Pathway Home

Perfect Timing

Timeless Moments

Without a Flaw

Yesterday's Love

A Modest Proposal

Hometown Girl

a novel by

Michele Ashman Bell

Covenant Communications, Inc.

Cover image: *Vintage Girl with Romantic Gift* © face2faith, courtesy of iStockphoto.com

Published by Covenant Communications, Inc.
American Fork, Utah

Printed in the United States of America.
First Printing: May 2011

17 16 15 14 13 12 11 10 9 8 7 6 5 4 3 2 1

ISBN-13: 978-1-60861-233-8

To my daughter-in-law Megan. I love you as if you were my own, and I'm so proud of the wonderful wife and mother you are. You are such a blessing to our family.

Acknowledgments

I'd like to acknowledge the outstanding efforts of Mothers Without Borders and the remarkable work they are doing in Zambia, Africa. My thanks to my daughter Kendyl for her sacrifice and service in Africa and for sharing with me the experience that changed her life.

Prologue

The boy lay on the floor, clutching his teddy bear in one hand. His face was completely numb, and it was more and more difficult to breathe. He knew he was bleeding on the floor, but his mom wouldn't be mad. She'd do her best to get the stains out, just like she had all the other times. And right now, stains were the least of her problems. This was the third night in a row his father had come home in a drunken rage, but tonight seemed especially violent—even for him.

A wave of nausea came over the boy, and he steeled himself against the urge to vomit. The blows to his head and face had left him dizzy and disoriented. He couldn't move his jaw, and one of his eyes was swelling shut. A tingling in his right side had gradually grown into a white-hot pain shooting down his back—but he didn't have time to worry about that now. His mom was taking a beating now, too, and she needed his help. He usually didn't interfere—his father outweighed him by two hundred pounds, and all he'd ever accomplished in the past was to secure further injuries for himself—but there was more fear in his mother's cries of pain tonight than he'd ever heard before.

The boy felt the fear in his chest tighten, making it hard to breathe. If something happened to his mother, he'd be left alone with his father. And he would rather die than have that happen.

Struggling to stand and nearly passing out from the new waves of pain, he took in several deep breaths to help calm the nausea. To his relief, it subsided enough for him to push himself off the spot on the floor he called a bed.

Steadying himself on his feet, he wobbled to the door and opened it a crack. He flinched at the heightened sounds of violence coming from his parents' bedroom. Part of him wanted to run down the stairs and out the front door, away, somewhere else, somewhere safe. But he knew of no such place. His grandparents lived far away, and the only other adult he felt comfortable with, Mrs. Nelson, his fifth grade teacher, lived a few miles out of town.

He briefly considered calling the police then just as quickly shut the idea out of his mind. He'd done it once before, and all that had happened was an officer being dispatched to investigate—then leaving just as quickly when his mother had been too frightened to say anything against her husband. The repercussions had been severe. His father had been enraged. Besides, he doubted he could even move his jaw to speak at the moment.

His mother's pleas for forgiveness for whatever she'd done wrong echoed through the hallway and brought on more of his father's vengeance. The boy cringed as he heard the despicable names his father called her.

Many times the boy's mother had tried to tell him that his father really was a good man at heart, but the boy didn't know how that could be true. If he were a good man, why would he beat them, why would he neglect them and subject them to the fear and horror that was their family's existence?

No, he told himself as he stood in the doorway, clutching the frame so tightly he felt his thumbnail chip under the pressure. He *hated* his father. The man was a beast who controlled them with intimidation and abuse. And the boy was tired of feeling frightened and hungry in the place he was supposed to be safe.

"John, no, please. I'll do better. I promise. I don't know what I was thinking. You're right, I shouldn't have answered the door. I didn't know it was the neighbor, though. I didn't talk to him for more than ten seconds—I told him he'd have to ask you to borrow the ladder. That's all, I swear."

"You're lying. You think you can do better than me, Lillian? You're old, ugly, and stupid, and no one would ever look twice at you. You're lucky I don't just kill you here and now to put us both out of our misery."

The boy heard a dull thud, and his mother let out a cry of pain. "John, please!"

His father laughed, a guttural, menacing sound.

Shaking and focusing hard so that he wouldn't pass out, the boy crept toward the bedroom door. If he could create a distraction, maybe his father would leave his mother alone and fall asleep or pass out like he usually did.

Looking around, he saw his father's shoes in the hallway, and an idea sprang to mind. It knew it might be the last idea he ever had, but he had to do something fast.

Grabbing the shoes, he threw them both down the stairs as hard as he could so they hit the front door, the bang reverberating up the stairwell. Then he rushed back to his room.

However, before he could even fully turn around, his father shot out into the hallway like a crazed bull out of the chute. "What was that?"

So frightened he was unable to think or speak, the boy froze.

"What did you do?" his father yelled, his eyes wide and unfocused with drink and rage.

The boy couldn't speak even if he'd wanted to. He tried to move his jaw, but all that resulted was another flash of white-hot pain.

Raising an iron fist, his father looked at the boy, his face growing redder by the second and his lips curling back like a mad dog's. "I told you to go to your room. Do you want me to make that ugly face of yours look even worse?"

As his father took one step toward him, something inside the boy snapped. A surge of adrenaline threw him into action, and before he knew it he was charging. With mute rage, he rammed into his Redwood-sized father.

Taken completely by surprise, his father lurched backward, teetering on the top step. The boy held his breath as his father seemed to regain his footing, his shocked expression settling back into a snarl.

But then, just as the boy was certain he was moments away from receiving the beating that would end his life, his father fell. As if in slow motion, the man launched backward down the stairs, the banister trembling under the weight of his body like a wrecking ball against a house of sticks. Head over heels, his body contorted freakishly then broke through the thin spiral banister and landed with a resounding boom on the ground, his head cocked at a ninety-degree angle, his eyes rolled back in his head.

The boy looked at the mangled human being below, watching for any sign of life, any chance his father had survived. And after several moments, when there was no movement, not even a slight rise or fall in his chest, the boy knew with a certainty that his father was dead.

And if he had been physically able, he would have smiled.

Chapter 1

"Amber Jeffries is dead," Chloe said quietly, looking up from the screen of her cell phone. Among the Butterfly Box girls, Chloe was known for her tender heart, and she blinked at the sudden tears in her eyes as the reality of the message began to sink in.

"Amber Jeffries from high school?" Lauryn asked in surprise as she removed a shopping bag from her suitcase. She'd brought everyone a gift from her design shop.

"The one who was on cheer with Ava," Andi added as she pulled her hair into a ponytail in preparation for her morning jog. The southern Utah weather was still pleasant, but even in June it paid to get out early, before the day got too warm.

"Not *that* Amber Jeffries," Jocelyn stated, as if saying it would make it true. "Right, Chloe?" Jocelyn finished lacing up her shoes. Andi had tried to get all of the girls to go running with her, but Jocelyn was the only one who would join her on the trail outside their hotel room. One of the things she loved about coming home to St. George was being able to run outside with the beautiful red rock scenery surrounding her.

She squeezed a glob of sunscreen into her hand and tossed the tube to Jocelyn. In the past she'd been a slave to tanning beds, working out, and strict dietary habits. But over the last few years, she'd come to grips with her eating issues and was more accepting of herself and her body. This had given her a greater amount of personal confidence and inner peace.

"The message is from Robin Frandson," Chloe said, holding up her cell phone and swiping at a tear that had fallen. "She was Amber's best friend in high school. I doubt she'd tell me this if it weren't *that* Amber."

"Shut up! That's crazy," Andi said. She pulled her ponytail through the back of her Lakers cap.

"She's really dead?" Jocelyn asked.

Lauryn's brow furrowed, and she narrowed her eyes slightly. "Did Robin say how she died?" She sat down on the bed and let the shopping bag slide to the floor.

"No. I'll ask her." Chloe entered the text then stared at the phone, waiting.

"I never really got to know Amber very well in high school," Andi said then shrugged. "I know this sounds rude, but I never felt like I was good enough for her."

"Whenever she and Ava got together, they acted like that," Lauryn said, her voice void of expression, as though she still couldn't believe it was true. "I felt it too."

"I was friends with Amber in grade school," Jocelyn said, "but she phased me out of her life when we got to junior high. She would still talk to me every once in a while, but we never hung out—unless she was with Ava."

"She intimidated the daylights out of me," Andi said.

"Me too," Chloe said, her voice steadier. "It's weird to think that she and Ava are both—" She stopped when her phone buzzed. She read the message then looked up, her expression lined with concern. "Whoa."

"What is it, Chloe?" Lauryn asked.

Chloe swallowed.

"What did she say?" Andi added.

Chloe looked at the message again.

"Chloe?" Jocelyn said, raising an eyebrow.

"Did Robin say how she died?" Lauryn asked.

Chloe nodded slowly, the color draining from her face. "She was murdered. Strangled in her apartment."

* * *

Although the news of their classmate's death cast a pall over the weekend, the girls did their best to enjoy the day together. This was their special weekend, the one they each looked forward to every year. The Butterfly Girls reunion was a chance for all of them to return to their hometown of St. George, Utah, where they'd all grown up together. Some years they changed locations, but coming home was as much a part of the experience as being together.

Ever since that first summer when Ava had passed away in the car accident on graduation day, they had reunited, sometimes traveling great distances to do so. Occasionally one of the girls couldn't make it, like Emma this year, but most of the time everyone came. The ritual was important to each of them—renewing and treasuring the special bond they'd shared growing up, one forged even more deeply after Ava's death. And though the festivities and locale changed occasionally, a few traditions never did—the most important being the Butterfly Box.

After a day of shopping and a late lunch at Durango's, their favorite Mexican restaurant, they returned to the hotel room they all shared. Although it was crowded to have everyone stay in one room, that was the way they'd always done it.

As she entered the room, Lauryn kicked her shoes off, which hit the wall with a sudden thump. Chloe raised her hand to her mouth and let out a sharp breath, turning to look at Lauryn in surprise.

"Chloe, you have to calm down," she said gently, seeing her friend's tense expression. "You've been jumpy all day." She reached for Chloe's hand and firmly held it in both of hers. "It's terrible what happened to Amber. But we are not in danger."

"I think I need to get home and be with my girls," Chloe said, turning away. She was the only Butterfly Box girl with children—and, as a consequence, her girls were spoiled rotten by their mother's four friends, who were affectionately called "aunts."

"There's no reason to think that just because Ava and Amber knew each other that their deaths were related," Jocelyn reasoned. "It's been fourteen years since Ava died. They aren't connected. I'm sure of it."

"I agree," Andi said firmly. "Unless there's more to all this, we can't freak out about it."

"Wait a second—wasn't there another girl in our class killed a few years back?" Lauryn said suddenly. "You know, what's her name?"

"Jessica Norton," Andi replied, remembering, and glancing at Chloe to gauge her reaction.

"Yeah, Jessica," Lauryn said.

"I thought that was a car accident," Jocelyn added.

"It was." Andi tried to keep the tone in her voice light. She didn't want to add to Chloe's concerns since she was already having a hard time as it was. "Anyway, I agree with Jocelyn. We're trying to see a connection where there isn't one. It's sad, but everyone dies—sometimes while they're still young. There's nothing more to it than that."

"You're right," Chloe said, pulling in a long breath. "I think I'm feeling vulnerable because of Roger. This whole restraining order thing has got me freaked out."

"He hasn't bothered you lately, has he?" Andi asked, saddened that Chloe and Roger's marriage was not only over but that he was causing her and her two young daughters so much grief. Wasn't it enough that he'd chosen porn over his family? Why did he think he deserved to have the girls live with him? He wasn't reasonable anymore. He was a completely different person than the man Chloe had married.

"Not lately, but the last time I saw him, he was pretty . . . angry," Chloe said softly, looking up at Andi.

Shaking her head, Andi wondered for the umpteenth time how her friend had gotten such a rotten break. She still remembered Chloe and Roger's wedding—they'd been the perfect couple, with a fairy-tale romance and a beautiful wedding. Roger had been Chloe's knight in shining armor—her prince, her hero. And all of the Butterfly Box girls had loved him—even Emma, who didn't like *anyone,* especially her friends' boyfriends. But when Roger had been trapped by pornography, his addiction had turned everyone's world upside down. Watching their marriage fall apart over the past few years had further convinced Andi that she was never going to find the right guy.

And yet, if she was honest with herself, it was what she wanted most in the world. As she looked at her friends, she had to admit she was jealous that Lauryn and Jocelyn both seemed blissfully happy. Emma—well, Emma was another story. She was still living in Greece with her new husband, and whenever anyone talked to her, she painted the picture of a fairy tale—going on and on about how beautiful their life together was, especially now that they were expecting a baby. But if Andi had learned anything over the past years, it was that fairy tales didn't often come true.

"I don't think I'll ever get married again," Chloe said after a moment of silence. "I don't know how I could ever trust another man."

Lauryn slipped her arm over Chloe's shoulders and gave her a squeeze. "You can't think that way. Not all men are like Roger. There are good, honorable men out there who would treat you like a queen."

"I think you two got the last good men," Chloe said with a half smile, nodding toward Lauryn and Jocelyn.

"Hey, don't forget, I never, *ever* expected to find a man like Jack," Jocelyn said. "That's how it seems to work out, though. Don't give up."

"It's hard not to," Andi answered for Chloe. "I know you have to kiss a lot of frogs to find your prince, but I'm going to get warts on my lips if I kiss any more."

Lauryn pulled a face. "That is a sick image."

"Agreed," Jocelyn said with a shudder. "Can you imagine how awful that would be?"

"See!" Andi exclaimed. "What's the point? Maybe we should just become roommates, Chloe. We can take care of each other in our old age. We can play cards at night and learn how to crochet."

"I'd love to have you as a roommate, and so would the girls." Chloe lifted a shoulder and smiled. "And I've always wanted to learn how to crochet."

Andi noticed the worried expression on Lauryn's face. "What's wrong?" she asked her.

"Well," she paused, "I mean, you can't give up. You can't just stop trying."

"Why can't I? Been there, done that." Chloe shook her head and waved her thumb like a hitchhiker. "No more men."

"But—"

"Listen, you guys," Andi interrupted, "it's not like this is the way we wanted our lives to turn out."

"Amen," Chloe said fervently.

"It's just the harsh reality of the situation, that's all." Andi sat back and folded her arms across her chest.

"So answer me this, then. Why did you sign up to be on that show, *Looking for Mrs. Right*?" Lauryn challenged.

"Yeah," Jocelyn said. "Why bother, if that's the way you feel about men?"

Andi swallowed and attempted to sound nonchalant, slightly embarrassed she'd told everyone about signing up for the show—although she could hardly avoid it, since she would be leaving for Hawaii the day after the reunion weekend. "I'm just going to have fun and to get exposure," she said defensively. "I'm not expecting to make it very far in the competition."

"What!" Lauryn exclaimed, her eyebrows shooting up. "I can't believe you said that. You're going to be great on the show, Andi. You have never looked more beautiful in your life!"

"It's true," Jocelyn said. "You look healthy and fit; your skin glows! I've always envied your skin and your cute little turned-up nose."

Andi covered her nose with her hand.

"I'd kill for your legs," Chloe said. "They're about six inches longer than mine."

"Okay, stop! You are embarrassing me," Andi said.

"Face it, Andi," Lauryn said, "you're beautiful, funny, accomplished, interesting . . . everything a man could want."

"Apparently not," Andi said dryly. "Otherwise I wouldn't need to be going on the show, would I?"

Jocelyn spoke up. "Let me ask you this. What if something *does* happen with you and *Looking for Mrs. Right*?"

She shrugged. "I haven't really thought too much about it," she answered truthfully. "I'm certainly not getting my hopes up."

"But—" Jocelyn started.

"Even if some guy did decide he liked me, the fact that he isn't a member would pose a huge problem." She turned to Lauryn. "You really think I'm interesting?"

Lauryn laughed. "Yes, I do. You've had a fascinating career, you've accomplished so many great things and traveled to so many interesting places, spending all that time in Africa and doing all that humanitarian work. You've always got something new and interesting going on."

Chloe and Jocelyn agreed.

"Well . . . thanks," Andi said, grateful for the ego boost they were providing. "And I actually do have something new to tell you about."

"See!" Lauryn exclaimed. "Just like I said."

"What is it?" Chloe asked.

"Remember how I told you I had submitted a book about my experience with my eating disorder? Well, I just found out it's getting published."

The three friends erupted with excitement.

Andi continued, encouraged by their enthusiasm. "Kirk, my manager, really thinks it's gonna do well, but I still worry. Do you guys really think people will buy my book and read my story?"

"Are you kidding?" Lauryn asked. "I've learned a lot about marketing lately, and for you to come clean on your eating disorder and how you overcame it, especially since you struggled with all of it as an adult, is going to appeal to a lot of people."

"The book is going to include a meal plan and cookbook, so hopefully it'll appeal to readers on different levels. My manager is even hoping to set me up on some popular daytime talk shows." She looked up at her friends, whose gazes were filled with excitement and hope for her. Then she added, "Admitting to others, especially you guys, that I actually had an eating problem was the hardest thing I've ever done, but it was also very empowering. If I can help others, it'll be worth it." She paused again, fighting a sudden flood of emotion. "Sorry." She cleared her throat and blinked her eyes to clear her tears.

Chloe reached forward and patted her on the knee. "It's okay, sweetie. Go ahead and let it out."

Andi nodded and laughed with embarrassment. "I'm good with this. Really, I am."

"When will it be released?" Lauryn asked.

"Soon! It's all happening so fast. Kirk thinks it'll be September or October. They're working overtime to get it out as soon as they can. As soon as I know more details, I'll let all of you know."

"I am so proud of you and what you are doing. This is really big," Lauryn said. "Since your book is also a cookbook, maybe you can go on the *Rachael Ray Show.* After that you'll probably get all sorts of requests for appearances. You'll let me design your wardrobe for your appearances, won't you?"

"Wardrobe? Man, I haven't even thought about that," Andi said as she found a napkin from last night's pizza run and wiped her eyes.

"Of course! We have to create your brand, really make you iconic. Who knows what this could lead to," Lauryn said.

"Well, yes, then, of course you can design it. I wouldn't have anyone else."

"I'll get Cooper to help me out, too. He's a great stylist."

Andi smiled. "Cooper?" She hadn't seen him for so long. She wondered if he even remembered who she was.

"Yes," Lauryn said. "He'll flip when I tell him about it."

"That means I'll need to come to New York for fittings and stuff?" Andi asked.

"It does," Lauryn said happily. "New York is the perfect place to start your book tour. After your appearance on *Rachael Ray* to kick it off, of course."

"I'll definitely need my personal hair and makeup stylist with me, don't you think?" She turned to Chloe.

Chloe placed her hand on her chest, and her mouth dropped open. "You want me to come with you?"

"If you can," Andi said. "I need all the help I can get. Can you get away?"

"Let me just say, the only good thing about Roger right now is his mom and dad. I absolutely love them. I couldn't have gotten through this without them. They adore their granddaughters and have promised to do all they can to help make up for Roger's mistakes. I'm sure they would help me out."

Andi noticed Jocelyn's turned-down mouth and sad eyes.

"Joss, you can come too, can't you? It won't be right without you there," Andi invited.

"Really?" Jocelyn's eyes lit up. "I would love to go." She clapped her hands together.

Then Andi remembered Emma. "I feel bad that Emma can't be with us. I miss her so much." She sighed, still feeling slightly betrayed by her friend's actions. Emma had shocked them all by marrying her Greek boyfriend without telling even one of her friends. And then, with hardly a good-bye, she had moved to Greece. "I bet she looks so cute with a baby bump."

"I bet so too," Lauryn said.

"That stupid Nickolas anyway," Chloe said. "Why did he have to take her so far away?"

"I wish I knew if she were really happy," Jocelyn said.

"Maybe we need to go pay her a visit," Lauryn suggested.

"We should!" Jocelyn agreed. "Actually, when Jack and I go to Tuscany for the trip I was telling you about, we could see about going on to Greece. I have a baby gift I haven't gotten around to mailing her anyway."

"I'm so jealous!" Andi said with a dreamy sigh. "I've always wanted to go to Italy and Greece."

"You'll just have to settle for Hawaii with the most eligible bachelor in the USA," Lauryn told her with a smile.

"Six weeks in Hawaii!" Chloe shut her eyes and sighed. "You are the luckiest girl I know."

"I'll probably be back in one week, right after the first cut," Andi said. "Still, it's a week in paradise."

"I looked at the link you e-mailed," Lauryn said, ignoring Andi's first comment. "That place you're going to stay is incredible."

"Wait, what link? I didn't see a link," Chloe said.

"You didn't? I'm sure I sent it to your account," Andi said.

"Oh! Didn't I tell you? I had to change my e-mail address," Chloe said. "I was getting all sorts of weird spam and junk mail. I'll send you my new address so you can send me the link. So where's the swanky place you're staying?"

"It's at the Makua Plantation Estate on Kauai," Andi said. "That's where *Looking for Mrs. Right* is going to be filmed. I guess they have all these cottages on the estate and then several mansions. It's an old sugar-cane plantation that's been turned into a spa and resort."

"You really are the luckiest girl I know," Chloe said.

"You should see the guy who's looking for Mrs. Right," Lauryn said, grinning. "He's the heir to the Makua cane sugar fortune—and he is *gorgeous*."

Chloe and Andi looked at each other with amusement.

"Hey," Lauryn said with a shrug, "I'm just sayin'."

"It's true, though," Andi said. "I have to admit, he's very good-looking, in pictures anyway. Who knows what he's like in person."

"It all sounds pretty perfect to me," Lauryn said. "And you've always said you wanted to live in Hawaii."

"I know, and at one time I also said I wanted to climb Mt. Everest—and there's not enough money in the world to pay me to do that!" Andi stated matter-of-factly.

Jocelyn laughed. "Why did you ever say that in the first place?"

"Don't you remember? I was dating Garrett the Granola Guy, as you all affectionately named him. He was big into mountain climbing." She giggled as she remembered. Garrett had certainly been good-looking, but it had required a little work to relate to him.

"Triple G!" Lauryn exclaimed. "Whatever happened to him?"

"He's in a wheelchair. He fell, climbing," Andi said. "I think I told you about it."

"That's right—I'd forgotten. That is so sad," Chloe said, frowning.

"It is, but he's doing really well. He's a motivational speaker now. He's actually pretty cool," Andi said.

"Why don't you hook back up with him?" Jocelyn asked.

"He's also married. His wife is a former beauty queen. Miss Texas or something. I'm not sure." Andi remembered reading about his wedding and wondering if she'd missed out on him. He was a member of the Church, but he wasn't active anymore—and that wasn't what she wanted in a husband.

A loud growl from Chloe's stomach made them all turn and stare at her then burst out laughing.

"Are we going to go out to dinner or what?" she said, rubbing her stomach. "I'm starving."

"Me too," Andi said, glad to change the topic. She hated having all her friends trying to help her with her love life—or, more accurately, her *non*-love life. They had good intentions, she realized, but did they really think she hadn't given love her best shot? It just wasn't in the cards for her.

The four girls left the hotel room, and, to Andi's relief, the discussion moved to more pleasant topics like sushi, chocolate, and shoe shopping.

* * *

The traditional ceremony of opening the Butterfly Box and taking turns by sharing the items each girl had placed in the box years earlier felt empty because of Emma's absence. Chloe's rhinestone hair clippie had a broken clasp. Jocelyn's secret white box had finally been opened, and she had found the love of her life and finally moved forward. Lauryn's crown didn't seem to sparkle like it once had, and Andi's bag of Tootsie Rolls didn't get devoured like usual. In fact, the candies had gotten so hard that none of the girls even wanted to eat them.

Andi had been given the box to take with her and keep for the year, until the next reunion. She'd had it before and knew that the bond of sisterhood and strength that came into her life from knowing her friends were praying for her and thinking of her would help her, especially as she embarked on a new journey. Her friends were there for her, and with their support, she could face the unknown.

After the Butterfly Box ceremony, everyone else crashed while watching *Sabrina,* but Andi didn't feel the least bit tired. Her brain wouldn't shut off. Grumbling under her breath, she finally pulled out her laptop and decided to work on the final contestant information for *Looking for Mrs. Right.* It needed to be in a week before she arrived for the show, and that meant tomorrow. Now was as good a time as any.

Most of the questions on the original application for acceptance required basic information, nothing too revealing. But this final questionnaire contained much more personal information. *Tell us about your past relationships. Were you ever engaged? Would you accept a proposal?*

How should I know? Andi thought, feeling her cheeks redden slightly. Luckily, she'd never officially been engaged. She'd been proposed to once before, but rings had never been exchanged.

She shuddered just thinking about how close she'd gotten to marrying Oscar. Clearly, looking back at her dating life, there were red flags all over the place with each and every guy. Her problem was she never saw them until she either got dumped or got slapped upside the head with reality. Thankfully, thus far it had always happened before it was too late.

She quickly typed in her answers and moved on. The producers already had her personal information so that they could do a background check, and she'd sent in her personality-type test and her three pictures—the least attractive of which was being used on the show's website. Of course.

All she had left now was the *All About You* portion of the questionnaire.

The questions that asked what her favorite date in her hometown would be and what her favorite romantic date would be made her laugh. Her idea of a great date wasn't exactly typical fare. She cringed a little at the idea of getting dressed up and having an elegant dinner at an expensive restaurant and going out to the theater or opera. She would much rather play tennis, take a picnic lunch up to the mountains, or go scuba diving. Or do something crazy like go up in a hot-air balloon or go bungee jumping. She shrugged as she entered the information. This was Andi, like it or not.

On the final page she was asked to disclose any and all personal information that the producers needed to be aware of, if in the event it surfaced unexpectedly, such as drug use, inappropriate photos or activities, legal issues, or history of STDs.

It felt good to answer no to all of the questions and have nothing embarrassing to confess to. *Unless they count stupidity when it comes to the guys I've dated,* she thought idly. That was her biggest flaw.

The only skeleton she had in her closet was her eating disorder, but she felt confident she had brought that issue under control and, as evidence, was even putting her story into print in her cookbook. Yet despite the fact that she was in a very healthy place, both physically and emotionally, she knew her disorder would be something she would deal with all of her life. And she was okay with that. She knew now how to get the help she needed whenever she slipped.

Hitting SEND on the e-mail containing her questionnaire took a slight weight off her shoulders, and she blew out a breath of air, glad she was done. She knew it was unlikely that going on this ridiculous show would help her achieve what she was after. But she also didn't feel she was being dishonest for her intent to go on the show. She wasn't opposed to meeting the love of her life; it was just that she lacked any faith that it could ever happen.

A message appeared telling her she had several new e-mails. The first one was from her manager, Kirk.

> *Everything is set for the show. I've taken care of all the arrangements and have attached your flight information and packing list. While you're there you can use your downtime to work on your next cookbook. I'm excited about your outline and ideas. I have a good feeling about all that's in store for you, Andi.*
>
> *Let me know when you arrive in Hawaii. Aloha! And good luck.*

She smiled. Kirk was her biggest fan and advocate. The publisher had told him they wanted Andi to do another book, with recipes and workout advice, and she'd already started on it.

The next message was from an unfamiliar name, but that wasn't surprising. Even though her workout videos were several years old, she still got a fair amount of fan mail and was determined to respond to all of it personally.

> *So, how does it feel to be a famous celebrity? I guess you think you're pretty hot stuff now, don't you? Well, I just hope you get what you deserve. Oh, wait, actually, I know you will. Aloha.*

A chill ran up her spine as she read the last words. Was it just because it was late and they'd all been freaked out by Amber's death today, or did that sound like a threat?

She read the e-mail again, knowing somehow that it wasn't the late night or her emotions messing with her. She was sure of it.

Chapter 2

"That's so creepy," Lauryn said. "I've had my share of rude e-mails and letters, but I've never gotten a threat like that."

"My manager is looking into it. He says it's probably harmless, but he is going to check it out. Besides, I'm going to be out of contact with anyone for a few weeks, so hopefully Kirk will get it taken care of. He takes good care of me," Andi said.

"Here," Jocelyn said, handing the Butterfly Box to Andi. "Don't forget this."

Andi took the box but paused for a few moments, running her fingers across the smooth jade butterfly inlay. "I really don't feel good about taking this," she said hesitantly.

"What? Why?" Jocelyn asked. "It's your turn, and you have a lot going on. You need it."

"I don't need it as badly as Chloe," she said quietly, glancing surreptitiously across the room. Chloe was blow-drying her hair and wasn't listening.

"Chloe said she's had her turn and refuses to take it again," Lauryn reminded her. "You haven't had it for four years. Just take it. I mean, we're all going to pray hard for Chloe anyway, right?"

"Right," Andi said, and Jocelyn agreed.

"Keep it," Lauryn said. "You have a lot happening in your life right now. You should have it."

"All right," she conceded reluctantly, "but I think maybe it's time to have two boxes."

"Or maybe each of us should have our own box," Jocelyn joked.

"That's not such a bad idea," Lauryn agreed, reaching down to grab a pair of socks out of her suitcase.

"Except I don't know if we could ever find anything quite like this," Jocelyn said. "It's not like my grandma got it at Wal-Mart."

"Got what at Wal-Mart?" Chloe asked, winding the cord around her blow-dryer as she joined them.

"We were just saying that maybe we all need our own Butterfly Box," Andi told her. "I really wish you'd take it instead of me."

Chloe's face brightened with her trademark winning smile. "It's your turn, sweetie. Besides, I'm feeling good about things." She shrugged and wrinkled her nose. "I think the dark cloud has lifted."

"Did you accidentally take some of my allergy medicine?" Jocelyn teased. Chloe laughed. "No. I just woke up feeling better about the future. I don't know why, but I'm going to enjoy the feeling while it lasts."

"It's good to see you smile," Jocelyn said.

"Thanks, hon. This weekend was just what I needed." Chloe stepped forward and enveloped Jocelyn in a bear hug and embraced Andi and Lauryn as well.

As they finished packing their suitcases, everyone chatted, filling one another in on the details of their lives that hadn't been discussed yet.

Jocelyn filled everyone in on more details of her and Jack's upcoming trip to Tuscany—and promised to try and find a way to Greece to see Emma.

To everyone's excitement, Lauryn announced that she'd found a highly recommended fertility specialist. She and her husband, Jace, had been trying, without success, to start a family, and a few months earlier, Lauryn had told the other girls in an e-mail that she would be looking into fertility treatments. And, although she was nervous, she was hopeful that taking this step would allow her and Jace to finally start their family.

Chloe began planning out loud for her trip to New York to help with Lauryn's preview, and everyone quickly joined in, already excited about what they would do, where they would eat, and how much fun they would have. They all decided to arrange the trip to New York for fall fashion week in September, when Lauryn would launch her new line.

Andi hoped the debut would coincide with her book release, but then again she loved New York City and wouldn't mind staying for both or having to travel there twice. And anyway, any excuse to see her beloved friends would be well worth the journey.

When the time came for the Butterfly Girls to part ways, it was, as usual, a tearful event. But behind everyone's tears were smiles and laughter as they embraced and promised to keep in touch until they would see one another again in New York.

"Listen, you guys," Lauryn said, "I know that there have been some weird things happening. Maybe it's coincidence, or maybe there really is something creepy going on. But just in case, let's all take extra precautions to be safe."

"I agree," Chloe said.

"If anything strange happens, we need to let each other know about it," Jocelyn added.

"Good idea," Andi said. "Until we know what's going on for sure, we need to keep each other posted on any weird happenings."

They spent the next few minutes giving farewell hugs and saying their good-byes then left in a flurry so flights wouldn't be missed.

Andi hung back, watching each of her friends drive away from the hotel; Chloe was dropping Jocelyn and Lauryn off at the airport and then driving back to her home in Cedar City. Andi was spending the night at her parents' house then would fly back to Los Angeles in the morning.

As Andi made the drive to her parents' house, she said a silent prayer for each of her friends, including Emma, whom they had desperately missed that weekend. She frowned, wondering if it was possible that Emma really was as happy as she insisted. Andi didn't know what she would do being so far away from her friends—without them, she didn't know how she would ever get through the challenges of life.

The thought of having the Butterfly Box in her possession filled her with warmth. It represented the faith and prayers of loved ones in her behalf, and she felt more confidence and courage to face whatever life handed her knowing that they were channeling an extra measure of their love toward her. She didn't know what the future held, but she was ready to meet it head on.

* * *

"Hi, Kirk, can you hold on a second?"

Andi readjusted her bag on her shoulder and scanned her surroundings until she found a quiet corner of the bustling airport. She was leaving for the reality show and had arrived plenty early that morning, not wanting to risk being late, and so she still had about ten minutes until her flight to Hawaii would board.

Seeing a group of unoccupied chairs near her boarding gate, she quickly made her way toward them then took a steadying breath. When she had woken up that Monday morning to finish packing her last-minute items, she had momentarily wondered if she'd been crazy to get involved with this show. And yet, as she forced herself to eat a piece of toast and some fruit to calm her rumbling stomach, she reminded herself that no matter what, she was on her way to paradise and that even now, many prayers were being sent her way.

"What's up, Kirk?" she asked as she sat down and placed her bag in the seat beside her.

"How are you feeling about the upcoming show?"

"I'm a little nervous, actually. I don't know why. I'm not really expecting anything to happen. I guess I'm just hoping that, at the very least, I won't make a fool out of myself on national television."

Kirk laughed. "I think if that was going to happen you would have done it by now."

She laughed with him. "Hey, I already have, remember? Falling off the exercise bench on QVC is still my most embarrassing moment. I never want to relive a moment like that again."

"Don't forget, your sales doubled after that. People just want to see someone real and someone they can relate to. All you need to do is just be yourself, Andi. You'll be fine."

"Thanks, Kirk." She tucked the magazine she had been reading into her tote bag and checked her watch. It was almost time.

"I also wanted you to know that I have a friend on the police force who knows a lot about online predators and bullying. He's going to follow up on that e-mail you received, but he says most likely it's harmless."

"Really?" she asked, relieved but a little surprised. The threat had sounded kind of ominous to her.

"He explained that people are much braver online than they are in real life. They will threaten and say things they would never actually follow through on. But he'll definitely check it out and see if he can find anything."

"Great. I haven't been stressing about it, but that's good to know."

"I told him about your friend Ava, and he said you ought to call the detective who is working on the case and let him know about it so he can put it on file. You never know if there is a connection."

"Thanks, I'll do that." The girls kept Detective Hutchinson up-to-date on each instance of suspicious activity. Here was one more to add to the growing list.

"Anyway, I know you'll lose your phone privileges once you get to the show, so I just wanted to tell you that I'm really glad you're doing this. Hopefully you'll get some work done on your next book while you're there, too. That deadline will be here before you know it."

"I will, Kirk. I promise."

"Okay, then. Go turn on that Andi charm. Who knows, maybe you will find love."

Andi smiled, appreciating his optimism but not sharing it. As long as they'd known each other, she and Kirk had never really seen eye to eye on the matter of religion or the fact that she was determined to find someone who shared her beliefs.

"I'm not getting my hopes up," she said. "But maybe by putting myself out there I'll be able to meet someone eventually."

"I'll be anxious to hear from you. Good luck. I have a good feeling about this, no matter what the outcome."

The call for her to board the plane came over the loudspeaker. "I've got to go," she said. "Thanks for everything. Give Laurie and the kids my love."

Andi hung up the phone then pulled her boarding pass from her purse and got in line. As she waited, she looked down the walkway toward the plane that would take her to an adventure of uncertainty. And as she reached the front of the line and had her boarding pass scanned, she swallowed, feeling the butterflies in her stomach flutter erratically. This was it. Pulling her shoulders back, she reminded herself of the three positive affirmations she had determined to think about daily: confidence, faith, and courage. With those three things on her side, she was well prepared to handle whatever came her way.

* * *

The view from Andi's window as the plane descended toward the island of Kauai captured her breath. Startling turquoise water, thick stands of palms, and verdant greenery welcomed her to the picturesque paradise. In all her travels, how had she never been here before?

Her stomach felt uneasy once more, and she drew in a calming breath, hoping to settle her nerves. More than anything, she was determined to make this a positive experience. Sure, she didn't have a snowball's chance in . . . Hawaii to find love with this guy, but that didn't mean she wouldn't have fun.

She looked down at the folder on her lap containing information about *Looking for Mrs. Right.* Flipping to the inside cover, she again studied the picture of the man who would be the center of attention for twenty-four beautiful women.

She reminded herself of what little she knew about this man. Michael Makua, heir to the Makua sugarcane fortune, was six foot one, had dark brown hair and eyes, and was thirty years old. The sugarcane plantation and factory had been established at the turn of the century by the Makua family and had grown into a major source of jobs and income for many of the islanders on Kauai. Michael's father was of native Hawaiian descent, and his mother was from a small town in Southern Idaho. Andi was curious to learn about their story and how the two had met.

She wondered, however, if she'd even get a chance to talk with Michael much with so many other women vying for his attention. There was plenty she wanted to ask him about—he was actually quite fascinating, at least on paper. He had an MBA from Stanford University, was an outdoor enthusiast, and was the founder of an organization that built homes for orphans in Africa and provided education and health care for them. He was an environmentalist and had a desire to become politically active and help solve some of the problems plaguing his island.

The picture provided of Michael showed him standing at the top of Mt. Kilimanjaro, the highest peak in Africa. The caption noted that he was there as part of a team from the California Academy of Sciences to study the glaciers and slowly disappearing ice cap that was feared to be gone by 2050.

She squinted and held the paper closer so she could see him better, but the photograph was too small and he was covered in climbing gear and protective clothing.

The flight attendant announced for the passengers to prepare for landing, so Andi slid the folder back into her carry-on and braced herself. Once she set foot outside the plane, she was stepping outside her comfort zone and hopefully into an exciting, worthwhile experience.

* * *

"You're a day early," Kirk said regretfully. "I can't believe I didn't catch this earlier."

"That explains why no one is here to take me to the hotel," Andi said, propping her two large rolling suitcases up against the wall outside the airport.

"I found the e-mail from the show's producer and realized my mistake after you were already on the plane," he explained. "But I was able to find you a room for the night, and you can report to the show tomorrow. I'm sorry about the mix-up, but maybe it will give you a chance to get rested and relax before all the craziness starts."

She wasn't upset—actually, she was a little relieved she would have a little more time before she became one of twenty-four bachelorettes. "Sure, I can soak up some sun and do a little shopping. It will be fun," she told him cheerfully.

"That's my girl. I didn't think you'd be too upset," Kirk said. "I had a hard time finding you a room at the last minute, but there is a beautiful place called the Sunset Bed and Breakfast. It's a trendy little place, very authentic Hawaiian. And it's not too far from the airport."

"Sounds perfect."

"Call if you have any problems," he said.

She slid her phone into her purse and looked for a taxi, feeling more enthusiastic by the minute that she had a full day to herself. Sleep, sun, and shopping were her three favorite pastimes.

"Can I help you, miss?" A short, smiling man approached her.

"I need to get to the Sunset Bed and Breakfast." She slid the strap of her purse over her shoulder and grabbed the handles of her two suitcases and her carry-on bag then followed him as he led the way to the curb.

"Very good, ma'am." The man hailed a cab, and in a few minutes she was looking out the window at some of the most beautiful scenery she'd ever seen.

Within five minutes the driver turned off the main road and followed a narrow lane that led to an expansive property with a sprawling lawn and a gorgeous Victorian mansion surrounded by palms, blossoming bushes, and every type and color of flower imaginable.

"Good job, Kirk," she whispered out loud.

"Excuse me, ma'am?"

"Oh, nothing. I'm sorry. This place is beautiful."

"Yes, very," the driver said with a grin as he pulled into the circular driveway in front of the mansion.

With her bags on the porch and the sound of gravel crunching as the car pulled away, Andi turned in a circle, drinking in the floral-scented breeze and pristine beauty surrounding her.

"May I help you?"

The man's voice startled her. She turned to see a handsome islander wearing a large-brimmed hat and leather work gloves, and carrying a shovel caked with rich, black soil.

"I was admiring how lovely this place is. The home and the grounds are just spectacular."

"Thank you," he said, dipping his chin. "Are you checking in?"

"Yes," she turned to the front doors. "This way?"

"That's it. They can help you inside. Just leave your bags and I'll bring them in for you." Her gaze shifted to his muscular arms, and she felt certain he could lift both of her heavy bags with one hand.

"Thank you," she said appreciatively, and he hoisted the shovel over his shoulder and strode off.

Even the hired help was beautiful.

Once inside the open, airy front reception area, Andi checked in and listened as the receptionist told her about the bed-and-breakfast's amenities. She would be staying in their nicest suite, which opened onto the pool deck and had a view of the beach and ocean.

When she got to her room, her bags were already inside and the windows were open to let in the fresh air.

The room was simply but elegantly decorated in white and soft lime green, and the effect was relaxing and peaceful. The lofty bed was covered with a fluffy, white down comforter, with pillows of greens and tropical floral patterns. The rattan backboard, chairs, and dresser completed the island feel, and the wide, sliding glass doors provided the only artwork needed—a view of the ocean.

She couldn't wait to get outside and wander around the property, intending to find the pool and Jacuzzi and check out the private beach.

Changing into her swimsuit and matching coral cover-up, she slid on her flip-flops and a beach hat in the same color then sent a quick text to Kirk to let him know that the place was perfect.

With her beach bag over her shoulder, she left her room through the sliding glass door and stepped outside into paradise.

Chapter 3

After a quick shower to rinse off the suntan oil and sand from the beach, Andi donned a colorful sundress, fuchsia shrug, and matching sandals, and went to have dinner in the small dining room where the other guests were seated and already eating.

The meal of grilled shrimp kebabs, salad, and breadsticks left her satisfied but not stuffed, and she decided that a treat of light pineapple sherbet was in order. As she took small bites, savoring the tart, sweet flavor, the breeze from the open patio lifted her hair slightly and swayed the leaves of the potted palms lining the walls. The sun dipped close to the horizon as she finished her dessert, and she decided to take a stroll along the beach to watch the sunset.

She removed her sandals and walked barefoot on the cool, soft sand. Her mind felt as tranquil as the gentle waves rolling in from the ocean, and she found that even her worries from that morning had somehow drifted away. She knew they were still there, but she just couldn't find it in herself to expend the energy to think about them right now.

As the sun hung low against the glistening ocean, Andi took several deep breaths and released them with a contented sigh. How did people get lucky enough to live here? She knew there were challenges to island life—she'd read about them in the local paper while she was tanning on the beach. Aside from the high cost of living, Hawaii dealt with problems of abandoned cars strewn along the roadways, homelessness, and drug abuse that had reached alarming proportions. She supposed even paradise had its problems.

A wooden deck chair invited her to sit, and so she kicked off her sandals and sat down awhile as a soft breeze teased the hem of her dress and pulled at tendrils of her hair. She dug her feet into the cool sand and let it slip between her toes as her body melted against the wooden slats of the chair.

Her thoughts turned back to the show, and she found herself increasingly curious about the other contestants. Would she be able to connect with the other girls and enjoy being around them, or would everyone be competitive and on guard? As she thought about the different possible scenarios and dynamics of the situation, she decided that since she wasn't out to win, she would make an effort to befriend the other girls. The experience would be much more fun if she could enjoy being with all the people involved—not just "Mr. Right."

The shadows lengthened, and the light soon gave way to the darkening sky. The beach was empty as far as she could tell, yet she suddenly had the feeling she wasn't alone. She sat up straighter in the deck chair and looked around, scanning the beach and trying to confirm the feeling. However, when she saw no one, she slowly eased back into the chair. And yet the feeling remained.

A chill ran up her spine, but she quickly brushed it off, chiding herself for being spooked so easily. The beach was wide open—she'd be able to tell if someone was watching her. But still, it was getting dark, and she decided to go back to her room. She wanted to get up early and jog on the beach anyway, which meant it was time for bed.

She wondered if there would be time for her to work out on the show. A slight smirk turned up the corners of her mouth. If not, her exercise would come from climbing the walls out of sheer desperation. Not only was staying in shape her personal passion, but it was her profession. As a well-respected fitness icon, she had a certain image to maintain.

Back in her room she got ready then climbed into bed and snuggled underneath the fluffy comforter, listening to the lapping waves on the shore and the rustling of the palms in the soft breeze. The scene was so incredibly perfect—and even after spending the day here, she was still tempted to pinch herself to make sure she wasn't dreaming. There was only one thing missing . . . having someone to share it all with.

She sighed and squeezed her eyes shut, trying to relax and allow sleep to overtake her. Most of the time she didn't mind being alone. She was independent and enjoyed having the freedom to do what she wanted. But at moments like these, freedom seemed like a small price to pay for a hand to hold along the beach at sunset.

* * *

The cloudless sky was rouged with a tinge of pink as the first hint of sunrise peeked over the horizon.

And, true to her nature, Andi was up and ready to see the sky's welcome banner and start the day with an early morning jog. She put her water bottle, scriptures, and journal in a tote bag. When she had finally accepted the offer to be on the show, she'd decided to do three things: keep a journal about the experience, read her scriptures every day, and say her prayers morning and night. She felt like this would be the best way for her to really stay grounded and not let all the drama of the situation get the best of her.

Crisp, clean air filled her lungs as she stepped out on the patio and looked out toward the ocean. Everything was still except the gentle roll of waves onto the shore. She followed the narrow cement path leading to the beach, placed her tote bag on one of the deck chairs, then began to warm up.

Nothing was more exhilarating than starting the day with an energizing workout, and Andi felt her spirits soar as she first stretched then did a few warm-up exercises, feeling the sand give way beneath her feet as they hit the ground. When she had finished, she felt empowered and strong, ready to face the day.

After taking a few sips of water, she walked across the sand to the edge of the waves, where the sand was wet and packed then began a mental run-through of the rest of her day—her first item of business choosing an outfit.

Lauryn had provided her with a killer wardrobe, and thanks to her and Cooper's help, she was going to be able to dress modestly but also have fashion-forward outfits—including her one-piece bathing suits. She knew her choice of modest clothing would set her apart from most of the other girls, but she was confident she hadn't sacrificed fashion sense to do so, and she felt proud of her choice.

She smiled and cleared her mind of anything but running then picked up speed and kicked up her heels, covering the long stretch of beach in a matter of minutes until she neared a rocky outcropping where the waves dashed against the rocks, creating a dramatic spray of water. Turning, she headed back the direction she'd started, keeping her pace strong and intense.

Several early-morning beachcombers waved at her as she jogged by, and a groundskeeper who was edging the grass along the walkway from the beach to the mansion nodded as she passed him.

She ran as far in the other direction as she could then doubled back and headed toward the starting point. When she was almost back to her chair, she slowed her pace, breathing heavily and eyeing the mostly full water bottle waiting for her.

Just a few feet from her chair, she gasped as she stepped on a broken seashell and felt a red hot pain shoot through her foot and up her leg.

"Ow!" she exclaimed, hopping on her left leg the rest of the way then collapsing onto the chair. A shell fragment was still wedged into the arch of her foot, and blood trailed from the wound, dripping generously onto the sand below.

Groaning in agony, she screwed her eyes shut and forced herself to breathe steadily, unable to bring herself to remove the shell until she got ahold of the pain. "Dang it!" This wasn't the way she wanted to start the show.

"Hey, are you okay?" The groundskeeper rushed toward her, a concerned expression on his face. As he got closer, she realized it was the same guy she had met yesterday when she arrived.

"I think so," she said through gritted teeth.

"Mind if I take a look?"

She nodded, and he grabbed the chair next to her and moved it in close. Folding her beach towel, he placed it underneath her foot and propped it on the chair seat. As she craned her neck to see her foot, she realized with some relief that the shell wasn't embedded as deeply as she'd thought—but that didn't make it hurt less.

"I need to pull out the shell," he said as he touched the side of her foot gently with one hand.

"How deep is it?"

"It should come out easily," he told her. "Are you ready?"

"I'm ready." She clenched her fists and scrunched her eyes tightly shut.

She felt his fingers on her skin and braced herself for more pain.

As he gripped the shell and jiggled the fragment, she felt as though a hot poker were touching a raw nerve. But then, suddenly, it was over.

"Not a very large cut, but it is deep," he said. "We need to get it cleaned out and bandaged. There's a first-aid kit inside. I'll go get it."

"I sure appreciate this," Andi said, feeling a tiny flutter in her heart when he looked at her. He had incredible eyes—thickly lashed and dark chocolate brown.

"My pleasure," he said, a wide, genuine smile lighting up his face.

While he left to get the kit, Andi examined her wound. It was hard to see exactly how deep it went because it was oozing blood. The bleeding would help clean it out, though, so she let it continue until the groundskeeper returned with the kit.

"Here we go," he said as he approached. "This tends to happen a lot, so I've become an expert medic—in seashell injuries anyway." He flashed his winning smile again as he knelt down next to her and opened the box containing medical supplies.

"This is probably going to sting at first." He took the lid off a bottle of hydrogen peroxide. "Ready?"

She nodded, clenching her fist just in case it did sting.

It did.

She caught her breath and flinched then relaxed as the pain subsided.

After swabbing the cut with cotton, he pressed a thick square of gauze onto her foot and held it tightly to stop the bleeding.

"I'm using a lot of padding since it's still bleeding, so it's going to look worse than it is," he said, "but once it stops, you can put a smaller bandage on."

"Okay," she said, watching as he deftly applied antibiotic ointment to a clean square of gauze with one hand. "You *have* done this before."

He shrugged. "One of the perils of walking barefoot on the sand. Most tourists don't have tough feet. Maybe we should warn them when they check in."

"Probably a good idea," she answered with a smile.

He secured the square by wrapping the arch of her foot with gauze then taping the end in place. "How does that feel?"

"Much better. It does look like I was attacked by a shark, though."

He chuckled then handed her several Band-Aids from the box. "You can use these later."

"Thank you. I'm glad you were out here when it happened."

"I am too. I was actually just about ready to leave."

He fastened the cover of the first-aid kit and stood, but his gaze caught on the books sitting next to her.

"Well, thank you again," she said, slightly puzzled when he didn't move.

He blinked and shook his head as if coming out of a trance. "I'm sorry, what did you say?"

"I just said thanks again."

"You're welcome. If you need more Band-Aids, they should have them at the registration desk."

"Oh, okay."

He tilted his head and suddenly asked, "You're Mormon?"

She looked over at the Book of Mormon and nodded in surprise. "Yes."

He nodded slowly, contemplatively. "My grandparents were Mormon."

"Really? That's great."

He nodded again then lifted his gaze to hers. "They both passed away. My mom didn't share their beliefs—she doesn't like to talk about it much." His gaze took on a curious expression. "I've never seen anyone read scriptures on vacation."

She shrugged. "It's a good book. Helps me keep my head together and deal with life when things get crazy."

"Yeah? Most people think alcohol does that."

She laughed. "This is just as addicting, but it's not detrimental to your health and it won't mess up your life."

"Interesting perspective. That's cool," he said, standing to leave. "Well, I hope you enjoy the rest of your vacation. Watch where you step."

"Funny, I heard that same line on my last vacation."

His eyebrows arched with amusement. "Where was that?"

"Africa. I went on a safari. We rode elephants."

The groundskeeper burst out laughing. "I can see why they warned you."

"Best advice I've ever gotten. Apparently my vacations have a catchphrase. Don't know if I like it, though."

He smiled. "Could be worse. How about 'prepare for a crash landing'?"

She laughed. "That would definitely be worse."

His watch beeped, and he looked down abruptly. "Oops, sorry. I gotta run." He took a couple of steps and turned. "Nice meeting you."

She lifted her hand in a half wave, but he had taken off in a jog across the lawn and out of sight. "You too," she said, wishing she'd at least caught his name.

* * *

It was time to check out of this little corner of paradise and report to the show.

Glad that her nerves had settled down, Andi took one last look in the mirror and adjusted her belt. She had on a slim-fitting, tea-length knit dress in a glorious rich lilac color with a V-neck and fluttery sleeves. She wore her hair, which was now back to its natural, golden-brown color, in long, loose curls, and she kept her makeup minimal, playing up her eyes with a hint of color that matched her dress. Her sandals were tan leather, almost the same shade as her skin, and she'd managed to hide the bandage on the bottom of her foot so it wouldn't show. She still couldn't put all her weight on the injured foot, however, since the cut from the shell still throbbed.

Overall she was pleased with her appearance. She felt classy and feminine—and not the least bit worried that if she bent down or stood up too fast, she'd be revealing more than she wanted to. All thanks to Lauryn and Cooper.

After showering from her morning run, she'd had a nice talk with Kirk, who reviewed her game plan with her for the show. Her pecking order and persona would be determined quickly—and Andi wanted to have as much say in how she was portrayed as possible. There would be the girls who gossiped about the other girls and created drama. There would be girls who were competitive and couldn't be trusted. And there would be girls who seemed to have something good going for them and were able to show their personality and garner support from the viewers. That was the category she planned to be in.

Since she was one of the older contestants, Andi hoped to create a big-sister image—hopefully not a mother image. She also wanted to be seen as positive and upbeat, not a whiner or complainer.

Her game plan with Mr. Right? Just to be herself. She wasn't a good enough actress to be anyone else. She was hopeful that this would be enough to keep her on the show for three or four weeks—just long enough to make an impression and be memorable without coming off as annoying to viewers.

Checking her room for any last items she might have missed, she buzzed the front desk to ask for help with her bags and prepared herself for the upcoming whirlwind. Enjoying the final moments of solitude and peace, she looked out the window at the half moon–shaped bay and watched the waves roll in.

Her cell phone rang, breaking into her thoughts.

"Joss? What's up?" she said happily.

"I'm so glad I caught you before you reported to the show," Jocelyn said. "I just got a call from Nickolas."

"In Greece?"

"Yes, I was as shocked as you are."

"What did he say? Is Emma okay? Is everything with her pregnancy okay?"

"Actually, that's why he called. She developed preeclampsia and went into labor. Her blood pressure was through the roof, so they didn't dare stop her contractions for fear she'd have a stroke. She had the baby. A little girl. She weighs three pounds, four ounces."

"What? The baby is here already? That's so tiny—will she be okay?" Andi asked the questions in rapid-fire succession, feeling her throat tighten with worry.

"Her name is Demetria, and she's doing better than anyone expected. Nickolas was actually quite moved by everything that had happened, and I could tell it had been a scary ordeal for them. He said Emma is doing well. They'll both be in the hospital for a while. The baby's lungs aren't very developed yet, and they have to watch her closely."

"That poor little thing. I hope she'll be okay. I can't believe Emma's a mother." Andi blinked quickly, not wanting to wreck her makeup but unable to stop the tears. "Demetria is a beautiful name."

"Isn't it?"

A knock sounded on her door.

"Oh no," Andi said.

"What's wrong?"

"I have to go. I can call you from the car."

"Okay—oh, wow. I can't believe you're really leaving for the show. I wish you could keep your phone so we could update you on the baby—and so you could tell us what's happening on the show," Jocelyn said.

"Me too. I'll see if I can check my messages occasionally or something. If you talk to Emma, will you please give her my love?" she asked quickly.

"Of course," Jocelyn said. "Good luck. You're going to be awesome."

"I sure hope so," she said, moving toward the door to answer it.

"Just have fun. You'll be great."

"I'll call you as soon as I get kicked off," Andi teased.

The knock came again, and Andi hung up the phone, still dazed at the news and filled with regret that they all couldn't be together with Emma and her precious new daughter.

"Ready, ma'am?" the tanned, wiry boy at the door asked.

She'd been hoping her friend from the beach would be the one to help with her luggage, but she smiled back and said, "Yes, thank you."

Without a backward glance, she stepped into the sunny outdoors.

Chapter 4

"Do you go by Andrea or Andi?" the man in the black pinstriped suit and maroon tie asked.

"Andi," she said, glancing at the other names on the clipboard as he nodded and wrote a note. One of the girls at the registration table handed her a manila envelope and her room key.

"The envelope contains information regarding the meeting tomorrow morning—it'll give you the time and place where you'll meet Mr. Right and have your one-on-one date. There's also a sheet for writing down some additional information we need to know for the show. Please return that to us at the meeting. You'll notice that you've been given an allowance for your evening meal and breakfast, which you can use at your discretion with room service. Except for the meeting tomorrow morning, you will not have any interaction with the other girls until after your one-on-one date, when all of you will move to the plantation bungalows."

Andi smiled. "Okay," she said, hoping her voice sounded even and nonchalant.

"Also, I will need you to turn in your cell phone," the girl said crisply, tucking a strand of short brown hair behind her ears and gesturing toward the girl next to her—who apparently had the job of confiscating the phones.

Andi had known that her phone would be taken from her, but she'd hoped she could keep it for a few more hours in case there was any update about Emma. However, not wanting to raise a fuss, she reluctantly handed her phone to the other girl, whose hair was pulled back into a long, thick ponytail with a bright pink flower clipped to it. The girl took it and dropped it into an envelope with Andi's name on it. Then she looked up with an exaggerated frown, apparently to show that she understood how hard it was to give up the use of a phone.

The contestants had been scheduled to check in every fifteen minutes, entering through one door and going out the other. Andi looked toward the exit door, stifling a sudden urge to giggle. She felt like she was signing up for some undercover spy mission or something.

The man in the pinstripe suit standing behind the girls cleared his throat. "We expect you to stay in your room until the meeting after breakfast tomorrow. I'm sorry, but use of the gym, pool, or any other hotel facility is off limits and grounds for dismissal from the show."

Andi nodded that she understood.

"Any questions?" he asked, raising an eyebrow.

"Aren't you going to give me a striped uniform and an ankle bracelet?" she asked with a deadpan expression.

The two girls burst out laughing, and Andi couldn't help but smile as well.

A grin tugged at the corner of the man's mouth, but he didn't give in. "Once you exit this room through the door behind me, you can use the elevators on your left to go up to the fourteenth floor, where you'll find your room. We do have several . . ."

"Guards," Andi said.

"Staff members," he continued, "who will remain in the hallway if you need anything."

The two girls at the desk had clapped their hands over their mouths and were clearing their throats to contain their laughter.

"That will be all. Welcome to *Looking for Mrs. Right,*" he said, writing something down on his clipboard.

* * *

As she dug into a meal of teriyaki chicken and rice with steamed vegetables, Andi sat on the deck and looked out over the private beach of the hotel. She had a nice view of the expansive pool below, where sunbathers were grabbing the last rays before the sun set.

"Well, there could be worse places to be imprisoned," she said to herself, spearing a piece of broccoli with her fork.

She'd spent the latter part of the afternoon watching TV. When she'd gotten bored with that, she had taken a bath and carefully shaved her legs then finally ordered dinner. As she took another bite of chicken, her eyes caught on a small family playing in the shallow end of the pool—a mother and father with a little girl of about two. She smiled as the little girl splashed at her mother then turned, giggling, to hug her father. It was still so crazy to think that Emma was a mother now. She wished fervently that she had her phone. She was anxious to hear how Demetria was doing. Maybe in the morning she could explain the situation to the producers and ask if they'd let her check her messages quickly. It was worth a try.

She sighed, pushing her fork around the plate to arrange the last grains of rice into a smiley face. She looked down and saw that the mother was wrapping her daughter in a fluffy blue towel and heading inside. The pool light had come on in the growing dusk, and a few sunbathers stood up to go inside as well. Andi stretched and picked up the empty plate, deciding that now was as good a time as any to go through the information packet she'd been given at registration.

She placed her plate on the counter by the door then sat down on the bed and curled her feet up under her, removing the stack of papers from the envelope. One look at the schedule and she realized that the girls were going to have a lot of free time at the beginning while Mr. Right went on his one-on-one dates. Most of the dates looked like they were scheduled around meals or evening dates. She whistled as she realized that somehow this guy was going to get six dates per day in over the next four days.

Andi found her name and time slot on the second day during lunch and smiled. Perfect. She had never been a schmoozy, romantic evening kind of girl—at least at the beginning of a relationship. The romantic stuff could come later.

Since she had no recent romances, job changes, or physical situations to report, Andi completed the other forms quickly then kicked back on the bed to scan the additional information provided about Mr. Makua to see if there was anything new from what she'd read on the plane.

She raised an eyebrow as she read about how Michael being both Hawaiian and Caucasian was a problem for some people on the island but that the financial status of the Makua family and the fact that they employed a large number of people on Kauai and were generous to the people had smoothed some of the tension.

She was surprised to see that the information packet included a brief history of Michael's romantic history. However, she realized as she read on that because of Michael's prominent status, especially in Hawaii, none of it was exactly a secret. He'd been linked to several high-profile celebrities and had associations with wealthy socialites on both coasts. One notable relationship was his prior engagement to the award-winning actress Hannah Grayson, whose last film was the highest-grossing movie of the summer.

Michael and Hannah had been on the cover of every tabloid when they first started dating and again when they broke up over Hannah's involvement with the film's leading man.

Andi barely remembered the story since she didn't usually pay much attention to tabloids. She figured that since most of the information was false anyway, it was a waste of time. She continued reading, frowning as she read reports of Michael drinking and causing scenes at clubs all over L.A., reports which had plastered the covers of newspapers and gossip magazines for months.

Apparently he'd cleaned up his act by becoming involved with charities and world organizations—something the information packet highlighted much more than the other information. Still, she wondered how sincere his efforts were and if he truly had changed or if his involvement was just a publicity maneuver to clear the family name.

Either way, she'd interacted with enough wealthy and famous people over the course of her career to know how to handle herself with them. She wasn't worried.

She jumped when a loud knock came at her door.

Padding to the door and peering through the peephole, she saw the girl with the ponytail and flower clip from earlier that afternoon.

"Hi there," Andi said in surprise when she opened the door.

The girl had a beaming smile on her face. "Are you enjoying your evening?"

"Uh-oh. Is that why you're here? I'm making too much noise partying?"

The girl giggled. "Actually, there's been a schedule change." She handed Andi an envelope. "You'll find everything you need in there."

"Oh," Andi said, lifting her eyebrows as she took the envelope. "Am I getting kicked off already? I shouldn't have made that prison crack earlier. I'm sorry."

"Nah, don't worry about it," the girl said. "My friend Maylea and I like you," she said confidentially. "Some of the crew members, too. One of them has a crush on you."

Andi smiled. She hadn't even met any members of the crew yet. Of course, they probably had access to the contestant files and information prior to all the girls showing up, but still. "Hmm, is he good-looking? Maybe if things don't work out with Michael . . ."

The girl laughed, bringing her hand to her mouth and crinkling up her dark eyes.

"I'm sorry, I didn't even ask your name."

"I'm Keilani," she said.

"Oh, okay. Thank you for bringing this, Keilani."

"You're welcome. Good night. And good luck."

Andi closed the door and smiled. At least someone liked her. She'd been pretty sure that the stone-faced man, whatever his name was, hadn't appreciated her humor.

She slid the seal on the envelope open as she walked back to the bed and, without looking where she was walking, accidentally stepped on her sandal with her injured foot.

She screeched, grabbing her foot and hopping on the other foot to the bed. Groaning, she examined her throbbing foot. To her dismay, the wound had been reopened and was bleeding again.

"That's just great!" she said, waiting for the pain to subside. Then she hobbled into the bathroom where she dabbed at the cut with toilet paper until it stopped dripping.

Searching through her tote bag, she found an extra bandage the groundskeeper had given her and put it on the cut. She knew she should have been wearing her flip-flops—she always wore them in hotel rooms. Just the thought of all the people who had walked on the floors and all the germs that probably thrived in the carpet made her skin crawl. But she'd kicked them off when she'd sat on the bed.

Hoping she didn't get an infection, she made her way back to the bed and saw the envelope she'd dropped there. Curious, she pulled out the paper inside and began to read.

Please be advised that your one-on-one date with Mr. Right has been re-scheduled for tomorrow evening beginning at 4:00 P.M. Be prepared with an evening gown for dinner and swim attire."

"You've gotta be kidding me!" she exclaimed, tossing the letter on the bed and rummaging around until she found the original schedule. Quickly scanning the page, she realized that there weren't even dates scheduled for the first evening. What was going on? She didn't want to wear an evening gown and go to dinner. And she most certainly didn't want to bring a swimsuit.

Early on, she'd vowed that she would never join Mr. Right in a hot tub. She'd watched other dating shows, and her biggest pet peeve was watching some girl in a skimpy swimsuit fawn all over the guy. She was certain she would throw up in the hot tub if they ever made her participate in such an idiotic activity. Besides, she reasoned, with her foot injury, getting in the water was not a good idea. Maybe the cut was actually a blessing in disguise to get her out of participating in hot-tub activities.

"Maybe he's punishing me," she muttered out loud, realizing that the producer probably hadn't been happy with her smart-mouthed remark earlier. But then again, how would he know that she wouldn't be chomping at the bit for a chance to jump in the hot tub with Mr. Right?

Then an alternate possibility occurred to her. "Or maybe Keilani and Maylea tried to do me a favor." Grimacing, she smacked herself on the forehead and laid down on the bed.

"Either way, it's my own fault," she said, rolling on her side and picking up the letter again to stare at it with dismay.

Picking up the remote, she clicked on the television and searched the channels, trying to find something to watch to take her mind off the date. She sincerely hoped that whatever she would accomplish by being on this show would be worth what she was about to go through.

* * *

It took every ounce of strength to keep Andi's jaw from dropping open as she entered the room where all the contestants were waiting for the meeting to begin. At first glance she was impressed by the sheer beauty of the other girls, but she was also fascinated by the broad range of style and persona in the group. Several girls, standing together, wore conservative yet fashionable business suits. Others had on colorful skirts and dresses that were fun, stylish, and feminine. And still others wore tight-fitting, low-cut dresses that revealed more than Andi wanted to see.

Wearing a black pencil skirt, a deep-red silk ruffled shirt, and black heels, Andi felt like she fell somewhere in the middle. Not too businesslike but not overly festive or—heaven forbid—trampy.

As she walked farther into the room, she felt all eyes follow her. Even in her line of work, where she often gave presentations to rooms filled with thousands of fitness fanatics, she had never felt as scrutinized as she did at that very moment.

Realizing to her dismay that she was breaking out in a sweat, she made her way to a table filled with refreshments where she poured herself a goblet of ice water.

"Hi, there," a beautiful blonde said as she sidled up to her. "This isn't intimidating at all, is it?"

Andi smiled. "You think so too?"

"Are you kidding? I felt every jiggle in my backside and was aware of every pore on my face as I walked into the room."

"For a minute I was sure I had toilet paper trailing from my shoe or something."

The girl laughed then stretched out her hand. "Hi, I'm Tara."

"Nice to meet you, Tara. I'm Andrea, but you can call me Andi."

"You've got beautiful calves—you must work out," Tara said as she studied Andi's outfit.

"Um, you could say that," Andi said with a smile.

"Ladies, ladies, would you all please take your seats?" The man wearing the pinstripe suit stood before them at a podium, and he was now wearing a lime-green shirt and tie.

Andi stayed with Tara, grateful to have someone to sit with. And as she nervously toyed with the hem of her shirt, she couldn't help but wonder how all of this was going to play out.

They sat next to a gorgeous girl with a thick mane of bronze-brown hair that hung in loose curls below her shoulders. She had incredibly vivid green eyes and almost blindingly white teeth. She gave Andi and Tara a quick smile as they took their seats.

"Welcome to *Looking for Mrs. Right,*" Mr. Pinstripe began. You have been carefully handpicked to be part of the hottest new reality show on TV. Of course, you are all familiar with *The Bachelor*. Well, our show is similar in that we are hoping that one of you ladies and our bachelor, Michael Makua, will find love."

A flutter of twittering excitement rose from the girls as they exchanged whispered comments and nervous smiles. The tension and excitement in the room grew stronger, and the man at the podium looked pleased.

"But," he continued, "our approach is quite different. Unlike the producers of *The Bachelor*, we think Mr. Makua should have a brief but intimate one-on-one date with each of you *before* he begins the elimination process. That way he can judge for himself whether there is an immediate connection on a personal level, rather than in a group setting. Once the one-on-ones are completed, he will eliminate half of you."

The collective gasp was matched only by the alarm registering on the girls' faces.

"I realize this may seem drastic, but *Mrs. Right* is only an eight-week show. So you will want to make a memorable impression with Mr. Makua.

Some of you will only have one chance to do that."

The girls began to whisper and exchange comments, which didn't go over well with Pinstripe.

"Girls, girls, please. We have a great deal of information to cover." He then began to explain the one-on-one dating process, including the fact that most dates would only last an hour or two. He also explained that Mr. Makua had the choice of whether he wanted to extend a date or not, so all contestants needed to be prepared in the event their date was rescheduled to accommodate Michael's other dates.

He also announced that everyone would be moving to the plantation right after the meeting, so they were to return to their rooms, pack their belongings, and meet downstairs, where they would be transferred from the hotel to their new accommodations. At first the girls would be split up and stay in groups of four in the small bungalows located on the property. Then, once Mr. Makua made the first cut, the remaining girls would move into the mansion.

"I'm sure you are full of questions, but we are on a tight schedule and need to check out of the hotel as soon as possible to allow you time to get settled and ready for your dates. Mr. Makua is anxious to meet all of you.

"As you leave to go to your rooms, you will pick up an envelope that will have your bungalow number and key. Chaperones will then escort you to the plantation. Any questions you have can be directed to them.

"If you've ever been on a television set, you'll know that it takes quite a large crew to film a show like this. After a few days you'll get used to having them around and constantly changing equipment, moving cable, and setting up shots. We ask that you try to accommodate them as much as possible."

He looked over the girls on one side of the room then slowly shifted his gaze to the others. "I wish you all the best of luck. And welcome to *Looking for Mrs. Right.*"

"I hope we're together," Tara whispered excitedly. "The rest of these girls scare me. Some of them act like they'd smother you in your sleep."

Andi laughed quietly. She was a strong competitor when she needed to be, but until the one-on-one dates were over, it was anyone's game.

The girls filed out of the room one by one. While Tara watched each girl as she left the room, Andi became distracted by the view from the window that overlooked a beautifully groomed golf course set against the open sea.

"Andi! We're together!" Tara exclaimed suddenly, startling her. She handed Andi her envelope. "I hope you don't mind, but one of the girls wanted to be in another bungalow so she traded with me."

"Sure, that's great," Andi said, hoping Tara calmed down once they got settled. The poor girl was going to have an aneurysm if she kept up this intensity for much longer.

"One of the other girls told me that during the next four days while the one-on-ones are going on, we can pretty much do whatever we want—go swimming and play tennis and use all the facilities. Tonight they're even having a big luau for us! Won't that be fun?"

Andi swallowed. "It does sound fun, but I won't be there," she said reluctantly.

"What? Why? It's for all the girls."

She lowered her voice slightly, unwilling to let this information be public knowledge just yet. "I have the first one-on-one."

Chapter 5

"I REALLY DON'T UNDERSTAND," TARA said. "The schedule clearly states that the first date begins tomorrow at eight o'clock in the morning—breakfast with Michael."

"Maybe they had to rearrange the schedule for some reason," Andi said, still debating over her black stretch knit cocktail dress or her teal shimmery silk one. The black was more comfortable and fit her style better, but the teal was showy and definitely had more "wow" factor.

"I guess. They did warn us that there could be changes."

MJ, one of the other girls in their bungalow, was busy painting her toenails a shimmery purple color. She looked up briefly, pushing back her blonde-streaked brown hair, which was cut in short, choppy layers that wisped around her face. "The producers can do anything they want. The show is more about getting ratings than it is about whether things are fair or whether we feel we were given the best chance to win Michael over."

Andi nodded her agreement—she liked MJ. Her personality was direct and honest, but she was also clever and funny. She was a software programmer, but contrary to the stereotype of a less-than-social introvert, she was cute and spunky, and Andi had immediately hit it off with her.

"Just be careful what you say in front of the camera," Myranda, their other bungalow mate, said. "They'll take things out of context and portray you however they want. My friend Jewel was on *The Bachelor,* and she said they could manipulate anything you said or did to make you look like a freak or really pulled together. They did whatever they needed to spice up the show." She looked thoughtful then added, "Of course, some girls come on the show for the sole purpose of causing the drama and getting the attention."

Myranda then turned back to the mirror, where she had been styling her long red hair into loose curls that hung down her back. Her skin was fair and freckly, and she had a darling upturned nose and startling blue eyes. She was thin, Andi noticed as she studied her briefly, but very shapely. Earlier she had mentioned that she was in real estate and had been very successful.

"So pretty much what you're saying is that not everyone is here to find love," Andi said, deciding on the black dress. She figured that if she was going to make a good impression, she needed to feel confident and comfortable. It was flattering to her figure and still beautifully modest. Bless Lauryn and Cooper, again.

"Ha!" MJ said. "Most of these girls are so desperate for their fifteen minutes of fame, they're willing to act like complete idiots to get noticed."

"So why are you here?" Andi asked her pointedly.

"Well," she said, screwing the lid back onto the nail polish, "I wasn't the one who signed up, actually. My sisters did. I just recently got out of a three-year relationship, and they figured this was a great way to get me back into the dating pool. I almost backed out at the last minute."

"How about you, Myranda? How did you end up on the show?" Andi asked.

She shrugged and wound another section of red hair around the curling-iron barrel. "I just thought it sounded like fun. I didn't think I'd actually get chosen, but I'm glad I did. Things have gotten kind of slow in the real-estate business lately, so I thought, why not?"

"Tara?" Andi said, sitting on the bed with her jewelry box to find the necklace Cooper had coordinated for her to wear with the dress. "What's your story?"

Tara smiled a little shyly. "I've never really done anything daring or bold like this in my life. I'm an autism specialist in our school district, I lead the church choir on Sunday, and I live at home with my parents. I didn't tell anyone that I applied for the show until I got the callback. My parents tried to talk me out of it, but I'd made up my mind that I needed to step out of my comfort zone and do something crazy once in a while."

"Well, good for you!" Andi said.

"What about you, Andi?" Tara asked. "How did you end up on the show?"

Andi opened her mouth to respond but found she didn't know what to say. If she told the others her thought process, they would think she had come on the show purely to promote her career. And while she hoped that happened, she wasn't opposed to finding love.

"Well, I haven't had a lot of luck finding love on my own," she said carefully. "I figured I didn't have anything to lose."

"Ah!" MJ shrieked suddenly, fanning at her toes frantically with a folded piece of paper. "Have you guys looked at the time? We're late!"

It was ten after the hour, and the luau had started at six.

"Where's my other sandal?" MJ said, walking around the room on her heels so she didn't smudge her paint job.

"Is this it?" Tara asked, kneeling down and pulling a sandal from under the bed.

"Yes. Thank you!" MJ carefully slid her foot into the sandal then grabbed her sweater. "I've heard it gets cool here at night. You two might want something to wrap around you when the sun goes down." She fluffed her hair in the back and gave Andi a sly glance. "You don't need one—you'll have Mr. Makua to keep you warm."

Andi burst out laughing, and Myranda and Tara joined in as well. However, Andi could tell they hoped MJ was wrong.

Once the three girls left, Andi began getting dressed. She hadn't wanted to get ready in front of everyone else. Even though the girls seemed wonderful and she knew she had gotten lucky with friendly roommates, she also knew they were all in competition together, and she felt uncomfortable having them scrutinize her clothes and appearance.

Glancing at the clock, she felt her heart skip a beat as she realized the driver would be there any minute to pick her up for the date.

"Calm down," she told herself as she fastened the necklace and took one last look in the mirror, happy with her choice. Outside, the sky was clear and there was a soft breeze. It was going to be another gorgeous Hawaiian evening, and she wondered if maybe they would be dining outside.

Just in case, she decided to grab a wrap. She chose a deep turquoise pashmina that added a little pop of color to her outfit and just enough coverage to keep her warm.

A knock came at the door. It was time.

Gripping her beaded clutch in one hand and slinging the bag with her bathing suit and towel over her shoulder, she opened the door.

"Good evening. My name is Morris. I'll be your driver this evening." The middle-aged gentleman bowed his head and offered a smile.

"Good evening, Morris," Andi said.

"You're ready?" he asked.

"I am."

"This way." He directed her down the hallway and out to a white limousine, where he opened the door and helped her inside.

"Oh! Hello," she said as she climbed into the limo and saw the cameraman sitting across from her. There was another man to the side, taking care of sound and lights, and two more in back, one adjusting a microphone and another fiddling with some unidentifiable technology. She realized she shouldn't have been surprised to see so many people waiting to accompany her, but she was a little taken aback all the same.

The man fiddling with the equipment had spiky, bleached-blond hair, and he looked up as she sat down. "Hi," he said, offering a hand in greeting. "I'm Caz. Short for Cazador. I'm the assistant director."

"Nice to meet you," Andi said, her eyes shifting to the other crew members.

He introduced her to two of the other men and then stopped when he got to the sound guy.

The sound guy, who had a bushy beard and long, straggly hair covered by a baseball cap worn backward, gave Caz a long look then turned his gaze to Andi and said, "It's Tom."

"Oh, right. Tom." He slapped the sound guy on the back. "Sorry," he said to Andi. "He's new; we just met."

Andi gave them all a smile, her glance resting briefly on Tom, who quickly looked away, a blush creeping up his face. But as they began to drive away from the bungalows, she felt his eyes on her and wondered if he could be the smitten crew member Keilani had told her about.

"We have some questions for you while we drive." Caz made some notes on a clipboard.

"Sure," Andi said, settling back into her seat.

When the cameraman and his associates indicated that they were ready to roll, Caz nodded and said, "Action."

Andi had been in front of a camera many times and was surprised that she felt so nervous with just the three men watching her.

"So, how does it feel now that you're about to finally meet Michael Makua?" Caz asked.

"A little like being strapped into a roller coaster at Six Flags and waiting for it to take off. It's thrilling and terrifying at the same time. It's thrillifying!" she said with a laugh. The men smiled but remained quiet, so she went on. "Michael seems like a fascinating man, and I'm looking forward to getting to know him. I think we'll have a lot to talk about because we have a lot in common."

"Like what?" Caz prompted.

She mentally reviewed everything she'd read as she responded. "Well, we're both into protecting the environment and educating people on how we can save our planet. We've both done humanitarian work in South Africa—I'm especially excited to talk to him about that. I'm attracted to a man who isn't focused on himself. He really seems committed to serving and making a difference. I really like that. I also love adventure. Michael seems to be very adventurous."

"Keep going," Caz said.

"Um, well," she thought for a moment, knowing that if she rambled and didn't plan her words carefully, they could be misconstrued. "Up to this point in my life, I've been unlucky in love. It wasn't easy for me to make the decision to come on the show, but I decided to take the opportunity and put myself out there."

"Does it scare you?"

"Of course it scares me. I've had my heart broken many times. I don't think I've put up walls around me, but I am going to have to let my guard down if I'm really going to get to know Michael and let him learn who I really am. It's not going to be easy, but I'm determined to try."

"What makes you different from the other girls on the show?"

She thought for a minute. "I haven't really had a chance to get to know them yet, but I would say nothing and everything. What I mean is that I'm just like all of the other girls in that we're all just doing the best we can, trying to figure out life and relationships and how to navigate the shark-filled waters of the dating pool. But I'm different in many ways because of my personal beliefs and goals. I don't know all the girls yet, but the ones I've met so far are incredible women."

"Are you intimidated by them?"

"I probably should be," she said with a laugh, "but no, not really. I don't get intimated anymore. I did when I was younger, but I really know who I am now, and I'm very comfortable in my own skin. If someone doesn't like me for who I am, there's nothing I can do about it. I'm not going to change to please them."

The car began to slow down.

"I think we're almost there," Caz said. "Is there anything else you want to say?"

"I've probably said more than I should. Really, I'm just here hoping to have a good experience and not do anything I'll regret."

"You aren't the spontaneous type, then, I take it?"

"Actually, I'm very spontaneous, but I don't take a lot of risks. Although," she smiled, "I guess being on the show is taking a risk, isn't it?"

The car came to a stop.

"That's good stuff, Andi. Thanks. We'll be here when the date ends to finish the interview."

The door opened, and Morris hurried around the car and reached inside to help her out.

Andi pulled in a calming breath. "How do I look?" she asked Caz and Tom.

Caz smiled. "Beautiful."

Tom nodded then looked away, but Andi caught a flicker of something in his eye—was it painful shyness and embarrassment? No, she decided as she pulled her gaze away. It was something else, something she couldn't put her finger on.

"See you in a bit," she said, deciding not to worry about it. She took Morris's hand and stepped out of the limo.

"Just follow the path around the back to the balcony," Morris instructed, taking her bag from her. "I'll put this inside."

Andi looked where he pointed and noticed another cameraman and sound guy ready to film her walking to the back of the cottage. She realized then that although she had often been in front of a camera, it was always with a specific purpose—to record a video or an interview. Not every little move she made.

Concentrating on her surroundings, she began walking up the path in front of her, admiring its borders of thick foliage and overflowing ferns and flowers. It was like a pathway to the Garden of Eden.

Her heart thumped in her chest. Was the date going to be enjoyable or awkward? Was Michael going to be what she expected, or would he be completely different?

There was only one way to find out.

As she arrived at the patio, she was met by the filming crew, who instructed the hair and makeup people to make some minor adjustments and add a little color to her lips. She made sure to thank them and make a mental note of their names. She liked calling people by their names and making sure they knew she appreciated what they did for her.

Ready for filming, she paused at the stairway leading to the balcony. On each step was a flickering candle lighting the way.

A man who quickly introduced himself as Silas appeared, ready to direct the shot. Andi saw his gaze slip appreciatively over her dress, and even though she felt confident in her modest choice of clothing, she still found herself suddenly wishing for an overcoat—at least until he left the room. She turned slightly, wishing Caz were there instead.

"Okay, people, let's do this," Silas commanded, still keeping his gaze on her. "Andi, we want you to go up the stairs then pause at the top, like you're anticipating this meeting but also a bit nervous. Can you do that?"

She nodded. That was exactly how she felt.

"Places!" Silas yelled, turning back to the rest of his crew, and Andi sighed with relief as he made his way up the stairs to man the camera.

A pretty girl with long, wavy black hair slapped the speed marker shut and the camera began rolling.

Andi tried to act natural as she climbed the stairs. She reminded herself to breathe and not look at the camera, but it was hard not to since both Silas and the camera were directly ahead of her.

At the top of the stairs, Silas took several steps back as she approached.

Just like she had been told, she paused and gazed out over the grounds leading to the beach at Hanalei Bay. It was an incredible sight, and she couldn't help drawing in a deep breath of air sweetened by the myriad of fragrances of flowers dancing in the gentle breeze.

Silas nodded and pointed to the far side of the balcony where a table was set with china, candles, and crystal goblets.

Wishing she were wearing jeans and that this was a sunny picnic, Andi resolutely walked to the dining area. Since no one was there at the table, she leaned against the railing and took another look at the view, wondering if the people who lived here took the incredible surroundings for granted.

"Cut!" Silas announced, startling her. "Good, Andi, you're very natural and relaxed. I want to get a few close-ups of you at the railing here. Let us see the anticipation in your eyes. You're about to meet a man who could possibly become your husband." He grinned. "And then, when Michael joins you, I really want to see that excitement on your face. He'll probably give you a hug, so be prepared so that you can stay relaxed and natural."

Andi nodded, glad that she seemed to be doing well.

Several adjustments were made to the camera angle, and the microphone man and gaffer had to move some cable and tape it down. There seemed to be hundreds of adjustments between takes, and she was surprised just how long each shot took.

"Okay, Andi, stand where you were by the railing and go ahead and look out at the view again. Then, when Michael comes out, you can turn and respond."

Andi took her place and looked out at the ocean once more. The sky was changing colors now as the sun dropped lower on the horizon, and she tried to keep her thoughts focused solely on the show in the sky.

Behind her a glass door slid open.

She caught her breath and held it.

"Good evening, Andi."

Andi turned and saw the man who'd spoken to her. Her mouth dropped open for a moment and then, using Cooper's favorite phrase, she whispered, "Shut the front door."

"Cut!" Silas said.

"I'm sorry," Andi said, covering her mouth. "I . . . I . . ."

Michael started laughing. And though Andi was mortified at what she'd just said, she couldn't help it. Standing in front of her was the handsome groundskeeper who had pulled the broken seashell out of her foot.

Chapter 6

"I'M NOT SURE I UNDERSTAND that reaction," Silas said, dropping his hands to his sides and looking at her oddly. "What was that all about?"

She glanced at Michael, who gave her the slightest shake of his head. He didn't want her to say anything to the director.

"I—I wasn't ready. I'm sorry," Andi said, feeling slightly off balance. "Can we try that again?"

"Michael, go back inside and come out again," Silas said. "Andi, do you need me to cue you for the reaction?"

Michael jumped in and answered. "Now that we've had a little *run*-through, I'm sure we'll get it right this time. We know what to do. Right, Andi? You don't need Silas to *jog* your memory for you, do you?" he asked with a grin.

"No, I've got it. My heart was just *racing* a little, and I got nervous." Andi returned the smile and laughed. What had Michael been doing taking care of a yard when he was heir to a fortune?

"Places, people," Silas said. He gave Andi a skeptical look. "Are you ready?"

She nodded, hoping she looked more composed than she felt. "Yes. I am." She could do this.

"And . . . action!" Silas commanded.

The door slid open behind her, and Andi reacted. Slowly she turned her head. Then, once she caught a glimpse of Michael, she smiled. Her smile grew as she walked toward him. He reached for her as she closed the gap, clasping her hands in his.

"Good evening, Michael," she said, looking up into his eyes.

"Good evening, Andi," he said, letting go of her hand and giving her a hug. "I'm so glad you could join me for dinner."

"Thanks for inviting me."

The conversation seemed stiff and formal and completely uncomfortable. She hoped that the entire evening wasn't going to be this way. She was dying to talk to him like a normal person and find out more about him.

"Would you like something to drink?" he asked, eyeing a bottle of wine chilling beside several crystal goblets.

"I would love something, thank you," she said. Pausing a moment, she said, "I'd love some water if you have it."

His eyebrows raised and he chuckled, clearly a little thrown that she'd requested something he wasn't prepared for. "Water. Okay, of course."

Knowing the scene would be edited and that they didn't have to guard every word and movement continually, Michael looked at Silas and said, "Do we have water?"

"Cut!" Silas yelled. Everyone on the set relaxed. "Yes, Michael. Of course we do. But you're supposed to drink wine," he said.

"I'm sorry, but I don't drink alcohol," Andi said. She was so used to letting people know she didn't smoke or drink that she didn't give it a second thought. Besides, she'd put it on her paperwork. She hoped she wouldn't have to defend her position about it.

"Oh, well, then, by all means, let's get her some water." Andi thought she detected annoyance in Silas's voice, but she didn't care. Not only was she not going to drink alcohol, but she didn't want to appear as though she was, especially on national television.

While some of the film crew scrambled to get her some water, she and Michael had a chance to speak off camera.

"You don't drink?" he asked.

"No, sorry. Apparently that's a problem," she said as Silas growled at someone to hurry up.

"Not at all. I admire that. You must be very health conscious."

"I am. Although it isn't the only reason I don't drink." She shrugged. "We can talk about it sometime. But first I have a question. What were you doing taking care of the grounds at the Sunset Bed and Breakfast?"

He glanced around, but when it seemed that no one was paying any particular attention, he said, "I was just as surprised as you were when I walked out and saw that it was you. Sunset Bed and Breakfast is one of the properties my family owns. I help manage it—and I'd rather be working outside than sitting at a desk."

She liked that. He was a rich boy, but maybe he wasn't the snobbish type.

She nodded her approval.

"How's your foot, by the way?" he asked.

"It hurts," she admitted. "But I'll be fine in a few days."

"People, let's do this!" Silas barked. "We're losing our light."

Someone came running with the crystal pitcher of water and placed it near the wine glasses.

"All right. Places, everyone." Silas stepped back then yelled, "Action!"

"Here you go," Michael said, pouring her a goblet of water. Then, to her surprise, he poured himself a goblet of water as well, leaving the wine bottle untouched beside them.

Their table was positioned at the edge of the balcony where they could look out over the ocean, and Andi found herself relaxing as she watched the waves loll in on the beach.

"So how do you like Kauai?" Michael asked, taking a sip from his goblet.

"I've never seen a more beautiful place in my life," she replied honestly.

"I'm glad to hear that—I love it here."

"It's like paradise."

He smiled. "It really is." Then he looked down at her feet. "I noticed you were limping. Did you hurt your foot?"

She raised her eyebrows in surprise. Why did he want to discuss this? "Um, yeah, actually. I was walking barefoot on the beach and stepped on a broken seashell."

"Was the injury serious?"

"I don't think so," she said hesitantly.

"I've had some medical training—do you want me to look at it?" he asked with a smile.

She laughed. "Sure." Now she could see where he was going with all this. Silas would love it.

She put her feet up on his lap, and he removed the sandal on her injured foot. Then he lifted her foot and looked at it closely. "Nice bandage job."

"It's all I had," she said. "It beat wrapping my foot in toilet paper. That was my next option."

He laughed out loud.

"I think I can do a little better than this. Just a minute." He slid off of his seat and went inside the building. She expected Silas to yell for a cut, but the camera kept rolling. She took a sip of water and gazed out at the ocean while she waited.

When he came back, she lit up—and was pleased to realize that the reaction was genuine. She actually was excited to see him.

"You didn't need to go to all this trouble," she said as he joined her on the bench and put her feet back on his lap.

"I don't mind. You don't want this to get infected."

Tenderly he peeled off the old bandage. "That's a nasty cut." He put some antibiotic ointment on it then applied a new bandage. "There. How's that?"

"Much better. Thank you."

"Now, how about some food?"

"Sounds wonderful."

"Here, let me help you." He whisked her off the bench and into his arms.

She couldn't help the surprised squeal that escaped her when he did it, and she wrapped her arms lightly around his neck as he carried her to her seat and gently set her down.

"I could get used to this," she said. "I feel like Cleopatra. Are you going to feed me grapes, too?"

He laughed. "Of course. I'll even fan you with palm fronds."

A tuxedoed waiter appeared to serve their meal, and as they enjoyed the hot bread and stuffed mushrooms that were the appetizers, they managed to relax and eat as though the cameras weren't even there.

"Tell me about Africa," she said. "I spent some time in Zambia, and I really admire what you're doing."

He nodded. "I'm sure you know bits and pieces from the tabloids—I wasn't in a very good place in my life a few years ago. But family and friends helped me sort things out, and when I was finally able to do that, I realized that the world didn't revolve around me—that there were people out there in pretty desperate situations. It wasn't until I was in my early twenties that I really understood what was going on in Africa." He took a bite of bread and continued. "Once I learned about the high rate of orphans caused by AIDS and how many of these children live on the streets, some of them taking care of younger siblings and having nowhere to sleep, no one to care for them, well, I had to do something. "

She nodded, knowing exactly how he felt.

"I realized that I'd been blessed to be in a position where I could help, where I could really do something and make a difference. So I traveled to South Africa. I've been to Zambia and spent time in the orphanages and visited some of the great facilities that exist to help get the children off the streets and get them educated. That's really the key, educating these children. It's the only way to improve their lives and their country.

"I helped build a school while I was there—but it still bothers me that the only children who could go to school there were the ones who had shoes and could walk an hour to and from school. I plan to go back again, and this time I want to take shoes to the children."

He looked up at her, and time seemed to stand still.

Andi felt her heart rate increase and wondered what was happening. This man sitting in front of her was incredible. Yes, he was good-looking and charming, wealthy, and privileged—and although he had a checkered past, it was obvious that he possessed depth and integrity and compassion. He also had a great sense of humor. Her heart fluttered every time their eyes met.

The evening shadows gave way to nightfall as they enjoyed a main course of scallops and butternut risotto followed by a rich dessert of chocolate-dipped raspberries and creamy slices of cheesecake. Andi sighed as she finished her last bite, sure she wouldn't be able to move after the meal she'd just eaten. But when Michael suggested they go for a walk, she eagerly agreed.

Silas, who had finally calmed down and seemed to be pleased with the way things were going, set up the shot as they began the walk from the balcony to the beach.

Michael held her hand in his. "Are you warm enough?"

"Yes, thank you."

"And you're sure you can walk on that foot?"

"Yes, it's fine." His thoughtfulness and consideration were refreshing. She hoped someday to meet his mom and thank her for raising such a considerate son.

Soft music floated down around them, and Andi wondered vaguely where it was coming from. She hummed quietly along with the island tempo as they set out across the walkway and asked on a whim, "So, do you play the ukulele?"

His laughter rang through the palm trees into the night. "Actually, I do," he said.

"Next time I'd love to hear you sing a song," she said.

"All right, I'll do it."

"What's the best part of living on an island?" She appreciated how he kept their pace nice and slow so she could walk on her injured foot—and she didn't mind at all that she had an added excuse to lean on his arm as she walked.

"We seem to be immune to some of the craziness in the world," he told her, turning to meet her gaze with dark, kind eyes. "Don't get me wrong—we have our troubles here on the island. Big problems. I'm doing what I can to help make life better for the people on Kauai, but for the most part, it is very relaxed and peaceful here."

"And what's the worst part of living on the island?"

He was thoughtful for a moment then said, "Dating."

"Really? I have a hard time believing you have trouble finding a date."

"You'd be surprised."

"Hence the show?" she asked.

"Yes. I mean, really, how could I turn down an offer to have twenty-four amazing women come to me?"

"When you put it that way, I guess you couldn't."

"Exactly. Besides, my mother is about ready to kill me. She's your typical mother, you know, wanting me to get married, settle down, and give her grandbabies."

"I've heard that song before," she said. "Dating isn't any easier on the mainland, but then I guess you know that."

"Far too well," he said with a laugh. "So I guess we're both very lucky. Without the show, we would have been left to our own resources," he said with a grin. "And frankly, I was running out of resources."

"Me too."

He looked out across the dark sand in front of them then turned to her with a mischievous sparkle catching his eye in the moonlight. "Want to go out on the beach?"

"Uh, well . . ."

"Here," he lifted her up into his arms again. "I'll make it easy for you."

"You like to sweep women off their feet, don't you?" She wrapped her arms around his neck.

"I can't help it. When I see a damsel in distress, I want to rescue her."

"I'll have to remember that," she said wickedly.

They laughed together.

Carrying her as if she were light as a feather, Michael walked near the water's edge then put her down. There was a cool breeze blowing off the waves, and Andi pulled her wrap tighter around her.

"Chilly?" he asked.

"Not too bad," she said tentatively.

"Here," he pulled her close and wrapped his arms around her. "Better?"

She felt herself melt into his warm, strong embrace. "Yes, much."

"I'm glad you chose to be on the show," he said quietly, holding her back ever so slightly to look into her eyes.

"Me too," she answered, never having spoken a truer statement in her life.

After a few more minutes, they decided to go back inside. The wind had kicked up, and the water was hitting the shore with a stronger force. The half-moon was covered with clouds.

Scooping her up once more, he carried her back to the walkway but didn't put her down when they reached it.

"You can put me down now," she said.

"Do I have to?"

She giggled. "No, I guess not. It's your show."

He laughed again, the rich, happy sound she was beginning to love.

The wind grew stronger, and it became clear that a storm was brewing. Part of her was relieved. That probably meant no hot tub—which she was grateful for—but part of her was disappointed. That meant the date would end.

"I want you to stay a little longer," he said as he walked back toward the cottage. "Since there's a storm coming, why don't we go inside? There's a fireplace where we can sit and talk. Would you join me?"

"Sure. But really, you can put me down now."

He lowered her feet to the ground but kept hold of her hand as they walked back to the house.

Silas ordered them to wait until the cameras were repositioned then cued them to climb the stairs to the balcony. When they entered the cottage, they found a fire burning, and, to their delight, the staff had put graham crackers, chocolate, and marshmallows out. On her paperwork, Andi had indicated that s'mores were one of her favorite treats. She shrugged slightly, unsure how they had caught on to this detail but overlooked the alcohol part.

"What's this?" Michael asked, looking at the treat with confusion.

"It's stuff to make s'mores," she replied.

"S'mores? I've never had one," he said.

"What? Really? Haven't you ever camped out?"

"Only in Africa. Otherwise, I've always had a chef and staff here. I don't think our chef knows how to make these."

"Well, I'm going to teach you. You haven't lived until you've had a s'more."

They took the sticks provided and skewered the marshmallows.

"Careful that you don't burn the marshmallow." She smiled. "Unless you like your marshmallows burned. Some people do."

"I don't know if I do," he said. "I've never roasted marshmallows before."

She held her tongue as he lit two different marshmallows on fire before he finally toasted the third without flames.

"Put it right here between the chocolate and graham crackers," she said. "And get ready."

He slid the marshmallow off the stick and squished it inside the crackers. Then, licking his fingers, he held the s'more in front of him and examined it.

"Go ahead, try it."

He took a large bite of the sweet treat. "Oh," he said, closing his eyes, "This is good."

She made her s'more and took a bite as well. "The perfect food," she said with a sigh.

"Where have you been all my life?" he said then quickly corrected himself. "I mean, where have these been all my life?"

Her heart skipped a beat. For a brief, glorious moment, she felt as though she was the only girl in his life. But then, just as quickly, she remembered: he was going to have moments like this with twenty-three other girls. The thought saddened her.

"Hey," he said, licking the chocolate off the corner of his mouth, "Everything okay?"

She flashed him a quick smile. "It's perfect. It really is."

"I think so too." They were sitting on a thick, plushy rug in front of the fireplace, resting their backs on large pillows propped against the couch. He edged slightly closer to her, and she felt her heartbeat speed up once more.

"Can I ask you something?" he asked.

"Sure?" She licked her finger, hoping that she didn't have food caught in her teeth.

"What is it you're looking for in a man?" He leaned back on one elbow and looked up at her. Then he reached for a square of chocolate and took a bite, offering her the other bite.

She didn't turn him down.

After she swallowed, she answered. "I'm looking for someone who knows who he is and where he's going. I want to be with a man who is committed and loyal to me and our relationship and who is willing to work together, even when things get hard."

He nodded.

"I want to be with someone who is my friend, someone I can laugh with and enjoy our lives together but also someone I can lean on when I need strength. And I want someone who has a strong belief system and values he's committed to."

"Do you think you just described me?" he asked seriously.

She laughed. "I don't know. I guess that's why I'm here, isn't it?"

"That's why we're both here."

"So, what are you looking for?" she asked in turn.

"Someone like you," he answered.

"Cut!" Silas ordered.

Chapter 7

"Michael, we need this show to last eight weeks. Plus, you have twenty-three other girls to meet. Can you please rein it in a little?" Silas asked him pointedly, an annoyed look on his face.

"Sure. Sorry. I didn't mean that so literally," Michael said, waving his hand flippantly.

Andi didn't know what he meant by that, and she decided to keep her mouth closed for the time being.

"Let's do that shot again, people," Silas ordered. "Andi, ask him the question again."

Everyone got into place, and Silas yelled, "Action!"

"So," Andi said, trying to put herself in the same frame of mind she had been in a few seconds ago. "What are you looking for?"

Michael smiled. "I'm a pretty traditional guy, but I still want a woman who's independent and strong and knows who she is. I just hope she'll still let me take care of her and pamper her, too. I want to laugh and cry together and understand and support each other. I want to be with someone who makes me want to be a better person just by being with her. And I want to be with someone who wants to be a wife and mother. Having a family, being a family, is very, very important to me."

"That's a tall order," she said, studying him closely.

"Maybe, but I'm willing to look until I find her." He reached out and stroked her cheek with his finger.

She shut her eyes, amazed that his touch could have such an electrifying effect on her. She told herself that when she got back to her bungalow, she would get her thoughts together. This was *not* reality, even though it was "reality TV." She couldn't allow herself to get caught up in it and lose sight of what her long-term goals were. The place and the way she got married had been fixed in her mind years ago, as a young girl.

"And . . . cut," Silas said, jarring them out of the moment. "Michael, let's get some footage of you walking her to the car." He began ordering the crew around and made a call for the limo to pull up in front.

"Guess that's that," Michael said softly.

"I guess so," she answered. "Would you hand my sandals to me, please?"

"You want to wear them? Is your foot okay?"

"Not that I don't like being carried around by you, but yes, it's fine." She slid her feet into her shoes and accepted his help in getting up.

"Thank you for tonight," he said. "It was a little strange with the cameras, but I enjoyed being with you."

"You'd better get used to the spotlight. You've got twenty-three more to go," she replied, feeling a little twinge of envy, which she quickly squelched.

He shook his head. "I can't imagine how they could be as wonderful as tonight was."

"I don't know. There are some pretty awesome girls in this group. I think you'll be pleasantly surprised."

"You two ready?" Silas hollered as he headed for the door behind the rest of the crew.

Michael raised his hand. "We're right behind you."

When Silas left the room, Michael turned to look directly at her. "We can't let anyone know we met before the show started," he said in a low voice, his tone serious. "I don't know if you read the contract, but it asks whether we knew each other previously. They'll ask you to forfeit your spot on the show if they find out," he whispered so softly she could barely hear him. "Our meeting was purely innocent, and you had no idea it was me, but I just want to be safe. I don't want you to leave the show."

"I won't say anything," she said, reaching for her clutch and wrap, touched that he was worried about whether or not she stayed.

He took the pashmina from her and draped it over her shoulders. "Ready?"

She nodded.

The cameras began rolling as they stepped onto the balcony. The wind was still blowing in gusts, and droplets of rain splattered across the walkway. He helped her down the stairs and held her hand as they walked to the limo.

She was surprised how comfortable she felt with Michael, even though she hardly knew him. Maybe it was the fact that they shared a secret together—but somehow it felt deeper than that. Either way, she marveled that they'd clicked so quickly. If he had a snobby, rich-kid mentality, she hadn't seen it. And as for his "checkered past," as he called it, she was more than convinced that he really had turned his life around. And she was willing to leave it at that.

"I guess this is good night," he said, turning to her as they stood next to the limo door.

"Thank you for a wonderful evening—and for carrying me around," she said, looking up at him with a grin. "You'll probably be sore tomorrow."

He laughed. "I'm used to lifting fifty-pound bags of sugar all day."

"I'm much heavier and not quite as sweet," she quipped coyly.

He laughed out loud. "Hmm, guess I'll have to find that out for myself, won't I?"

She raised her eyebrows at the implication. "I guess so." Although she was very attracted to Michael, she didn't want him to kiss her—not yet, anyway. She didn't want to be one of those kiss-on-the-first-date, make-out-in-the-hot-tub reality-show types.

"Good night," he said then pulled her toward him. She returned the embrace, breathing in his subtle cologne and feeling the strength in his arms. As soon as he loosened his grasp on her, she stepped out of his embrace and took a step toward the car.

"Good night," she said quickly.

Before the driver got out to open the door, Michael stepped up and opened it for her. The expression on his face was a mix of disappointment and confusion, and she was certain now he had wanted to kiss her. Maybe they could talk about it sometime.

"Take care of that foot," he said.

She smiled. "I will."

Inside the car she met Caz and his crew ready to get her post-date thoughts. However, they graciously allowed her a few moments to gather her thoughts and get settled as the car drove away. She exchanged a glance with the soundman and was glad to see that he didn't turn away from her smile this time. In fact, he returned her smile and turned back to his equipment. She chalked her earlier impression up to nerves on her part and said a quick prayer that the interview would go well.

Before the cameras started rolling, Caz asked, "So what's the deal with the water?"

"What do you mean?" she asked, thinking for a moment that he was asking about their walk along the beach.

"Or, the bigger question is, why don't you drink alcohol? Are you a recovering alcoholic?"

"Me?" she choked out. "No. Hardly."

"Then what? I don't understand."

All eyes turned to her, waiting for her answer.

"Part of the reason is that I work in the fitness industry, and I try to discourage people from drinking because of the harmful effect it has on the body."

"What's the other part?" Silas asked.

"Religious reasons," she said. "Smoking, drinking, drug use—anything harmful—is against my beliefs."

He pulled a face. "Sounds like a fun religion."

"It works for me," she said simply.

"Well, the producers will want you to keep your religious views on the down low," Caz said. "You know, don't talk about it, especially on camera. Don't get me wrong—they don't want you to go against what you believe in, but they also don't want you to get all preachy about it."

"I won't unless someone asks me a question. I'm not going to lie," she told him, "but I will try my best not to bring attention to my religious beliefs, and I certainly won't address the matter in front of the camera." From experience, she already knew that her actions spoke louder than her words anyway.

"Good," Caz said. "Let's get this interview going, then. We're almost back to your bungalow." He cued the cameraman and soundman. "Tell me, Andi, how did you feel the night went, and what did you think of Michael?"

Andi couldn't stop the immediate smile that felt like it set her aglow. "I thought tonight went really well. I was very comfortable with him—it felt as though I'd known him for years. He's warm and considerate and a lot of fun. We really hit it off, right from the beginning. I was surprised to learn just how accomplished he is and how much time he spends trying to help improve some of the problems on the island as well as around the world. He's quite an important guy around here, but he's very approachable and down to earth."

"What was going on with your foot?"

Andi laughed. "I cut my foot earlier on a broken seashell, and he was sweet enough to bandage it up for me. It hurt to walk on it in my sandal, so he carried me out to the beach. I guess you could say he swept me off my feet."

"How does it make you feel to know he'll be with twenty-three other girls in the next four days?"

"Actually, I'm okay with it. I think he and I really connected and were very open and honest with each other. If he wants to keep me around and get to know me better, I would be very happy about that."

"Good," Caz said. "Anything else?"

"Um, yeah. I thought it was cute that he'd never had s'mores before. It was fun to make them together, and I was glad he liked them. We're definitely different when it comes to lifestyle, but he's not pretentious at all and doesn't seem to mind that I don't come from a wealthy background." She paused for a moment then shrugged and added, "I guess that's all."

"All right, then," Caz said. "We've got everything we need."

The driver killed the engine as the car stopped, but when Andi looked out the window, she frowned. "I'm sorry, I don't think this is the right place," she said, looking to Caz.

"Actually, we've moved you to a new place. We're keeping the girls who've gone out with Michael away from the girls who haven't. You'll be alone tonight, but we'll have someone posted outside your door to keep you safe. You'll get some company as the day progresses tomorrow."

"Oh, I see," she said, taking the change in stride.

"All of your belongings have been transferred here. Let one of the crew members know if they happened to miss something."

Morris opened the car door for her, and she shifted to step out of the car. But before she did so, she turned back to the crew. "Thank you," she said to Caz and Tom. "Have a good night."

"Don't mention it," Caz said, giving her a nod as he scribbled something on a notepad. Tom was busy gathering up equipment and gave her a brief grunt in reply.

She left the limo and walked up the path to her new bungalow.

Luckily, her extensive travel had gotten her used to being alone in new surroundings and unfamiliar situations. She understood the reasoning behind the seclusion and had, in fact, felt some concern about returning to the three girls in her bungalow and being bombarded with questions.

"Aloha," an elderly Polynesian man said as she approached. "You must be Andrea."

"I am," she answered.

"Very good. Here is your key. My name is Kana, and I will remain outside your door this evening."

The wind had calmed a little, and rain was falling softly as she tried to duck underneath the almost nonexistent roof ledge.

"But you'll get rained on," she protested, feeling the raindrops begin to seep beneath her pashmina.

"No worries, I have shelter," he said, pointing to a covered golf cart.

"You're sleeping in that?"

"No. No sleep. I will stay awake until I am relieved at three. It is kind of you to worry about me, but I am used to it. This is my regular shift."

"Well, okay," she said, shielding her face from the rain.

"You must get inside," Kana said. "The storm will get worse before it gets better."

"Good night, then, Kana."

"Sleep well."

She hurried inside and shut the door. The bungalow was laid out and decorated exactly as the other one; it had a large main room/kitchen, two bedrooms with two single beds in each, and one large main bathroom. Her belongings had been deposited into one of the rooms, and upon quick inspection, she determined that they were all accounted for.

Feeling a wave of sleepiness overtake her, she changed into her pajamas and got ready for bed. Glad she could sleep late in the morning, she took an extra minute to hang up her dresses and other clothes so they wouldn't wrinkle. She wasn't sure how long she would be here, so she didn't unload her suitcase just yet. She hoped to stay put for a few days at least, but one never knew here.

After reading her scriptures and saying her prayers—a simple nightly ritual that would surely become complicated once her roommates arrived—she crawled into bed and pulled the covers up to her chin. There was a bit of a chill in the air, which was made worse by the rattling of the windows against the worsening storm.

She listened to the raindrops ping against the window, and her thoughts drifted to Michael. Once again she felt a rush of relief and satisfaction at how the night had gone. There was something really spectacular about him—he definitely had a well-rounded personality, his approach to life was admirable, and his thoughtfulness and incredible good looks made him a catch. But even beyond those qualities, there was something very grounded and real about him that topped the list. He was completely different from what she'd expected.

She felt a thrill of excitement as she thought about the prospect of spending time with him again and getting to know him—although she knew that wasn't going to be easy with all the competition of the show. She determined once more to simply do the best she could and maximize any time she had with him.

For now, she needed sleep. It had been a very long and full day.

A flash of lightning and an immediate crash of thunder sent her deeper under her covers but wasn't enough to keep her awake. Soon she was with Michael again, but this time, in her dreams.

Chapter 8

ANDI AWOKE TO THE SAME tune of drizzling rain. Peering out the corner of her window at the gray skies and soggy world outside, she felt bad for the girls who'd been scheduled for outside dates that day.

She also noticed that the golf cart was gone. She had considered it thoughtful of the producers to keep an eye on her, but she wondered whether their motives were to keep her safe or to keep tabs on her.

Shrugging and deciding it didn't matter much either way, she searched for the card listing her options for room service. She wasn't terribly hungry but didn't have anything else to do so she ordered some breakfast. The TV had been disconnected to keep her from watching any coverage about the show, Michael, or any of the girls participating on it.

As they often did, her thoughts drifted to her friends and what was going on with them, especially Emma's baby and Chloe and Roger. She was anxious to check in with them at the first opportunity and see how they were doing.

Feeling antsy as she waited for her breakfast and the other girls to show up, Andi pulled out the material for her book and began writing. Kirk would be proud of her. So far this book had been much easier to write than her first one, which had been therapeutic but extremely emotional.

After breakfast and a few hours of writing, she heard the crunch of gravel outside the front door. Sliding her writing back into the flap of her suitcase, she looked to the doorway. She had company.

Still dressed in comfy sweats and with her hair pulled up in a ponytail, Andi suddenly wished she would have taken time to get ready for the day. But it was too late for that now.

When she opened the door, a girl who looked like she'd been standing under a fire hose burst past her.

The girl swore and dropped her suitcase onto the floor. Then, not even bothering to say hello to Andi, she stormed straight to the bathroom.

A young man carrying the rest of her bags came through the door. He too was soaked clear through. Andi hadn't realized how hard it was raining until they showed up.

She didn't even have a chance to thank the young man, who dropped the luggage on the floor and took off, slamming the door behind him.

"Great," Andi said under her breath, looking at the pile of matching designer luggage. She knew the current housing arrangements weren't going to be permanent, but this girl seemed high maintenance already.

A few minutes later, Andi forced a smile as the girl came back from the bathroom wearing only a bra and underwear. She tossed her soaked clothing onto the floor and went straight to her luggage—still without acknowledging Andi. Then, wringing out her long blonde hair with one hand, she rummaged through several suitcases before she found what she was looking for and pulled on a pair of fuchsia-pink Juicy Couture sweatpants and jacket, both heavily embellished with blinding rhinestones.

Finally dressed, the girl looked up at Andi, seeming to notice her for the first time. "Hi."

"Hello," Andi said.

"I'm Kimmie." She lifted her long, wet hair off her neck with an unpleasant expression on her face. "That was the worst date I've ever been on in my life!"

Not knowing what to say, Andi decided to remain silent.

"The rain totally ruined it, but even without it, the date would have been a disaster. Who does Michael Makua think he is anyway? Hawaiian royalty?"

Andi had to ask. "What happened?"

"We were supposed to go to this lovely spot that overlooked the ocean and have breakfast then go for a walk on the beach, but since this *monsoon* arrived, we couldn't do that. So we had breakfast indoors and pretty much talked about him the entire time and all his *save the planet* junk and all the stuff he does in stupid Africa!"

Andi's eyes opened wide, but she managed to keep her mouth clamped shut. Was this woman serious?

"He hardly asked me anything about myself. I'm a freaking swimsuit model, I get invited to all the posh parties in Hollywood, and my acting career is really starting to take off. Yeah," she flipped her hands toward herself and said, "he could've had me, but he's such an idiot, he doesn't even know what he's losing."

"You didn't get kicked off the show, did you?" she asked tentatively, hoping the answering might be yes.

"Not yet, but there was zero chemistry between us. All the money in the world couldn't make up for his lack of personality. Whoever ends up with him has my sympathy."

Andi wondered briefly if she and Kimmie had been on dates with the same person. If Michael had anything going for him, it was personality.

Kimmie suddenly narrowed her eyes and gave Andi a careful look. "How was your date with him? Did you go out last night?"

"It went well," Andi said carefully. "We actually had a lot in common, so we had plenty to talk about."

Kimmie eyed her, sizing her up. "Yeah, it figures."

Andi felt as if she had just been slapped. The woman had just insulted her! However, she simply shrugged. "I actually found him charming and quite fascinating." Then she turned and went back to the chair where her notebook was.

Without a reply, Kimmie dug her blow-dryer out of her suitcase and took it to the bathroom. Andi rolled her eyes, glad she was gone.

Kimmie stayed in the bathroom redoing her hair and makeup for the next hour, and Andi continued to work until she noticed that the sun was shining and the clouds were moving away. She smiled. Now she could go outside and avoid the dark cloud named Kimmie that was inside with her.

Putting away her notebook and pen, she found her light jacket and pulled it on before venturing out. She'd have to be careful not to run into any of the girls who hadn't been on their date yet. It was mandatory that she not have contact with them.

The plantation was large but still very quaint. There were at least thirty bungalows of various sizes, along with a lovely reception hall, a restaurant, banquet room, spa, pool, and a laundry facility for guests. It even had a small church on the premises.

Of course, the plantation also contained business offices, as well as the main home known as the Mansion. Andi wondered how it would be, once the group of contestants was whittled down enough, to move into the Mansion for the remainder of the show.

As she left the bungalow, Andi spotted a comfortable-looking bench, nearly dry from the sun, which looked like the perfect place to sit and gather her thoughts. The beach was empty except for seagulls busy dipping and soaring and scavenging for food. The air was fresh and fragrant, and the sun was warm on her skin.

She closed her eyes and drew in several deep breaths. Any concerns were suddenly nonexistent in the beauty and quiet of the moment.

A sigh escaped her lips as a breeze played with a few tendrils of hair at the base of her neck, and she smiled, caught up in the perfection of the surroundings. Could she give up the craziness and the convenience of living in the city for this magic?

Yes, she thought with a nod. In fact, she could get used to it very easily.

"Good morning," a man's voice said.

Andi jumped, her eyes flying open. "Oh!" she scanned around her quickly, finding her nighttime caretaker, Kana, standing near her with a rake in his hand. "You startled me."

"My apologies," he said, putting his hand on his heart and bowing his head.

"That's okay. I didn't hear you walk up."

"I saw you and wondered if everything was okay," he said then gestured to the surrounding plantation. "After that storm, there's some cleaning up for me to do."

"I can imagine. Was there any damage?"

"Not really. Just branches and debris. Nothing too terrible. Are you enjoying yourself?"

She shrugged. "Yeah, I guess. I mean, don't get me wrong, the plantation is incredible. I'd really love to go exploring and see all of it, but I'm not allowed to yet."

He nodded. "When you are able to go exploring, I have some bicycles you can use to ride around the grounds. It's a great way to see the plantation. It's quite a beautiful place," he said proudly.

"I hope I stay around long enough to see more of it," she said sincerely.

They both jumped as the front door to the bungalow banged open and Kimmie stormed outside. "There you are! I've been looking all over for you," she called in a shrill voice.

Andi and Kana exchanged glances. The bungalow only had four rooms. It didn't take a brain surgeon to figure out she wasn't inside.

"How in the world am I supposed to get food? I'm starving! I didn't get a bite to eat at that ridiculous breakfast."

"I'd better help her," Andi told Kana in a low voice. "It was nice seeing you again."

Kana dipped his chin, "And you also." He looked at Kimmie and frowned, not saying anything to her.

Andi prayed the next four days would pass quickly.

* * *

Throughout the course of the afternoon, two more girls were moved into the bungalow—Danee and Becca, whom Andi found she adored. Danee was fun-loving, chatty, and friendly, and when she arrived at the bungalow with a smile and hugs all around (which Kimmie refused), Andi immediately liked her. She was athletic and outdoorsy, with a shoulder-length page-boy haircut, large green eyes, and a constant smile, and she immediately recognized Andi from her appearances on QVC. Becca was equally as warm and friendly but much more sophisticated and almost intimidatingly beautiful. She was tall, thin, and tan, had gorgeous blonde hair, and a contagious laugh.

From their reports, Becca's and Danee's dates had gone well. They both adored Michael and reported that he was easy to get to know. Andi hoped if she stayed around, they would too. The discussion of their dates didn't go over well with Kimmie, who pouted and stomped around the bungalow until she finally shut herself in her room.

"This day is a wastin'. Let's go to the beach," Danee said in her darling Southern drawl. She was a landscape designer from Atlanta and practically lived outside.

It took some convincing, but the girls even got Kimmie to join them. Spending time at the beach was the only activity allowed since the beach was so close to their bungalow and no one else was out there.

Pulling lounge chairs together in a row, they got settled and applied sunscreen then relaxed back in the warmth of the Hawaiian sun.

Kimmie was the only one who had been to Hawaii before. Her last boyfriend had been a pilot, so she'd been able to travel all over the world. Danee had never been farther than two hundred miles away from Atlanta, and Becca had grown up in Phoenix but had moved to the Bay Area in California to be with her boyfriend, who had dumped her one month after she'd moved.

Becca wasn't the only one with dating horror stories. Even Kimmie had been burned royally by the airline pilot because he felt like she would be "too high maintenance" to take care of if they got married. This had apparently been a shocking revelation to her, and she told the other girls with a confidential whisper that he probably had women in every city he flew to and just didn't want to give that up for her.

"So, did you notice how buff our Mr. Makua is?" Becca said, bringing the conversation back to their immediate prospect for love. "He's got incredible shoulders."

"You can tell he's strong," Danee said, lighting up.

Andi didn't tell them that she knew firsthand how strong he was because he'd carried her around practically their entire date.

"Kimmie, what did you think of Michael?" Becca asked, having missed the earlier tirade.

"I don't really see what all the fuss is about," she answered crabbily.

Becca turned toward Andi and Danee and mouthed the word *wow* to them. Then she rolled over onto her stomach and said, "After some of the freaks I've dated, it's nice to meet a man who's good-looking and successful and doesn't act like he's entitled to take advantage of you. I'm so sick of men attacking me on our first date and acting like it's my duty to be intimate with them. Call me old-fashioned, but I actually want some respect from my date."

"I don't think it's old-fashioned," Danee said. "I feel the same way."

The conversation was interrupted by a golf cart driving toward them. When it stopped, a young Asian girl wearing a beautiful turquoise Hawaiian-print blouse and white pencil skirt got out.

"Excuse me, ladies," she said, flashing them a smile. "I'm here with a message. You have been invited to the Grove Banquet Room for dinner this evening at seven. The dress is casual."

"Finally. Food!" Kimmie erupted.

"There is a map in your bungalow that tells you how to get to the banquet room," she said, casting a glance at Kimmie. Then she climbed back into her cart and drove away.

"It'll be nice when these one-on-one dates are over," Danee said.

"It's ridiculous that we have to sit here and do nothing," Kimmie complained. "Honestly, at least give us our phones and a TV, for crying out loud."

"It's just to keep us from having contact—"

"I know why!" Kimmie burst in. "I'm just saying it's ridiculous."

A silence ensued until Kimmie's outburst settled onto the sand and blew away with the ocean breeze.

"I'm hot," Danee exclaimed after a moment. "I'm going in the water. Y'all joining me?"

"I will," Andi said.

"Me too." Becca jumped up. "Come on, Kimmie."

"You guys go ahead; I can't get my suit wet," Kimmie replied, closing her eyes.

Danee burst out laughing. "I'm sorry, but did you just say you can't get your swimsuit wet?"

"It's a bathing suit, for *sun* bathing," Kimmie said with irritated emphasis. "There's a difference—a five-hundred-dollar difference."

"Say what?" Danee took off her sunglasses and looked closely at Kimmie's black and gold lamé suit. "Is that real gold or something?"

"No, but it's real Balenciaga, which is as good as gold."

"Well, Kimmie, it's very . . . shiny," Danee said, a smile tugging at the corner of her mouth. She shrugged then ran for the water. Andi and Becca followed after her.

Andi wasn't sure about getting her foot wet, but she decided she'd rather risk an infection than stay with Miss Haute Couture and hear her whine about everything.

The water was brisk at first but soon felt wonderfully refreshing. Andi and Becca both knew how to body surf, so they spent the next half hour teaching Danee how to wait for a wave then swim with it and let it carry her back to shore.

Spending a few carefree moments playing like kids on the beach was refreshing, and it reinforced her feelings that she truly was glad to be here. She wasn't as much about winning as she was about making this experience worthwhile. And today had become such a day.

* * *

The following days passed quickly as more girls joined the ranks of those who had been on their one-on-one date with Michael. The contestants had once upon a time been instructed not to discuss Michael or their dates, but Andi soon realized that the producers wanted them to talk in order to create as much drama over the situation as possible. In fact, they even spent time baiting the girls with talk of what everyone else was saying about the dates.

Andi hated to disappoint them, but she wasn't going to play their game.

Kimmie, on the other hand, managed to stir up as much controversy as she could. Somehow a rumor got started that Kimmie and Michael had actually kissed on their first date. Andi was certain that Kimmie herself had started that one.

With cameras rolling even when the girls spent time together at the pool, on the beach, or riding bikes around the plantation, Kimmie managed to position herself right in view of the camera lens whenever possible. However, to Andi's relief, she soon realized that there were only a handful of girls like Kimmie who seemed to be after TV exposure and who were willing to do whatever it took to get it. As Andi got to know the rest of the contestants, she found the majority of them to be extremely interesting and accomplished.

On the evening of the fourth night, all the girls were invited to dinner and were told to dress in their nicest formal gowns. They weren't told whether Michael would be making an appearance or not, but it seemed obvious what was going to happen.

At eight o'clock on the dot, their transportation arrived, and the girls, either twittering with excitement or mute with nerves, climbed into the limousines. When her turn arrived, Andi took a breath and climbed in, gathering her gown around her. She was certain the moment of truth had arrived—it was time for eliminations.

Chapter 9

In the room full of high-strung females, a large television crew, and a table laden with food and various types of alcoholic drinks, Andi sat back and observed the way small clusters had formed and the dynamic of each group.

Kimmie was surrounded by five other women, all of them wearing uncannily similar skin-tight minidresses. They were so low cut and bare that Andi found herself turning completely away from them so she didn't have to worry about viewing any "wardrobe malfunctions."

Becca was laughing and having fun with another group of girls, several of whom Andi had gotten to know during a volleyball game earlier in the day. They were happy, down-to-earth women who had the same purpose in doing the show as Andi did—to have fun and see what happened.

Several smaller clusters of two and three girls were tucked away in corners. Some of them had seemed nice to Andi upon first meeting, but she had gradually gotten the feeling that behind the friendly façade, they were capable of subterfuge. Trusting her instincts, she had decided to keep an eye out for them.

The rest of the contestants just seemed to be making the rounds trying to meet and greet as many of the other women as they could. Danee was one of them. As she finished working the room, she came to stand beside Andi.

"So, what do you think?" Danee asked her. She slid her stilettos off and pointed and flexed her feet.

"About what?"

"The show, the other girls, meeting Michael?"

"I'm starting to get used to being on the show, I guess, but I'm more convinced than ever that I'd never want to be a celebrity with the paparazzi following me all the time."

"What are you talking about? You already are a celebrity," Danee said, giving her an inquisitive look.

"Only to the fitness industry," Andi clarified. "Really, most people here don't even know who I am—and I actually like it that way."

"A couple of girls have mentioned that they have your DVDs and some of the products you've endorsed on QVC."

"That's nice to hear. Still, I'm no one special. Believe me."

"You're just being modest," Danee said. "I like that about you. And you know what?"

Andi shrugged.

"I think you're going to do very well on this show. You're beautiful, famous, and a really unique person. He'd be crazy not to choose you."

"Thank you, Danee," Andi replied, flattered by the compliment, "but really, I don't see how it could ever—" She stopped, remembering what she'd been told about sharing her religious views with others. "I don't see that ever happening. I mean, Michael's probably looking for someone completely different than me. I'm not glamorous enough for him. Besides, I'm pretty sure I'm the oldest one here. He's going to go for someone younger and hotter."

"That's crazy," Danee protested, rolling her eyes. "You're not giving yourself enough credit." She snagged a glass of wine as a waiter walked by carrying a tray of goblets. "Let's have fun tonight and not let any of these Barbies get to us. Here's to 'real' women."

Andi toasted her with her goblet of ice water, and the two women giggled as a flock of Barbie girls walked by, one of them tugging her strapless dress up, one of them pulling her minidress down, and another trying to keep upright on a pair of six-inch stilettos.

Once the buffet had been set up, the girls lined up to fill their plates, after which they found a seat at one of the four round tables set up in the garden area.

Most of the girls, Andi noticed, hardly took any food, but Andi couldn't resist all the fresh shrimp and fresh fruit. She hadn't eaten much that day and was famished.

Danee waited for her at the end of the buffet line and together they walked to the candlelit tables looking for Becca, who was supposed to save them a seat.

When Becca saw them she gave them an enthusiastic wave. Andi smiled, thinking again how much she liked these two girls. She was grateful to have them for roommates, even though it was only temporary.

A small three-piece band began to play lovely Hawaiian music for them as they dined, and soon the feeling in the room relaxed as everyone enjoyed the dinner and the soothing music.

The pineapple was especially sweet and delicious, and Andi decided she wanted a little more. Taking her plate to the buffet table, she placed a few more slices on her plate then turned to head back to her table.

"Is everything okay, miss?" an employee standing behind the buffet table asked her. The woman appeared to be a supervisor rather than a waitress.

"It's incredible," Andi said. "I don't think I've ever had pineapple this good in my life. And that shrimp is to die for."

"Take some more," the woman urged. "Apparently none of the other girls eat, so there's plenty."

"I can't resist," Andi said, putting a few more shrimps on her plate. "Everything is delicious. Thank you so much. The whole place is really lovely."

"Thank you," the woman answered, a smile lighting up her expression. Then she gave Andi a wink. "You seem to have figured out how to eat and stay thin."

"Believe me, I'll be up early running, but it's so worth it."

The woman shook her head. "Some of these girls don't eat enough to keep a bird alive."

"I think some of them are nervous about Mr. Makua showing up," she said.

"You aren't nervous?"

"It doesn't really make sense to be nervous. Each of us has already met him."

"If you don't mind me asking, how did your date go?"

"I think it went really well—at least as far as I'm concerned, it did."

"What do you think of Mr. Right?"

Andi couldn't keep herself from smiling. "He's pretty incredible—a lot more down to earth than I expected. I really liked that about him. We have a lot in common."

The woman gave her another smile. "Well, good luck."

Andi thanked her again then returned to her seat.

"Who was that?" Becca asked when she returned.

"I think she was the supervisor. Just asking how I liked the food." Andi dipped one of the shrimp into cocktail sauce and took a big bite.

A couple of girls across from her stared enviously at her plate. Andi noticed they'd barely eaten their meals. She shrugged, feeling sorry for them. The shrimp was divine.

A table of desserts was ready when everyone finished eating, and Andi was amused by how many of the women didn't eat their food but managed to find an appetite for dessert. She herself was too full of fruit and shrimp to indulge in cheesecake, brownies, or ice cream.

While the other girls swarmed the dessert buffet, Andi decided to wander the garden and look at the amazing tropical flowers that filled the air with their intoxicating fragrance.

Andi meandered along a winding pathway lit by candles and tiki torches and thronged by fern- and flower-filled gardens. She stopped to admire a bush loaded with delicate pink plumeria blossoms, shutting her eyes and pulling in a lungful of their sweet scent.

"Smells good, doesn't it?" a male voice asked.

Andi jumped. She smiled when she saw Michael standing a few feet away. "Hi, there," she said. He stepped toward her, and they hugged in greeting. "How has your week been?"

"Long," he said. "How has yours been?"

"It's been fun, actually. Very relaxing."

"I'm jealous," he said.

"It's good to see you."

He smiled, obviously pleased. "You too." He nodded toward the flower. "That's my favorite fragrance."

"It's heavenly."

"How come you're not inside?" he asked, a curious look on his face.

"I didn't want dessert. And I needed a little time away from all the girls."

"I know what you mean."

They both laughed.

"There you are, Michael!" Silas exclaimed. "Oh." He paused when he saw Andi. "Hello, Andi."

"Hello, Silas," Andi said easily, determined to be friendly despite the prickle of unease she felt when he appeared.

"We need you inside," Silas said to Michael. "Both of you, actually."

"Okay," Michael said. "We'll be right there."

"It would be best if Andi went inside first. Then after a few minutes, you can make your entrance," Silas instructed.

"All right," Andi said, her gaze lingering on Michael. "See you both inside."

She followed the path back to the reception area, where the girls had been moved after finishing dessert.

"Where have you been?" Danee asked when Andi showed up.

"I didn't want any dessert, so I went to look at the flowers. Did I miss anything?"

"Just Kimmie throwing a fit because one of the girls accidentally tipped her cherry-covered cheesecake into Kimmie's lap."

"What? Oh no, poor Kimmie."

"You're kidding, right? Poor Kimmie? It was all I could do not to laugh. Besides, it wiped right off. It wasn't that big of a deal. She just created a big scene. The poor girl who did it was crying afterward. And, of course, the cameras caught it all."

"Of course."

"I think we're getting a visitor, and I'm not talking Santa Claus."

Andi laughed and glanced around. "Are the cameras rolling now?"

"I don't think so, but you never know. I feel like they have hidden cameras all over the place," Danee said. "I'm glad you came back when you did, though. They're about ready to make an announcement."

Silas walked to the front of the room, and the girls applauded.

"Good evening, girls. I hope you had an enjoyable dinner."

Everyone glanced at Kimmie, who looked beautiful in spite of the mishap. Andi had to admit, she was an incredibly attractive woman. If only beauty went a little further than skin-deep.

"We have a few surprises for you tonight. I am going to introduce you to Mark Sterling, the show's host," Silas continued. "He will tell you how the rest of the evening will proceed. As always, ignore the cameras and just be your beautiful selves."

The girls clapped as Silas held out his hand for Mark to join him.

When Mark stepped from the back room, Andi recognized him as a former entertainment reporter for a Los Angeles–based news program. He was often seen interviewing celebrities at red-carpet events and even did a little acting on the side.

"Thank you for that warm welcome," he said to the girls as the thunderous applause died down. "I can honestly say this is definitely the sweetest job I've ever had."

The girls cheered, clapped, and giggled.

"Now, I have some good news and some bad news for you." He looked over the crowd to gauge their reaction. "The good news is we are going to have a visit from the guy who makes everything *right* about this show, our own Mr. Michael Makua."

An eruption of cheers and catcalls came from the group of girls.

"The bad news is—" he looked them over one more time, his brows teasingly lifted "—well, the bad news is, half of you will be going home tonight."

A cry of disbelief filled the room, and looks of panic filled many of the girls' faces.

To Andi, it seemed a little drastic to eliminate half of the girls all at once, but the producers had warned them that this would happen.

Judging by the facial expressions around her, no one felt safe—well, except Kimmie. For some reason, she looked as though she'd been given a free ticket straight to the finale.

Mark tried to calm everyone down by telling them, "Keep in mind, our Mr. Right would like to spend some time tonight getting to know some of you just a little better before he makes his decision." He paused, letting the news sink in. "At the end of the night, we will have a lei ceremony. Those who don't receive a lei will go directly back to their bungalows, pack their bags, and return home."

Danee discreetly leaned closer to Andi. "I'm so nervous," she whispered. "Is it a good thing or a bad thing if he wants to talk to me? On our date, I first felt like we really connected, but now that I've had a chance to think about it, we really didn't. I don't want to go home yet. Did you know I quit my job to be on this show?"

"I didn't know that," Andi said, surprised. "But Danee, you don't need to worry. He's not going to send you home."

"You really think that?"

"I really do. You are an incredible woman; you really seem like his type," Andi told her with complete sincerity.

"Oh, Andi, I hope so," she said then gasped along with the rest of the girls. Michael had just walked in.

With the cameras rolling and the girls offering plenty of reaction, Michael took his place in front and even hugged a couple of girls as he walked into the room. It appeared by the dreamy-eyed look on most of the girls' faces that each of them felt as though she were his one and only, the one who would receive a proposal and engagement ring at the end of the show.

Andi wondered if these girls were really intent on finding love or just on winning.

No matter what, Andi didn't envy Michael's predicament.

"Good evening, ladies," Michael said. He looked extremely handsome in his black suit, white shirt, and deep burgundy tie. The white against his tanned skin and dark brown hair made him even more attractive, not to mention how stunning he was in the suit.

Andi felt herself getting caught up in the moment—Michael, the location, and the heightened competition all appealed to her. She told herself to stay focused and not get caught up in all of it, but she couldn't help it—at least a little.

"Tonight is going to be a lot of fun. Even though we are going to send a few of you home this evening, I want you to know how hard this decision is and also how happy I am that I got to spend time with twenty-four amazing women. In real time, it would have taken me about a decade to get dates with that many beautiful, accomplished women."

Polite laughter followed.

"So, let's relax. I think there are some fire pits and a bar outside, so please make yourselves comfortable. I'll try to greet each of you personally, but if I don't get to you, please don't hesitate to pull me aside."

Several of the girls looked at each other and laughed. He didn't realize what he had just said. As competitive as these girls were, he would be lucky to have five minutes alone with anyone.

The double doors to the garden opened, and the girls were encouraged to go outside. However, the problem was that none of the girls wanted anyone else to have time alone with Michael. No one would leave.

Snapping out of the moment she'd been caught up in, Andi shook her head to get her brain functioning again. She took Danee by the arm and said, "Let's go out. We can see him when he gets outside. Where's Becca?"

Poor Becca was standing near the Barbie section, looking lost and forlorn.

Danee rescued her, and together the three girls went outside and found the bar. Becca and Danee each got another glass of wine, and Andi opted for a soft drink. They took their drinks to one of the fire pits, where they sat on the cushioned bamboo love seat and chairs.

The other girls slowly trickled outside, and a few joined them at the fire pit.

To Andi's amazement, Kimmie had somehow managed to morph into a charming, witty, life-of-the-party alter ego of herself. Danee and

Becca noticed it as well, and with growing nausea they watched Kimmie work her way through the group keeping up a façade of being kind and friendly. Occasionally she glanced over to see if Michael or the cameras were noticing.

After twenty minutes of Michael hanging with the entire group, he began pulling girls aside and taking them to a secluded spot where they could talk privately.

Those who hadn't had private time with Michael watched closely for his return then did their best to catch his attention, hoping to be the next one to have an intimate moment with him.

When Michael chose Kimmie, she turned and gave the rest of the girls a quick wave, her expression one of pure triumph. She might have thought she'd fooled everyone, but at that moment all the girls knew what she was capable of.

Because Andi had already had private time with Michael, she didn't feel the anxiety some of the others felt. However, Danee and Becca were both close to heart failure by the time Michael returned with Kimmie. That is, until they saw Kimmie's expression. After spending the last four days with her, they immediately recognized that the expression they were seeing was definitely not her "happy face."

"I don't think that went as well as she wanted it to," Danee said quietly to Andi and Becca.

"Doesn't look that way," Becca said. "I hope that means he saw through her. Can you imagine being married to her?"

Andi agreed with them but didn't join in the conversation, refusing to gossip. But they were right—Kimmie had raised the bar on being high maintenance. In fact, the bar was so high, an Olympic pole-vaulter would be intimidated.

"Look, Michael's coming our way," Becca said, smoothing her dress and shifting anxiously.

Andi felt her heart flutter but knew he wasn't coming for her. Or was he?

Chapter 10

"Good evening, ladies," Michael said, his baritone voice soft.

The girls offered a greeting in response, and Andi once again found herself thinking how handsome he looked in his suit. He had a slight tilt to his grin and a dimple in one cheek that gave him a boyish charm Andi found irresistible. Dang, he was a hunk!

"Can I borrow you for a minute?" he asked Becca.

Becca kept her eyes on Michael as she accepted his hand and walked away with him.

"I hope this is a good thing," Dance said. "She really doesn't want to go home on this first cut."

"He's got a tough job tonight," Andi said, trying to picture how difficult it would be to make such a decision after only one date with each girl.

"Hopefully the one-on-one dates helped him sort the girls he connected with from the ones he didn't. Did you feel like you made a connection with him?"

Andi didn't answer for a moment. The truth was, yes, she felt like she'd connected with him faster than any man she'd ever dated. And that's what made the whole situation so difficult. She knew she could really like this guy, but she could never marry him.

Moments later Becca and Michael came back from their visit. Andi couldn't tell by her expression whether things had gone well or not. She wouldn't have to wonder long, though—Mark Sterling had just joined the contestants outside.

"All right, girls. I'm going to steal Michael for a few minutes so he can make his final decisions, and then we'll be back to have the lei ceremony. You ready, Michael?"

"No," Michael said.

The girls laughed, and Mark looked slightly taken aback.

Michael took a deep breath. "Actually, I take that back. I'm as ready as I'll ever be."

"Okay, then. Girls, we'll meet you inside," Mark instructed. Then the two men left, leaving the girls in silence.

"Ladies, we need you to come inside now so we can freshen your hair and makeup," a woman named Shauna, who oversaw the hair and makeup crew, told them.

Once inside, Silas gave them further instructions. "We will place you in two half circles for the elimination. Those of you who are given a lei will return to your spot. Those without a lei will be asked to leave. After the final lei is given, you can say your good-byes. "

With the announcement made, a somber group of women began re-applying lipstick and getting hair adjustments. Then they made their way to the stage and platforms that had been arranged for the back row of women to stand on.

The previously chatty and excited contestants spoke very little as the tension in the room grew by the minute.

"I don't have a good feeling about this," Becca said sadly after she'd been fluffed and sprayed. "He's such a nice guy, and we had a really great—but short—conversation, but I didn't see anything in his eyes, you know?"

"It was dark," Danee said. "You probably couldn't even see his eyes."

Becca smiled. "Maybe. I hope I'm wrong. I'd like a chance to go out with him again."

As cameras were set up and all the technical adjustments were made, a woman Andi hadn't met began placing girls on the steps in what appeared to be a random order.

Andi was placed next to Kimmie on the center of the back row.

"Are you sure you want me in the back?" Kimmie asked the woman.

"That's where Silas wants you," the woman told her,

"Really? Where is he? I'm sure there must be some mistake," Kimmie said, craning her neck to look for him.

"He's . . ."

Kimmie walked away before the woman could finish.

The woman's gaze connected with Andi's. Andi shrugged, expressing sympathy for her. Returning the gesture, the woman shook her head and finished placing the girls.

A few moments later, the woman received instruction through her headset. Then, shaking her head, she asked Eliza, a tiny blonde with a cute, bobbed haircut and large green eyes to step up to the back row. In her place at the front stood Kimmie.

Andi's mouth dropped open, but she quickly shut it and wiped any reaction off her face. She did not want the cameras to capture her being appalled at Kimmie's gall—even though inside she was.

With all the girls in position, it was time for Michael to enter the room. The room became deathly still as he made his entrance alongside Mark Sterling.

"Good evening, ladies," Mark began. "As you all know, it is time for our first lei ceremony. I'm sure Michael wouldn't mind me telling you that he's had a very difficult time making the decision of who to keep and who to let go. But after a lot of thought, he's made his final decision."

Mark turned to Michael. "Are you ready?"

"I'm ready, Mark."

"All right, I'll leave you to it." Mark stepped to the side and out of the way as Michael stepped up to a lovely carved wooden stand that had colorful floral leis hanging from it.

The first three women he called were all tall and thin, with dark hair and tanned skin. Andi wondered if that was a coincidence or if he was simply drawn to girls with this body type and style. Then he called Eliza's name and shattered that theory.

She found herself holding her breath as four more girls were called.

It was obvious that all around her, nerves were strung tight and sparking. The girl standing beside Andi was literally shaking. Andi wanted to put an arm around her, but she knew Silas wouldn't approve.

Michael paused and looked at the girls, dragging out the agony. Andi wondered if contestants were going to start fainting from the heightened tension.

"Danee," he called.

Without missing a beat, Danee made a beeline for Michael and accepted his lei with a giggle of joy and a hug. Andi found herself breathing a sigh of relief, genuinely glad that Danee had made it.

Two more girls were called, both of whom Andi didn't know at all. That left one more girl. Kimmie and Becca were still standing. Andi was determined to keep her cool, but her palms were clammy with sweat.

Mark stepped forward. "Michael, there is only one lei left. Are you ready to make your final choice?"

Michael nodded.

He looked the girls over again and smiled. Andi felt light-headed from standing so long.

"Kimmie," he said.

Andi felt her face go numb. So, they hadn't clicked like she'd thought they had. Heat soon replaced the numbness. She suddenly felt stupid thinking they'd had such a great connection. Had she made it all up? She hoped the camera wasn't right on her face because she was certain it was as vivid red as the bird of paradise in the floral arrangement next to Michael.

After he placed the lei over Kimmie's head, she put her arms around his neck and gave him a lingering hug. Andi hadn't felt so nauseated since she'd had swine flu last winter. It was better this way, she told herself, swallowing the hurt. Now she wouldn't have a chance to get attached to someone she couldn't have anyway.

"Ladies, could I have your attention?" Mark said

Even Andi's ears felt hot. Why did she care? She knew from the beginning nothing would become of this. But to be kicked off on the first cut stung more than she'd anticipated.

Was it possible she'd been cut for political reasons? For the wine thing? Michael had been so gracious about it. Maybe Silas had encouraged Michael not to keep her. Maybe he thought that eventually her beliefs would come out and mess up the ratings.

"Michael has something to say."

Stepping up to the microphone, Michael gave the girls an understanding smile. "First of all, thank you to all of you who will be staying, but especially to those of you who will be leaving. You are all such beautiful, talented, and accomplished women, and I feel fortunate to have been able to meet you this week."

Andi managed to calm down and put a pleasant expression on her face. At least now she could go home and get back to work on her book and be with her friends. With everything each of them had going on, she felt like she was needed to offer support and help any way she could.

"I have a small surprise I was saving for last," he said. "I've decided to give an extra lei for the best one-on-one date. And that lei goes to . . . Andi."

For a brief moment, Andi had to close her eyes and anchor her composure. She felt like laughing and crying at the same time. But she didn't. She left the platform, purposefully avoiding Kimmie's eyes.

Her gaze locked onto Michael's as she approached him. They both smiled.

"Andi, will you accept this lei?" he asked when she stood in front of him.

"Yes, I would love to."

After he put it around her head, they hugged. "Sorry," he whispered, "were you worried?"

"You want me to be honest?" she whispered back.

"Of course," he said as they stepped back.

She didn't have a chance to answer. He gave her hand a squeeze as she walked away.

It was impossible to miss the heat of Kimmie's glare as she took her place beside her. But Andi didn't care. Michael was a wonderful, incredible man, and he deserved someone equally wonderful and incredible. Kimmie was not that person.

"Ladies, you may take a minute to say good-bye."

Very few girls congratulated Andi, but Danee and Becca each gave her a hug.

"I'm so sad you're leaving," Danee told Becca. "He didn't get to know you like we did—otherwise, he'd know how much he was missing out on."

"There must be someone really amazing out there for you," Andi told her. "I'm going to miss you."

"Well, if I can't be Mrs. Right, I want it to be one of you. Or . . . basically anyone except Kimmie," Becca said wickedly.

They tried to hide their laughter and hugged again.

Once the farewells had been said, the remaining girls were given wine glasses. Andi's was empty this time since no water was readily available, and they toasted to surviving the first cut of the show.

The girls were then allowed to mingle for a while and enjoy the moment. After a while, Kimmie, who had snuggled right up to Michael's side, said, "Why don't we all meet back at the hot tub?"

Most of the girls squealed with excitement at the suggestion and tried to coax Michael into agreeing. Michael cast a glance at Silas, who nodded his approval.

"Sounds great. Let's do it," he said.

Andi swallowed. This was the part of the matchup reality shows that left Andi less than impressed. She got uncomfortable watching when things got steamy, so she changed the channel. And she wasn't about to be part of it now.

Michael was whisked away before the girls could swarm him when the cameras stopped, and the girls were sent in cars back to their bungalows to change clothes. Earlier, everyone had been instructed to have their bags packed and ready in case they were going home, so by the time they arrived, Becca was already gone. She'd left a note to both Andi and Danee but not one to Kimmie. Of course, Kimmie didn't seem to care. She'd made it clear she wasn't there to make friends.

Keeping to herself and blatantly ignoring the others, Kimmie went straight to her room to change. Danee and Andi changed in the other bedroom. They didn't say anything about Kimmie just in case she could hear them, but Andi knew Danee was thinking the same thing she was: Kimmie was psycho.

Dreading what lay ahead for the evening, Andi accompanied Danee to the car then waited another ten minutes for Kimmie. But still, they didn't complain. There were ears and eyes everywhere.

Kimmie finally stepped out of the bungalow and strolled to the car, showing no urgency. Andi and Danee exchanged looks of annoyance but said nothing when Kimmie finally got in the car.

It was obvious that Kimmie had redone her hair and makeup and even slathered on some type of tanning lotion. Her skin glistened a sparkling bronze color, which was breathtaking against her daffodil-colored bathing suit. From what Andi could tell, she had somewhere between ten to fifteen bathing suits with her, all of them couture designs. Andi's biggest concern was that her own suit might still smell like the ocean. She hadn't had a chance to wash any of her clothes, and her other suits were still wet. However, she felt confident that her swimsuits were every bit as beautiful as Kimmie's. Cooper and Lauryn had done an amazing job with her wardrobe, and that included swimwear. She was proud to wear their designs.

Wishing she could just go back to the bungalow and go to bed, Andi put on a happy face and joined the throng of girls at the pool and hot tub.

Cameras and lights were set up to capture the fun, and while most of the other girls had shed their cover-ups, Andi kept her fun, flouncy cover-up on. No doubt she was the only one wearing a one-piece suit, but she noticed to her relief that at least some of the girls had a sense of modesty.

Kimmie, on the other hand, was the ringleader and center of attention. Afraid that this was going to turn into something akin to a sorority party, Andi kept her distance from the pack, and she and Danee joined two other girls who weren't into making fools out of themselves on national television.

"Hi," Andi said, introducing herself. "I'm Andi, and this is Danee."

"I'm Maria," said the girl with shoulder-length brown hair and a generous Julia Roberts smile.

"I'm Arial," the other girl said.

Andi almost asked if she was kidding. Arial had long, red, wavy hair to the center of her back, a cute turned-up nose, and gorgeous blue eyes. To top it off, she wore a sea-green bikini.

"So," Maria asked Andi, "did that extra lei come as a surprise?"

"A total surprise. I was already thinking about what I was going to do when I got home." Andi watched as two of the girls pushed another girl into the pool. If they even came near her, Andi planned on putting up a fight—and she was pretty sure she'd win, too. People had a tendency to underestimate her strength because of her size. At five foot six and a hundred and twenty pounds, she didn't look like she could drop a full-grown man to his knees, but she could.

"That must have been some first date," Arial continued.

Andi couldn't help noticing that Arial was perched on the chaise lounge resting on one hip with her feet curled to the side and leaning to the side on one arm. Was she going to start singing "Part of Your World"?

"We had a nice time together," she said, biting back a grin. "We seem to have a lot in common." She and Michael had clicked—there was no other explanation. It was all chemistry.

To Andi's surprise, Kimmie actually let herself get thrown into the pool. However, she was less than surprised when Kimmie slowly came up out of the pool and slicked her hair back, looking like a scene out of a movie just as Michael walked outside. How she'd timed that so perfectly, Andi would never know. But Michael definitely noticed her, and all the other girls noticed Michael noticing her.

Tara, a petite blonde with an athletic build, was the first to greet Michael. Her action triggered the others to join in.

"Come on," Danee said, getting to her feet. "We'd better join the others."

The four girls congregated with the rest of the group as Michael told them how nice it was to see them and how much he was looking forward to getting to know them better.

Andi stayed toward the back of the group, watching with amusement. Some of the girls seemed so desperate. How could Michael not see through it? Or could he? The swarm of girls and barrage of questions and attention seemed to overwhelm him.

Andi noticed him glancing around at all of the girls then locating Andi in the back.

He mouthed a word to her then was slammed with more questions from the girls.

Andi smiled as she realized that he'd just said, "Help!"

Chapter 11

WITH A SMILE, ANDI CONTINUED watching the chaotic scene, feeling a bit disgusted by some of the girls who were acting like they were college coeds on spring break.

Kimmie held up her hands to quiet the others and said in a silky voice, "So, Michael, are you ready to get wet?"

"Uh," he looked around as the girls closed in on him, "do I have a choice?" Kimmie shook her head, smiled wickedly, then lunged for him. He put up some resistance but in the end landed in the pool, with Kimmie and four other girls leaping in after him.

The rest of the women, except Andi and Danee, headed for the large hot tub, knowing Michael was bound to head that direction.

"Well," Danee asked, "pool or hot tub?"

"Too cold for the pool," Andi said, deliberately keeping her eyes averted from the splashing scene.

"Hot tub it is, then."

As Andi sat on the edge of the hot tub, just letting her feet dangle in the steaming water, she found herself content to simply listen to the conversations around her. A couple of the girls were complaining about Kimmie—one even saying she hoped Kimmie drowned—but quickly clammed up when the sopping-wet pool crowd approached.

"Any room left?" Michael asked. Kimmie was attached to his side like a barnacle and smiled triumphantly to the others. Andi knew her game—she was out to intimidate as many of the girls as she could. But Andi wasn't worried about her. Being in the competitive fitness environment, she knew how to deal with that vibe. She did feel sorry for the others who weren't as thick-skinned as she was.

* * *

Andi was ready to go back to her bungalow. To her surprise, being in the hot tub had actually been fun, and she'd enjoyed getting to see the playful side of Michael—and the crazy side of some of the girls.

She was impressed with the way Michael could tease and have fun without excluding anyone. She was also impressed with the way he worked himself away from Kimmie and managed to have short conversations with each of the girls.

As the party wound down and the hour grew late, the director let them know it was time to wrap it up for the night.

Andi sighed with relief and smiled as she saw Danee's dreamy expression. She was thrilled that Michael had spent some time talking to her and had nearly fainted when he had tucked her hair behind her ear.

Wrapping up in big beach towels, everyone started climbing out of the hot tub. Andi shivered despite the plush towel and swung her legs over the side to step out. But just then, Michael said her name.

She turned.

"Hey, got a minute?"

A couple of the girls were still in the hot tub, not willing to leave until he did. They looked at Andi with interest.

"Sure," she replied nonchalantly, despite the fact that her heart had just skipped more than one beat.

"I just wondered if you had an answer to that question I asked you earlier." He smiled at her with mischief in his eyes.

She bit her bottom lip in an attempt to suppress a smile, but she couldn't help it. He was so darned irresistible.

"Well?"

"Girls, your rides are here," one of the crew yelled.

"Yes, and the answer is—I was." She decided to answer him honestly. She *had* been worried when he didn't choose her.

"You didn't need to be," he told her, his voice softening.

She gave him a nod. "Okay."

The two girls looked at them with confusion and annoyance in their expressions then climbed out of the hot tub.

Michael stood and stepped out of the water then held out his hand to help Andi.

"Thank you," she said, hoping he knew she was grateful for more than just his assistance right then.

He gave her hand a squeeze and flashed a knowing grin. "You're welcome."

"Michael!" Silas barked his name. "Could we get you over here for some spots?"

"Gotta run," he told her. "See you soon."

As she waited for some of the crew members to move cable and the boom microphone, Andi wrapped her towel closer around her shoulders and allowed herself a small grin. She couldn't help feeling excited. He liked her.

Most of the girls had already gathered their things and were waiting for their ride. Andi quickly gathered her cover-up and bag and was about to shove her feet into her raspberry-pink ballet flats when she let out a loud scream.

A purplish blue centipede, nearly five inches across, was sitting inside one of her shoes.

Michael came running, followed by all of the girls.

Andi was frozen by the immediate shock of seeing such a gigantic insect on her shoe but managed to point at the creature.

Stepping protectively in front of her, Michael looked where she was pointing. The girls who had rushed to see what was going on screamed and retreated quickly.

"Centipede," he said with a tilt of his head. He stepped toward the creepy-crawler and looked closer. "I've lived here all my life, and this is only the second time I've seen one. We hardly ever get them here on the plantation. Sure glad it didn't bite you."

"Is it poisonous?" Andi asked, shivering as chills raced up her spine.

"You could have ended up in the hospital," he said then turned toward the crew. "Someone bring me a jar," he yelled.

The crowd of girls and some crew members watched as someone rushed forward and handed Michael a jar. Then, in one quick motion, he scooped up the centipede. The long creature squirmed wildly inside, sending some of the girls packing.

One of the film crew took the jar from Michael and escorted the multi-legged insect away from the set.

"That guy looked like he could take on a small animal," Michael said, turning to Andi.

She shuddered again at the thought of putting her foot inside her shoe, but Michael laughed softly and put his arm around her. "Hey, it's okay. He's gone."

She relaxed, giggling a little as well, and leaned her head on his shoulder. "I'm sorry. I almost stepped on him, though. It totally freaked me out."

"I wonder where he came from. They usually stay out in the fields." Michael stepped back and looked into her face. "You okay?"

She nodded. "Spiders and bugs just really give me the creeps." She was surprised he didn't know this, since she'd mentioned it on her paperwork.

"No need to apologize."

At that moment, Silas called over to see if everything was okay. Michael replied in the affirmative then led Andi to the group of girls waiting for their ride. She was met with sympathetic glances and assurances from most of the girls that they were terrified of insects too and didn't blame her for being so frightened.

As Andi took a moment to finally put on her shoes, she looked up and saw Kimmie staring daggers at her. Looking back down at her shoes, she caught her breath, amazed by how much animosity she'd seen in Kimmie's eyes. *I was almost eaten by a killer bug,* she thought, annoyed. *And you're jealous because Michael noticed?* But all the same, a chill ran through her veins. Kimmie had made herself clear. She needed to raise her defenses.

* * *

The main house, the Mansion, was a sight to behold. It was a massive sixteen-thousand-square-foot building of plantation architecture design, indicative of the style and era of 1936, the year it was built.

With enough rooms that each bedroom had to be shared by only two girls, three in the largest bedroom, the gorgeous structure was comfortable and inviting. Andi felt a burst of gratitude that she would be rooming with Danee. She was still spooked about the centipede incident and made extra sure she watched where she stepped and clapped her shoes together before putting them on.

Andi and Danee's room was upstairs and had a balcony overlooking the palms and gardens of the plantation. At the moment, Danee was relaxing on the bed while Andi hung up her gowns and other clothes. Neither of them had enough clothes to fill the enormous closet they shared.

"You have some really beautiful gowns," Danee said, stretching. "Where do you shop?"

"Most of my wardrobe was designed and provided by my friend Lauryn Alexander."

"Your friend is Lauryn Alexander?" Danee's expression froze in disbelief.

"We've been friends since junior high," Andi told her with a shrug. "Since I don't really own evening and cocktail gowns, she helped me out with a few things. Dresses mostly, and swimsuits. Oh, and a couple of casual outfits. And shoes." She grinned. "Well, okay, she pretty much got me all my clothes. I really didn't have anything nice enough for the show, and I wasn't in a position to go buy a new wardrobe."

"You are *so* lucky. I love her designs," Danee said wistfully. "That swimsuit and cover-up last night—were those Lauryn's designs?"

"Actually, they were designed by her partner, Cooper D'Angelo. All of my shoes are by Cooper too."

"Those red pumps with the little embellishment on the toe are to die for."

"Aren't they?" Andi picked up the shoes. "What size do you wear?"

"I'm a seven and a half," she said.

"These are an eight, but they fit kind of tight. You can try them if you want."

Danee jumped off the bed and slid her feet into the shoes, admiring the fit and look on her foot and leg.

"They look good on you," Andi said sincerely.

"I'm surprised they're so comfortable."

"You can borrow them anytime you want," Andi replied, turning back to the closet.

"Serious? Andi, that is so sweet. Thank you."

With her suitcases finally empty, Andi sat down on her bed and relaxed against the pillow. "So what was your impression about last night?"

"Other than the fact that they have five-inch bugs around here? Girl, how did you not pass out cold? I would have for sure. That thing looked like it crawled out of a prehistoric nightmare!"

Andi laughed. "I'm embarrassed that I freaked out like that."

"Are you kidding? We were all freaking out with you!"

She nodded. "I hope everyone will forget about it soon, though. I don't want to be known as the insect girl or something."

"To be honest, I was glad to have something to pull the spotlight away from Kimmie." Danee lowered her voice. "She is so annoying. Please tell me that Michael sees past her phoniness."

Andi shrugged. "I don't know. She seems to know what she's doing. And it doesn't hurt that she's drop-dead gorgeous."

"Ugh!" Danee exclaimed. "Not when you know her like we do." She took the red pumps off, paused thoughtfully before she put them in Andi's side of the closet, then said, "I noticed you had a chance to speak privately with Michael."

"Oh?" Andi shifted onto her hip and rested her head casually on her hand. She had nothing to hide.

"Yeah, everyone noticed. What did you guys talk about?"

"Nothing really," Andi answered truthfully. Anyone who had overheard the conversation would probably be confused. "He was curious if I was surprised that he'd given out the extra lei. Of course I said yes, since I had pretty much expected to be going home until he did that."

Danee smiled unconvincingly. "Of course."

"So, yeah, it was no big deal." She looked at Danee, whose expression hadn't changed. "Really."

"I think he really, really likes you," Danee said.

"I can't tell what he thinks," Andi said truthfully. "I'm very comfortable with him, almost like we're old friends, but, Danee, I think he's looking for more than a friend." Even as she said the words, she hoped they weren't the truth. Yes, she did think they had a connection, but was it romantic? She didn't know yet. She was definitely attracted to him—evidenced by the flutter in her heart when she was around him. But that didn't mean he felt it.

Besides, what he was looking for and what she was looking for were two different things. Aside from marrying a member of the Church in the temple, she wasn't sure about marrying someone who had the checkered past Michael had. Not that she was perfect, but Michael's prior relationships would always be around to haunt him. The tabloids and Internet would make sure of that.

"That's the truth. What is he looking for?" Danee's shoulders relaxed, like she was finally convinced. She paused then a moment later added, "I have a confession."

Andi's eyebrows arched. "You do?"

Danee nodded and covered her face with her hands. "Yes. I've totally fallen for him. I mean, head over heels. I think he is the most amazing man I've ever met," she said, shaking her head helplessly.

Andi was taken aback. "Danee, how can you know this after one short date?"

"Oh, believe me, I know. I've had enough boyfriends to know. I—I just can't tell how he feels about me yet. I hope we get to have another date soon."

Andi nodded, deciding to let the love thing drop. "I think they split us up into three different groups and go on a group date. Then after that he'll choose someone he wants to have another one-on-one with."

Danee's eyes lit up.

Andi smiled, but she didn't pursue the conversation further. Danee had become her friend on the show, but it was clear that Andi had been warned. Danee had thrown down the gauntlet, staked her claim. She was letting Andi know that she intended on winning Michael for herself.

* * *

Standing at the dock, Andi and three other girls—Arial, Eliza, and Mandy—waited for Michael to arrive. It was their group's turn to spend time with Michael. They were going on a boat ride that would take them up the Nā Pali coastline, where they would stop and eat lunch, snorkel, and enjoy the incredible scenery.

The other three girls had on bikini tops and shorts and were consequently shivering like a pack of Chihuahua puppies. Andi had on hot-pink terry-cloth Capri pants and a matching hoodie jacket over her swimsuit. It was one of Lauryn's new activewear outfits, a line that was going to launch in the fall. For the umpteenth time, Andi made a mental note to find something wonderful to bring back from Hawaii to give to Lauryn and Cooper. She couldn't have had a better wardrobe for the occasion.

"I'm freezing my tail off," Mandy whimpered. She finally unzipped her bag, pulled out her towel, and wrapped it around her waist. "I thought it was warm in Hawaii."

"Maybe it will be a warmer on the boat," Eliza said, wrapping her arms around herself.

"I hope so. I'm shivering so hard my teeth are getting loose." Mandy started dancing around to stay warm.

Silas and the crew had holed up in their van while they waited, and just then the van door slid open and Silas climbed out.

"Okay, girls. Michael will be pulling up any minute. We're ready to roll cameras."

Andi understood that this meant they were supposed to pretend it wasn't cold, that they were happy to be there, and get excited when Michael showed up.

Moments later Michael's ride pulled up, a glistening black luxury Hummer.

Mandy quickly shoved her towel back into her bag and smiled for the cameras.

Michael stepped out of the Hummer and gave them a wave. He wore large movie-star sunglasses, bright yellow Hawaiian-print swim trunks, and a white Ed Hardy hoodie. Even he was prepared for the cool temperature.

"Dang, he's hot!" Arial said under her breath.

The other three girls burst out laughing. Normally, Arial was reserved and shy, so the comment was totally out of character and caught them all off guard.

"What?" she said, flipping her red hair indignantly. "Tell me you're not all thinking the same thing."

"Oh, don't worry," Eliza said. "We are."

"Good morning, ladies," Michael said as he approached. "Don't you all look lovely."

He gave each of them a peck on the cheek and a brief hug. "Do you girls need a jacket? It's a little chilly this early until the clouds burn off."

"That would be awesome," Mandy said, shivering slightly. "I would kill for a jacket."

"I'll see what I can do."

The boat had pulled up to the dock and was running, waiting for them to board. Michael strolled over and talked to the driver, and a few minutes later came back with three unattractive but warm sweatshirts. They were much too large for the girls, but none of them seemed to care.

Andi was impressed by Michael's thoughtfulness—and simultaneously grateful to be wearing her own hoodie.

"Shall we board?" he asked once they were covered up.

The crew, including Tom and Caz from the limo, followed Michael and the women as they walked to the boat, the wind whipping around their legs and pulling at their hair. Andi had pulled her hair into a ponytail, but the other girls fought to keep theirs out of their faces. Did any of these girls have a practical bone in their body? Did they just think they were going to stand on the deck of the boat like cardboard cutouts in a sexy pose all day?

Andi suddenly felt her age—and was grateful for it. She'd gotten past the suffer-for-beauty phase of life and had finally learned that it was possible to be beautiful and practical at the same time.

Andi was the last one to accept Michael's assistance as they climbed on board.

"Excited for today?" he asked.

"Extremely," she answered as he steadied her with his hand while she stepped over the side and onto the landing inside. "I've seen this coastline in so many movies, but I've always wanted to see it in person."

"It's going to take your breath away," he told her, fixing her with a steady gaze.

She smiled, deciding he was definitely worth all the fuss each of the girls made over him.

Reminding herself to keep her wits about her, she pulled in a breath to calm her heart while she sat down next to the other girls. She hadn't reacted this way to a man in a long time. The feeling was exhilarating but terrifying. She couldn't fall for him. She couldn't. But she was afraid she was.

Chapter 12

"Hey, Poki," Michael said to the driver, reaching to shake his hand.

The stout man accepted his hand then pulled him into a hug, and they slapped each other on the back.

Poki had long hair pulled into a ponytail, was shirtless, and had a pair of Hawaiian-print swim trunks worn low on his hips, his rotund belly hanging over the waistband. Around his neck he wore a puka-shell necklace and another necklace made of braided hemp with a shark tooth on it.

"You gonna let me blow the conch shell?"

"You think you'll be able to do it today?" Poki asked with a lopsided smile. "You sure you want to embarrass yourself in front of the ladies?"

"I'll take my chances," Michael said.

Poki's son Kaleo busied himself getting the boat ready for the trip while Caz, Tom, and Silas positioned themselves so they were out of the way. Next to them was another boat with a cameraman that would follow along next to them.

Poki disappeared for a moment then reappeared with a large, beautiful shell about the size of a football.

The four girls looked at each other and giggled, not sure what was going to happen next.

"First, I will show you what it's supposed to sound like," Poki said. "Then we will let Michael try."

Poki stood with his feet spread, drew the shell ceremoniously to his lips, and blew. A long, loud wail like a foghorn blasted from the shell.

The girls clapped and cheered.

"Okay, Michael," Poki said. "Let's see what you can do."

Michael stood and lifted the shell to his lips. Taking a deep breath, he blew hard into the shell. Out came a sputtering squeak and a lot of screeching. Arial stepped backward, startled, and the others chuckled.

"Good thing we aren't fishing today," Poki said. "You've scared them all away."

Michael tried again, with a little more success.

"You girls want to try?" Poki asked.

The boat had pulled away from the dock by now and was slowly churning its way out to sea. The wind kept the waves choppy and the boat rocking.

"I will," Arial volunteered.

Poki was busy helping maneuver the boat through the rolling water, so Michael explained the technique.

"Have you ever played a brass instrument?"

"Like a trumpet?" she asked. "No."

"Good, then you won't make me look bad," he teased.

He showed her how to purse her lips together so they vibrated as the air passed by. Arial proceeded to try it several times without the shell then put the shell to her lips.

Spit flew as she blew into the hole at the base of the shell. A little bit of air escaped, but there was no sound at all.

After a few more unsuccessful attempts, she gave up and Mandy picked up the shell. She'd played flute in junior high so she had a little more to work with.

Her first attempt was similar to Arial's, but after a few more tries, she managed to get a decent sound out of the shell. Everyone applauded as she sat down.

Eliza seemed a little hesitant, so Andi stood, hoping she wouldn't humiliate herself.

"Remember," Michael said, "it's not like this." He puckered up and blew out a breath, like he was blowing out birthday candles. "It's like this." He flattened his lips and pursed them together.

Andi nodded then gamely picked up the shell, hoping she didn't look as dumb as she felt.

He nodded, encouraging her. "That's it."

"Hold on!" Poki shouted as the boat suddenly rocked hard against the waves and tilted side to side.

Andi reached out to grab onto something and stumbled backward, dropping the shell. In one swift movement, Michael caught her and held her tightly as the boat plowed through the open, churning sea.

When the water settled a few moments later, she knew she would be able to regain her footing—however, Michael hadn't let go.

"I think I'm good now," she said, feeling the eyes of the other three girls on her.

"You sure?" he asked, a mischievous glint to his eye.

"Yeah," she said with a smile. "I'm ready to try this."

She stood once more then held the shell up to her lips and blew. Nothing came out, and her face went bright red.

They both burst out laughing.

"Don't try to blow so hard," he said.

She tried again and managed to get some sound out. And after a few more attempts, she was able to get a longer sustained honk from it. It wasn't as powerful as Poki's, but it was acceptable.

"I'm impressed," Michael said, and Andi basked in the rays of his warm smile.

"Me too. I didn't think it was so hard."

Andi sat down and looked at Eliza, wondering if she was going to try her hand at the conch too. The girl's face was pale white.

"Uh-oh, you aren't doing well, are you?"

Eliza shook her head.

"Are you going to—?"

Eliza nodded.

Andi spied a bucket out of the corner of her eye and grabbed it just in time.

Luckily Eliza hadn't had much for breakfast, and Andi held up a towel to cover her while she emptied her stomach.

Once she was done, Michael got some crackers and a soda from Poki to help settle her stomach. Poki took the bucket from Andi and gave her a grateful smile for her help.

Because they had so far to travel to reach their destination, Eliza had some time to lie down and rest. Mandy and Arial huddled together under their towels as the boat charged ahead, and Andi moved off the bench seat so Eliza would have room to stretch out. She moved instead to a seat on a side bench with a view of the coastline.

The sheer, three-thousand-foot cliffs and jagged outcroppings of land were made of vibrant red earth and covered with lush green overgrowth. Occasionally white-plumed waterfalls tumbled over precipices in a breath-taking plunge onto the sloping drop-offs and razor-sharp ridges.

Andi felt like she had been transported to another place and time.

"It's beautiful, isn't it?" Michael said as he sat down next to her.

"It's even better than I'd imagined," she said, scooting over to give him some room.

They settled into a comfortable position looking outward, nestled close so they could hear each other over the roar of the engine and splashing waves.

"Where does the water come from?" she asked, pointing at another large waterfall.

"The Nā Pali Coast gets nearly a hundred inches of rain a year."

"That's why it's so green," she said, nodding. "I can't take my eyes off it."

He leaned closer so their foreheads were touching, pointing at the jagged cliffs. "There's a trail that runs along the ridge there. It's a beautiful hike."

"Ah," she sighed, "that sounds incredible. I'd love to do that hike."

He nodded and gave her a squeeze with his arm.

For one magical moment, it felt like the two of them were the only ones on the boat, floating along in paradise, sharing the experience together.

"Hey, there," Mandy interrupted, "mind if I take a turn with Michael for a few minutes?"

Andi looked up at the girl and faked a smile and a cheery response. "Not at all."

Michael tightened his grip around her hand for a brief moment then let go as she stood to change seats.

Mandy slipped quickly into the vacated spot, and Andi balanced herself as she walked over to the vacant seat near the other girls, who looked like they'd both fallen asleep.

With the constant bouncing of the boat, Andi searched for a different seat and spied one near the galley that would shield her and allow her to sit facing backward so she'd have a better view.

Out of the corner of her eye she watched Mandy and Michael talking and laughing and felt a tinge of something unpleasant inside. Was it jealousy?

Knowing it was silly to sit and watch Michael interact with the other girls, she glanced around the boat and spied a ladder going up to the flying bridge.

Steadying herself against the bumpy ride, she climbed the rungs to the upper deck and found Poki at the wheel. He smiled when he saw her and motioned for her to join him.

"It's quite a sight, isn't it?" he asked.

"You're right about that," she answered.

"You are lucky. We have many waterfalls for you today."

She smiled. "They're breathtaking."

They stood silently for a moment, watching as the boat roared down the coastline.

The wind whipped at Andi's hair and clothes, challenging her balance, but there was something daring and exciting about the powerful force.

"Have you lived here all your life?" she asked after a moment, feeling like she was yelling. They had to speak loudly to talk over the noise of the boat.

"Oh yes. I have never left the island, except by boat, like this."

"Really? Never?"

"No."

"Do you ever want to?"

"Why? I live in paradise. Is there anywhere more beautiful? More peaceful? This is where my heart is, where my family is. I am happy here."

"That's wonderful, Poki. It really is."

He dipped his chin in gratitude. "We are getting close to the spot where we will stop and snorkel. Then we will have lunch. Have you ever seen a sea turtle?"

"Just in pictures."

"Then you are in for a treat. You will be amazed."

She found a seat once more and allowed her mind to drift as she waited. She found herself wishing fervently that she were here with her friends and not twelve other girls vying for Michael's affections. She'd never been one to play games when it came to relationships with men. If she liked a guy—or didn't like a guy—she told him. Keeping him guessing or stringing him along made no sense to her. She'd never been in a situation like this and wasn't sure how to act.

She felt a painful little twist in her stomach as she realized how isolated she was from the world. So much was going on in each of her friends' lives, and she missed being able to call them and talk to them. Not only that, she could use their advice right now.

Pulling in a long breath, she let the air out slowly as she said a silent prayer for each of them. They weren't just her friends—they were her sisters. She loved and missed them.

The top of a man's head appeared through the opening in the floor, and she soon saw Michael's smiling face. She smiled in return. He was so blasted beautiful, she couldn't stand it!

"I wondered where you were," he said, squeezing in next to her on the small seat.

"I wanted to see the view from up here," she told him.

"I'm sure Poki didn't mind having some company either, did ya, Poki?" Michael said loudly.

Poki made a hang-loose sign with his hand, and they all laughed.

They rode for a moment before Michael asked, "Everything okay?"

"Everything is great," she answered. "I was planning on coming back down in a few minutes."

He slid his arm around her. "Good. I was excited to bring you here today. It's just too bad everyone else had to come with us."

His face was only inches away from hers. She wondered what kinds of things he said to the other girls when he was alone with them.

"We don't go quite to the end of the coastline," he explained, and Andi let the negative thought slip away. "There's a wonderful place to have lunch and do some snorkeling."

"Poki told me about the sea turtles," she said. "I really hope I get to see one."

"I hope so too," he said. "You don't scuba dive, do you?"

"I certified about five years ago but haven't had a chance to dive as often as I'd like."

He raised his eyebrows and was thoughtful for a moment.

She wondered what that look meant, but she didn't have time to ask, since just then one of the cameramen came looking for them and gestured for them to come back down.

By the time they reached the cove where they were going to eat lunch and snorkel, the fog had burned off and the waves had calmed. The rest of the girls gladly shook off the bulky sweatshirts they had sported for the duration of the ride, and Andi grinned as she saw the pile of them strewn at the bottom of the boat.

Kaleo and Poki spread out bread, lunch meats, cheeses, and other sandwich condiments as well as salads, drinks, and thick, chewy macadamia-nut-and-white-chocolate-chip cookies.

Everyone made their own sandwich and then, as waves lapped gently against the boat, they ate and enjoyed the beautiful scenery and secluded cove.

Andi wasn't shy by nature, but she felt strangely reserved in this setting, while the other girls seemed to feel a need to demand attention by being loud, overly talkative, or constantly giggling, especially at everything Michael said.

"Who needs sunscreen?" Michael asked.

The other three girls flew into a frenzy, and the cameramen ate it up. Michael slathered lotion on each of their shoulders then looked at Andi and asked, "Would you like some sunscreen?"

"Actually, I already put some on, but I'd be happy to put some on you," she replied.

The other three girls' expressions fell, and Mandy looked downright irritated. Andi hadn't planned for it to happen this way—it just had. But it definitely worked to her advantage.

She avoided the daggers thrown her way from the other girls and focused on Michael.

"Sure, thanks," he said, handing her the tube and turning his back to her. She proceeded to generously rub lotion over his neck, shoulders, and back. The man had chiseled muscles, and she knew that he didn't have them just from pumping weights in a gym. They came from hard work, and that made her appreciate them even more.

"There," she said, giving his shoulder a final pat. "I think that'll do it."

"Thanks, Andi. "

"I think it's great you wear sunscreen—even with your dark complexion. All it takes is one bad sunburn," Arial said in a rush. "You just can never be too safe. With my fair skin I have to be really careful."

Mandy's expression as she listened to Arial nearly caused Andi to burst out laughing. It was as if she were saying, "TMI. Newsflash—nobody cares."

While Eliza and Arial prattled on about sunburns and delicate skin, Michael decided that it was hot, which it was, and that he was ready to dive into the water.

"I hope that stuff is waterproof," he said, jumping to his feet, "'cause I'm going in! Who's joining me?"

This was where Andi didn't hold back. She loved the water and snorkeling and was anxious to see what was swimming around below them. The three hood ornaments in the boat could sit and watch them for all she cared. She was getting in.

Michael gave her a wink as he perched on the edge of the boat. "Ready?"

She got up beside him. "Set."

"Go!" they yelled together and dove in.

Chapter 13

The lukewarm water was fabulously refreshing. Andi felt free and energized as she burst to the surface, joined a moment later by Michael.

"Man, were you a diver in high school or something?" he asked.

She laughed. "Hardly. You?"

"Both," he said. "You have a nice dive—I'm impressed."

"Thanks. I got into swimming a few years ago. I love it. It's such great exercise."

"It shows," he said.

They were both treading water, bobbing on the glimmering teal green ocean, their bodies only inches apart.

"Thanks," she said. "You too." He smiled as his leg bumped against hers, sending a shiver of chills up to her spine.

"Geronimo!" Mandy shouted as she dove into the water, sending a splash of water their way.

They wiped their eyes and watched as she swam to the surface. Andi felt a bubble of annoyance for a moment at the intrusion. She was already tired of doing this. She wanted to spend time with Michael all by herself. There was so much she wanted to learn about him, so many questions she wanted to ask him.

Sputtering as she broke the surface, Mandy swam right up to them and acted as though they'd be thrilled to see her. "This water is amazing!"

Just then, Kaleo threw a handful of bread into the water toward the front of the boat. Seconds later, a frenzy of activity swirled in the water in what looked like piranha devouring their evening meal.

"They don't eat meat, right?" Andi said, bobbing up in the water to try to see the fish.

Michael laughed out loud, his voice echoing inside the cove. "No, we're safe."

She must not have looked convinced, because he added, "I promise. Now, should we do some snorkeling?"

"Love to," Andi said quickly.

"Um, sure. That sounds like loads of fun." Mandy seemed tentative but not about to be outdone. "Let's do it."

"You two going to join us?" Michael called to Eliza and Arial.

"Sure," Eliza said.

"Sounds good," Arial echoed.

Andi avoided rolling her eyes. It was obvious that water activities weren't really their thing. She felt a little sorry for them, but if they wanted to spend time with Michael, it had to be on his terms. He was a water lover—and it wasn't hard to guess that he would want to be with someone who enjoyed it as much as he did.

With Poki and Kaleo's help, everyone donned snorkel gear then jumped off the back of the boat. Andi and Michael cracked up when they looked at each other through their goggles. Even with a black mask and a squashed-up nose, he was still the most attractive man she'd seen in—well—forever.

"Let's find some sea turtles," he said then pulled the snorkel tube into his mouth.

Andi nodded her head and inserted her tube as well.

Then, without waiting for the others, they both submerged themselves and began swimming away, their flippers in exact synchronization.

He took her hand and they swam together, looking through the water for marine and plant life. Strong beams of sunlight streamed through the water, illuminating the ocean like magical spotlights.

Andi didn't know the names of most of the fish they saw, but the water was teaming with fish of all colors, sizes, and varieties. It was a thrilling sight.

To Andi's disappointment, after several minutes, Michael appeared to have a moment of conscience and signaled for them to stop swimming so they could wait for the others to catch up.

While they waited, Andi turned slowly in a circle, looking for other interesting sights. To her delight and surprise, a sea turtle floated in the distance, about fifteen feet under.

She turned and grabbed Michael's hand and pointed in the direction of the turtle. When Michael caught sight of it as well, his eyes lit up with excitement behind his mask.

They started swimming slowly toward the turtle as they waited for the other girls to follow. Andi glanced back over at Michael and flashed him a thumbs up. She didn't necessarily enjoy having to split Michael's attention with the other girls, but she truly appreciated his thoughtfulness in including everyone in the group.

Throughout the rest of the afternoon, the group was fortunate enough to see several turtles and countless colorful fish. It was an otherworldly experience, to say the least, and Andi could have continued swimming and exploring much longer, but Poki signaled them to come back to the boat. They had a long ride back ahead of them, and apparently it was time to return.

Michael, continually the conscientious host, served up the cookies that had been overlooked at lunch. The girls were given fluffy, thick towels to wrap themselves in, and with the warm sun shining overhead, the ride back was much more comfortable.

It was difficult to talk over the roar of the engine, so Michael took this chance to pull each girl aside and chat with her one-on-one.

Never knowing when a camera would catch an awkward reaction or expression, Andi kept her expression neutral and her feelings buried deep. She realized Michael had to do what he was doing, to get to know the girls and see if he had any connection with them—but that didn't mean she had to like it.

In her opinion, in wasn't hard to tell which girls were Michael's type and which weren't. Out of the three other girls on the boat, Mandy seemed like the only one Michael would be interested in. She was interesting and beautiful and wasn't afraid to let her feelings show. And, true to Andi's prediction, Michael seemed to show her a little more interest than he did the other two.

Arial didn't seem to connect with Michael on any level, and Eliza was in a world of her own. As for herself, Andi felt like she and Michael were extremely compatible and had a lot in common. If that was what he was looking for, then she was his girl.

She stopped her thoughts and groaned inwardly, mentally slapping her forehead. What was she doing? It was one thing to think he was a hunk and to enjoy spending time with him—who could help that? But when it came right down to it, she couldn't win. She swallowed hard, hoping she wasn't giving the camera a grimace. This was such a mistake. Why was she here allowing herself to fall for a guy she couldn't have? If—and she knew that *if* was the key word still—Michael somehow ended up choosing her, she would be going against her greatest goal in life. She had promised herself that she wouldn't marry outside her faith and outside the temple. And she wondered if he could truly ever leave his past behind. He lived a completely different lifestyle, and she wasn't sure she could ever just accept all the partying and women from his past, even if he did change.

Why had she let Kirk talk her into this?

She watched the coastline pass by as the boat cut through the waves, water spraying off the sides, occasionally sending a cool mist her way.

Her throat ached as she forced herself to see things as they were. She really, really liked this guy. Even though it had only been a relatively short amount of time, she knew that out of all the guys she'd ever dated, Michael was closest to the person she'd imagined marrying. She loved his heritage and ethnicity. She loved his sense of humor and zest for life that fed her own energy and passion for the causes she was passionate about and the way she approached living. There was a hand-in-glove fit here that she'd never experienced before.

Crap. Now what did she do?

Her mind spun as she considered the possibility and realized that there was only one real solution here. She had to get him to kick her off the show. It was the only way. She had to leave before it got serious, before it would be too hard to leave.

"Hey," Michael said, jolting her from her thoughts as he sat down next to her and slid his arm around her shoulders. "Can I sit by you?"

She knew she needed to say no, but having his arm around her, feeling the fit of it envelop her so perfectly, made it impossible to utter the word.

"I've loved spending time with you today," he said. "And I have a surprise for you when we get back."

The difficult thoughts that had raced through her mind moments before slid away far too easily. She was trying to ignore him, to fight against her heart, but she couldn't. He had a surprise for her. A surprise!

He was perfect. There was no other word. Perfect except for one thing—one monumentally gigantic thing—and that would never change.

"I thought you'd be happy," he said, looking disappointed.

"I am," she reassured him, quickly putting a smile back on her face. "I—I just don't know what to say. I'm flattered. Thank you."

He smiled. "You're going to love it." He tucked a strand of hair that had blown across her face behind her ear. "Have I told you how beautiful

I think you are?"

She didn't tell him that even though he never had told her that, he had made her feel that way right from the start.

"No," she said, feeling shy.

"You are. I love the little dip in your chin and the curve of your nose. I get lost in the color of your eyes, and your smile turns my knees to jelly."

She burst out laughing. The other girls flipped their heads and looked at them, their expressions ranging from annoyance to anger.

Andi tried to wipe the joy from her face, but she couldn't help it. This guy had gotten to her.

"I'm sorry," he said, looking suddenly unsure. "Did I embarrass you?"

"Hardly!" she said. "I've always hated that divot in my chin, my nose is too turned up on the end, and my eyes are the color of dirt. But I do have a nice smile. Three years of braces made sure of that."

Now it was his turn to laugh. "Is that what you see in the mirror?"

"Every morning."

"I wish you could see yourself through my eyes," he said sincerely. "It's pretty amazing."

Her breath caught in her throat. Was this guy even human? Seriously. She almost felt like pinching herself to make sure this wasn't a dream.

"Wow," she said, feeling a knot form in her throat. She swallowed hard to remove it. "That is definitely the most incredible thing anyone has ever said to me."

"It's true. I think you're really something, Andi."

Their gazes locked, and for a moment no one else existed.

A long, loud blast sounded from the conch shell, breaking the spell. It was Kaleo. They were nearing the dock.

"Let's pick up this conversation later," he said.

"I'd like that."

They moved apart, and Michael resumed his role as the center of attention and star of the show. Smiling widely at the other girls, he strode toward them, and Andi watched the tension surrounding them melt away. Dipping down, he picked up the conch shell again, having a little more luck with it this time. The other girls tried as well, but Andi declined. She was ready to get off the boat and find out what her surprise was.

A few minutes later, they pulled up to the dock and Kaleo tied them off. Then, after the film crew climbed out, Michael helped each of the girls step onto the dock. He had to catch Eliza, who didn't have her land legs back quite yet. Then, once she was steady, he came back for Mandy and Andi.

"Thanks for a great day, ladies," he said. Then, adding a touch of mystery to his voice, he added, "But it's not quite over yet."

Several of the girls squealed with excitement.

"I have something special planned." He looked at them with mischief in his eyes. "As you know, I'm kind of an extreme-sports kind of guy."

Andi felt the bottom of her stomach drop. This couldn't be good.

"Some of you might be familiar with the treetop ziplines we have on the island."

Swallowing, Andi dreaded what would come out of his mouth next.

"We just opened a new line I haven't been on yet. It happens to be the longest in the world," he said proudly. "Before we take you back, we're going to make a quick stop." He smiled wickedly. "I'll see you at the top!"

The other girls couldn't seem to stop talking the entire way to the jumping off spot for the zipline. Andi, however, hung back, unable to bring herself to admit she was terrified of heights. As a young girl she'd been dared by her brother to climb up a tree in exchange for a chance to play on his new game system. He didn't think she'd do it. To his utter shock and surprise, she had nimbly climbed her way to the top without much trouble. Going up turned out to be a lot easier than going down. However, she'd happened to find the fast route when the branch she was standing on had split off the trunk and crashed to the ground, taking her with it.

She's spent most of that summer in a cast up to her hip on her right leg. It had taken months after the cast was removed to get her strength and movement back, and for a long time afterward, she had felt like she couldn't play sports or keep up with the other kids because her leg was weak. Year after year of not participating in activities and in PE at school had been the start of her battle with being overweight—one she'd overcorrected by developing an eating disorder, which she had ultimately conquered. However, she'd never overcome her fear of heights.

When they arrived at the top, Michael greeted each of them with a hug and a kiss on both cheeks. Andi was the last one to get out of the car.

"Excited?" he asked her.

Afraid she'd throw up from nerves if she opened her mouth, she just smiled and shrugged, hoping it would suffice as an answer.

"Girls, we need you over here," Silas called. He wanted to set up the shot and arrange the girls' order down the zipline. There would be a helicopter overhead to get some arial shots of everyone flying down the mountain.

Feeling weak-kneed and light-headed, Andi stood at a distance, doing some of the relaxation breathing techniques she'd learned in yoga. From what Silas said, even small kids went on the zipline. If they could, then of course she could too, she told herself.

As the girls were outfitted with the equipment, helmet, and harness, Michael joked and teased everyone. He was charming and wonderful, and Andi knew she needed to quit worrying and just have fun, but she was about ready to pass out. Fear of falling paralyzed her.

The man who was helping the girls put on their gear must have noticed her hesitancy.

"First time doing a zipline?" he asked.

"Yes," she answered, trying to keep her voice level.

"Heights make you nervous?"

"Yeah. A little." She gave him a half smile. "Actually, a lot. I fell out of a tree when I was young. My right leg was in a cast for three months."

"You're completely safe. Nothing's going to happen," the man said, attaching another carabiner to a line.

"Nothing? How can you be sure?"

"Well, of course there are always fluke accidents, but we've never had a problem. Yesterday we had a seven-year-old boy do the same zipline you're doing."

"Promise?" she asked, raising an eyebrow.

"I promise."

Hesitantly she allowed him to strap on the gear. Maybe she could close her eyes all the way down. It's not like she had to steer the crazy thing.

"Hey," Michael called when he saw her, "you about ready?"

She gave him a smile.

"She fell out of a tree when she was little," the guy informed him over her shoulder.

Andi cringed. If she'd wanted Michael to know her concerns, she would have told him.

"You did?" he said, stepping closer to her. "So I take it you're a little nervous?"

"A little," she lied.

"You will not believe how much fun it is," he assured her, rubbing her shoulder. "I promise. Trust me on this."

He reached for her hand and led her to the line of girls waiting to take their turn.

"You can do this," he said once more.

She nodded, unable to speak right at the moment. But despite that, she was determined to conquer her fear. She didn't have a choice. It wasn't on her terms or her timing, but it was now or never. This was important to him. She had to do it.

The next thing she knew, the first girl was attached to the zipline and sent flying. When it came to her turn, Michael was there to help her.

"Okay, just relax and enjoy the ride. You couldn't be safer. I promise."

Andi closed her eyes and breathed, pushing away the image of falling.

"You all right?" he asked softly.

She opened her eyes and looked into his face, "Yes. Now I am."

"I'll see you at the bottom," he said. Then, quickly, he gave her a kiss.

Before she had another chance to think about what she was doing, the employee gave her a shove and off she went.

Chapter 14

She was so surprised, she didn't even have a chance to scream. In an instant she was bouncing and swaying, feeling free and airborne, with the wind rushing through her hair and the sound of the zipline whirring above her. To her surprise, after a few moments, Andi felt secure enough in her harness that she dared to open her eyes. Just below her was the tree line of the lush green forest. Instead of screaming, though, she cried out in amazement. It was breathtaking. She felt like she was flying.

The ride was smooth and exhilarating, so much so that she forgot to be afraid. With each passing moment, she found herself enjoying it more and more.

The tour was a series of six ziplines that skimmed the tree line, which occasionally gave way to a breathtaking waterfall or thickly forested valley. Instead of the lines stopping and starting at various points like most ziplines, the lines on this tour were one continuous path. Andi's feet never touched the ground until she hit the final line, which picked up speed with the sudden drop in elevation and then slowed as the line flattened out, allowing her to coast in for a smooth landing.

The camera crew as well as the three girls ahead of her waited at the bottom and clapped as she came to a complete stop.

"That was awesome!" Andi cried as the worker helped her find her feet again then began unhooking her from the zipline. "I can't believe I did it!"

The worker directed her from the platform, where she took her place with the others as Michael came swooping into view.

"Wahoo!" he hollered as he neared the end. The girls clapped and watched as he deftly hit the ground running then slowed to a stop.

"Unbelievable!" he said, smiling broadly. "That was amazing!"

"Thank you, Mr. Makua," said the young man helping Michael out of his harness. "We're so glad you could join us."

"Hey," Michael said directly to Andi, locking his gaze with hers. "What did you think?"

"That was just so amazing!" Mandy said, stepping in front of Andi. "You looked so good up there in that harness."

She took a few steps closer and tried to cozy up to Michael, but he didn't play along. Giving her a quick, one-armed hug, he approached the others.

"What about you ladies? Did you like it?"

The three of them answered affirmatively and received individual hugs from him.

"You okay?" he asked Andi as he stepped back from hugging her.

She smiled and nodded. "Yes, surprisingly. I'm great, actually. I loved it."

"Good. I'm proud of you."

"I'm proud of me too," she quipped.

He enveloped her in another giant hug. "I'm guessing that not many people know you're terrified of heights," Michael said. "But you conquered that fear today, didn't you."

"All I know is that I loved it and can't wait to do it again. So, yeah, I guess I have."

He held her for another moment longer, and when the hug ended, he kept an arm around her waist. "By the way, did any of you notice Mount Waialeale? It's usually hidden by the clouds."

"Was that the big mountain in the distance that you could see from the third line?" Andi asked.

"That's it." He looked at the other girls and casually let his hand drop from Andi's waist, allowing her to return to the lineup. "It's the wettest place on earth."

"On earth? Like, the whole earth?" Arial asked.

Andi bit the inside her top lip in an attempt not to smile.

"Yes," Michael said without drawing attention to her remark. "It gets over four hundred inches of rain a year. It's actually a volcano, and we're lucky we saw it today—the summit can be covered by clouds for months at a time."

Andi shook her head, continually amazed at the many wonders on the island.

"Michael?" Brandon, Silas's assistant producer who was taking care of filming, motioned Michael over to him. The crew had been in a huddle while Michael had been pointing out Mount Waialeale.

The girls exchanged curious glances as Michael joined the crew.

The conversation was brief, and when the huddle broke, Brandon said, "I'll send someone to go on ahead, then, and set up the shot."

Tom raised his hand to volunteer. Andi caught his eye as he did so, and he offered her a brief smile before turning back to Brandon.

"Great, you go ahead—tell them we'll be there in fifteen minutes," Brandon told him. He then turned to one of the other crew members and spoke to him privately. The young man, who had dreadlocks tied back with a leather strap and was wearing a Jamaica T-shirt and Nike basketball shorts, nodded to Brandon then took off running.

Andi didn't know what to think, and judging by the confused expressions on the other contestants' faces, neither did they.

They'd been standing in the sun for a while now, and Andi was feeling her neck starting to burn. She noticed a patch of shade and took a couple of steps to the side to take advantage of it.

Mandy noticed her and joined her immediately. Andi suppressed a smile. She couldn't tell if her motive was to get out of the heat or stay close to Andi. Andi had felt a competitive vibe from Mandy from the start, and she knew the other girl viewed her as a threat.

Moments later, the dreadlock guy returned with a box in one hand and a bunch of water bottles under his arm. Brandon took the box, and Dreadlocks handed out the water bottles.

"For you, miss," he said, his pearly white smile gleaming against his ebony skin. He handed a bottle to Arial, then Mandy, then Eliza, and finally Andi.

Taking a refreshing drink, the girls made small talk in the shade while they waited to find out what awaited them next.

"Looks like we're going to be here a while." Mandy discreetly wiped her forehead then found a small boulder and sat down. Eliza sat on a smaller rock beside her while Arial continued standing with Andi.

"I'm going to fall asleep standing up," Arial said quietly. "I was so nervous for this date today, I didn't get any sleep."

"You want to find a place to sit?" Andi said, looking for another boulder or other place to sit.

"That would be—" She covered a yawn.

Before Andi could reply, Brandon called to them. "Girls, we're going to set up a shot here. Michael has something to tell you."

Immediately the girls exchanged glances, each of their expressions reflecting different emotions. Eliza looked frightened, Arial looked anxious, and Mandy looked completely confident in herself. Andi didn't know what to think.

The sound guy helped get microphones on each of the girls and did a quick sound check. Once they were mic'd, Brandon instructed them to go back into the shade then spaced each of them apart in a staggered line. "Okay, girls, just remember not to look directly at the camera and to stay engaged in the moment."

"Michael, we're ready for you," Brandon called.

"Do I look okay?" Mandy asked anxiously. "What's my hair doing?"

Eliza helped her smooth some stray strands.

"Why aren't there hair and makeup people?" she demanded, an edge creeping into her voice.

"I think this was a spur-of-the-moment thing," Arial said.

That was Andi's guess too—she'd learned to expect the unexpected on the show.

"Places everyone!"

The crew members held their positions, Brandon yelled, "Action!" and the marker clapped shut.

From across the clearing, near the landing platform for the zipline, Michael emerged from the trees carrying an orchid lei.

"Hi, ladies. I'm glad to see you all survived the zipline."

The girls laughed politely.

"It's been quite a fun-filled day, and I've really enjoyed getting to know each of you better. I hate to see it end." He looked down at the strand of purple flowers in his hand then back at the girls. "And for one of you, it won't. I would like to invite one of you to join me for a one-on-one date this evening."

Eliza and Arial looked at Andi. Mandy lifted her chin as if readying herself for the lei.

Andi could think of a dozen reasons why he would want to choose the other girls instead of her, and so it didn't surprise her to see him walk toward Mandy. The girl had made her feelings for Michael quite clear, and Michael probably wanted to see if he felt the same way about her.

Before Michael got to Mandy, though, he turned slightly and took several steps in Andi's direction, and the next thing she knew, he reached up and put the lei over her head.

"Would you join me?" he asked.

"I'd love to," she said, suddenly feeling light-headed. In the back of her mind, she could hear something screaming at her to wake up. This relationship couldn't go anywhere. She ignored it for the time being. They hugged, and it was settled.

"Ladies," he addressed them all, "thank you again for a wonderful time."

Andi smiled, excited for the date but dreading getting into the car with the other girls. She knew they would be upset with her and jealous because she got the lei. She even felt guilty because she knew she was taking away someone else's chance of having a relationship with Michael. But she wanted one more date with him, one last time before she asked him to kick her off the show. It was the only right thing to do. She would talk to him tonight, after their date.

The microphones were removed, and the girls walked toward the cars, which were ready to head back to the Mansion.

"Andi," Michael said. "You're staying a little longer."

"Oh?" She glanced at the other three girls, who didn't even attempt to hide their annoyance at the fact that she'd been chosen over them.

"Right this way, ladies," the driver of their car said. He opened the door and ushered them inside.

Andi sighed. She knew the mudslinging would start as soon as the car door was shut and that when they met up with the rest of the group at the Mansion, there would be plenty more mud to share with those girls.

She stood alone, waiting to find out what was going to happen next. Brandon was on his cell phone, obviously talking to Tom, who had gone ahead, letting him know they were on their way.

A dark cloud lingered behind the three girls, and the fact that Andi knew she needed to talk to Michael about leaving the show only made her feel worse.

"Hey," Michael said, "are you okay? You don't look too happy about staying."

Andi forced herself to snap out of the gloom. "Sorry—I was just thinking about something. I'm very excited."

"Good." He held her at arm's length and looked into her face. "I didn't want our time together to end. I have another surprise for you."

"You do?" He would have a hard time topping the surprise lei.

"Since you had so much fun on the zipline, I made arrangements for us to go on another one."

"What? Really?"

"It's a tandem line, and we'll see some incredible waterfalls and valleys from this one. There are a couple of places I'll show you that were used in the first *Jurassic Park* movie."

"That sounds amazing—and I'm not even nervous this time," Andi replied truthfully. "Especially knowing we'll be together."

He smiled. "I hoped you'd say that. Since we have a short drive ahead of us, I thought we could take that time to get to know each other better."

"I'd like that."

"You two ready?" Brandon called.

Michael nodded then took Andi by the hand and led her to the Hummer.

As they sat in the back, Andi felt herself relax, leaning slightly against Michael. It was nice to have a moment with him without the microphones and cameras in their faces.

"This has been quite a day," Andi said. "You really know how to pack a lot of fun into a short amount of time."

"I'm glad it's not over yet." He studied her face for a moment.

She suddenly worried that there was something on her nose or in her teeth. "What?" she asked hesitantly.

"Nothing. Just admiring how beautiful you are."

"Michael! My hair's a mess, and I don't have any makeup on."

"You don't need it. I like seeing your natural beauty. It suits you. Some of these other girls seem to think more is better."

"I guess you could say I'm a 'what you see is what you get' kind of girl."

He nodded his approval.

"Whether I'm in Africa building houses or off to an appearance at a fancy dinner, I'm pretty much the same person. You strike me as the same type of person."

"I'm not out to impress anyone or prove anything to anyone. I guess I'm comfortable with who I am."

"That's good. I've finally reached that point in my life too. It feels good."

He smiled at her, holding onto her hand and focusing his gaze into her eyes. She'd never talked to a man who appeared so completely engaged in a conversation before.

"Tell me about your work in Zambia with Mothers Without Borders. Didn't you put on your paperwork that you're planning to go back next spring?" Michael asked her.

"I am. Last time I was there, we were making bricks and trying to build houses for the complex that will house the AIDS orphans. I'm anxious to go back and see how much has been done since I've been there and, of course, to do more. I'm also hoping to see some of the wonderful people I met while I was there. Many of them are HIV positive, and some were already dying of the disease. Some of them have already passed away." Her voice grew soft. She couldn't talk about the ones who had died without getting emotional. Leaving Zambia had been all the more difficult because she knew she would never see some of the people she had grown to love.

Michael reached up and stroked her face.

"This will be my third trip, and they've asked that I help lead the expedition. The women in this organization are amazing."

He looked surprised. "Aren't men allowed?"

"Oh yes, of course. But it was started by a woman, and most of the expeditions are made up of women. Men are welcome, though. And needed."

"Hmm," he said thoughtfully.

She went on to tell him more about how the organization worked and some of the projects that were going on to help the children, and before she knew it, they had arrived at the new zipline.

Andi was surprised at the level of comfort she felt with Michael. She kept waiting for him to say or do something that would throw up a red flag. But he just kept getting better and better.

The crew was quickly setting up for the shot, and Brandon called the helicopter back to confirm that they were ready to film Michael and Andi as they rode each zipline.

Standing out of the way as the cameras were set, Andi watched the work that went into filming the show. She was used to the waiting that was involved in film work, but usually she had her phone or computer with her to help her pass the time.

"Let's find a bench in the shade and talk," Brandon said, coming up beside her and Michael.

Andi readily agreed—the sun was blazing hot. Michael escorted her over and assisted her while she sat down. Brandon passed out water bottles, and they all paused to drink. Brandon even requested that every crew member stop and get some water and a short break from the sun.

Brandon then explained to Michael and Andi that they would do the zipline in tandem and that the cameras would catch the action from the top but the helicopter cam would follow them down the mountain.

After making sure Michael knew what he was doing and that he'd done it before, Brandon gave a final nod.

"All right, everyone. Places," he called.

Michael and Andi donned helmets, then they were each handed a harness. Andi stepped into the straps that fit around her legs, and the employee helped secure them around her shoulders and back then fastened them in front.

When they were set, the employee clipped the hooks onto the trolley.

"Remember, landing is a little trickier in tandem," he said. "You'll want to anticipate the platform earlier."

Michael nodded. "Got it."

Andi felt a few nerves kick in but nothing to quell her excitement. It didn't really matter what they did—anything with Michael was bound to be fun and adventurous.

"You don't need much of a running start—the grade is pretty steep," the man told them as a final piece of instruction.

"Okay," Michael said, turning to Andi. "Ready?"

She blew out a nervous breath and nodded. "Ready."

Syncing their steps, they took off running and threw themselves into the air off the platform.

The zipline caught their weight and sagged slightly, creating a floating sensation. The feeling was every bit as unbelievable as the first time, and maybe even more so—because now Michael was right here with her.

Michael shifted his position so he could put his arm around Andi. "How are you doing?" He had to yell over the sound of the trolley whirring along the cable at high speed.

"Awesome!" She held onto the strap with one hand and Michael with the other.

"Look!" he yelled, pointing off in the distance.

The sight of thick jungle growth below them, rugged with verdant green mountains in the distance against a startling blue sky, was breathtaking. The island was truly one of God's masterpieces.

They neared the platform ahead, and Andi prepared herself for the landing. She felt their speed decrease and realized that the zipline was designed to flatten out before the platform to help slow them down.

When their feet came in contact with the wooden platform, they both ran with the momentum, slowing to a stop after several steps. Then they unhooked themselves from the cable and hiked over to the next platform, which would take them through a long narrow canyon with a large stream and waterfall.

Michael held Andi's hand as they followed the trail to the next starting point.

"I still can't believe you actually live here," Andi said.

He nodded. "I took it for granted as a kid, growing up. I didn't fully appreciate it until I left home and traveled and spent time in Africa. Sometimes you have to leave something or lose something to know how much it means to you."

The employee at the station waved and greeted them when they came into sight then quickly attached their harnesses to the trolley as they got ready for takeoff.

Then Michael counted to three, and they once again took off running, pushing a little harder this time to get some good speed on the zipline.

When the cable caught their weight, the line sagged slightly and the weightless floating sensation returned.

Andi was once again enjoying the scenery all around her when suddenly she felt one of the straps around her leg give way.

Chapter 15

Andi screamed and grabbed at Michael, her leg dangling dangerously and pulling her weight to one side.

"What's wrong?" he yelled.

"The strap broke!"

"What? Are you all right?" He craned his neck, attempting to see what had happened while at the same time wrapping his arm around her tightly.

"I think so," she said, her heart pounding wildly as she saw the drop below and the rugged mountain stream directly beneath them.

"I've got you, Andi, you're—"

And then the strap around her other leg broke.

Andi screamed loudly and grabbed for Michael but slipped from his grasp. She gasped as the harness around her arms caught, keeping her from falling—but she had no idea how long it would hold.

As she dangled precariously, certain that she was moments from falling to her death, the ground below them dropped off into a crashing waterfall, and the spray sent a blast of mist upward that caught Andi's legs.

She screamed again and fought harder to hang on.

"I've got you!" Michael called out. "I'm not letting go. You won't fall."

Using his arms and legs to steady her, he managed to pull her up a few inches to where he could wrap both arms around her.

Shaking badly now, she buried her head in his chest and prayed the shoulder straps would hold. She knew Michael was strong, but if her other straps broke, she doubted he could hold on to her under the present circumstances.

She prayed they would get to the next platform quickly.

"Almost there," Michael said, leaning close to her so that she would hear him.

Keeping her eyes closed, Andi continued praying. She was aware of the pain as Michael's fingers dug into her skin as he fought to keep a steady grip on her, and she squeezed her arms tighter around him to help.

"We're here," he said. "Just bend your knees. I've got this."

With all her strength she bent her knees and held the position, her hamstrings cramping at the intense contraction of her legs. Then, what felt like an eternity but was only moments later, they made contact with the platform.

The impact threw Andi from Michael's grasp. She gasped sharply as she felt his arms let her go, but her shoulder straps held, keeping her from catapulting off the platform.

Michael pulled her to him once more and helped steady her as she stumbled to find her feet and stop the momentum. When they finally came to a stop, she collapsed into his arms and let him hold her while she got a grip on her emotions. She felt like crying, but instead she focused on her breathing and calming down. She was okay.

The employee approached, but Michael held up his hand. "We need just a second." He cupped the back of Andi's head with large, steady hands and kept her close against his chest. His racing heartbeat matched her own.

After a full minute, and after the reality of what had just happened finally settled in, Michael loosened his hold on her.

"Are you okay? Tell me honestly," he said quietly, his eyes serious.

Andi caught the surge of emotions his question triggered, and she drew in another breath before blowing it out and answering. "Yes. I think so."

"Andi, I can't believe this. I'm so sorry."

She nodded. "I know. But we made it. I'm glad your straps held."

He pulled her close again then addressed the employee, telling him what had happened and requesting the use of his walkie-talkie to call for a Jeep to pick them up. He also demanded to talk to the manager and the owner to find out what had happened to Andi's harness. Then he released Andi from his embrace so that he could look at the faulty straps.

"This looks like it's been cut," Michael said upon closer inspection. He showed the employee.

"That's a brand-new harness," the worker said, shaking his head. "It's been inspected and tested. I've worked here since we opened, and I've never seen anything like this."

"Someone's got some explaining to do," Michael replied angrily. "I promise, Andi, I *will* get to the bottom of this."

* * *

Michael sent Andi home in a car while he stayed and did some investigating on the harness, letting her know that he would see her again that evening for their date. Now she stood in the quiet outside the Mansion for a moment, praying. Her heart was full of gratitude that she had been protected and kept from falling to her death. She was grateful for Michael and his quick reaction and strength. And she was thankful that even though she should be freaking out, she wasn't. She felt surprisingly calm. Of course, that could be attributed to the fact that she was still in shock—when the gravity of the situation hit, she might crumble. But for now, she was grateful.

"Stay with me, Father," she whispered as she walked to the front door and opened it. She dreaded having to face the girls, having to tell them what had happened and deal with their jealousy of her being chosen for a second one-on-one date. But despite the bad vibes from the other contestants, she was glad Michael had asked. They needed to talk. As much as she cared about him, she knew he needed to understand the position she was in—and why she couldn't stay.

To her relief, no one was directly inside the Mansion, and she walked up the stairs and went to her room. After a long shower, she slid on a pair of sweatpants and a T-shirt. She knew that soon she would receive details about what time to be ready and what to wear for her date. But until then she wanted to be comfortable.

She straightened her side of the room then put away some of her clothes and made her bed. She had left in a rush that morning and left her side a mess. She was glad to get things organized and delay having to explain her experience or her upcoming date to anyone else. Her thoughts were jumbled, and she didn't feel like talking.

Just as she was about to lie down and rest for a few minutes, a knock came at the door.

Reluctantly, she answered the door and found one of the young assistants there.

"I have a note for you, miss," the girl said with a smile.

"Thank you." Andi took the note, expecting the details of the date.

The young woman remained standing in the doorway.

"Is there something else?"

"Yes, you'll need this," the girl said, handing Andi's cell phone to her.

A sick feeling curdled her stomach. She slid her finger under the sealed flap and opened the note.

We've received an urgent phone call from Miss Jocelyn Emerson. You have been allowed special phone privileges so you can return the phone call. Please advise us of any extenuating circumstances.

Sincerely,
The Producers

Chapter 16

After issuing instructions to return the phone when she had completed the call, the assistant left Andi to be alone. As soon as the door closed, she used trembling fingers to dial Jocelyn's number. What was urgent enough that she was allowed a phone call? Her mind whirled with possible scenarios. Had something happened to Jocelyn? Was it Emma or the baby? Was it good or bad news? She went through each of her friends and worried about what was possibly going on.

"Hello, Joss?" Andi spoke, her voice constricted with worry.

"Oh, Andi, thank goodness you called." Joss's voice matched the concern in Andi's heart.

"What's wrong? What happened?"

"It's Chloe. She was in a horrible automobile accident. Horrible," Jocelyn managed to say as her voice shrunk to a whisper.

Andi shut her eyes. "How horrible?" Her face scrunched up, fighting the emotion threatening to explode.

"She's in a coma," Jocelyn said with a deflating noise. "They were surprised she made it through the night. She was banged up pretty bad. Her car rolled down an embankment. Luckily the girls weren't with her."

Her head suddenly felt too heavy, and Andi sat down on the bed to cradle it in her hands. "How did it happen? She's one of the most careful drivers I know."

"I know. It doesn't make sense," Jocelyn said. "They think her brakes went out on her."

"Her brakes!" Andi exclaimed. "Her dad's a mechanic. He keeps her car in perfect condition."

"I know. It just doesn't make any sense."

Andi's breath caught in her throat. "Oh, Joss. I can't believe this."

"We don't think it was an accident."

"Neither do I," Andi said as her hands began to tremble again. "I don't know what's going on, but there's something else you should know about." She then told Jocelyn about her near-death experience on the zipline.

"But how . . . why . . . ?" Jocelyn asked. "Is this just a coincidence?"

Andi thought for a moment, trying to sort everything out somehow. "My gut instinct says no—not with the timing."

"I think we all need to watch our backs. For some reason, we are all in danger."

"I do too," Andi agreed. She couldn't bear the thought of losing Chloe.

"I have to ask, Andi. How did you even agree to doing the zipline? You're terrified of heights."

"I know. I was so proud of myself. I mean, I was having fun until this happened." She pinched the bridge of her nose, trying to keep the tears at bay. "I need to come home. I have to see Chloe."

"No," Jocelyn said quickly, "stay put. I'll let you know if anything changes. She wouldn't want you to bail out on the show."

"After what happened this afternoon, I don't know if it's safe for me to stay. Besides, I want to see her. Especially if . . ." She couldn't bring herself to say it.

"That is not going to happen," Jocelyn said firmly. "She's going to pull out of this. Nothing is going to happen to Chloe."

"But I'm not sure if it's safe for me to stay here."

"Well, until you decide for sure, I'll take care of things here. I'll let you know if anything changes."

Andi sighed. Jocelyn was right—for the moment. She wanted to talk to Michael before she made any decisions. "Okay."

"So, except for the insane zipline experience, how is everything going?" Jocelyn asked, clearly trying to lighten the mood. "How is he?"

"Who?" She couldn't think of anything except Chloe in the hospital.

"Michael. How is Michael?"

"Um, well, Michael. He's handsome, charming, funny, down-to-earth, caring, thoughtful—basically everything a woman would ever want in a man."

"I'm sorry, Andi? Is this really you?" Jocelyn said.

"Very funny."

"I can't help it. That's the last thing I expected to hear—that you've fallen for him."

"I didn't say I've fallen for him!"

"You don't have to. I can tell. You like him. Admit it."

Andi couldn't help the smile that preceded her words. Thinking of Michael did that to her. "I can't lie. I do like him. He's really amazing. We have so much in common."

"Plus, he's wealthy. That's a bonus."

"I don't even care about that. Honestly, it doesn't matter to me. He's hardworking, fun, and ambitious. That's enough."

"What about him not being a member of the Church?"

Andi felt the knot in her stomach tighten. "It's the only thing that doesn't make him perfect."

"Be careful, Andi. I know you can take care of yourself, but . . . it'll only make things harder if you fall in love."

"I know. Believe me, I know."

Andi heard voices outside her door and knew she needed to get off the phone.

"I gotta hang up," Andi told her. "Please give Chloe my love and call me the minute you get any more information about her or about what happened with the car."

"I promise. Love you."

"Love you too."

Andi hung up the phone and felt her throat close off as tears finally spilled down her cheeks.

She didn't feel like seeing anyone at the moment.

Remembering there was a back entrance to the room, she quickly made her way to the adjoining bathroom and waited near the door to the hallway until whoever was out there left. She just needed a moment of privacy to digest the news and to wrap her head around what was happening.

Opening the door just a crack, she scanned the hallway and saw a small congregation of contestants several feet away. They were being filmed as they were talking.

Taking advantage of the opportunity, Andi raced across the hall to the door leading down the back stairs and let herself outside, where she found solace in the garden.

In a quiet corner, where palm fronds and ferns created a cocoon of cover, she found a small cement bench and sat down.

Her tears fell swiftly as she thought about Chloe lying in the hospital in a coma, perhaps close to dying, and her two sweet daughters possibly losing their mother.

It was more than she could stand.

What if Chloe did die? And what if it had been intentional? What if it was murder? And what had happened today? Had there been a defect, or had someone tampered with her harness?

She pulled her knees up to her chest and wrapped her arms around her legs, laying her forehead on her knees. And then she truly wept.

She needed to be there with Chloe. She needed to be near her loved ones and friends. Michael was wonderful, but there was no future with him. Right now her place was at home.

She wasn't sure how long she stayed in the garden but knew she needed to make an appearance before the producers sent people out looking for her. Wiping her eyes on the sleeve of her T-shirt, she followed the path back through the garden to the Mansion.

Right outside the back entrance, she saw Kana, the groundskeeper, working on a sprinkler head near the steps.

"Good afternoon, miss. How are you—"

She sniffed quickly so she wouldn't have to wipe her nose on her shirt.

"Something is wrong. You are not well?" he asked urgently.

"No, I'm fine," she said. "I just got some bad news about a friend, someone who's like a sister to me."

"Oh, miss, I am sorry to hear this."

"Thank you."

"Is there anything I can do?"

"No. Just pray for her."

"I will do that," he said, and his kind eyes and caring expression actually soothed her pain. "All will be well," he assured her. "Don't you worry."

She appreciated his encouraging words and smiled. "I sure hope so."

Knowing her eyes were red and puffy, she wondered if she should go to her room first and freshen up before she returned the phone, but she decided not to. She didn't really care what anyone thought at this point. She was leaving anyway.

The young woman who had given her the phone in the first place greeted her when she stepped into the producer's office, which was located in a building just twenty feet from the Mansion.

"Is Silas available?" Andi asked. "I think I'd better talk to him."

"Actually, he's out on a shoot but should be back soon. Would you like to wait?"

"Sure, I guess."

"Did you make all the calls you needed to make?"

"I just made the one."

"While you have the phone, you're welcome to use it," the girl said kindly. "You can just go wait in his office, and I'll notify you if he's coming this way."

"Really?"

"Why not? It might make you feel better. They won't know."

"Thank you," Andi said gratefully then did as the girl told her and went into Silas's office and shut the door. Then she quickly dialed Chloe's mother's home phone.

"Hello?" Even over the phone the woman sounded weary.

"Janette, this is Andi. I just got the news about Chloe."

"Andi, dear. How sweet of you to call."

"How is Chloe? Has there been any change?"

"Actually, yes. The doctors got some response from her just a bit ago. They said it was a good sign."

Andi took her first calm breath since she'd gotten the news.

"It's so hard to see her lying there," Janette said. "She's such a tiny little thing. She's been through so much."

"I know. I can't imagine how hard this is for you." She sat in one of the chairs in front of the desk. "I was thinking I would come and be with you at the hospital."

"But aren't you doing that reality show?"

"Yes, but Chloe is more important."

"Oh, Andi, you're so sweet. There's just really nothing you can do if you come. We're just sitting and waiting until something changes."

"I'm just so worried."

"If you'd like to join us, we're going to fast for her till tomorrow. That would be lovely if you could participate. Just keep her and those sweet little girls in your prayers. I would hate to see them lose their mother."

"I would love to fast with you. Please give her my love."

"I will, dear. Do a good job on your show. I hope you're the winner."

Andi laughed. Janette probably wouldn't even watch the show.

She hung up, feeling a little more encouraged and slightly less anxious about Chloe. Now that the adrenaline of the afternoon was beginning to wear off, she wondered if maybe it was a coincidence that she'd gotten a defective harness. She tended to have that kind of luck—especially when she was shopping. If there was a missing tag on one shirt in an entire pile, she managed to find it.

Quickly scanning through her texts and e-mails, she was relieved to see that even though there were hundreds, none of them looked urgent or important.

Emerging from Silas's office, she handed the phone to the receptionist. "Thank you so much. That really helped me."

"Good, I'm glad. Let us know if there's anything you need."

"I will. They're going to call with an update for me if something changes—will that be okay?"

"We'll let you know when the call comes," the girl said, offering a sympathetic smile.

"Thank you again," Andi said.

Climbing the stairs to her room, Andi tried to imagine Chloe in her bed, completely unconscious. It just didn't seem possible.

The hallway was empty when she arrived at her room, and an eerie silence filled the Mansion. Where was everyone? Shrugging and deciding she was grateful for the alone time anyway, she entered the room then immediately dropped to the side of her bed and poured her heart out in prayer. She pleaded for Chloe's life. She pleaded for the family to be strengthened. And she pleaded for Chloe's daughters to be protected and comforted. She expressed gratitude for the safety she'd been blessed with that afternoon on the zipline. And then, she thanked Heavenly Father for Michael.

She began her fast then, exercising all her faith that if it was the Lord's will, Chloe would be healed.

She crawled onto her bed and curled up in a ball as she released more tears and let her emotions drain away. What was going on?

* * *

"Andi, wake up. You're wanted at the door."

"Huh?" It took Andi a minute to clear the fog from her mind as she woke up out of a dead sleep. She saw Danee in front of her.

"You're wanted at the door. It's Mark Sterling."

"Mark who?"

"Sterling, the host of the show!"

"Oh, okay," she said, climbing off the bed as she tried to figure out what was going on and when Danee had gotten there. Knowing she looked like a train wreck, she was tempted to stop and fix her hair and face but knew it would take too long to do that much damage control.

"Good evening," Mark swallowed when he saw her, "Andrea."

"Hey, Mark," she said, pushing a mess of hair out of her eyes.

"I've got a dinner invitation for you from Michael." A cameraman was behind him, ready to film her reaction.

"I'm not feeling well," she said, unable to see herself surviving any date—even one with Michael—when she was feeling such overwhelming concern and heartache for Chloe and her family, not to mention the fact that she was now fasting. She and Michael would have to talk later. She couldn't imagine trying to be perky and happy in front of the cameras. If she and Michael could be alone, it would be different. But every word would be captured on film. She just couldn't do it.

"Uh, yeah, I can see that," Mark said. "Um, hold on."

He spoke quietly to the cameraman, who then spoke over his headset to someone else.

Andi sat on a chair and waited. She just wanted to crawl into bed and pull the covers over her head.

"Okay, I think we've got it figured out. We'll let Michael know you aren't well and that you won't be able to join him tonight."

"Great. Thanks, Mark." She got up to shut the door.

"You do realize this could hurt your chances on the show if you don't go out with him," Mark said as she closed the door.

"Yes, but that's just the way it is. If Michael doesn't care that I'm not feeling well, then I guess he's not someone I'm really interested in anyway."

Her answer took Mark by surprise. He seemed like the type who was used to having girls throw themselves at him. She had no use for men like that—ones with an overly healthy ego.

"Dude, let's go," the cameraman said.

Andi shut the door and fell onto the chair again, relieved that she didn't have to go on a date in her current state of mind. More than anything she wished she had her phone so she could find out if there was any news on Chloe.

"Wow," Danee said, coming over to stand by her. "I could tell you twelve other girls who would kill to have that invitation."

"Well, hopefully one of them will have a chance now. I just don't feel up to going out, especially with a camera following us around all night."

"Do you need a doctor?"

"No, I'm not sick. It's personal." She liked Danee but didn't want to involve her in her private life. "I just want to go to bed."

"I'm going to dinner. Do you want me to bring something back for you?"

"That's so sweet of you, but I'm fine. Thank you, though."

"I won't be long." Danee grabbed her purse. She was wearing a cute cotton sundress with a brightly colored wrap around her shoulders. "I'm really sorry about whatever it is that's going on."

"Thanks, Danee. I appreciate it."

After Danee left, Andi sat where she was for a moment and then, for lack of any other ideas, decided she should try to make herself more presentable. She had to do something. All she could think of was Chloe lying in a hospital bed, fighting for her life.

She washed her face and brushed her hair and changed into jeans and a T-shirt. Then she wandered to the window, which looked out over a grove of palm trees and beautifully manicured grounds. This was such a lovely place, but right now it was the last place she wanted to be.

Chapter 17

Chloe occupied Andi's thoughts most of the night. When she did sleep, nightmares of falling woke her up. A constant prayer ran through her head and her heart that Chloe would be okay and that somehow everything would work out the way it should.

A brisk morning shower helped Andi wake up and feel refreshed. As she blow-dried her hair, she decided it would help her mood to get outside and go for a walk. She wished there were some way to go see the sights on the island—after all, she didn't know how much longer she would be here, and, anyway, she needed a distraction.

Her wish came true.

Danee and Andi were just finishing getting ready for the day when a knock came at the door. They looked at each other, and Danee let out a squeal of excitement—the day's itinerary was here.

"Good morning!" Mark Sterling said loudly when Danee opened the door. "Well, well, look who's back from the dead."

"Good morning, Mark," Andi said flatly.

"Now, that's not the warmest reception for a guy with an invitation, is it?" He dangled the square white envelope from his fingers.

"Who's it for?" Danee asked.

"Sorry, doll," Mark said with a slight eye roll. "Maybe next time."

"Me?" Andi was dumbfounded. After turning Michael down last night, she was certain she would be on her way out the door before breakfast.

"I guess Michael doesn't take no for an answer," Mark said, shrugging.

Andi took the envelope and slipped open the flap with her finger. "Ouch!" she exclaimed, examining the already-bleeding paper cut on her index finger.

Danee handed her a tissue, which Andi wrapped around her finger until she could find a Band-Aid.

She read the invitation:

> *Michael would like to request your company on a helicopter tour of the island. He will meet you at the helicopter pad at eleven o'clock. Please dress casually.*

"What does it say?" Danee asked anxiously.

"He wants me to go on a helicopter ride with him this morning." Andi folded the invitation and put it back in the envelope, her mind already searching for the right outfit to wear.

"Oh . . . that sounds so fun," Danee said. "He really likes you. You and Kimmie."

"Kimmie?" Andi asked.

"Yeah, when you weren't able to go last night, he asked Kimmie instead."

"Well, good for Kimmie," Andi said slowly, keeping her thoughts to herself. She wasn't going to be known as a complainer or a gossip.

"He took her to see Waimea Canyon," Danee explained.

"What! Dang, that's one of the places I was hoping to see while I was here." Andi had done some research before she arrived and had read about Waimea Canyon, which was also known as the little Grand Canyon. Growing up in Southern Utah, she'd come to love the red sand and beautiful formations in nature, especially the Grand Canyon. She'd heard about Waimea and had wanted to see the red dirt and deep canyon on the lush island.

"I'll leave you girls to get ready, then," Mark said in a dull voice. Clearly he felt his time was better spent around the girls who worshipped the ground he walked on.

"Am I supposed to be going somewhere?" Danee asked with surprise.

"Didn't you read the schedule downstairs? You and the rest of the girls are going to the Hideaway Spa for treatments," Mark told her. "I think they're leaving at ten, so you might want to hurry."

Danee glanced at her watch and gasped; she had less than fifteen minutes to get ready.

"Thanks, Mark," Andi said, moving to close the door.

"Wait a second. You seem very familiar to me," Mark said to her and narrowed his eyes a touch. "Have we met before?"

Andi thought a moment and studied his face. Now that she looked closely, she realized she had seen him before, and not just from TV. "Now that you mention it, I think we might work out at the same gym," she told him.

His mouth dropped open. "That's right! Of course! You're that workout chick. That ab-machine girl."

"I am," Andi said.

"Well, well," he said, giving her the once-over from head to toe. "I was just thinking you looked like you were in great shape."

Andi smiled at him, unfazed by his patronizing comment.

"You know," he said, keeping his voice low, "if things don't work out here, maybe we could get together back in L.A."

"I make it a rule to never date guys from my gym," she said. "It gets too awkward."

"I'll change gyms, then," he said.

"Why don't we see what happens here first," she told him, wondering why he was being so dogged in the face of blatant rejection.

"Okay," he said, "but remember, I know how to find you."

The gym Mark went to was a total pick-up scene, a place Andi despised and only went to because it was near her apartment. However, she had a free membership to several other gyms. She'd have to start going to one of them now.

"I won't forget," she said, finally getting the door closed.

With Mark gone and Danee busy throwing on her bathing suit and packing her beach bag, Andi took a moment to think. With her luck, she didn't know if going up in a helicopter right now was all that smart. But how could she turn Michael down again? She mused on that for a moment. Maybe she could voice her fears to him and he'd understand and change their plans. A nice, safe walk on the beach would be a good choice—although, of course, there were always tsunamis to worry about.

Deciding not to think about that possibility for the time being, she looked through her wardrobe to find something to wear. While other girls wore short shorts or strapless sundresses, she had chosen figure-flattering walking shorts and T-shirts and adorably stylish sundresses that looked like they belonged on the Riviera or a yacht in the Mediterranean.

"Gotta run," Danee shouted as she left the bathroom, leaving a cloud of perfume behind her. "Have fun."

"You too," Andi called after her.

Andi realized with sudden gratitude that any other contestant would probably be giving her grief because she was getting extra attention from Michael. And although Danee wasn't happy about the fact that Michael hadn't requested a special date with her yet, at least she was a big enough person to not take it out on Andi.

Wearing white walking shorts, a yellow cotton knit shirt with a wide boat neck, and a pair of large, yellow hoop earrings, Andi took a look in the mirror to check her reflection. The color of the shirt popped against her deeply tanned skin and the sun-kissed highlights in her hair. She almost chose a pair of white ballet flats then decided to dress up the outfit with a platform sandal. Michael was six foot two, so she could wear heels with confidence.

With only a few minutes before she had to go downstairs to catch her ride, Andi took a moment to get on her knees. Her prayers were full of gratitude as well as concern for Chloe and for the rest of her friends and their safety.

Ready for a memorable outing with Michael, Andi got to her feet, gathered her scarf and a white straw D'Angelo bag, and headed downstairs.

* * *

"I'm surprised none of the girls has said anything about what happened on the zipline yesterday," Andi told Michael after he enveloped her in a close embrace.

"We're keeping it completely confidential right now," he replied, pulling back slightly. "We don't want this to hit the news before we have a chance to investigate. From what I gather, though, everything checks out with how the zipline companies safety check their harnesses after every ride. If there is even a small tear or sign of wear, they retire the harness."

"I appreciate all you're doing to figure this out. And for rescuing me yesterday. You're my hero, you know." She wasn't teasing. It was true.

"I don't know what I would have done if you had fallen. I was ready to do whatever it took to make sure that didn't happen."

"I know." And she did. She was certain that even if it meant risking his own life, he would have done so in a heartbeat if it meant protecting her. This wonderful man was beyond amazing. "So, a helicopter ride, eh?"

"Have you ever been up in a helicopter before?" Michael asked through the earphones. The helicopter was firing up, and the blades made a deafening sound.

"In New York City. It was pretty awesome."

"I bet. What were you doing there?"

She explained about Lauryn and her design studio as the helicopter took off. The conversation ebbed and flowed as they lifted into the air, and Michael acted as her personal tour guide, telling her in detail about all of the sights they would see from the air.

"After what happened yesterday, are you sure this is smart?" Andi asked during a lull in the conversation. "I mean, I seem to be some kind of magnet for trouble."

Michael laughed. "I'll take my chances. As long as you're okay with it, I'm not worried. This is one of my favorite things to do on the island."

She had to admit that she was a bit frightened, but being with Michael helped her feel safe. "I think I'll be just fine."

It felt wonderful sitting with Michael's arm around her as he pointed at various landmarks and points of interest. She was grateful for the headsets they wore so they could talk to each other over the noise of the whirring blades.

The pilot took them up the Nā Pali coastline, sweeping close to cascading waterfalls and rocky outcroppings. To her delight, the flight took them directly over and then inside Waimea Canyon. By helicopter was "the only way to see it," according to Michael.

The canyon was everything she expected and more. It was both massive and breathtaking, similar to the Grand Canyon but strikingly different because of all the greenery.

At times, Andi was not only speechless but choked up as the beauty of the island unfolded before her and Michael's rich voice spoke in her ear, telling her of places he wanted to take her, special spots he wanted to share with her.

From below, the ocean sparkled with rich hues of turquoise, teal, and aquamarine. She'd never seen colors so vivid and beautiful.

"Michael, this is the most incredible experience I've ever had," she told him, overwhelmed by the expansive scenery before her eyes. "It is paradise. It really is."

Their eyes connected, and he smiled, his expression filled with joy for her appreciation of his island.

"I didn't think it could get better—until now," he told her.

Her heart flipped right over. She hadn't felt that kind of reaction in . . . well . . . ever.

"Andi, I'm glad you didn't come with me last night."

Her eyes widened with surprise. "Huh?"

He laughed. "Only because this way we were able to take this ride together. It took some work, but I convinced Silas to do this."

"I'm really, really glad you did." She felt like a giddy schoolgirl, weak and giggly, in his arms.

"I knew you'd love it."

"I do. I love everything about it."

He tilted the microphone away from his mouth as he leaned closer to her. She did the same.

She couldn't stop herself any more than she could stop one of the waterfalls tumbling over the rugged coastline.

Their lips met, and she felt as if she were floating on air without the helicopter's help.

"Wow," he said as he pulled back.

She could only nod. It wasn't possible to put into words how she felt at that moment.

"There's somewhere else I want to take you—it's called the fern grotto," he said, his hand still resting lightly on her cheek.

"I read about that," she said, managing to find her voice. "It's at the top of my list." The grotto was an overgrown lava cave covered in tropical ferns. According to the article she'd read, it was the most romantic spot in all of Hawaii. Her heart thumped wildly at the thought of being there with him.

"I promise you, we will see it together." He kissed her again. And again.

"I would love that," she said, lacing her fingers into his. She wasn't sure how it was possible to feel so absolutely comfortable with him, but she did. He was the most amazing man she'd ever met.

And they could never be together.

Chapter 18

"MICHAEL, ANDI, I'D LIKE TO see you in my office." Silas had met them at the door after their memorable ride and ushered them inside. Usually Michael was dropped off at his quarters after a date, but Silas had requested that they both come see him.

When they were seated, Silas looked at both of them, his expression disapproving. Andi felt like she'd been sent to the principal's office but wasn't sure what she'd done wrong.

"We've received word that the paparazzi were at a certain bed-and-breakfast before taping of the show began. Michael, I guess they wanted to get pictures of you to use for who knows what."

"Yes?" Michael prompted, seeming unconcerned by Silas's tone.

"Well, surprise. Look what they found."

He handed them a photo. In the picture, Andi was sitting in a chair and her foot was on Michael's lap as he bandaged her cut.

"This is ridiculous! I was working on the grounds; she was staying at the inn. She got cut on the foot by a seashell, and I took care of it for her. We didn't even learn each other's names!"

"The paparazzi doesn't care. The pictures speak for themselves."

"What do you want us to do about it?" Michael asked, sitting back in his chair rigidly.

"You need to cut her at the next lei ceremony."

"What!" Michael exploded, jumping to his feet, his chair rocketing back. "That's ridiculous, Silas. I won't do it."

"Then she is in breach of contract, and we will have to let her go. Having you cut her will at least allow her to avoid a scandal." Silas spoke without emotion.

"Allow *her* to avoid a scandal or allow the *show* to avoid a scandal? Come on, Silas. The audience won't believe that I wanted to get rid of her. It's obvious that I have the strongest connection with her out of all the girls."

"We can take care of that in editing."

"This is insane!" Michael exclaimed, sitting down heavily. "I would think you would love having this publicity for the show. It'll get people talking about it."

"The network has given us strict guidelines, and they will not appreciate learning that you and one of the candidates had a prior relationship."

"But we *didn't.* Can't you just issue a press release and do damage control?" Michael insisted.

"You think the public will believe it?"

Michael nodded.

"Well, I'm here to tell you they won't," Silas replied in a clipped tone. "No matter how innocent your meeting was, these pictures will tarnish the show. People already think reality shows are orchestrated and contrived. In their minds, these pictures will prove it!"

Michael's grip strangled the armrests.

"Michael," Andi said, resting her hand on his forearm, "It's okay. Let me go. It's for the best."

"I won't let you go." He grabbed her hand and held it tight.

She realized she had no choice but to have the conversation she'd been dreading all day. It would help him understand that her leaving the show would be the best thing for everyone in the end.

"Silas, could we have a minute?" she asked. Her last desire was to help Silas. For some reason, he'd always rubbed her the wrong way, but the truth was, she and Michael couldn't be together. In some ways this was an answer to her prayers, even though it was extremely painful.

Silas sighed but left the room, and Andi turned her chair toward Michael, taking both of his hands in hers.

"I can't believe this," he said. "I am so sorry, Andi."

"I know. Me too, but . . . well, it might be irrelevant anyway. There's something I've needed to talk to you about."

"What?" His brow narrowed. "Is something wrong?"

"It's just that," she cleared her throat, "well, you see." She looked at their hands clasped together and knew that in a few moments he would let go and that would be the end of it.

"Just say it, Andi. You can tell me anything."

"Okay, here's the situation. I think we've connected in some really wonderful ways."

"Me too."

"We have so much in common, and I think you're . . ." She swallowed. "I think you're one of the most amazing men I've ever met."

"Thank you, Andi. I feel the same way about you. But why do I sense there's a problem?"

She blinked as her eyes prickled with tears. "Because there is. It's because of my religion. I could never marry anyone who isn't a member. It just wouldn't work."

He looked somber and asked, "It's that important to you?"

"Yes."

He raked his hand through his hair. "So this goes beyond the not drinking–not swearing thing."

She nodded. "It's more than that."

"My mother's got Mormons in her family." He pulled a face. "They sound so strange. How can you be one of them? My mother doesn't even like to talk about what happened when she was younger, it's so painful. She grew up in a Mormon community, and the people were horrible to her. She still has issues."

"Well, then, it's good I said something to you now. It wouldn't work out. Your mother probably wouldn't want you to keep me on the show. And, like I said, I could never marry anyone who doesn't belong to my faith. I've dreamed of getting married in one of our temples since I was a little girl. I know you don't understand, but it's the only way I'll get married."

He released a sigh of frustration. "I can't believe this. Why did you even come on the show, then?"

She closed her eyes for a moment and wished he hadn't asked. As she'd expected, he wasn't happy with her. She didn't want to make him angrier by saying that she hadn't expected to connect with him and that she'd wanted to boost her career. "I was sure I would be one of the first kicked off because I'm so different."

"That's what attracted me to you the most. That's what I like about you." He looked away.

"I don't know what to say." The tears threatened once more, but she did her best to hold them back. "I'm so sorry. I didn't think anything would ever happen between us."

"But it has happened. And you're willing to walk away from it?"

She shut her eyes then nodded. "It's not easy for me, but it's that important to me."

"Then I'll join your church," he said resolutely.

"That's so sweet of you," she said. "But I wouldn't want you to join my church unless you understand it and really believe it."

"Andi, I don't want you to leave." He gripped her hands in his own.

"I have to," she told him. "I just don't see how it could work out."

"Are you saying you don't have feelings for me at all?"

She swallowed. "I would be lying if I said I didn't. That's what makes this so hard. But we're on different paths. Our paths crossed, but we're still heading in different directions. And now with these pictures . . . I guess it just wasn't meant to be."

It was all she could do to keep her emotions in check as she looked at his pained expression.

"All right. If this is how it has to be, then I can't stop you from leaving. But I want you to know how hard it's going to be to tell you good-bye."

She didn't speak for fear she would break down. She nodded once then kept her head down.

"Come here," he said, taking her in his arms.

The door opened, and in stepped Silas.

"Have you figured this out, then?" he asked, glancing between them.

"Yes," Michael said in a low voice. "It's taken care of."

"Good. We'll film the lei ceremony tonight. She'll be on the plane tomorrow."

Silas remained in the room, preventing them from speaking further, which meant they wouldn't get to say a real good-bye. But perhaps it was better that way. A real good-bye would have been too difficult.

Chapter 19

"You've been quiet all afternoon," Danee said as she came to stand beside Andi at the bathroom vanity. "Is everything okay? Are you feeling all right?"

"I'm fine," Andi said, finger-combing through the spiral curls in her hair then giving them a spritz of hairspray. She felt bad that three of the evening gowns designed by Lauryn and Cooper wouldn't be seen on the show. She'd been hoping to give Lauryn's design house some exposure. Cooper had even orchestrated a huge blog campaign in conjunction with the show to promote their fashions.

But she knew it was out of her hands now.

As she put on earrings and a bracelet, she thought about the situation with Michael and winced at the pain in her heart as she thought about how soon she would be leaving. Why did the paparazzi have to get that picture?

Still, she knew that when it came down to it, the photograph was probably a blessing in disguise. Leaving now would prevent her from getting more attached to Michael. She found herself thinking of him way too much as it was.

"It's time," Danee said, breaking into her thoughts. "Should we go down?"

"I'm ready," Andi replied as she slowly let out a breath.

When they stepped outside their room, they met several of the other girls making their way down to the banquet room, where the lei ceremony would be held.

Each contestant was offered a glass of wine when she entered the room, and since there was no water available this time, Andi just turned down the offer. She wasn't going to push the issue now that she was leaving.

The girls mingled for about fifteen minutes, making small talk and laughing together about their trip to the Hideaway Spa. Andi noticed that most of the girls avoided her. Thank goodness Danee didn't abandon her. She shrugged slightly. They would all be surprised when she left that night.

"I guess I have you to thank for a wonderful evening with Michael last night," came a voice from behind Andi.

Andi shut her eyes, trying not to groan audibly. Kimmie!

Putting on a fake smile, she turned. "I'm glad it worked out for you."

"Oh, it worked out perfectly. I've never connected with a man like I've connected with Michael. It's like we were made for each other."

Andi knew it was pointless to let Kimmie get to her. The woman was just messing with her.

"He took me to Waimea Canyon. It was so incredible. You'll have to visit there sometime. Of course, it won't be the same if you're not with Michael." Kimmie twirled a strand of hair around her finger as she gave a long sigh. "I could tell he wanted to kiss me."

Andi refrained from telling Kimmie about her own date and the kisses she'd shared with Michael. She would find out in due time when the show aired.

Kimmie continued. "To see us together, you'd never know that Michael and I had just met."

"That's nice, Kimmie." Andi searched the group for Danee; she needed a reason to get away from Kimmie. Where was she?

"I think it's fascinating that two people who are complete strangers can have such strong chemistry. I mean, until the show, I didn't even know who Michael was, then, *bam,* it's like the Fourth of July."

"I thought you said your first meeting with him didn't go well." Andi didn't care if this was a touchy subject. She was asking anyway.

"It was because of the rain," Kimmie responded immediately. "Every time we've been together since has been wonderful. We're really getting close, which is really remarkable, since I didn't have the advantage of knowing him beforehand."

Andi froze. Why would Kimmie say that?

Luckily, before she had time to respond, Danee returned from the ladies' room, and Andi seized the opportunity to get away from Kimmie.

"We'll have to chat later," she said to Kimmie. "I think Danee needs me."

Kimmie's eyebrows arched and she shrugged. "Sure."

Andi rolled her eyes as she walked away. Something fishy was going on here, and she wasn't sure what to make of it.

"Hey, did you try that dip?" Danee said when Andi rushed up to her. "It's incred—"

"Get me away from that woman," Andi said in a low voice.

"What were you two talking about anyway? She's trouble. You should stay away from her."

"Believe me, I didn't go looking for her."

"She's used to having Daddy get her anything she wants. If she can, she'll get Michael, too. Hopefully he's smart enough to see through her."

A flutter passed through the group as they heard the signal that the cameras were rolling and Mark was about to join them. The girls formed a half circle, with Andi on one end and Kimmie on the other. Andi never looked directly at her, she but felt Kimmie's eyes on her.

Kimmie knew something. Andi didn't know how, but she was sure of it.

Mark walked out from a back room and greeted all the girls. He talked about the group dates they'd all participated in and then the two private dates Michael had had with Kimmie and Andi. He explained that tonight was going to be a special night, but for two contestants, it would be the end.

The girls exchanged glances and worried expressions, but Mark quickly cracked a joke and got them all to laugh. Andi looked around her and realized that she was ready to leave. The only thing real about this reality show were the feelings she had for Michael, but even then, she couldn't be entirely sure. Being here in Hawaii, under these circumstances, was not "real." Once the show ended, all of it would end.

"So, ladies, if you are ready, let's bring out Mr. Right." Mark stepped back, and out walked Michael, looking amazing in a gorgeous white linen suit. He had a presence about him, an instant magnetism that made every girl standing below him go weak at the knees.

"You all look beautiful tonight," Michael said. "I've looked forward to seeing you, even though I'm dreading what I have to do."

"Michael, it's been quite a week for you. You've been busy with dates and getting to know these lovely women," Mark said. "What are your thoughts?"

Michael chuckled and scanned the group of women in front of him, starting with Kimmie and ending with Andi. She noticed with a painful twist in her chest that his gaze remained on her for several seconds longer than the other girls.

"I want to say how much I've enjoyed having a chance to get to know each of you ladies a little bit better. I am so impressed with each of you and what amazing women all of you are."

"They really are amazing," Mark echoed. "But we do have to say good-bye to two of them tonight."

Michael nodded.

"So, if you're ready, I think these lovely ladies are anxious to know what you've decided."

"I'm ready." Michael stepped up to the stand, where the beautiful purple orchid leis hung.

Andi pulled in several breaths, determined to keep her composure strong and her chin high. She couldn't decide if she was glad she had come on the show or not. It was an experience she would never forget but definitely not one she would repeat again.

A heavy tension hung in the air. None of the girls wanted to leave. Most of them were smitten with Michael, and several of them were convinced they were his soul mate.

Instead of focusing on leaving, she concentrated on the fact that in a few days, she would be in St. George visiting Chloe. That's where she needed to be. That's where she wanted to be.

Mandy, Eliza, and Arial received leis, and the tension shimmered in the air with four leis left to go.

"Maria."

Maria walked to Michael and stood in front of him as he put the lei around her head and rested it on her shoulders. He kissed both of her cheeks, and she returned to her spot.

"Tara."

Tara was someone Andi had hoped to get to know better. Her work as an autism specialist fascinated Andi. Tara was also wickedly funny. Andi could definitely see Michael being compatible with Tara.

There were only two spots left.

"Kimmie."

Kimmie flashed a triumphant smile in Andi's direction then practically ran to Michael. She threw her arms around him and hugged him tightly. When he asked her if she'd accept the lei, she said, "Yes!" with far too much enthusiasm. Andi groaned inwardly, noticing that most of the other girls had a queasy look on their faces. No one really liked Kimmie.

One spot left.

Andi hoped Michael chose Danee. He hadn't really spent enough time to get to know her, and Andi was convinced he would really like her if he just gave her a chance.

"This is your final choice," Mark said. "When you are ready."

Michael cleared his throat and smiled at the women.

Andi felt her heart skip a beat when his gaze traveled her direction.

I don't want to go.

The thought caught her by surprise, and she did her utmost to will it away. It didn't make sense to even entertain the idea that something could ever come of a relationship with him.

It was time to go home. For many reasons.

Michael stood in silence, and as the seconds ticked by, the silence grew awkward.

Finally, Michael turned to Mark. "Could I have a minute?"

Mark's cool demeanor melted for a moment. His eyes shifted to Silas, who nodded. Then Mark said, "Of course, Michael."

The two men walked out of the room, and Andi let out a breath. The only other girl left besides Danee and Andi was a girl named Candace. Andi didn't know Candace very well, but the girl was pretty and seemed nice. She wore a lot of designer-brand clothes and had an air of wealth about her, but she was nothing like Kimmie.

Andi reached for Danee and gave her hand a squeeze. The girls relaxed their stance a bit while the cameras took a break. *How can anyone really ever find true love on a reality show?* Andi wondered as she waited. The contestants were chosen at random and according to what they could bring to the show. It was more about ratings than true love.

The thought strengthened her resolve that she was glad to be leaving.

The girls talked quietly, except for Kimmie, who felt a need to act surprised that she'd received a lei. She made sure everyone could hear her, especially Andi, down on the opposite end of the line.

"I'm going to throw up," Danee muttered.

"Nerves?" Andi asked.

"No. Kimmie."

Andi and Danee laughed.

"If he's smart, he'll choose you," Andi said. "You deserve a one-on-one."

"Thanks, Andi," Danee said, giving Andi a hug. "I'm sure it's going to be you, though."

Andi shook her head. "No. You'll be staying. Just don't let Kimmie bully you."

"Don't worry."

"Places, ladies," one of the crew said.

One of the men counted down, and the cameras began rolling again.

Michael's expression seemed strained when he returned. Andi felt sorry for him. He was really struggling with making his choice.

"Michael, are you ready to give out the final lei?" Mark asked.

Michael nodded.

He picked up the lei and looked at it for a moment before looking up at the women.

Then he said, "Andi."

Andi blinked and wondered if she'd heard him correctly. Danee gave her a little push.

As Andi walked up to Michael, her heart pounded in her chest. What was he doing?

"Andi, will you accept this lei?"

She honestly wondered if she should say no. Maybe that would help him out. If she said yes, they were both in big trouble.

Before she could think it through properly, she found herself saying yes.

He slid the fragrant orchid lei over her head and rested it on her shoulders then kissed her on both cheeks and hugged her.

"You like to live dangerously," she whispered.

"I tried, but I couldn't do it," he whispered back.

She blocked the other girls out as she walked back to her spot. What had Michael just done?

Mark said something in the background, and Danee and Candace were allowed to tell Michael good-bye. Andi remained stunned. She didn't want this to get ugly for either her or Michael.

She needed to talk to Silas and tell him she was willing to go home.

After the cameras stopped rolling, Andi searched for Silas to let him know she wanted to talk to him, but he wasn't anywhere to be found. Neither was Michael.

The girls were told to go back to their rooms and prepare to go to the hot tub.

Andi cringed. She really didn't want to participate in this again. How many hot-tub scenes did a reality show need?

When she got to her room, Andi found Danee packing and crying.

She decided to walk out to the garden for a moment and let Danee finish in private. The poor girl needed some space.

The cool air held a whisper of plumeria and felt good against her skin. She appreciated Michael putting himself out there and asking her to stay, but she was afraid it wasn't worth it.

"Aloha," a voice said.

Andi jumped and turned to see Kana standing a few feet away, hand-watering flower baskets.

"Kana!" She put her hand over her racing heart.

"I am so sorry. I didn't mean to frighten you."

"That's okay. I'm a little jittery right now." Her nerves were stretched to the breaking point. Between her accident, Chloe's accident, and Michael's change of mind, she felt like a long-tailed cat in a scissor factory, as her grandfather used to say.

"Is something wrong? Do you need help?" he asked, turning a switch on the hose to stop the flow of water.

"I'll be fine, but thank you," she said. "I just need to get a good night's sleep and start fresh tomorrow. Speaking of sleep, is that something you ever do? You seem to be at work twenty-four hours a day."

"Ah, it may seem that way, but I get plenty of sleep. I work a lot, but I enjoy what I do very, very much and don't think of it as work."

"Must be nice to have a job you love so much."

"I feel very fortunate."

She nodded as her mind drifted back to her concerns.

"Patience and time will solve almost any problem," Kana said softly. "Try not to worry. Things have a way of sorting themselves out."

It would take a magic wand to sort out all of her problems.

"Thanks, Kana. I'm glad I bumped into you. I appreciate your advice. Your wife is lucky to be married to someone with such a kind heart."

"Ha! You haven't seen Kana play golf," he said with a laugh. "I'm not so kind then."

She laughed with him. "I'm not sure golf counts. I've had to fight the urge to throw a few clubs when I'm playing."

"Broke my favorite nine iron that way," he said.

They laughed again, and Andi realized she'd probably better get back inside. "Thank you again. I hope you don't have much more work to do."

"Almost done," he said.

With a wave, she walked back inside the Mansion and headed for her room. Just as she rounded the corner to the staircase, she heard someone call her name.

There, standing near the registration desk, was Silas, a stony expression on his face.

Chapter 20

"GOOD EVENING, ANDI. I WAS wondering where you'd wandered off to. Is there something important out here in the garden?"

Her heart fell. Silas probably assumed she was up to something.

"I just needed a breath of fresh air. I ran into the gardener, and we had a little chat."

"I see," Silas said, nodding calmly. "I was wondering if you had a moment."

"I'd really like to say good-bye to Danee," she said, glancing toward the doorway.

"This won't take long, I promise."

And so, since she really didn't have a choice, she followed him to a room off the main lobby.

"Sit down," he said, and gestured with his hand.

She sat.

He sat across from her. Between them was a glass table with a tropical flower arrangement on it.

"Well, Michael sure surprised us tonight, didn't he?"

"Yes, he really did."

"If I didn't know better, I'd think you two had planned it."

She felt her eyes narrow. "That's ridiculous. We didn't talk again after our meeting. I was under the impression that I was leaving. My bags are half packed."

His expression remained impassive, and she knew he didn't believe her. "Well, whatever actually happened, there's not much we can do about it now. We do need to do everything we can to avoid any negative press. I don't like making threats, but we can't afford to have a scandal on the show. In fact, if word gets out that something like this is going on, we could be in danger of cancellation. Which means I'm out of a job. We all are."

"Silas, please understand. It was a complete fluke that I ended up staying overnight at the bed-and-breakfast where Michael was working. I mean, why would I assume that the guy cleaning the pool or weeding the flower beds was Mr. Right? He put a bandage on my foot. That's it."

"Well, tabloids will print what they want—and what they want isn't usually the simple truth. The media misrepresents people in pictures all the time. And the only way to put a stop to this getting leaked is for you to leave the show."

"I did *not* ask Michael to give me the lei. Maybe he's the one you should be talking to."

"He refuses to listen. I knew we were in for a rough ride when we decided to go with him this year. He may be one of the fifty most eligible bachelors in the United States, but he's also one of the richest, which makes him think he can do as he pleases."

Andi had a hard time believing that Michael behaved like a spoiled rich boy. From everything she'd seen, he was hardworking, easygoing, and lacked the ego most men of his status possessed. Of course, she'd known him barely two weeks. She supposed he could behave differently when he wasn't around her. Yet she'd met him when neither of them knew the other was part of the show, and he had nothing to prove to her then.

"What would you like me to do, Silas?"

"I want you to quit the show. It can be for any reason you choose, or we can just say it's because of personal reasons. If Michael won't kick you off the show, then it's on your shoulders. If you don't go now, you could end up as the last one standing, and we can't let that happen."

Whether he meant to offend her or not, he did. But oblivious, he continued. "I know you have some acting ability because of your career in front of the camera, so I'm sure you can pull this off. Michael is going to ask you to accompany him on another date, and I want you to tell him then that you're leaving."

This was a lose-lose situation. If she stayed and fell further in love with Michael, she lost, because in the end, they could never marry. If she left, she lost literally. Silas left her no choice.

"All right, Silas. I'll tell him."

He looked pleased but hid the smile she knew must be just beneath his calm façade. "We'll arrange a meeting for you to talk to him—on film, of course."

She nodded.

"I'll let you know when that meeting will take place."

Andi stood but didn't speak.

Silas opened his mouth then seemed to think better of it and released a drawn-out breath. "That's all."

Turning away, Andi walked toward the door, her vision blurred with tears. There were no more stops to pull. She was leaving.

* * *

"You ready to go to lunch?" Maria asked Andi as she sat on the chair by the door and put on her wedge-heeled sandals. They'd become roommates after both of their previous roommates had been sent home.

"I'm not hungry," Andi said, laying her head heavily against the couch cushion.

"But you didn't have breakfast, either. Don't you feel well?"

"I'm fine, Maria. Really." Andi picked up the yellow legal pad again. She had been trying to come up with ideas for her book, but her brain felt numb

"I can bring you a sandwich and some fruit. Maybe you'll be hungry later."

Andi's stomach was churning and upset. The thought of food made her nauseated, but Maria was so persistent that Andi was afraid she'd never give up.

"That would be nice. Thank you."

"Okay. Well, I'll be back in about an hour."

Maria paused before leaving then opened the door, walked out, and closed it behind her.

Andi appreciated some alone time with her thoughts. She knew she needed to leave, but she'd never felt more blue in her life. Michael had gotten to her. He'd managed to sneak past the barriers guarding her emotions and get to her heart. Knowing she would never see him again made her stomach feel like it was twisting itself into hundreds of square knots.

She knew her heart had a tendency to drive her actions more than her head, and this tendency caused her more problems when it came to relationships than anything else in her life. Not this time, though. No matter how difficult it was, no matter how much it hurt, she was leaving.

The blank paper stared back at her, and she knew she wasn't going to get any real work done until she'd put all this behind her. The movement of palm leaves out the window caught her eye. She needed a break.

Slipping out the back way, she stepped outside into the brilliant sunshine and fragrant air. She followed the narrow cement path that wound through gorgeous flower beds and trickling fountains until she reached her favorite cozy corner with a bench and overhang of ferns that gave her the privacy she craved to sit and ponder her predicament.

Being here in Hawaii, meeting some of these wonderful women, and having these incredible experiences would be memories she'd never forget. And even though leaving was going to break her heart, she was glad she'd come. There had been several times in her life that she'd taken a risk and stepped outside her comfort zone in hopes of making something good happen. The first time had led to getting her exercise videos produced, and the second time had led to her becoming the spokesperson for *The Chiseler,* the ab machine that became a QVC best seller.

"Aloha!" a man's voice broke into her thoughts.

She jumped and turned to find Kana walking toward her. He wore a large-brimmed straw hat and carried a pair of pruning shears in his hand. She laughed inwardly that their meetings always seemed to catch her off guard.

"Aloha, Kana," she said, happy to see him. She'd hoped to have a chance to tell him good-bye and thank him for being so kind to her.

"A beautiful day, isn't it?" he said.

"It is," she said. "And so is this garden. I'm really going to miss it."

He frowned. "Miss it? Are you going somewhere?"

"Well, you know, we never know how long we'll stay on the show. I could be gone tomorrow."

"Oh, now, that's a load of fertilizer if I've ever heard one. Mr. Makua would be crazy to let you go."

She smiled. "I've really appreciated your kindness, Kana. I'm going to miss it here."

His forehead wrinkled. "Is everything okay, miss?"

"No, but sometimes you have to do the right thing, even though it's not what's easiest."

"Is it Mr. Makua? Has he done something?"

"Oh no, not at all. He's actually quite possibly the most wonderful man I've ever met." She knew she needed to stop talking. Silas wouldn't want her blabbing to the hired help about being forced to leave the show for a ridiculous reason.

"I hope I get to see you around here for many days to come," Kana said.

"No matter what happens, I hope to come back here someday. If I do, I'll come by and say hello."

"Please do, miss." He tipped his hat and gave her a smile then left her to herself.

Glad that she hadn't unpacked completely, she decided to go to her room and get her things together. She knew it wouldn't be long before she met with Michael and gave him her news.

* * *

Andi twisted the strap of her purse until it was permanently kinked. Michael would be joining her any minute.

Silas had arranged for them to meet on the terrace of the restaurant on the plantation property that overlooked the beach and had a panoramic view of the ocean and coastline in both directions.

The cameras were set up, and the crew was waiting for Michael to arrive. Andi kept to herself instead of chatting with the crew, trying to decide exactly how to tell Michael she was leaving.

Chloe's accident was not only a legitimate excuse but also a perfect excuse for her to exit the show. Michael couldn't take it personally, and she might garner some sympathy from viewers. Of course, Silas would make sure her announcement was used to further the purpose of the show, which was to create drama.

A commotion inside the restaurant told her that Michael had arrived. Several of the crew members came out onto the terrace and began to position last-minute lights and other pieces of equipment.

As luck would have it, Silas had been called away to attend to another crisis, so Brandon would be helping with the shot. He had explained to her what the producers wanted for the scene, and she understood what she needed to do.

One of the crew members asked Andi if she needed a drink, and she gladly accepted a bottle of cold water. Nerves always made her mouth dry.

"All right, Andi, we're ready to begin shooting," Brandon announced as he stepped out onto the terrace from the sliding doors. "Michael will come through this entrance. You walk over to meet him, then both of you will sit over there on that sectional lounge in the shade to have your conversation."

Andi nodded in understanding and pulled in a calming breath. The turmoil of seeing Michael, telling him she was leaving, and saying good-bye was causing her incredible distress. She dreaded what was about to happen and would be glad when it was over.

A soft wind pulled at her long hair and fluttered the hem of her sundress. She'd paid particularly careful attention to dressing for the final meeting. Not only did she want to show off one of Lauryn's cutest dress creations, but she wanted to leave Michael with a positive impression.

She was ready.

In position, Andi waited for her cue, closing her eyes briefly to say a quick prayer. She needed help, guidance, and strength to go through with this.

"Action!" Brandon announced.

Andi turned and saw Michael slide open the glass door, a giant smile on his face as he walked onto the terrace.

Just seeing him made Andi smile. She couldn't help it. That was the effect he had on her.

She got to her feet and walked toward him. When they met in the middle, they kissed briefly and embraced. She closed her eyes, trying to memorize the feel of his arms before she stepped back, but he held on to her for a moment longer than she had expected.

"I've missed you," he said softly.

Her heart responded in a clenching ache.

Finally releasing his hold on her, he asked, "Shall we sit?"

She nodded, and he led her toward the cushioned sectional in the shade beneath the overhanging umbrella.

They sat down and got comfortable, then Michael angled himself toward her and took one of her hands in his. "So, you wanted to talk to me?"

"Yes," she said softly, unable to meet his gaze.

"Is everything okay?"

"Actually, no. I have a bit of a dilemma, and I just wanted to meet with you to tell you that . . ." She took a breath to stop her emotions from surfacing. "I have to leave."

Alarm filled his expression. "What? No! You can't leave now. I wanted to take you scuba diving and hiking."

Tears stung her eyes, and she blinked quickly to clear them.

"Why, Andi? Why do you have to leave?"

"My friend, who's like a sister to me, was in a terrible car accident. She's in a coma, and they don't know if she'll make it or not. I need to be there with her. I would never forgive myself if something happened to her and I wasn't there."

"Andi, I'm so sorry." He pulled her into a hug and held her while she gathered her emotions. "What can I do? How can I help?"

"She's getting the best care possible. All we can do is pray."

He hugged her again.

"This experience has been so wonderful," she said, sniffing back her tears. "Thank you for everything. I've loved being here."

He nodded somberly. "I was looking forward to spending more time together and getting to know you better."

"Me too," she said. "These other girls are really amazing, though. I know you'll find someone special. I hope you do. You deserve someone wonderful."

He pulled her toward him until their foreheads touched. "If this is really what you feel you need to do, then I'll support you. But I'm going to miss you."

The look of pain in his eyes added to the ache in her heart.

"I'm going to miss you too. Thank you for being so understanding."

He circled his arms around her and held her tightly. "Tell your friend she's lucky to have you."

Andi chuckled despite the tears still coursing down her cheeks. "I will."

They released their embrace and pulled back to look into each other's eyes. Then Michael leaned in and kissed her, his lips lingering on hers for a moment. She kept telling herself to stay strong, to rein in the tears. She could cry all she wanted to later. She didn't want to seem pathetic.

Michael finally sat back and looked down at their clasped hands before he cleared his throat and said, "I'll walk you out."

He stood and pulled her to her feet. They didn't speak as they walked across the terrace to the glass doors. Just before they stepped inside, Michael stopped, picked a fuchsia plumeria blossom from a vine, and slipped it behind Andi's ear then gave her a kiss.

"Here's a little bit of Hawaii to take with you."

Andi put her hand on her heart. "I already have a lot in here," she told him.

They stepped inside the restaurant, which was completely empty besides the film crew, and Brandon yelled, "Cut! Let's reposition at the bottom of the stairs before they go out front to the cars. You two?" he said, turning to Michael and Andi. "Come to the entrance, and we'll get you walking out." For Brandon, this moment was about getting the perfect shot, creating reality TV for viewers. But when he and the crew went down the stairs, reality stayed behind with Michael and Andi. And it was painful.

"Do you really have a friend to go home to?" Michael asked. "Or did Silas put you up to this?"

"I really do. She's fighting for her life, and I need to be there."

"Then I want you to go. But I will come and find you. You are the one I choose, Andi. I already know that."

She felt like a dagger had been thrust straight into her heart.

She shook her head, and confusion filled his eyes. It took everything she had to say, "No, Michael. We have no future together. I have made a decision to stay true to my beliefs. I never meant to hurt you. I didn't think we would connect . . ." She swallowed, feeling like she'd played a cruel joke on him, "like we did."

"Andi, I know you feel something for me. Doesn't that mean something? You know I have feelings for you."

"I do," she squeezed her eyes shut. "Like I said before, it's complicated. There's more to a relationship than love."

"I know that, but how do you know we couldn't work something out? Why can't we just try? After the show."

Because I may not have the strength to turn you away again.

"You're assuming you won't find someone else during the show. You've got some really amazing girls to spend time with."

"Michael!" Brandon's voice carried up the stairwell. "We're ready."

"I hate that we don't have time to talk about this!" He took her hand and squeezed it tightly.

"Action!" Brandon yelled.

"We'd better go," Andi whispered.

With her hand held tightly in his, Michael escorted her down the stairs in silence. She knew her reasons had sounded unreasonable to him and that he was probably angry with her because she had come on the show knowing they could never be together. And it broke her heart.

By the time they got to the bottom of the stairs, she was ready to burst into tears again. She felt like she'd deceived him. He was a wonderful guy, and he didn't deserve that.

They walked out of the entrance, still saying nothing. She didn't dare look at his face; she didn't want to see the disappointment on it.

"Well, I guess this is it," he said, stopping by the car door.

"I am so sorry," she said, forcing herself to look in his eyes. "I wish things could be different." She hoped he knew what she was trying to say. She hoped he understood that she wished they could have a future together. It just wasn't meant to be.

"I hope your friend gets better soon." He reached for the door handle, and her heart thumped painfully. She wasn't ready to leave.

"Thank you for everything, Michael." He looked away. He *was* angry. He was ready to shove her into the car and send her away. But what did she expect?

He opened the door and she stepped forward, ready to get inside, but he caught her arm. She froze, her heart caught in her throat.

He pulled her into a crushing hug and held her against him like his life depended on it. She couldn't keep her tears in. She was heartbroken to be leaving, but more than that, she was heartbroken she'd found the perfect guy and couldn't have him.

Even with tearstained cheeks and her nose running, he kissed her.

When the kiss ended, Michael pressed his lips to her forehead. "You really are sweeter than sugar."

She laughed in spite of it all.

With nothing left to say, he helped her into the car, and when she was seated, he closed the door.

The reverberating slam sent a shudder through her body. It was over.

Chapter 21

"LET'S DO THAT SHOT ONE more time from inside the airplane," Silas said to the crew.

Andi took a deep breath and tried to stay patient. She couldn't even leave the show without being filmed. She'd climbed the stairs to the small aircraft three times already. How many more takes did he need?

"And . . . action!" Silas yelled.

Grasping the railing, Andi began to climb the small portable stairway that led to the nine-seat Cessna turboprop private plane that would take her to the airport in Honolulu. The private plane allowed them to avoid paparazzi and to take their time getting the parting shot they needed, which made a commercial flight impossible. The cameraman had also told Andi that the smaller aircraft flew at a lower altitude so she would have unparalleled views of Hawaii's magnificent coastlines, mountains, frozen lava flows, plunging waterfalls, and even frolicking whales. At least leaving would be scenic, albeit painful.

Most of the crew members had told Andi they were sad to see her go and were sorry about her friend. Even Tom, whom Andi had finally decided was just painfully shy, had murmured that he was sad she was leaving. Silas, however, was all business. She wouldn't miss him much.

Just as Silas had instructed for the shot, Andi climbed the portable stairway leading into the plane then stopped and looked back over her shoulder, supposedly to signify her reluctance to leave and her sadness at ending her time on the show. She wasn't sad to leave the show, but her heart did ache for Michael.

"And cut!" Silas ordered. He listened on his earpiece for any further instructions then announced, "That's a wrap."

Andi was ready to get going already. It was hard enough keeping her game face on through the retakes. She needed some private time to deal with the emotions churning inside her.

The captain opened the door to the cabin and said, "Good afternoon, miss. We'll be taking off shortly. If you want to sit on the port side of the craft, you'll be able to see a lot of the coastline as we leave the island." He pointed to the rows of seats on the left side of the plane, and she nodded.

Feeling a little like she was having an out-of-body experience, Andi took her seat and fastened her seat belt. She checked her phone for any current messages and, seeing none, put it back in her purse. It had taken a good hour to scroll through all her messages and missed calls. Most of them were unimportant, some needed to be directed to Kirk, and a few needed attention once she got home. The rest were calls and messages regarding Chloe's situation and condition. Even Emma had checked in from Greece and wanted to get regular updates on Chloe's improvement. She had also sent some pictures of her baby, Demetria, who was out of intensive care and growing stronger every day. Even though the baby was barely five pounds now, she had a head of thick, dark hair and incredibly big, brown eyes.

Andi felt suddenly overwhelmed by all the thoughts swirling in her head regarding the show and her friends. She leaned back on the headrest and shut her eyes as the engines roared to life.

A sudden shimmy ran through the plane, bringing her upright abruptly, but then the calming steady hum of the engine took over. She looked out the window and watched as the film crew loaded equipment in the van. Standing, watching her, was Tom. When their gazes connected, he quickly turned and helped load some cable.

Pulling her notepad from her bag, she began making notes of things she needed to do when she got home. This helped pull her focus away from Michael and all the drama she was leaving behind. She regretted leaving the beauty of the island and not having been able to visit the many sites she'd dreamed about.

She hoped to return someday under more normal circumstances. This was definitely a place she wanted to visit again, if she could handle the memories.

Holding onto the armrests as the plane taxied, Andi watched out the window. The time she had spent in Hawaii seemed like a dream. Would she still think Michael was as wonderful when she was away from him and out of paradise?

Probably.

The engines roared louder, and the plane shot forward, slowly lifting, until the back wheels bumped then left the ground.

Through blurred vision, Andi stared out her window, amazed as ever at the view of the beaches and ocean below. It reminded her of being in the helicopter with Michael, and the memory brought a sharp stab of pain to her heart. She thought about the kisses she'd shared with him. They were etched into her heart and would be difficult, if not impossible, to erase. How long would it take to get him out of her system?

She hadn't slept well the night before, and soon the dull roar of the plane had her eyelids feeling heavy. She relaxed back into her seat and shut her eyes tightly to keep tears from forming. This wasn't the way she wanted to leave the show. Or Michael.

As she drifted to sleep, she couldn't fight the images of his face, fresh in her memory. She pictured standing beside him at the top of a lush green precipice looking over the ocean as the wind brushed against their faces and waterfalls crashed below them. She felt safe, secure, loved, and happy in his arms.

* * *

Andi woke with a start as the copilot rushed from the cockpit with a fire extinguisher in his hands, charging down the aisle to the back of the plane. Smoke-tinged air assaulted her lungs, and she began to cough.

Belted tightly to her seat, she twisted around as best she could in an effort to see what was going on, but she already knew. The plane was on fire.

The aircraft was tilted forward at an alarming angle, and fear paralyzed Andi's heart. A quick glance out the window showed nothing below but ocean.

After several minutes, the copilot stumbled down the aisle back to the cockpit.

"What's happening?" Andi shouted over the noise of the screaming engines.

"Fire in the cargo hold!" he responded. "Stay seated; we're landing."

She looked out the window at the water getting closer, and all she could see was the waves and whitecaps.

The pilot was trying to slow the plane, but the water was approaching at an alarming rate.

Father, please don't let me die this way!

She gripped the armrests and prayed for deliverance with every fiber of her being. Would she feel it when the plane crashed? Would she know when it happened?

Please, no. Father, help us!

To her amazement, the outline of land appeared at the edge of the water, and she saw a beach and land and trees. At least they wouldn't go down in the ocean.

A runway appeared out of nowhere, and Andi braced herself for the landing.

Clenching her eyes shut, she prayed with all her might.

With spine-jarring impact, the plane slammed onto the runway. Tires screeched against the tarmac, but the plane began to slow and finally came to a stop.

They'd made it.

Chapter 22

"Excuse me, miss." A young nurse in hospital-green scrubs addressed Andi as she entered the room. "Another reporter is here to talk to you.

Andi groaned and sat up in her bed. "Is it that same guy from *Celebrity Update*?"

"I'm afraid so. He's quite persistent." The nurse checked Andi's chart then wrote something on it. "It looks like you can be released as soon as the doctor comes to check you. How is your neck this morning?"

"Sore, but better than yesterday."

At the insistence of the show's producers, Andi had stayed the night in the hospital for observation after the rough landing the previous day. The producers had also requested that she not speak to reporters until an investigation surrounding the plane's mechanical problems was completed.

She shuddered as she remembered the horrible feeling in her stomach as the plane had begun to fall. The mild whiplash and bruising where her right knee had slammed into the seat in front of her seemed like a blessing compared to how bad it could have been if the plane had actually crashed.

Clinging to the hope that the incident was random and not directed toward her, Andi was more than happy to not discuss the situation with anyone, especially the media. The last thing she wanted was to be the topic of tabloids and celebrity gossip columns. In fact, the only thing she wanted was to go home, where she could move on with her life and put the show and Michael behind her, if that was even possible.

Michael. Just the thought of his name brought a pain to her heart, a pain that no medication or brace or treatment was going to cure. She wasn't sure how she was going to make herself forget about him, but leaving Hawaii was a start.

Maybe having a pain in her neck would help take her mind off the pain in her heart.

"I'll let the reporter know you're not having visitors. I'll warn you, though, there's quite a group of them out there waiting for you."

"There is?" Andi closed her eyes, cringing at the thought of facing a mob of reporters.

"There's a back entrance," the nurse said, offering a smile. "I'm sure we can arrange a shuttle to the airport to pick you up back there."

Andi rested a hand on her heart. "Thank you. I appreciate your help." She raised an eyebrow. "You don't have a disguise handy, do you?"

"Actually, I do—if you think dressing like a vampire would draw less attention," the nurse said dryly.

Andi winced as she laughed, the movement sending sparks of pain through the muscles of her neck.

"Sorry," the nurse said, "no laughing. Doctor's orders."

"I'll try to remember that."

"We'll get you out of here. I promise. I'll go find the doctor and tell him you're ready to go home."

Home. It was time. Despite the fact that she had no idea what she was going to do with herself, she needed to go home. Chloe needed her. She needed to make decisions about her future. She needed to get as far away from Michael and Hawaii as she possibly could.

* * *

Wearing a neck brace and favoring her right leg, Andi limped softly into Chloe's hospital room, holding her breath as she approached the bed where her friend was sleeping. According to Chloe's mother, Chloe had briefly woken up from the coma the day before, but only for a few minutes. It was a good sign, but they wouldn't know the extent of damage from her accident until she was fully awake.

Pulling a chair close to the side of the bed, Andi sat down and reached for Chloe's hand.

"Hey, sweetie," she said, trying to keep her voice cheery. "It's Andi. I'm back from Hawaii."

There was no sign of recognition or response.

"I'm so sorry about your accident." She reached to smooth a strand of hair from Chloe's forehead. "I've been so worried about you."

Emotion from her own ordeal combined with concern for her friend made it all but impossible to stop a tear from dribbling down Andi's cheek. They were both lucky to be alive. And if she was honest with herself, she was worried that everything that had happened wasn't a coincidence. Wiping the tear away with her sleeve, she vowed to be more wary of shadows and to keep a better watch over her shoulder.

"Chloe," she addressed her sleeping friend again, "you have to fight. You have to get better. If . . . if someone *is* targeting us, we can't let them win." The words were meant as much for herself as for Chloe. They'd already lost Ava. She couldn't bear the thought of anything happening to any of the other girls.

"Be strong, Chloe." She kept ahold of her friend's hand as she rested her head against the back of the chair. She shut her eyes and sent a plea heavenward, asking God to help Chloe get better and to watch over and protect all of her friends. Then she slowly drifted off to sleep.

* * *

"You sure it doesn't hurt your neck to do this?" Chloe asked as Andi pushed the wheelchair through the elevator's open doors into the foyer.

"It's fine," Andi told her. "It hardly hurts anymore."

Andi was so happy that Chloe was finally staying awake for longer periods of time during the day that she would walk through fire for her if she had to. "I am a little surprised the nurses trust me after what happened last time I took you out, though," she said wryly as the automatic doors opened outside to the hospital grounds.

"Hey, that could have happened to anyone." Chloe reached back and patted Andi's hand.

"Oh, I'm sure people get wheelchairs caught in the elevator doors every day."

Andi cringed, thinking about Chloe getting squished between the two doors.

Chloe waved away the statement with a flip of her wrist. "So tell me, have you heard anything from Michael?"

Andi took in a deep breath, wondering when she would stop feeling like she'd had the wind knocked out of her every time his name came up. She had been sure he would call after the scare of the fire and emergency plane landing. But the only person she'd heard from was Silas, who'd called on behalf of the show. He'd wanted to make sure she wasn't talking to reporters, and he wanted to remind Andi that she had signed a strict confidentiality agreement when she went on the show, so she couldn't discuss matters with anyone, which included Chloe.

And Chloe wasn't exactly making it easy.

"You can tell me," she coaxed. "You know I won't tell anyone."

"I wish I could, but I'm already on the producer's bad side. If I don't follow the contract, I can't even begin to imagine what kind of legal action he'd take."

Chloe sighed and then shrugged. "It's going to be crazy watching you on TV with all those other girls. I feel awful thinking that you came home for me."

"Don't. You're more important to me than anything happening on the show."

"I was just sure he was going to choose you. From what I heard before you left, you two have so much in common."

It was true. Surprisingly, she had connected with Michael more than she'd ever connected with anyone before.

"So what now?" Chloe asked.

Andi swung the wheelchair around and parked it by a bench in the shade. The day was already hot and dry—nothing like Hawaii.

"Hmm?" Andi said, thinking about the warm air in Hawaii that smelled like perfume. Then Chloe's question caught up with her. "Um, well, I'm working on a few things. I've been asked to head up an expedition to Zambia in the spring for Mothers Without Borders. I'm going to be doing some fundraising for them through the fall and winter."

Chloe nodded her approval. "I hope that someday I can go with you."

"That would be really cool if you could, Chloe. You'd love the people, and they would love you."

A young couple walked by, the man holding one arm around the woman, who looked to be very overdue to have a baby. His gentle and caring attention to her caused both Andi and Chloe to sigh.

"How sweet is that," Chloe said. "Roger was so cute with me when I was pregnant with the girls. He hardly let me lift a finger—"

Andi looked over as Chloe stopped talking.

Chloe looked down at her hands. "Around the house."

Roger had apparently come by the hospital several times since Chloe's accident. He smelled of alcohol and cigarettes. The last time he had come to visit, Andi had hardly recognized him. He looked twenty years older and forty pounds thinner.

"So you're still moving to the rehab facility tomorrow?" Andi wanted to get Chloe's mind off her ex-husband.

"Yep. I hear the food isn't as good, but it will be nice to get out of here."

"Just give me a call anytime, and I'll bring you Durango's or anything else you want. Breakfast, lunch, or dinner."

"Thanks," Chloe said with a weak smile. "I'll let you know my phone and room number when I get there."

Andi nodded. "Can I just call you on your cell?"

"I don't have it anymore," she said, shaking her head. "It got lost in the accident. My dad's taking care of getting me a new one."

Andi's phone rang. "Speaking of phones," she said and looked at the caller ID. It was Kirk. "Do you mind if I take this? It might be about that creepy e-mail."

Chloe shook her head, and Andi answered the call.

"Hey, Kirk."

"How's it going?" Kirk said. "I'm glad you answered."

"I'm good. I'm with Chloe right now. They let me bring her outside."

"Really?" Kirk asked with a grin in his voice. "Even after what happened?"

She covered the mouthpiece with her hand and hissed to Chloe, "Not everyone's forgotten about the elevator-door incident."

Chloe shook her head and rolled her eyes.

"So, what's up, Kirk?"

"I was wondering if you're up to making some appearances. There's a fitness convention in Boca Raton six months away, and they're looking for a keynote speaker. Are you interested?"

"Yeah, sure," Andi said. "Hopefully it's on a topic I already have prepared."

"I'll make sure it is. What about the workshop in Vegas? Have you given it any more thought?"

"I think I'm gonna pass. I need more time."

"You've been home two weeks," he said. "How much more time do you need?"

Spoken like a true man, she thought. What she would give for a switch in her heart to turn her emotions on and off like men seemed to do.

"Can't really say, Kirk. I promise I'll let you know. I am working on the book, though. I can probably get it done by the end of the month."

"That's great. I should hear back from Addison and Campbell in the next few days to let us know when they want you to go to New York to meet with them."

Addison and Campbell was the publisher for her book. And a trip to New York sounded like a great distraction from sitting around and thinking about Michael. She was all for it. "Just name the day and I'm there," she told him.

"Sounds good, Andi. Tell Chloe hi for me."

"I will."

"Wait, one more thing. I almost forgot. We got a call from a man named Drake Hampton. He's a wealthy developer and is opening a five-star resort in Nassau. I believe he called it Paradise Bay Resort and Spa. He wants to invite some celebrities down to help with the grand opening and called to see if you'd be interested. All expenses would be paid, and you'd receive a hefty sum for your appearance."

"Me? I'm hardly a celebrity," Andi responded, genuinely surprised.

"Actually, you are. Now more so than ever. And the reason he is asking you is that a large part of the resort is their state-of-the-art spa and fitness facility. He said the board met, and your name was at the top of their list. I can smell an endorsement in there somewhere, which means commercials and advertising. It would be a great gig to be the face of a place like that."

"When is it?"

"I need to get more details. But Drake said he would love to meet you when you go back to New York. He also thought it would be helpful to talk on the phone before then."

"All right, you can give him my cell number," Andi said hesitantly. "What's his last name again?"

"Drake Hampton. Sounded like a great guy on the phone. I'll get in touch with him."

"Thanks, Kirk."

She closed the call and put her phone in her back pocket. Ever since she'd come home from Hawaii, she hadn't felt much of a desire to launch back into work. In fact, she didn't know when she was going to go back to California. Staying in St. George felt comfortable and relaxed, and right now it felt good to have some time and space for herself.

To help keep her mind off Michael and everything that was going on in Kauai, she had been coming to see Chloe every day at the hospital and even babysat her girls a few times when their grandmother needed a break. She also took long walks along the trails in the red hills around St. George and spent time working on her book. Overall it was the most relaxed she'd been in a while.

The only problem was, she couldn't stay busy 24-7, and when her mind wasn't occupied with something else, she found herself wondering which one of the girls from the show had won Michael's heart. Had they spent the night, or several nights, together? Had he proposed? She wasn't naive enough to think that he couldn't fall quickly for someone else. With her out of the picture, it was the perfect chance for someone to move in on him.

"Hey, Andi?"

Andi shook her head and looked at Chloe. "I'm sorry, what did you say?"

"Thinking of Michael again?"

"No," she said quickly.

"Andi."

"I wasn't thinking of him, exactly. I was thinking of the women who were on the show who were all very glad I left."

"I bet. I wonder which one he ended up choosing."

"Ugh! I sure hope it's not Kimmie."

"The rich, bratty one?"

Andi nodded, knowing she'd probably told Chloe too much already. "I know he's wealthy and comes from privilege, but you wouldn't know it. He's so down-to-earth and real. Probably more than any other man I've ever known."

"It's interesting to see you like this."

"Like what?"

Chloe raised her eyebrows and lowered her chin.

"Like what?" she asked again.

"It's obvious you really fell for him."

"No, I didn't," she countered. "And what do you mean, it's obvious?"

"Oh," Chloe shielded her eyes with her hand as she looked at Andi. "The faraway looks, the longing in your eyes, the moments of silence when you're thinking about him."

Andi bent over and felt her friend's forehead. "Funny, you don't feel like you have a fever."

"I'm perfectly fine," Chloe said with a giggle.

"You're delirious. What pain meds are you on?"

Chloe laughed. "Tylenol. I'm not making it up. You fell for him, admit it."

"I'll admit we had a lot in common, I'll admit we connected well, but that doesn't mean I fell—"

Chloe tilted her head and wore an expression that told Andi she wasn't buying a word of it.

Andi sighed and nodded once. "Yeah, I fell. Hard. But it doesn't matter. He's found someone else, and I'm out of the picture. Besides, he doesn't belong to the Church, and I'm determined to wait for someone who will marry me for time and all eternity. Someone who hasn't lived a fast-paced, tabloid lifestyle. I don't think I could deal with that."

"You're right," Chloe agreed. "Absolutely. Except, remember, when I married Roger he was as pure as the driven snow, and look how he ended up. Michael didn't know differently, so be careful how you judge him."

Andi pulled a face. "It makes it easier to accept not having him in my life."

Chloe gave her a smile. "I know. Don't give up. If it's right, it will work out. I really believe that."

"Now," Andi grabbed the handles of the wheelchair, "let's talk about something else, please."

Andi pushed Chloe toward the small garden area where the scent of flowers filled the warm summer air. Memories of the gardens in Kauai flooded her brain once more, but she fought them back and pushed them down deep. She wondered how long it would take to erase Michael's memory or if she ever would be able to.

Chapter 23

Despite feeling hollow inside, Andi tried to resume a normal life. The problem seemed to be figuring out what normal was anymore. She spent hours each day staring at her computer, trying to come up with information for her cookbook, but somehow she inevitably ended up searching the Internet for information about the show. She was dying to find a scoop or a leak in information to know whom Michael had chosen. But so far she hadn't come up with a single leak.

Luckily she had plenty of time to visit with Chloe on the phone or via Skype every afternoon. Andi was amazed at how far Chloe had come in her rehabilitation and how she'd become such a strong woman.

During her fifth game of solitaire that afternoon, her phone rang. She didn't recognize the number and nearly didn't answer, but curiosity got the best of her.

"Hello," she said, moving the red queen of hearts onto the black king of spades.

"I'm trying to reach Andrea Martin," a man's voice said. His voice sounded vaguely familiar, but she couldn't place it.

"This is Andrea," she said, turning over a red jack of diamonds. Perfect. Just what she needed. She put it on top of the red queen of hearts then moved a column of cards on top to complete it.

Come on, she thought. *I need the ace of clubs.* She clicked on the deck as another card turned over and then another one.

". . . so I was wondering if we could meet and talk about it." The male voice stopped talking, waiting for her reply.

She turned the final card over and let out a frustrated sigh. Nothing. "I'm sorry. Who did you say this was?"

"My name is Drake Hampton. Your manager, Kirk, told me it would be okay for me to call."

"Oh, yes, of course, Mr. Hampton. I apologize." She quickly turned off the game and focused on the phone call. "What can I do to help you?"

"I'm not sure how much Kirk told you, but I am the manager of a new resort we're building in Nassau. It's a spa but designed for families as well as couples and individual guests. We want to promote a high-class, family-oriented atmosphere and think you are the perfect spokesperson to do that."

"Really?" Andi asked, flattered but still a little skeptical.

"Yes. Absolutely. We've looked at a lot of fitness celebrities and, frankly, none of them fits the image as well as you do."

"Thank you, Mr. Hampton. That's very nice of you to say."

"It's true. We are targeting a family demographic, and, frankly, our resort is state-of-the-art in every way. I think you'll be quite impressed. We are close to launching our website, and I can send the link to you as soon as it is available so you can take a closer look at it. Besides our hotel and spa facilities, we are building a water park that will rival anything out there. In fact, we were able to lure two of Disney's top executives to help us brand our theme park, and we'll have our own characters and logo."

"It sounds wonderful. I'd be very interested in discussing this further with you."

"If you'd be willing, I'd like to fly you out to New York so we can meet in person—go over the details and discuss the contract."

"When would you like to do that?"

"What's your schedule like?" he asked.

She tried not to laugh out loud. Schedule? Seriously?

"Let me take a look," she said, rustling a few papers near the keyboard. "I'm pretty open right now. You've caught me at a good time."

"Wonderful. Why don't I work out the details and call you back with flight information."

"That would be great. Oh, and you don't have to book me a hotel. I can stay with a friend."

"No need. We want to cover all your expenses," he insisted.

"That's kind of you. But if it's all right with you, I'd really rather stay with my friend. I don't get to see her much."

"I understand. All right, then. We'll leave those arrangements to you."

"Thank you. I'm looking forward to meeting with you. Will Kirk just fly out and meet us?"

"Kirk?" he asked.

"My manager."

"Right, yes, of course, Kirk. We definitely want him there as well."

She wouldn't make a move without him. As managers went, Kirk was very protective and loyal. She would be lost without him. His wife and two kids were almost like family to her. She felt very blessed to have him on her side.

"We're very happy you're interested, Ms. Martin," Drake said. "I'll be in touch in the next day or two."

They said good-bye, and for a moment after she hung up Andi sat in stunned silence, looking at the phone in her hand. Had that conversation really just happened? Being a spokesperson for a resort in the Bahamas meant she would have to travel to Nassau occasionally and spend time at the resort. This was possibly the sweetest gig ever. And it was just what she needed to take her mind off Mr. Right.

Without wasting time, she texted her friends the good news then called Kirk. She wanted to tell him everything.

* * *

"I went ahead and set up a meeting with Addison and Campbell. They're anxious to talk to you about setting up some appearances and a book tour. I think they just want to meet you also. They're very excited about the potential your cookbook has. They want to get you on all the daily talk shows, you know, *Regis and Kelly, Rachael Ray,* and the morning shows too. Hopefully it won't conflict with Mr. Hampton's plans. Are you sure you don't want me to just come out now? I have another client I can meet with while I'm there."

She could tell he was dying to come to New York. "That would be great, Kirk. Sure. I'd love to have you there."

"Okay," he responded without skipping a beat. "I'll get my flight booked and let you know when I'll be there. I'm telling you, Andi, your ship has finally landed. The *Looking for Mrs. Right* show, a book deal, and a spokesperson offer all in the same year? Get ready. Your life is about to change drastically."

* * *

The ride into the city from the JFK airport took forever. Traffic was terrible, and Andi had never seen rain literally coming down in sheets like it was. She checked her texts, waiting to hear from Lauryn to see if she should go straight to her apartment or to her design house. Part of her wanted to go to the design house so she could see Cooper. Right now she needed some of his upbeat craziness.

On the long flight, her thoughts had drifted to Michael. By now the show had ended. He'd made his choice. For all she knew, he was with *her* now. Whoever *her* was. It was hard not to dwell on the fact that he was with one of those other girls when it very well could have been her—if things had been different.

Life seemed to be full of wanting things you couldn't have. As a child, she remembered wanting toys, a bike, shoes, and clothes. As a teen, she'd wanted a car, a boyfriend, to be popular, to be prom queen, to be thin. As an adult, material things didn't matter as much. Now she wanted security, happiness, good health, close relationships with family and friends, and a husband and children.

There were things she could control and things she couldn't. She hoped her feelings for Michael would fade soon. He was starting a life with someone else. He was not an option. Energy spent thinking about him, wondering about him, wanting him was energy wasted.

She needed Cooper desperately. He would take her mind off of Michael.

* * *

"So where's Cooper?" Andi asked after she unloaded her bags inside the lobby of Lauryn's design studio. She gave her friend a hug and looked over her shoulder.

Lauryn smiled with an amused expression on her face. "Gee, Andi, I'm fine. Thanks for asking."

"I'm sorry. How are you? You look amazing," Andi said. Lauryn seemed to get more beautiful with every passing year. There was a confidence and inner peace about her that radiated past her gorgeous exterior. She had on black tights and flats, a poofy skirt that looked like a knee-length ballet tutu, and a darling deep-pink Betsey Johnson sweater with big red roses on it.

"I'm fine," she said. "I was kidding. And I'm sorry to tell you this, but Cooper won't be back for a few days. He had to go to Atlanta for some meetings."

Andi stuck her bottom lip out in a pout. "Ah, I was looking forward to getting hit with some of that Cooper enthusiasm."

Lauryn gave her another hug. "He'll be home soon. You're stuck with me till then."

"I'm thrilled to be stuck with you," Andi said sincerely.

"You might be surprised when you see him," Lauryn said.

"Really? Why? Did he dye his hair green? No, wait, did he shave his head? What's he done?"

"Nothing like that. He's still as crazy as ever, but ever since he joined the Church, he's, well, how do I put this . . ." She thought for a moment. "I guess you could say he's more grounded. His approach to life and relationships is different."

"Wow, I don't know what to think. I loved him just the way he was."

"I think he's even more wonderful now," Lauryn said. "There's a depth and purpose to him that was kind of missing before, when all he cared about was fashion, fame, and fun."

"Hmm." Andi thought about Lauryn's description of the "new" Cooper. "I think I'll like these changes."

"Trust me, you will. And he's dying to see you again. You two always had a connection."

Andi smiled. It was true.

"You look wonderful, Andi. How is your neck?"

"Doing much better. When I get tired or stressed, it seems to hurt more. It will be fine, though. Could have been so much worse."

"Are they investigating the fire?"

"Not yet. So far I'm just hearing it's a mechanical problem that started the fire. They aren't sure yet. The pilot was a hero, the way he landed the plane safely."

Lauryn shut her eyes as if trying to block the image of something worse happening.

"There were some weird things that happened over there," Andi told her after a moment. "I know it sounds crazy, but—"

Opening her eyes, Lauryn sighed and shook her head. "I just don't want to believe it's possible. I don't want to believe that someone could have actually done something to the plane that would make it crash. Andi, who would do something like that? Who could possibly want to hurt you, or any of us?"

"Like Chloe?" Andi suggested.

"No, that was an accident," Lauryn insisted. "Wasn't it?"

"Chloe doesn't think so." She paused then added, "I thought the same as you for a while after the accident, but I've decided that we at least need to consider the possibility that someone is out to get us. Whether or not it's true, we need to take every precaution we can." If there was something fishy going on, their best defense was to have their eyes wide open and their defenses in place.

"I don't want to believe—"

"I know you don't," Andi said, "but it isn't going to hurt us to be on our guard."

"Living in the city makes me that way anyway," Lauryn said. "I'm worried more about all of you than I am myself."

"I suppose Emma is out of harm's way for now. Anyone who would want to mess with her husband is insane."

Lauryn nodded then said, "How about that little Demetria? Is that baby darling or what?"

"I can't believe Joss and Jack are going to get to see her when they go on their trip," Andi said. "I'd love to go to Tuscany and travel around Italy—and take a little side trip to Greece, just for fun."

"Why don't we?" Lauryn said. "We could find time to get away. I have enough frequent flyer miles for me, you, and Chloe."

Andi's mouth dropped open. "That's the best idea you've ever had. What are we thinking? Of course! If they won't come to us, we'll go to them."

"Besides," Lauryn added, "they can't really travel with Demetria anyway right now. She just barely got out of the hospital."

Lauryn pulled up Emma's baby's picture on her cell phone, and they both gushed over how adorable she was. A few minutes later, the front door opened, and in walked Lauryn's husband, Jace.

"Andi!" he exclaimed when he saw her. He gave her a giant hug that lifted her off her feet. "It is so good to see you. How was Hawaii?"

Lauryn tried to shush him secretively, but Andi saw her.

"Sorry," Lauryn said, "I didn't want him to bring up a painful subject."

"Oh, sorry. Was I not supposed to ask?" he said.

"It's okay," Andi answered. "Kauai was incredible. I think I could live there. And the show was an experience I'm glad I had but would never do again. I was really anxious to find out who he's chosen, but sometimes I'm not sure I even want to watch it when it comes on TV."

"What?" Lauryn exclaimed. "You have to."

Andi shook her head. "I'll wait and see how I'm feeling when it comes on. But right now it would be just a little too painful."

"Well, we're glad you're here with us," Jace said. "I made arrangements for dinner. I hope that's okay. I thought we should celebrate." Jace put one arm around Lauryn and the other around Andi. "It's good to see you girls together again."

"I wish everyone could be here," Lauryn said.

"Chloe told me that she would seriously try to come and visit while I'm here," Andi told her.

"How long are you staying?" Jace asked. He'd moved to the reception desk in the lobby and was sorting through some papers.

"I don't even know. I have meetings with my publisher and meetings with a man representing a resort being built in Nassau."

"What's that about?" Lauryn asked. Her phone beeped, indicating an incoming message.

"I'll tell you all about it at dinner. I'd love your input."

Andi saw Lauryn's cheerful expression suddenly fade. "Lauryn, is something wrong?"

"I think I just got a text from a wrong number."

"What did it say, honey?" Jace got up from the desk and walked over to his wife.

Enjoy your success while it lasts.

Jace pulled a face. "Huh?"

"If I didn't know better, I'd think it was that crazy Hungarian, Lazslo Molnar. But he's locked up for another year. I doubt they have cell phones in prison."

"Are you talking about that guy you worked for who tried to sabotage your first fashion show?" Andi remembered how all of the Butterfly Girls had worked together to help Lauryn make a big splash in the fashion world of New York.

"That's the one." Lauryn let Jace take her phone so he could read the message again.

"Don't respond unless you get another message from the same number," he said, frowning. "This doesn't justify a reply."

Lauryn thought for a moment. "Still, it's just one more thing, you know?"

Andi agreed. "We can't be too careful with everything that's happened. I'll let the others know."

Lauryn nodded then said, "Okay. Well, enough of that. Let's go eat. I'm famished."

Andi laughed. "I still remember the first time I heard you say that back in seventh grade. I'd never heard that word before then."

"You guys were horrible the way you teased me about it."

"We thought you'd made it up. *Famished.* Such a weird word. Don't you think, Jace?"

Jace didn't answer. He was still looking at the phone. "I'm sorry, what?"

"Nothing," Lauryn said. "Honey, is everything okay?"

"You got another text."

Lauryn furrowed her brows. "From who?" she asked hesitantly.

"Same number."

"What did this one say?" she asked, her voice edged with fear.

"'I hope you like surprises.'" Jace's expression darkened, and he snapped the phone shut. "Okay, that's it. I'm calling the police."

Lauryn and Andi looked at each other then stepped together and stood arm in arm while Jace made the call.

"This is getting scary," Lauryn said.

"I'm convinced Chloe's accident was no accident," Andi said quietly. "I don't think the plane was either."

"Who's doing this? How is he finding us?" Lauryn whispered with desperation.

"And why?"

Jace hung up the phone. The look on his face wasn't a happy one.

"What did they say?" Lauryn asked.

"We can file a report and get it on record, but there is no actual threat. The police can't do anything."

Both Andi and Lauryn heaved a sigh of frustration.

"I know there's a connection to Ava," Lauryn said.

"I do too," Andi added. "We need to call Detective Hutchinson. He'll want to know."

"I have an idea," Jace said. "Let's sit down after dinner and write down everything we know in connection to Ava's death. Any suspicious contact, any weird experiences. Anything. We need Emma and Chloe to do the same and let us know so we can get their input. I know Detective Hutchinson has this information, but maybe we can see a pattern or find some clues."

Andi smiled, feeling relief that they were taking action. "We'd better do it before someone is . . ." She stopped when Lauryn's expression became alarmed. "Sorry. I was going to say injured, but that's already happened."

"Come on," Jace said. "I'm not going to let anything happen to either of you. Let's go eat."

Chapter 24

JACE PROVED TO BE THOROUGH in his method of compiling information about the accidents surrounding each of the Butterfly Girls. Up until recently anything unusual they had to report seemed random and unrelated. But when they looked at everything that had happened in the last few years combined, there were a number of incidents that left them thinking something suspicious was definitely happening.

Emma had the least to report, most likely because she lived out of the country. Most of the contact had come in the form of text messages and e-mails, and Andi found herself feeling uneasy at just how simple it was for a person to get personal information off the Internet. She realized that she, in particular, needed to go to all her social networks and eliminate any personal information that could lead a predator to her door or her friend's doors. Because she was something of a public figure, she was easily accessible, and someone who knew what they were looking for could find it.

After Chloe got her new phone and transferred all her data and messages, she had discovered several from an anonymous number. A couple of the messages seemed harmless, yet they were still strange. But one, which had been received after her accident, left them convinced something scary was going on.

Next time you won't be so lucky.

The message had been texted later in the day after her car accident.

Jace proved to be the voice of reason and kept them all from going into panic mode. Having him actively doing something to help expose whoever was behind the messages gave the girls a level of encouragement that the culprit would be found before something serious happened. At least they hoped so.

* * *

"I'm sad you can't come for the meetings," Andi said over the phone to Kirk as she walked across the busy street on the corner of Broadway and 54th. She was on her way to Lauryn's studio. It was such a beautiful day that she had decided to walk instead of take a taxi.

"This meeting in L.A. came out of nowhere, but it would be great for my career if it worked out."

Kirk had been offered a position at an agency in Los Angeles, which would help him build his client base and get his name out to bigger fish in the entertainment industry. Most importantly, he would still be able to remain as Andi's manager.

"When is your meeting?" she asked.

"In two days. I have some other business to take care of while I'm there, though, so this works out well. Tell Mr. Hampton I will be available the first of next week if he wants me to fly out then. A lot of this we can do over the phone. Just have him fax the contract to me so I can look it over. Don't agree to anything or be too anxious. They will want you even more if they know that you're in demand."

"Am I?" Andi said, stepping up onto the curb.

"Are you what?"

"In demand."

"I'd say you are, now that you're willing to look at some of the offers that come your way. I'm glad you're finally getting over that Mr. Right guy. I still think the exposure will boost your career, but I feel terrible it was such a traumatic experience for you. Oh, which reminds me, I think I might be able to get you on the *Rachael Ray Show.* I talked to their producer and told her about your cookbook. She was especially excited about your participation in the *Looking for Mrs. Right* show."

She stepped across a large puddle as she crossed the street again, getting closer to the garment district where Lauryn's shop was located.

"Thanks, Kirk. I'll call you after my meetings, then."

"And I'll call you after mine."

With the plan settled, they hung up just as Andi came to a stop in front of the shop. Looking up at the building, she felt a wave of pride for her friend. Lauryn's success had come about from hard work, believing in herself, and persistence in the face of huge challenges. Andi admired Lauryn and all she had achieved.

She decided to snap a photo of the shop with the camera on her phone to send to the other girls.

And then, well aware of her lack of photography skills, she took another photo just in case the first one didn't turn out. She was notorious for cutting people's heads off in photos and taking blurry pictures.

Forwarding the pictures to her friends, she entered the shop. There, dressed in cutting-edge fashion with jet black hair and fingernails, was Cooper, talking on the phone.

His expression lit up like Times Square when he saw Andi. Her heartbeat quickened when she saw him. They'd always had a connection. And now that he was a member of the Church, she could actually be open to dating him—a fact she'd considered multiple times since her trip to New York had been planned.

Seriously, how cute was he!

"I will fax it over to you first thing in the morning, darling," he said to whomever he was speaking to. "It's to die for. I'm not kidding. The colors and textures are *amazing,*" he said with typical Cooper enthusiasm. "Bye, then," he said then hung up the phone. An explosion of energy and excitement followed.

"Andiiiiiiiii!" he shrieked, drawing out her name as he navigated around the desk and ran to her. His hug nearly broke her ribs, but she didn't care. A greeting like that was hard to top. "I've missed you!"

Andi tried to respond but had no wind in her lungs until he put her feet back on the ground. "I've missed you too! I was so sad you weren't here when I arrived. I thought you were coming back tomorrow."

"I blew off the last meeting. It was a waste of time, and I wanted to get back to see you."

He hugged her again and kissed her cheek. "It's been way too long. And look at you." He stepped back and looked her over from head to toe, then his eyes went back to her face. "The Hawaiian sun looks good on you. You look amazing."

"Thanks, Cooper. You look pretty amazing yourself."

"I do, don't I?" he said matter-of-factly. "I've discovered Zumba and a killer boot-camp workout. I've lost twenty-five pounds. Uh-huh," he said, turning to the side and smoothing his hand across his flat stomach. "Not quite a six-pack, but I'm working on it."

"That's wonderful. Let's hit some classes together. I have a couple of friends who teach right here in the city."

"That would be great." He sighed and shook his head. "Did I tell you I've missed you?"

She smiled. "Yeah, but it feels good to hear it again."

"Would you allow me to monopolize your time while you're here? There's so much to catch up on."

"Sure, I'd love that. As long as Lauryn doesn't care if I steal you away from work."

He dipped his chin and raised his eyebrows. "It would take an act of Congress to keep me away from you. And I'm not even sure that would do it." He reached for her hand. "Now, what brings you here?"

"To New York, or LC Designs?" LC Designs was the name of Lauryn and Cooper's shop.

"Both," he said, pulling her to the black leather couch to talk.

"Well, I came to New York for some meetings. One with my publisher and one with a new business venture."

"Exciting stuff," he said. "And how did everything go on the show? I know you can't talk about it, but was it worth it? Are you glad you did it? You're not engaged are you?" He flipped her hand over to see if there was a ring.

"No, I'm not engaged," she told him. "And the show was . . . interesting. I'm not sure I'm glad I did it, yet. However, I do have to tell you, I seriously had *the* best wardrobe of anyone on the show. I got so many compliments and told every girl where all my clothes came from. Hopefully you'll get some business from them. Oh! I even mentioned it on camera. It would be great if they kept that in the show."

"And how was Mr. Right? From what I've read about the show on the Internet, he was born with a silver spoon in his mouth. How self-centered and spoiled was he?"

Andi's heart dropped. Michael was probably perceived that way by everyone who didn't know him. She knew it was possible that the Michael she met wasn't the real guy, but she couldn't help remembering their first meeting and how down-to-earth he was—the meeting that had ultimately gotten her kicked off the show.

What would have happened had she stayed? The question would haunt her for the rest of her life.

"Actually, he was a really nice guy. He didn't seem spoiled at all."

"Really? With all those Hollywood actresses after him? And all the trouble he's gotten into, and Daddy bailing him out when he gets into trouble? That's hard to believe."

"Yeah, I guess it is. But he's really turned his life around. He wasn't anything like that on the show."

"Hmm, I guess I would be the first to admit that people really can change. Good for him. I think that's pretty cool."

Andi gave him a smile. He was right, and she was beginning to see how much Cooper had changed. In a very good way.

Cooper's brow narrowed. "Hey, what's that look? You didn't fall for him, did you?"

She laughed and pushed his words away with her hand.

"I hope not. Hey, no one loves reality TV as much as I do. I mean, if I wasn't too old, I'd audition for *American Idol.* I know I could win," he said matter-of-factly. "But these dating shows are so orchestrated and edited to create drama—it's all a bunch of garbage. Don't you agree?"

"There is a lot of drama. And I'll be honest. Anyone could fall in love in Kauai. It's paradise. Complete paradise."

"Well, I happen to think we have a part of paradise here in Manhattan. And I'm going to show it to you." He lifted her hand and kissed it. "Starting tonight. Do you have dinner plans?"

"Nope, nothing."

"Then you're mine. And I've got the perfect outfit for you to wear. You're still a size four, right?"

She shrugged. "I think so."

"Let's go try it on. I need to make a few phone calls for reservations, and then we're off."

Caught up in Cooper's whirlwind, Andi didn't have time to think about Michael. Which was good. She had to somehow purge him from her mind. And Cooper was the perfect person to help her do that.

Chapter 25

Under Cooper's attentive care, Andi found herself captivated by a magical side of the city she'd never experienced before.

Their first stop was an early dinner at The View, New York's only revolving rooftop restaurant. Forty-eight stories above Times Square, they were given a window-side table where they could enjoy the ever-changing view.

Cooper took care of the ordering, giving special instructions for the head chef, who was a good friend of his.

"We want to start with the grilled quail salad and fig vinaigrette, and then we'd like the seared salmon," he said, not even glancing at the menu. "Oh, and could you have Henri add a side of the gingered basmati rice?"

"Very good, sir," the waiter said. He bowed and took a step back before retreating to the kitchen to place the order.

"Cooper, this place is incredible," Andi said, looking out at the bustling city below.

"It's a great way to see the city without having to go to the top of the Empire State Building," he said.

"Which I've never done."

"I know. I remember how you wanted to last time you were here, but there wasn't time. Will this suffice?"

"Definitely. The view is incredible. So, what are we looking at right now?"

"Hmm, well, right now we're facing west, so that's New Jersey over there, and that's the Hudson River. That building with the flat top is the AT&T building, and right by it is the Intrepid Sea, Air and Space Museum."

"Worth visiting?" she asked.

"Yes, definitely. We can add it to our list while you're here. I'll try to point out different spots of interest as we rotate around."

"How long does it take to complete the circle?" She broke off a piece of her warm sourdough roll and buttered it.

"One hour. We'll probably be leaving as this view comes back around."

As they discussed different areas and buildings in the city, the waiter arrived with their salads. Andi allowed herself to relax completely, enjoying the exquisite cuisine and an animated, entertaining conversation with Cooper. He made her feel like she was the most important person in the world as he flooded her with attention and compliments.

By the time they finished their salmon, Andi was filled and satisfied with good food and good company.

"Here," he said, taking her deep pink, lime-green, and turquoise paisley pashmina from her. "I'll do that." He draped it around her shoulders and gave her a small kiss on the forehead. "You look absolutely ravishing tonight. Have I mentioned that?"

She laughed. "Probably a dozen times. I think it's the clothes, though."

"That dress is only as beautiful as the wearer," he said, handing her the floral beaded clutch purse in the same exotic palette that he'd given her to wear with the outfit. The splash of color against the classic black jersey knit dress was stunning.

Several heads turned as they walked out of the restaurant. Andi was definitely more comfortable in jeans or activewear, but she had to admit that it felt incredible to get dressed up and go out on the town.

In the elevator, Cooper circled one arm around her and gave her a squeeze. "I'm so glad you're here."

She rested her head on his shoulder. "Me too. Dinner was wonderful. Thank you."

"I hope you're not tired," Cooper said, "because the evening has just begun."

She leaned away from him, looking at him from the corner of her eye. "Oh, really?" Tingles of excitement tickled her neck.

"I seem to remember that last time you were here you wanted to see *Wicked* but weren't able to get tickets."

Her eyes grew wide, and her mouth dropped open. "You didn't."

He smiled.

"You didn't!" she exclaimed again.

"I did."

"Oh, Cooper. You are amazing!" She threw her arms around his neck and gave him a giant hug. "Thank you, thank you, thank you. I can't believe you would go to all this trouble."

"I want to make this date memorable for you. We have a lot of lost time to make up for." He hugged her back, lifting her off the ground. They laughed together then quickly stepped apart as the elevator came to a halt and the doors opened to a handful of people waiting to come in.

The evening air was just the right temperature, so they walked the short distance to the Gershwin Theatre, holding hands and enjoying the chaos and energy of Times Square.

Cooper, ever the attentive gentleman, kept her close to his side and held her hand tightly as they crossed the crowded streets. Taxis honked in protest at having to wait for the pedestrians, and vendors on the sidewalks called for tourists to check out purses, watches, and photographs of the city and celebrities.

"I can't believe we're actually doing this," she said, soaking everything in.

"I hope you'll stay for a while," Cooper answered. "I have so many places I want to take you and things I want to show you."

She smiled up at him, once again grateful to have him to help her get the recent past out of her system.

Billboards advertised other Broadway shows, and video screens the size of buildings played trailers of upcoming movies, televisions shows, and advertisements. Andi couldn't believe how busy it was. The main triangle section of Times Square was closed to traffic, but it was packed with tourists.

"Do you enjoy living here?" Andi asked, wondering if she could see herself living in Manhattan.

"Are you kidding? This is the best city in the world. Everything you want is here. Of course, it's all I've ever known, but I can't imagine living anywhere else. Besides, to be in the industry I'm in, I would have to live here or London or Paris. Maybe someday when the company is more established I would consider moving, but Lauryn and I are still making a name for ourselves." He shrugged. "But who knows, maybe someday. It would be hard to leave, though."

They walked through the breezeway toward the entrance and ticket counter.

"Could you see yourself living in the city, or are you strictly a West Coast girl?" he asked her as he opened the door for her.

"There are so many things about California that I'd miss, but I travel so much with my job, I could visit there once or twice a month anyway. I guess I'd be willing to try it."

"Well, if you stay long enough, you'll get to see what it's like living in the big city. Maybe you'll want to stay," he said, locking eyes with her.

"You keep doing stuff like this, and you won't be able to get rid of me," she replied.

Cooper picked up the tickets, and they entered the theater, ready to continue their magical evening.

* * *

On the taxi ride back to Lauryn and Jace's apartment, Andi and Cooper sang songs and discussed the many exhilarating moments of the play.

They had gone out for dessert after the show for New York cheesecake and crème brûlée.

"This has been the perfect evening," Andi told him. "Really, Cooper. How can I thank you?"

"You being here is thanks enough," he said, meeting her gaze. "It's funny, but you'd think in a city this size, with all of these people, it would be easy to meet someone. But it's not, especially if you have specific qualities you're looking for in a date."

"I have the same problem in California," she said. "Although there are a lot more members of the Church there, I still have had a hard time finding someone I want spend time with and get to know better."

The taxi pulled up in front of Lauryn's brownstone.

Cooper paid the driver and got out with her then took her arm to walk her up the steps and make sure she got inside safely.

When they got to the door, before Andi buzzed the apartment to have Lauryn let her in, she thanked Cooper one more time.

"This night has been the best—" She stopped and looked at Cooper, who was waiting for her to finish, but she suddenly knew she wasn't being completely honest. It definitely was one of the best nights she'd had, but she could think of another date that had been even more memorable and special.

Luckily Cooper read her half-completed comment the way it was originally intended and pulled her into a hug. "I'm glad you enjoyed yourself tonight," he said. "It's been all my pleasure. I felt like I was experiencing the city for the very first time with you."

When the hug ended, Andi turned to press the buzzer, but it seemed that Cooper had another idea.

The next thing she knew, Cooper kissed her. It was short and sweet, and she waited, hoping to feel tingles of excitement and joy, but all she felt was . . . nothing.

She smiled awkwardly, and he looked into her face.

"I'm really glad you're here," he said, pulling away slightly.

Choosing to leave the comment where it was, she smiled again then turned and pushed the button. A buzz quickly responded, and she and Cooper opened the front door and went inside.

"You coming up?" she asked when Cooper continued walking to the elevator with her.

"I want to make sure you get up to her place okay, and I thought I'd say hi to Lauryn and Jace."

"Oh, okay," she said, hoping they were still awake. It was close to midnight, and she was ready for bed. She had two meetings the next day and wanted to be at her best.

When they reached the apartment, they found that Jace was the only one still awake. Lauryn had a headache and had gone to bed. Andi found herself slightly relieved. She didn't want to seem ungrateful to Cooper, but she really needed to get some sleep anyway. And she needed some distance to think about that kiss.

Jace and Cooper talked about a problem with the computer at the shop and discussed a few other incidental business concerns as well as the Mets game they were going to that weekend. Then Jace excused himself to go to bed.

Luckily Cooper took it as his cue to leave. "Well, I guess I'll say good night, then," he said, looking slightly wistful.

"Thank you again for a wonderful evening," Andi told him. "I'll see you soon."

"Are you free for lunch tomorrow?"

"Uh, let me confirm my appointments, and I'll get back to you on that."

"Sounds good." He smiled at her again. "You looked beautiful tonight."

"Thanks to you," she said, trying to keep the tone light and distant.

Apparently she hadn't quite succeeded because Cooper leaned in and kissed her on the cheek.

"Good night," Andi said.

He stepped through the door but seemed hesitant to leave.

"I'll talk to you tomorrow," she said, urging him along.

Once in the hallway, Andi gave him a friendly wave then closed the door.

She didn't like how she was feeling but knew she needed to let the reality of what had happened sink in before she could truly analyze what she felt. Once that happened she was sure she would be fine with all of this. She liked Cooper. A lot. Always had. And now that he'd made his move and shown her that he liked her the way she liked him, she knew she should be extremely happy.

She wanted to be extremely happy.

Or at least moderately happy.

But all she could think about was Michael.

* * *

"I'll find out this afternoon if I get to go home Friday," Chloe told Andi.

"I bet you're so sick of that place."

"It hasn't been too bad. I've gotten to know a couple of the nurses really well, and believe it or not, the food hasn't been that bad. I just miss being with the girls so much."

"What about your salon?" Andi was getting ready for her meeting with her publisher and was trying to decide whether to wear a tan jacket or a cream sweater set, both of which belonged to Lauryn.

"The girls have been wonderful to cover for me, but they are ready for me to come back. I'll just have to ease into it, though."

"Well, listen to the doctor. We don't want you back in the hospital."

"What about you? Do you have your appointment today?"

"Yes! I'm so excited but nervous. I'm not sure what to expect."

"I'd better let you go so you can get ready. Tell Lauryn and Jace hi from me. And Cooper. Have you seen him again?"

"Uh, yeah. A few times. I'll let him know you said hi." Andi didn't want to make a big deal out of her and Cooper dating. She just wasn't sure yet how she felt about it.

"Call me after and tell me how the meeting goes. Good luck, Andi. You're gonna be awesome."

"Thanks, Chloe. Good luck with your doctor's appointment. I hope you get good news."

The girls hung up, and Andi held the two options up, looking at her reflection in the mirror. She decided on the jacket. It looked more businesslike, almost like she knew what she was doing.

Once she was dressed and had her hair pulled back in a smooth ponytail, she took time to say a prayer before she left for her meeting. This was a big opportunity for her, and she didn't want to mess it up.

* * *

"Call me as soon as you're out of the meeting," Kirk said. "I can't believe I'm not there. I should be there."

"Kirk, it's fine. You said yourself that this meeting is just to get acquainted with me and to talk about the promotion. I've got it covered. I'm sure they'll want to meet again when you can be here."

She waited for the DON'T WALK sign to change then moved with the crowd of men and women in business suits, all talking on their mobile phones.

"You're right. I'd feel better about missing it if things were going better here. I can't believe my meeting got canceled and they didn't tell me about it until today!"

"No kidding. It was really inconsiderate of them. So are you just turning around and going home?"

"I've got a few things I can take care of while I'm here, so I'm staying overnight." He sighed again. "These people had my e-mail, home, and cell phone numbers. How did they miss telling me?"

"I'm sorry," she said, taking the phone away from her ear to see who else was calling. It was Cooper. "Hey, I've got a call coming in. I'll talk to you in a few hours, okay?"

She hung up with Kirk and answered Cooper's call.

"Good morning," he said. "What's going on?"

"Actually, I'm on my way to a meeting with my publisher."

"Well, listen to you, Miss Author. I'm impressed."

"I know. It's so cool to say that. I'm pretty excited. I'm going to get the details about my book release and book tour."

"Hmm, sounds like I need to sit down and sketch out a few possible outfits for your appearances. Something trendy and sassy but professional, too."

"That sounds good," she agreed, smiling.

"In turquoise. That's your best color. And something in black. Black always works, no matter what the occasion."

"I agree. It's so sweet of you to go to the trouble."

"Well, aside from wanting you to look fabulous, it's also a way for us to advertise. We're generous, of course, but we also have ulterior motives."

Andi heard Lauryn yell in the background, "Speak for yourself, Cooper."

Cooper wished her luck, and then Andi got off the phone, realizing she was standing in front of the office building where the publisher was located. "Here goes nothing," she said under her breath with a smile as she walked up the steps.

Chapter 26

"THEY ONLY GAVE YOU FORTY-FIVE minutes?" Kirk asked incredulously. "I thought the meeting would go several hours."

"I'm telling you," Andi assured him, "we covered everything that you would possibly want to know. Mr. Addison Jr. is so kind and optimistic about the possible success of my story and cookbook. And Spencer Phillips, the marketing guy, was awesome. He was really glad to meet me in person. He said it's easier to convince radio hosts and television producers to book their authors as guests when he knows them personally and knows what angles to use to pitch them."

"Good, good," Kirk said. "I guess that's good, then."

"Mr. Addison seemed very positive and said that they'd be happy to meet with you in person, over the phone, or conduct further business over e-mail, whichever worked best for you."

"Okay, I'll contact them and figure that out."

"They're going to send you an outline of what we covered at the meeting so you can talk to them if you have any questions."

"I appreciate that," Kirk said. "All right, then. I'll watch for that, and we can talk before I contact them. What time is your next appointment?"

"I wish I knew. Mr. Hampton was supposed to call or text this morning when he found out his schedule. I guess I'll just keep myself open so when he calls, I can meet with him."

"We'll talk later. You can reach me anytime today on my cell."

"Thanks, Kirk."

Andi stopped to look in the Betsey Johnson window and drool over the darling clothes and accessories. Since she was in between jobs, she didn't go inside. She'd just gotten her Visa card paid off and didn't trust herself.

The vibration of the phone in her hand told her a call was coming in. It was Cooper.

"Hey, Cooper," she said, wandering farther down Fifth Avenue.

"So things went well?"

"It was a great meeting. I'm so excited. I may be hanging around New York for a while after all."

Cooper let out a whoop of joy, and in the background, Andi heard Lauryn scold him for startling her. However, when he told Lauryn why he was making so much noise, Lauryn released her own excited squeal of delight.

"Everyone's happy on this end," Cooper said. "This is very good news. Are you free for lunch, then?"

"I am. I'm still waiting for Mr. Hampton to call and tell me what time and where we are meeting, though."

Cooper found out where she was and suggested they meet at a deli on Fifty-First and Eighth Street. It was midway between them and would only take about fifteen minutes to walk.

Feeling on top of the world after the positive meeting, Andi nearly skipped all the way to meet Cooper.

As she hurried toward the deli, she smiled just thinking about the meeting with her publisher and how she'd connected with the team assigned to making her book a success. The only point at which she'd gotten a little uncomfortable was when the marketing people got excited about the incredible timing of her book and her appearance on the *Looking for Mrs. Right* show. They were convinced it would amp up sales of the book and capture an even younger demographic. She hated thinking that she might be seen as going on the show merely to further her career, yet her actions spoke contrary to her intentions. She also knew that when the show was edited, they could spin her situation to make her look any way they wanted her to look, good or bad.

Regrets about ever going on the show were beginning to surface. She was gaining momentum with her career, with the release of her book, and with the opportunity to be a spokesperson for the resort in the Bahamas. If it weren't for that touchy spot in her memory, she would be on top of the world right now.

But there was nothing she could do about it now. She groaned and blocked the thoughts from her mind. She didn't want to deal with the "reality" of the reality show.

Waiting to cross the street, she felt a buzz from her pocket and saw that a new text had come through. It was Jocelyn. When she opened the phone, her breath caught in her throat as she saw that Jocelyn and Jack were at Emma's house; she'd sent a picture of her holding baby Demetria.

Andi stopped amid the bustling street for a moment so she could gaze at the little angel in Jocelyn's arms. Emotion flooded her as she thought about Emma and her baby. She longed to go to Greece and see Demetria for herself.

They texted back and forth for a moment, then Andi told her about the meeting with her publisher and that she was meeting Cooper for lunch. That brought an immediate response from both Jocelyn and Emma and a request, which was more of a demand, for pictures of them together as well as the assignment to tell Cooper hello.

Andi promised to let them know how things went after lunch, and Jocelyn promised to give her the real scoop on Emma and what was going on with her and the baby.

Grateful she had worn decent shoes to walk in, Andi kept a brisk pace as she cut straight across to Eighth Street then headed toward Fifty-First.

She'd stayed up for a little while after Cooper left the previous night, trying to figure out her feelings and her strange reaction to his kiss. She was attracted to him, she knew that for certain, and she had wanted to date him for a long time. Logically, she knew that she was finally getting her chance with him. This was what he wanted too. The stars were aligning for them. He'd joined the Church, he had a great career and future ahead of him, and she loved his personality and positive outlook on life. He made her laugh and feel like she was amazing.

She should feel lucky to have his affection. It was as if the powers of heaven had orchestrated the timing for them to finally get together.

After analyzing and replaying the night over in her head, she decided that his kiss had caught her off guard and somehow had forced her to process the finality of her and Michael. It was time to move on, and she was lucky enough to have Cooper to help her do so.

She tried to call Chloe while she walked, but Chloe didn't pick up. Hoping that meant something good, Andi left her a quick message and told her that the meeting went great. She'd call her later.

She didn't have to search long to find the appointed meeting spot. There in front of the deli, waving a bouquet of flowers, was Cooper. She couldn't help but laugh and break into a run to meet him. He was like a bright ray of sunshine waiting for her.

He gave her a quick kiss in greeting and handed her the flowers. "Congratulations on a great meeting," he said. "I knew they'd love you."

She buried her face in the blossoms and inhaled their intoxicating fragrance. "These are gorgeous. Thank you," she said, giving him a hug. "You didn't need to do this."

"I wanted to. I'm so proud of you."

"Thanks." She loved that he seemed as excited for her as she was for herself. Moments like this were so much more fun when there was someone to share them with.

"I thought we could grab our food and sit outside to eat. There's a little grassy area with benches nearby. It's such a beautiful day."

She nodded. He was right. It was a beautiful day.

With bags of food and drinks in hand, they walked together to the tiny triangle of a park and found a bench in the shade. A soft breeze blew, and in the distance salsa music was playing. It was complete bliss.

They ate and talked nonstop as Cooper explained all the exciting developments happening with LC Designs and some of the connections they were making in the fashion industry. Lauryn's gowns had been featured at a recent celebrity event, and orders were pouring in from all over the world. Cooper's accessories had been included in several fashion magazine spreads on current trends, and even the First Lady was a fan of his handbags and shoes.

"Oh, I didn't tell you," Andi said during a lull in the conversation. "Jocelyn texted me a little while ago. She's in Greece visiting our friend Emma."

"The one who just had a baby?"

"Yes. She's actually there, right now. I'm so jealous." She showed him the picture of the baby. "I have to go see her sometime. I miss Emma, too."

"That's a very cute baby. And I don't say that about many babies."

"Cooper!"

"Hey, it's not personal. The babies can't help it." He grinned and took a bite of his sandwich.

"It's personal to the babies," she said. "And their mothers."

He laughed. "Emma's baby is beautiful. I wouldn't say so if I didn't mean it."

"I'll tell her you said so. They're going to send more pictures. Oh! Speaking of pictures, they want us to send a picture of me and you."

Cooper smiled. "Let's do it."

For the next five minutes, they took pictures of themselves with Andi's phone. It took a few tries to get the angle of the phone right to keep one person's head from being cropped off. Finally, some teenage girls walked by, and Cooper asked them if they would take the photo.

"We look freaking awesome together!" Cooper said a few minutes later, looking through the shots.

"You look like a rock star, and I look like a . . ."

"Movie star," he completed the sentence for her.

"Hardly," she said but appreciated the compliment. She sent several of the pictures to Jocelyn, laughing at the one where Cooper pulled his "male runway model" expression. She added a note for Emma and Jocelyn to look closely at his eyes because one of them had crossed just as the picture was snapped.

Being with Cooper was comfortable and easy, she decided as they sat together, shoulders touching. She really liked that he spoke his mind, and she felt like they could talk about anything. She still wasn't completely comfortable with the hand-holding and occasional kiss he slipped in, but she figured she'd get used to it. At least she hoped so.

They threw away their garbage, and Andi was planning on walking back to the shop with him when a text from Drake Hampton came through. He was ready to meet.

"Do you want me to come with you? I'm not sure I'm comfortable having you meet a strange man alone."

"We're going to be in a public place," she said. "Really, what could happen?"

"I don't know. Anything. I love this town, but I'll be honest, there are a lot of crazy people here."

"I'll be fine. I'm sure the people at Starbucks will come to my aid if I start screaming my head off."

"You'll call me as soon as you leave your meeting?"

"I promise."

"You know where you're going—where Broadway and Sixty-Third is?"

"By Lincoln Center, kitty-corner to the Manhattan temple, right?"

"Right."

Cooper gave her another kiss for luck and told her he'd put her flowers in a vase for her while she went to her meeting.

"Good luck," he said.

She waved to him as she walked away.

"Remember to scream really loud if he tries anything," he called after.

Several people on the street turned and looked at him.

"What?" he said with a shrug, and they turned and hurried away.

Andi shook her head and laughed. She liked the fact that he was protective of her. She liked the feeling of being taken care of.

It seemed like things were starting to fall into place for her and her friends, and Andi walked with a light heart and anticipation. Maybe they really had been reading too much into coincidences by thinking that recent accidents and problems had been connected. On a sunny day like today, where everything seemed right, it did seem a little far-fetched.

She smiled at this thought and turned her mind to her upcoming meeting. This spokesperson job could be incredibly cool. She'd never been to the Bahamas but would welcome the chance to go there, especially with all her expenses paid.

She texted Kirk that she was on her way to the next meeting, knowing he was waiting anxiously to hear how things went. They would talk on the phone afterward to thoroughly discuss each meeting's outcome and options before decisions were made. He was a stickler for details and never left anything to chance.

She kept up her brisk walk, realizing that one of her favorite things about Manhattan was having most things within walking distance. Back in California, the only walking she did was on the treadmill at the gym. She didn't live in an area that had parks or trails where she could conveniently or safely go for walks outside. With her lease almost up, she wondered if it was time to relocate, maybe here to New York.

She walked past a shop selling bundles of flowers and felt a pang in her heart when she took a breath of the floral-scented air. A particular fragrance caught on her memory and reminded her of the flowers in Hawaii, triggering a sudden rush of emotion.

Keeping Michael out of her thoughts was proving to be challenging; she never knew when something would remind her of him or her time with him. She shook her head, trying to clear away the memories. Hopefully once the show was aired and she saw him with the other women, and ultimately with the woman he chose at the end, she would find closure.

Within several minutes, she arrived at Starbucks and waited outside for a moment to gather her thoughts and focus her mind on the meeting. She had a list of specific questions Kirk wanted her to ask. He wouldn't be pleased if she didn't get the answers he wanted.

A sudden tingle went up her neck and she turned, expecting to see someone directly behind her, but aside from several women waiting to cross at the light, a shop owner sweeping the sidewalk, and a man walking a dog and talking on his phone, there was no one else around.

Shrugging it off and chalking it up to Cooper's paranoia catching up to her, she squared her shoulders, ready to go inside.

Mr. Hampton had told her not to worry about finding him. He knew who she was and would find her, so she stood off to the side, watching out the window for anyone who might look like the man on the phone.

Several customers walked in and got in line, but none of them approached her. Since the coffee shop was located next to the Julliard School and the School of American Ballet, she noticed a lot of younger people in line, some of them still in dance attire.

While reading Kirk's response to her text, she became aware of someone standing next to her.

Thinking she was in someone's way, she stepped to the side then looked up.

The man smiled at her. "Andi Martin?"

Andi smiled. "Yes, you must be Mr. Hampton."

"Please, call me Drake."

Drake was completely bald and wore sunglasses, which he didn't remove. He wasn't much taller than Andi, maybe five foot ten, and wore black pants and a black shirt.

"Would you like something to drink?" he asked and smiled crookedly, one side of his mouth quirking up at a strange angle.

"Actually, I just came from lunch. Maybe a bottle of water?"

He nodded then walked to the counter to place his order. She waited while he gathered his cup of coffee and her water bottle and paid for them. Then he led her to a table in the corner, near a window.

"It's nice to finally meet you in person. I hope you don't mind, but I've done a lot of reading about your career and what you've been involved in."

"No, of course not."

"I guess you just finished the *Looking for Mrs. Right* show? How was that?"

"I can't really talk about it, but I'll just say it was interesting."

He chuckled and nodded. "I never watch those shows, but they seem to be popular."

She nodded, studying him to try to get a better handle on him. She couldn't tell how old Drake Hampton was. Being bald seemed to age him, yet she felt he was much older than she was. Late thirties, maybe. His skin was mottled in a way that seemed to suggest age as well, but it was too smooth for that.

"So," she said, uncomfortable with the silence he had left hanging, "tell me about your resort. It sounds like quite a place."

"We're very excited about it. This whole thing, this plan, has been a dream of mine for almost twenty years. I've had to be patient, but it's finally starting to happen exactly the way I've planned it."

Andi sensed an intensity behind his words, and she could tell that he was extremely focused and driven. Since she had a tendency for those qualities herself, it was easy to see them in other people.

"So, tell me about the resort," she asked again.

Apparently he wasn't finished talking about his vision and plan, so he continued telling her how important it was to meet the right people at the right time and to be patient for things to happen when they were supposed to because then certain things were meant to be.

While she was happy for him, she also wanted to get to the point of their meeting. "I'm glad you're finally going to be able to see your vision come to life."

He smiled his odd smile again then broke into a laugh. "Yes, I guess you could say that."

She smiled back, thinking about Cooper's reference to crazy people. Drake was beginning to move toward that category. She just wanted him to get on with it.

"So," he said, clapping his hands and rubbing them briskly together, "I guess you're wondering how you fit into all of this."

"Yes. I'm excited to hear your thoughts."

"You will be part of our marketing campaign and basically be the *face* of our resort and spa. You will be on commercials, advertising materials, and make appearances sponsored by the resort."

"Sounds wonderful. When does all of this start happening?"

"We've had some setbacks on construction: permits, weather, labor disputes. However, we have our grand opening scheduled for this time next year, and we're still going to shoot for it. One thing I've learned is that you can buy pretty much anything with cold, hard cash. My investors are from the Middle East. I can't give you names, but I'll just say money is no object. We'll get it done."

She wasn't sure what to say. It was all very well that he was determined and convinced that this was all going to fly, yet she wasn't sure what he needed from her right now.

"We have a team of marketing experts I've recruited from some of the best firms here in Manhattan working on the campaign right now. We'll want to do photo shoots with you here and, when portions of the resort are ready, there in the Bahamas on-site. We want to get brochures and material ready to send to travel companies, large corporations, and event planners."

Andi nodded, trying to wrap her brain around all of it.

"Andi, this is going to be huge. And we want you to be part of it," he concluded, taking a sip of coffee and raising his eyebrows.

"I still don't know how you came up with me. There are so many other—"

"We looked at hundreds of other options while we were making our decision; pop stars, actresses, and other fitness professionals. None of them had what you have to offer. We need someone who looks like a celebrity but offers a wholesome image to promote our family-oriented atmosphere."

She couldn't help but feel flattered. "Well, thank you."

"I would like to discuss the offer and details of the contract with your manager. I know he couldn't join us today, and that's okay. I wanted a chance to meet you in person—you know, give us both a chance to get to know each other and see if this is the right fit." He cleared his throat and added, "And now that I know, I would like to take it to the next level. But . . ."

"Yes?"

"It depends on if you're interested." He leaned back in his chair and took another drink of his coffee, letting his words hang between them.

She would be crazy not to jump at this chance, yet she had learned from Kirk not to appear too anxious and willing. Part of negotiating her fee was letting them know her time was valuable and that she was in high demand.

"I'd like to think about it, but I have to admit it sounds like a great opportunity. Of course, that depends on whether we can work out all the details."

"Of course," he said.

"So," she sat up tall in her chair, "I guess the next step then is to get Kirk involved, right?"

"Right. I've got his contact information and will be getting in touch with him today."

"Is your website ready yet?"

"We're waiting for our artist's rendering of the facility so we can post it before we go online. But it should be within the next few weeks. I'll let you know. I'd love to be able to announce you as our official spokesperson for the resort at that time. We can also send out press releases and start getting you in some of the local papers. We need to set up a photo shoot first, though, so we can release a photo along with it. We have an art department finalizing our logo so we can add that to it."

She nodded. "This all sounds very exciting."

"Yes, it is. I've been waiting a long time for this, Andi. I really hope you'll be part of it."

He reached over to shake her hand, which she withheld for just a moment then offered. Something caught her off guard, but she didn't know what. A flash of déjà vu washed over her.

He tilted his head, his expression reflecting concern. "Everything okay?"

A quick shake of her head cleared the sensation. "Sorry, yes. Everything is fine."

"Good, good. I've really enjoyed meeting you today. That Hawaiian sun looks beautiful on your skin, but wait until you have a tan from the Bahamas."

She smiled. "That's enough to make me ink the deal right now."

He laughed. "We'll have a celebration when we make it official."

They said good-bye, and a moment later Drake was in a taxi, heading down Broadway, while she began walking toward Lauryn and Cooper's studio. It was a bit of a distance, but she didn't mind. She wanted to process everything, and it would give her a chance to talk to Kirk.

Being outside amid the busy streets and crowded sidewalks pulled her thoughts away from the uncomfortable feeling that lingered. So much was going on, and her mind was in overdrive processing it. It was like there were three different tornados swirling around inside her, stirring up her emotions, keeping her from feeling settled and secure. She loved new adventures and opportunities, but there was a little too much going on right now for even her liking.

Chapter 27

"How did you like the papaya salad?" Cooper asked.

"It was delicious." She smirked and added, " I'm glad we both ate it because I reek of garlic."

Cooper laughed and sniffed her neck. "It smells wonderful on you."

She hunched her shoulder and pulled back because it tickled. "I've eaten a lot of Thai food but never that particular dish." She raised her hands and wiggled her fingers. "It's kind of fun eating with your hands."

At the mention of her hands, Cooper took both of hers in his and kissed her knuckles. "I'll remember that." He led her away from the restaurant toward the crosswalk. "How do you like those heels? Are they comfortable?"

"Cooper, I could run a marathon in these shoes, they're so comfy. If they weren't high heels, I'd think I was wearing my cross-trainers. The design is brilliant."

He smiled broadly, his eyes lighting up. "Lauryn's the one to thank for the idea, but I will take credit for the design."

"You've given me so many new clothes and shoes. You're spoiling me."

He shrugged and blinked. "Guilty as charged. But I'm having so much fun doing it. Besides, everything looks so incredible on you. You understand that there is something in it for the company, don't you?"

"That's what you say, but I think I get more out of it than you do."

"When that show airs, we're expecting all sorts of response. We've got good friends in high places in the media world, and you don't need to worry—we're expecting an impressive reaction."

"Okay. Whatever I can do to help," she agreed, shrugging.

"That's my girl. So, shoes are comfy, the night is young, and we both look beautiful. I'm thinking we should do something about it."

"Oh?" She grinned. Cooper always seemed to have something up his sleeve.

"When was the last time you went dancing?"

"Not too long ago, but I'm not sure it's possible to dance too much. Why?"

"I want to take you somewhere."

It didn't take much convincing. She was all for the idea. Besides staying busy, surrounding herself with noise and activity was just what the doctor ordered.

"You lead the way."

* * *

"You want a piggyback ride?" Cooper asked as they approached the steps to Lauryn and Jace's apartment several hours later.

"I have exactly fifteen steps left in me," she said wearily. "I think I can make it."

He offered his elbow to assist her. "How'd you like my friend's club?"

"I loved it. I don't go to clubs much—well, actually, I don't go to clubs at all—so I wasn't sure what to expect. It wasn't at all like I thought it would be. I really enjoyed myself."

Cooper nodded. "Jerome tends to draw the upscale, couples crowd, not so much those who are looking for a place to pick up dates or a one-night stand."

"It seems to be working. And it was fun to run into some of the members of your ward there."

"There are a lot of couples who like to go out dancing in our ward. And that's their favorite place."

"I can definitely see why," Andi replied. "And I like Jerome. He seems really cool."

"We went to school together. He's really worked hard to get where he is today. I'm happy for his success."

"It sounds like you've had a lot to do with it."

When they reached the landing just outside the door leading into the building, they lingered there for a moment. It was close to one in the morning, but there was still a lot of noise and traffic on the streets.

"Ah, not really. I helped him organize a few events to launch his place and got some write-ups in the paper," Cooper said modestly.

"He basically gives you credit for his success," Andi said. "He told me it would never have happened without you."

"He's done a lot for me," Cooper said.

Andi smiled. Cooper wasn't typically the most humble person, but most of the attitude was for show. Now, when he had a legitimate reason to take credit, he didn't. She liked that quality in him.

"Well, it's late," she said. "I'd better let you get to bed. You have to go to work in the morning."

"Not if you'll play hooky with me," he tempted.

"Hooky . . . hmm," she said. "What did you have in mind?"

"Oh, I'll think of something. Breakfast, jogging in Central Park, museum . . ." He slid his arms around her waist and pulled her close.

"Tell you what, give me a call in the morning if you're serious. But I don't want Lauryn getting mad at me if you're supposed to be working."

"Deal." He leaned in and gave her a kiss. She shut her eyes and concentrated on the feel of his arms around her and his lips on hers, waiting for something to happen. She was old enough to know that fireworks weren't a guarantee for a solid relationship, but she was hoping that at least a sparkler would light up.

Nothing. Absolutely nothing.

When the kiss ended she gave him a wide smile. "Thank you for another wonderful evening. I can't believe how many great date ideas and connections you have."

"Hopefully you'll be around long enough to find out. It could take months, even years."

He was so fun, so sweet, so incredible. More than anything, she wanted to feel some romantic feelings for him. But somehow those feelings continued to elude her.

She looked up at the soft curve of his smile and sighed. He was so deserving of a woman to love and pamper. It was his nature to do so. Anyone would be a lucky girl to have him fall in love with her.

"Good night, Cooper. Thank you again," she said softly.

He leaned in close to give her one last kiss on the cheek and was gone.

* * *

Andi expected to be alone in the apartment when she woke up. It was close to ten, and Lauryn and Jace were nice enough to let her sleep in after coming in so late.

However, when she walked out of the guest bedroom into the living room, she found Lauryn sitting at the kitchen table working on her laptop.

"Hey, I didn't expect to see you here." She covered a yawn as she walked to the kitchen table and took a seat.

"I needed to take care of a few things from home. Sometimes I get more done here than at the office because I don't have as many distractions."

Lauryn looked incredibly striking in a black-and-white houndstooth skirt with a crisp, white shirt that had a large ruffle around the neck and down the back. The outfit was pulled together with black pumps, a fat black belt, and black hoop earrings. Simple but elegant.

Thirsty, Andi walked to the refrigerator and got out a water bottle. Offering one to Lauryn as well, she plopped down on a stool beside her. Lauryn pushed her laptop aside while they both took a drink.

"I talked to Chloe for a minute this morning," Lauryn said. "She tried to call you but said you didn't answer."

Andi looked at her phone and saw the missed call. "What did she say?"

"They are letting her go home Friday. She's so excited."

"This really is a miracle that she has recovered so quickly." Andi glanced out the window at the clear, sunshine-filled sky. It was going to be a beautiful day.

"That's what the doctor told her." Lauryn screwed the lid onto her water bottle. "So, how did things go last night? I wanted to stay up so we could talk, but I fell asleep on the couch and didn't even hear you come in. Must have been pretty late, huh?" She raised her eyebrows and smiled as though she knew a secret.

"Yeah, it was pretty late." Andi took a drink.

Lauryn watched her, waiting.

About to take another sip, Andi tilted the bottle toward her lips when Lauryn exploded. "Well?"

Andi flinched at Lauryn's outburst. "Well, what?" she asked.

"How is it going between you two? You've been spending a lot of time together on some incredible dates. That must mean something."

"The dates have been incredible. Cooper has been incredible. Everything about him is. He's handsome, funny, attentive, thoughtful, generous, and amazing."

Lauryn's expression lit up, and she clapped her hands, but Andi finished with, "I just can't picture myself seriously dating or married to him."

"Wait a minute. How can you say that already?"

"Lauryn, I adore Cooper. I want to feel all tingly inside and weak at the knees, but it's just not there."

"Sometimes love takes time to grow," Lauryn said gently.

"I understand that. And I'm still willing to try and see if it will. I would love to be in love with him, and I hope I do fall head over heels for him, but it's not there yet."

Lauryn nodded. "Okay, I can accept that. Just as long as you're giving it a chance. He's worth it. Any girl would be lucky to get him."

"I agree. Don't think I don't know, because I do. He's amazing in every way. It's just that . . ."

"He's not Michael?"

"Michael?" Andi echoed, not wanting to admit that Lauryn had verbalized her thought.

"Come on, Andi. You told me yourself that you'd never felt such an immediate connection with a person as you did with Michael. Obviously you want that with Cooper, too."

She opened her mouth to speak, but Lauryn cut her off. "That was just a bunch of hype and circumstance," she continued. "There was nothing real about it. Nothing. He's probably nothing like the guy you met."

Andi turned her head and looked out of the corners of her eyes. "Huh?"

"It was probably all a show for him too. I doubt there was anything sincere about him and who he portrayed himself to be."

This wasn't the first time Andi had wondered the same thing. She had honestly felt Michael had been sincere and that their connection had been genuine, but now that she was away from him and the island, she had to wonder if any of it had been real.

For her it had been.

"How did you feel with Jace when you first met him?" she asked Lauryn. "Were you swept off your feet and head over heels in love with him?"

"Well, yeah," Lauryn said.

"Right from the start?"

Lauryn paused to think for a brief moment. "Yes."

"That's what I want—it's how I always imagined it. I hope I eventually feel that way with Cooper, I really do, and I'll give love a chance to grow. I just wished his kisses didn't leave me feeling, well . . . nauseated."

Lauryn pulled a face. "They do?"

"Yeah. But he's trying so hard. And I am too."

"Good, then things are bound to work out." Lauryn gave her a reassuring smile.

Andi returned her smile, but her heart didn't participate.

* * *

The next few days flew by, and Andi found it wasn't hard to go through the motions and continue accepting Cooper's invitations. She honestly and sincerely enjoyed being with him. He made her laugh. He treated her like a queen.

They ate lunch together, went on dates in the evening, and worked out together. He ran circles around her and lifted weights with a vengeance. He was everything she could ever want in a man, and she was determined to have a change of heart and one day wake up and be in love with him. She was praying for a miracle to happen.

Chapter 28

ANDI HUMMED QUIETLY TO HERSELF as she rode the subway heading toward Times Square, where she was meeting Cooper for lunch. Most of the time, she walked where she needed to go because she enjoyed the exercise. But today she was running late and had too far to go to walk. The subway dropped her right where she needed to go.

The train was packed, and she didn't have a seat, so she hung on to one of the metal poles to keep her balance as the subway raced through the tunnels.

She watched with interest as passengers exited and boarded the train at each stop. She'd always enjoyed people-watching, and New York provided her with plenty of entertaining characters. Almost to her destination, she shifted her weight and held tightly as the train neared the next stop.

Her gaze landed on a woman sitting a few feet away reading a tabloid. The headline jumped out at her in large black letters: "Caught on Camera!" The picture below took her breath away.

It was Michael. And the woman he was with . . . was her!

* * *

Andi blinked, told herself to breathe, then blinked again. Surely it was her imagination.

But there she was, with her foot in Michael's lap, the day she'd cut her foot on the beach. What was their picture doing on the front of the *National Enquirer*?

She took a step toward the woman, wanting to ask if she could look at the paper, but the train came to a screeching halt at the next stop, and a flood of people disembarked, including the woman.

Wondering how it was possible that the photo had been released, she tried to call Silas, the show's producer. How had he let this happen? Her phone beeped, indicating that she had no service until she got above ground, leaving her with nothing to do but wait anxiously until her stop—the longest five minutes of her life.

As soon as the door opened, she bolted for the stairs leading to the street and pushed the send button. As the call went through, she raced for the nearest magazine stand to find the paper.

Silas's phone went to voice mail.

"Of course!" she exclaimed, waiting for the beep. "Silas, this is Andrea Martin. Could you call me as soon as you get this message? I'm assuming you've seen the *National Enquirer* today." Hanging up, she dialed Kirk's phone but got his voice mail as well. Just her luck.

She looked up and down the street for a magazine stand then decided to try the Duane Reade store. Hopefully they would have the magazine in stock.

Trying to appear calm as she charged inside, she found the section carrying periodicals and there, in full color, was the picture of her with Michael. Under the main caption were the words, "Scandal Rocks Paradise."

Keeping her sunglasses on, she took the magazine up to the counter. To her horror, one of the women at the registers was reading the tabloid. Andi kept her head down, hoping neither of them recognized her.

Her hand shook as she handed her money to the cashier.

"You wanna bag for this?" the woman asked.

"No, that's fine."

The woman counted out her change then handed the magazine to her. As she did so, her eyes locked on Andi's face for a moment. Not giving her a chance to make the connection, Andi snatched the paper out of her hand and dashed outside.

Trembling, she leaned against the building and held the paper in front of her to get a good look at the picture sprawled across the front page. A jumble of emotions whirled around inside her then slammed into her heart. Seeing Michael's picture took her breath away. Every memory flooded back—his smile and dark brown eyes, the laughter and fun they had shared, their talks, walking on the beach, and the way she had felt in his arms.

Quickly her feelings changed to embarrassment and anger. Who could have done this? She quickly read the article about her and Michael meeting up before the show began to air and how he'd planned on choosing her even before he met the other contestants. The article then went on to describe how supposedly the producers had found out and forced him to kick her off the show. Each word she read made her angrier. They were all lies, and the people who read the tabloids would believe them.

The article pointed out that Andi was a fitness celebrity and listed all her credits from workout DVDs to products she'd endorsed. No punches were withheld, and she felt every blow. Somehow, the article didn't seem to damage Michael's public standing, but she came off looking like an attention-seeking, manipulative celebrity has-been.

She felt the vibration of her phone in her back pocket and quickly answered, hoping it was Silas.

"Where are you?"

"Cooper! Oh, my gosh. I totally forgot about you."

"What? Thanks a lot."

"No, I don't mean that. I'm here in Times Square. I'm right by Duane Reade. Where are you?"

"I'm by TKTS, where we were supposed to meet. Hey, is everything okay?"

"No, actually."

"Stay put, I'll be right there. What's wrong?"

While he walked the two blocks to her, she told him about the tabloid, trying to keep her voice from shaking. He promptly reminded her in a matter-of-fact way that it was all garbage, but he agreed that people would still believe it and that it could very well leave a lasting stain on her name.

Andi was so happy to see him coming up the sidewalk a few minutes later that she ran up to him and gave him a hug. "Oh, Cooper!" she cried.

He held her as she buried her head in his neck and let down her guard. For a brief moment she felt safe and secure. Cooper kept a tight hold on her and soothed her, telling her it would all be okay.

"Do you mind if I look?" he asked.

She handed him the paper, and he scanned the picture and article. "Wow! That's not slanderous or anything," he said with sarcasm when he was finished. "I'm guessing you made an enemy on the show, because it sounds like someone is out to get you."

"I know." She looked away from the picture. It was just too upsetting. Was this experience going to haunt her for the rest of her life?

Cooper then folded the paper, picture side in.

"Well?" she asked.

"Not filled with warm fuzzies, is it? And I thought you were such a nice girl," he teased.

She slapped him on the shoulder. "This isn't funny."

"I know, I'm sorry. Really, though, Andi, only idiots believe these papers, and you don't care what idiots think."

But actually, when it came down to it, she did. She'd been careful her entire career to make choices that would leave a good perception of her in the public eye. Was this photo going to undo all the good?

Kimmie! She pictured Kimmie's scowling face with sudden clarity. Kimmie had to have something to do with this. But why would the woman go to such lengths to cause her trouble? Wasn't it enough that she'd had to leave the show early? What else did the woman want?

"Let's go someplace where we can talk," Cooper said, breaking into her thoughts and leading her around the corner to a small deli.

A few minutes later, Andi picked at the contents of her turkey on whole wheat, her appetite shot by nerves.

"What did your manager say?" Cooper asked before he took a bite of his meatball sandwich.

"I got his voice mail. Hopefully he'll call me back soon."

Cooper nodded. "You need to let him take care of this. You don't want to feed the story by overreacting," he counseled. "You haven't done anything wrong. Let your actions prove that."

She pulled in a calming breath. "You're right. I'm acting like I'm guilty. Michael and I didn't even know we were going to be on the show together." She reached for Cooper's hand.

"Sweetie, celebrity scandals happen all the time. In fact, most of the time they boost the celebrity's career."

"I don't want a boost if this is what it takes."

He shook his head. "Don't worry about that. Let your manager handle this. But just in case, I'd keep your sunglasses on and maybe wear a hat."

She scowled at him. "You're not funny."

"Oh, come on now." He touched her nose. "It's going to blow over quickly. You won't be tabloid fodder for long. And anyway, you look great in hats."

"I don't like being fodder. I don't even know what fodder is."

"I don't either, but you're the prettiest fodder I've ever known." He leaned forward and kissed her forehead. "What can I do? How can I help?"

"Buy me a mask or send me to China for a few months."

His face lit up. "I'm actually going to China in a few weeks. I've got to meet with our manufacturer over there. Is your passport current?"

She laughed. "It is."

"Come with me."

"Really? You're serious?"

"I am."

She considered a moment then said, "Let me find out what's going on with my book release and tour and I'll let you know. They'll probably cancel my book and my tour. I've brought shame to everyone who knows me."

Cooper rolled his eyes and shook his head slowly. "I've never thought of you as a drama queen. I think you need to stay away from Times Square for a while. All these Broadway shows are getting to you."

She chuckled. "I think so too. We'd better leave before I break out in song."

He laughed out loud.

They left the deli and walked down the street hand in hand. He'd managed to help her feel better, more hopeful, less ashamed. She wondered how big celebrities learned to ignore the headlines and paparazzi.

This was a whole new ball game, and she was wishing more and more that she'd never done that stupid show to begin with.

* * *

"Thanks, Kirk," she said as they wrapped up their conversation. "I appreciate you getting right on this. I knew you would, but I'll be honest—it freaked me out when I saw that picture on the subway."

"I'm telling you, Andi, if we play our cards right, this could really work to your advantage."

"I just want it to go away."

"I know, but it is what it is, and we might as well take advantage of it. I'll give *Extra* and *Entertainment Tonight* a call and see if they want to do an exclusive. I've also had another thought."

"What's that?"

"Could it be possible that the producers leaked the story to generate interest and focus on the show? It's going to start airing in a few weeks, and they could be stirring up some controversy just to draw attention to the show. It's all about drama, you know that."

"Well, they'll have plenty of that on the show. That's all it was," Andi told him.

"Hang in there and keep a low profile. You could be a target for paparazzi."

"I will. And thanks again. I'm glad the Addison and Campbell people were cool about it."

"They reminded me that there really is no negative publicity. They're actually thrilled with the timing, especially front-page news."

Andi rolled her eyes. It wasn't their reputation getting dragged through the mud. "Have you heard back from Drake?"

"No. I called and told him I needed to talk to him, but I haven't heard from him. I'm sure he won't have any problems with this either. Don't worry, Andi. Tomorrow you'll be yesterday's news, literally. Another pop star will shave her head or something like that."

"Thanks, Kirk."

Andi paced the floor in Lauryn's apartment. She was ready to turn off her phone and lie down. She had a horrible headache.

Just as she was about to hold down the button to shut down her phone, a call came in. It was Drake.

Tempted to not answer—she was sick of talking about the tabloid story—she finally let out an exasperated breath and said hello.

"Good afternoon, Andrea. I just got your message."

"Does that mean you haven't—"

"I've seen it." His voice reflected his displeasure.

"Oh. I wanted to warn you."

"Is it true?"

"Absolutely not. Yes, we did meet prior to the taping of the show, but at the time neither Michael nor I knew who the other was. We met purely by accident."

"I see."

He seemed skeptical but continued. "Well, I wish I could say the board isn't going to have a problem with this, but the thing that appealed to them the most was that you had a wholesome image. I am a little worried about this new development."

"I'm sorry. I did nothing wrong, though. I cut my foot on a seashell, and he put a bandage on it. That's all."

"Yes, people can appear to be one way and be something completely different," he said. "You have to be careful who you trust."

"I thought I was being careful," she said.

His response was slow in coming. After an awkward pause, he finally said, "I'd better make a few phone calls. I had your photo shoot set up, but

I think we'd better postpone it until I hear back from the board members."

Disappointment filled her. "I understand."

"I'll be in touch, Andrea."

They hung up, and Andi plopped down on the bed then covered her eyes with one arm and groaned out loud. She was so frustrated with the situation. At first she hadn't been excited about the thought of talking to any entertainment reporters, but if it gave her a chance to tell her story, she wanted to do it.

Angry tears leaked from her eyes, and she put her other arm across her face, wanting to block out reality. She was a good person. She hadn't done anything wrong. Why would someone do this to her?

Instead of going to China with Cooper, maybe she needed to go to Greece and visit Emma for a while. She needed some distance from her problems, which, she realized, was just another way of saying that she wanted to run away from them for a while. Sometimes reality was just too hard to deal with.

Chapter 29

FOR THE NEXT FEW DAYS, Andi stayed in the apartment. She didn't want to chance getting recognized on the street or running into any paparazzi. Instead of answering her phone, she let her voice mail screen calls and only returned those from friends and family. Kirk was doing all he could to put out fires and warned her to stay off the Internet—she wouldn't like what she read there. He also told her that she should be glad she didn't have a lot of skeletons in her closet because it was at times like these that they came out.

Cooper was being especially thoughtful and supportive, but Andi turned down any offers to get together, despite the fact that she was going a little bit stir-crazy. She needed to get her head together about so many things, Cooper included.

Her phone buzzed, and she saw that Chloe was calling.

"Hey, Chloe," Andi said, muting the television. She was watching reruns of *Friends* and nibbling on dry Frosted Mini-Wheats.

"How are you, sweetie?" Chloe asked. "Any updates?"

"No, nothing. Which I guess is good. Kirk thought he might be able to get me an interview on one of the entertainment-news programs, but we're still waiting to hear from them."

"I would love to see you get a chance to set the record straight."

"Me too. Kirk warned me that I'd have to be careful what I said, though. He said he'd go on air with me if it happens."

"I think that's probably smart," Chloe concurred. Then she added, "Hey, I called because I wanted to tell you something. I've been thinking about going to Greece with you."

"What? Really, you have?"

"Yes. I want to do it. I want to go."

"Chloe, that's great. And besides, Joss just got back. We'd have an awesome time."

"My friend is looking into some flights for us. Are you sure Emma wants us to come? I don't know how to read her anymore."

"She was so happy when I told her we were thinking about it. I could hear the baby in the background. I can't wait to see her."

"I just need to get some dates from you so we can lock in the airline tickets."

Andi was having a hard time figuring that out. She had to work around her book release and tour and hopefully her obligations to Drake and the resort. "Kirk said he'd call and get things pinned down for me in the next two days. I'll let you know as soon as he calls."

"Sounds good. My mother-in-law is happy to watch the girls whenever it works out. I don't know what I'd do without her."

Andi sighed. "Roger broke both your hearts, didn't he?"

"She's just sick about what's happened to him."

"Have you talked—" Her phone beeped. She didn't recognize the number, however, so she didn't answer.

"Do you need to answer that?"

"No. I'm not talking to anyone. My voice mail tells them to call Kirk if they have questions for me."

"That's smart. Hey, I've got a customer here for a weave so I gotta run. I'll talk to you in a few days."

They hung up and Andi stood to get a drink of water. She had spent time earlier that morning dusting and vacuuming around the apartment, and she was doing laundry, too. Lauryn wouldn't accept payment for her stay, so she figured the least she could do was clean to earn her keep.

The dryer beeped, so she obligingly folded a load of laundry and started another load. Afterward she put together a pan of lasagna she'd bought ingredients for. The one place she did feel comfortable going was the grocery store next door. She could slip in and out without notice and had done so a couple of times in the past few days.

With dinner baking, the house clean, and nothing else to do, she decided to listen to her messages just in case something important came through. She was still waiting for Drake to respond about the photo shoot, and she didn't want to miss a call about her interview.

She deleted message after message, glad she hadn't answered the phone. How people got her number she'd never know. A couple of other tabloids wanted to talk to her, claiming they were interested in her side of the story. She was glad she'd referred them to Kirk. He could take care of them.

She was setting the table as she listened to messages, stopping only to press the delete button. But just as she was reaching for glasses from the cupboard, the final message began to play, and the sound of the voice jarred her so hard she knocked one of the glasses off the shelf. It landed on the edge of the counter and shattered.

"Andi, this is Michael. We need to talk."

* * *

"Andi, are you okay?" Lauryn asked as she came through the door. Andi was frozen in position, staring at her phone with broken glass surrounding her.

She couldn't answer for a moment. The voice had frozen both her muscles and her brain. She'd missed his call!

"He called," she choked out.

"Who did?" Lauryn asked, her eyes sweeping over the broken glass.

"Michael. He called me."

"Michael, from the show?"

Andi managed to nod. "He wants to talk to me."

"Can he do that? I thought you weren't supposed to have any contact with each other until after the show ended on the air."

"We're not supposed to. If the media found out that we were talking, if the show found out we were talking, we would be in so much trouble."

Lauryn frowned and sucked in a breath. "Well, I wasn't going to tell you, but I think I'd better. You really need to watch your actions. There are paparazzi all over downstairs. They must have discovered you're staying here with me."

"Lauryn, I am so sorry to get you involved in this."

"You don't need to worry about me. Luckily I can have the driver pick me up at a private entrance so that they don't bother me. Same with work. I can be dropped off by a back elevator. It's temporary. Things will get back to normal soon."

"I hope so. Staying indoors is making me crazy."

Lauryn nodded. "You can come to my office, or we can go somewhere you won't be recognized for a while."

"Chloe just called and said she'll go to Greece with me. Are you sure you can't get away?"

"You know what? I just had a client reschedule, and I actually have a window of opportunity in the next couple of weeks. I'd need to work it out with Cooper, but I might just be able to swing it," Lauryn said, a sparkle of excitement in her eyes.

"That would be wonderful. I feel like I've caused you so much trouble already just staying here. And now this."

"That's a bunch of garbage, Andi. You can stay as long as you want. Jace and I aren't home that much anyway, so it's no imposition for us."

"I hope not. I'm sure I won't be here much longer. In fact, with the way things are heading, I might need to head back to L.A. right away. I'll have to see, after I talk to Kirk."

"Don't leave on our account. I love having you here." Lauryn looked squarely at her friend. "So, are you going to just stand there and make me wonder what Michael wanted, or are you going to call him?"

She shut her eyes and sighed heavily. "Yes, I'm going to call him."

Lauryn got the broom out of the cupboard and began sweeping up the floor. "Good. You go make your call. I'll get this cleaned up."

Andi looked at her phone. "I'm sorry about the glass."

"Don't worry about it. Jace does it all the time."

"I'm scared," she said quietly before she turned to leave.

"It will be okay," Lauryn assured her. "You have to know why he called."

"I do, but hearing his voice made me remember how much I liked him. It's going to be too hard."

"You have to do this, Andi. I'm here. I'll help you."

"I know you will." She held her fist to her heart, trying to calm its erratic beating. She wanted to drop her phone and run as if it had suddenly become a bomb, ready to explode if she dialed.

"Just get it over with. Like a Band-Aid."

"You're right." She blew out a quick breath and stretched her neck to the right then to the left.

"Good grief, Andi—you're not running a marathon."

"I know!" Andi exclaimed, jumping up and down. "I'm so nervous."

"Here." Lauryn reached for the phone. "I'll call him."

"No!" Andi jerked her hand back. "I will. I'm good." She nodded. "I can do this."

Lauryn gave her a level stare.

"I'm going." Andi went into the bedroom and shut the door, deciding it was wise to be prayerful first. She needed divine guidance so she would handle this phone call correctly.

After a quick plea for help and strength, she pushed the button that revealed missed calls. Barely breathing, she found the message Michael had left and pushed the button to call the number. Was he going to pick up? What would she say when he did? What was she doing?

His ringback tone, a breezy tropical tune, transported her for a split second back to the island, back to paradise.

Abruptly the song ended and his voice mail came on, a generic voice stating only his phone number and giving instructions to leave a message after the beep.

She hung up before the beep sounded.

Disappointment filled in where the fear had been. She was dying to hear what Michael had to say, to know what he wanted, especially when he was willing to talk to her and risk a breach of contract.

She had convinced herself that she would never see or hear from him again. It felt surreal knowing that she might have heard his voice again, heard his beautiful laugh.

At least now she could say she tried.

The buzzing of her phone startled her, and she tossed it across the bed. It landed on the floor, the sparkly pink cover popping off in several directions.

She dove across the bed and grabbed the phone.

It was Michael!

Without another thought, she pushed the talk button. "Hello?"

Chapter 30

"Andi? Is that you?"

Andi forced herself to breathe then answered, "Yes, hi. Michael?"

"Hi. Wow, it's great to hear your voice. How are you?"

She squeezed her eyes shut. "I'm good, I guess," she replied. "How about you?"

"I'm doing well, thanks."

They didn't speak for a moment. She wanted to let him lead out on the conversation.

"Actually, that's not true," he finally said. "I'm sure you know why I'm calling."

"Is it okay that you're calling me?" she asked tentatively.

"No," he said. "This has to stay between us."

She groaned. "I'm sorry, but the friend I'm staying with knows."

"Okay, then, between the three of us," he said. "She won't tell anyone, right?"

"Right." She'd have to remember to tell Lauryn to not say anything to anyone. Especially Cooper. He would flip.

"I'm assuming you've seen the *Enquirer*?"

"A couple of days ago."

"What was your first thought?" he asked.

"Honestly, my first thought was how big my head looks for my body. Then I thought how good the picture was of you. And then I wondered how it got leaked to the press."

Michael was laughing. "Those were your thoughts, in that order?"

"Yes. It took it a minute to register."

"Same for me. I wanted to let you know that the show is trying to get to the bottom of this, and I'm sure Silas will be calling your agent to tell him how he'd like you to handle the media."

"I'm surprised I haven't heard from Silas yet—maybe he's called Kirk, though." She let out a breath. "I've never been tabloid fodder before."

"I'm really sorry," he said. "It's all my fault. I wanted to talk to you so I could tell you how bad I feel about it. I would never do anything to hurt you intentionally."

His words went straight to her heart, and she knew then that time hadn't lessened her feelings for him. They were as strong and as painful as ever.

"It's not your fault, Michael. We did nothing wrong. We didn't even know who we were talking to."

"Tabloids don't care about the truth—they just want a story. The picture gave them all the "proof" they needed, whether the story was accurate or not."

Andi swallowed. "My reputation has definitely taken a hit. I'm probably going to lose a job over this."

"Oh no, Andi. I am so sorry," Michael said. "Can I make a call or do something to help?"

"My manager is trying to fix things."

"Please let him know I'll do anything I can to help."

More than anything, she wanted to tell him how much she missed him and how wonderful she thought he was, but she knew those were feelings she would keep to herself and hopefully forget about one day.

"Do you have any idea how the picture got leaked?"

"I have my suspicions, but I don't know for sure. Hopefully Silas will get to the bottom of it, but I can't help but think that, in some way, all of this was an intentional ploy to build interest in the show," he told her.

"I've wondered that too."

She heard him sigh heavily. "Please just know, Andi, that I will do what I can to protect you."

She shut her eyes, hanging on the words.

"I miss you, Andi. When your plane had to make the emergency landing, it took the entire crew to hold me back from flying out to be with you. Are you okay?"

Absolutely relieved to know he'd wanted to be there, she replied, "I'm fine. I can't turn my head anymore, but I'm fine."

"What! Andi, no!"

She laughed. "I'm just kidding. It was scary, but I'm doing fine."

"I want to see you."

She wasn't sure where the strength came from, but she managed to say, "That wouldn't be wise. It would completely jeopardize the show. And legitimize the photo."

"You're right. I know you're right."

Hearing those words tore at her heart, but they didn't lessen the fact that she and Michael really couldn't have a future together or the fact that he was involved with the woman who was left standing at the end of the show.

She tried to keep the conversation steered in a positive direction. "It's hard for me too. Hopefully this will all blow over soon; then I'll be able to show my face outside again."

"Andi, really? You aren't going out?"

"I'm keeping a low profile for now. I don't want to give any more fuel to fire up the paparazzi."

"Where are you, anyway?"

"I'm staying with a friend in New York. I have some things here to take care of."

"When are you going back to L.A?"

"I don't know. Why?"

"When the show is over, I want to see you."

"Michael—"

"Andi, we had a connection we can't ignore. We owe it to ourselves to see what that means."

"But there are fundamental differences in our lives."

"I know, I know—the religion thing."

"It's important to me. I can't explain it all to you right now, but it is. It makes all the difference in who I marry, where I get married, and to my children."

He was silent.

"I'm sorry, Michael. I haven't stopped thinking about you since I left, but some things just aren't meant to be."

"I understand."

She bit her bottom lip hoping to keep her emotions in check.

"Well, guess this is good-bye, then." He cleared his throat. "Take care of yourself, Andi."

"I will. You too."

They didn't say good-bye. The conversation ended there. And then Andi let herself sink to her pillow and cry.

* * *

Wearing sunglasses and a large brimmed hat, Andi walked along the quiet, secluded paths of Central Park, grateful to finally be outside and get some fresh air. Lauryn's driver, Randolph, had worked for several Broadway stars and knew how to avoid the paparazzi. He was happy to help Andi escape the confines of the apartment.

Even though she had to stay in disguise, she didn't care; it felt wonderful to be free for a while.

The vibration of her phone in her pocket broke her thoughts. It was Kirk.

"Silas finally called," he said.

"What did he have to say?" She found a large rock and sat down.

"He's convinced someone from the inside leaked the picture and the story. He admitted that they've had trouble with crew members keeping confidentiality agreements, so he's trying to find out which one of them did this. He says he's very upset, but honestly I get the feeling he's kind of glad it happened. The show is getting a lot of buzz and attention."

"At my expense, and Michael's."

"Exactly. I've told him that I've contacted several of the entertainment shows and offered them an exclusive interview with you. He's not completely opposed to it, but he wants a day to think about how he'd like things handled. I gave him until tomorrow to get back to me."

"Good. I appreciate you taking care of this. Did he speculate about who he thought it was? He didn't say anything about any of the contestants, did he?"

"No. I fished a little, knowing how suspicious you are of Kimmie, but he said he was certain it was a crew member. He said he'd look into it. Oh, and he also told me that we should get a report soon regarding the investigation on the plane accident. I guess a plane in Portland had the same trouble back in 2007 and had to land suddenly."

"Great. Flying already makes me nervous. I don't like hearing that this type of thing happens often."

"Flying is still twenty-nine times safer than traveling in an automobile."

"And how do you know that statistic off the top of your head?"

"I did a little research, just in case you got a little nervous to fly."

"It doesn't have anything to do with your personal fear of flying, does it?"

"Maybe, a little. But it was mostly for you."

She laughed. "Well, thank you. Because if I end up going to Greece to visit Emma, there's no way I'm taking a boat there."

"Let me know as soon as you make your plans. Also, let me know if you talk to Drake. He's not returning my phone calls."

"Mine either. I'll feel terrible if I lose this job because of that picture."

"We'll get your name cleared," he reassured her. "That will help."

"I hope so. I'll stay in touch. Thanks, Kirk."

She glanced at her watch. She only had a few minutes until she had to meet Randolph, and she still had quite a ways to walk.

At that moment, she saw a movement out of the corner of her eye, and she jumped to her feet. Her heart lurched inside her chest. Had she been discovered?

Trying to remain calm and unruffled, she began walking, listening carefully for any movement behind her, but there was nothing. She could have sworn she'd seen something.

Picking up her pace, she walked briskly to the appointed meeting spot, grateful that she was traveling through a more populated area of the park. Chills went up her neck as she thought about having someone following her.

Breaking into a jog, she pushed ahead, hurrying to get to the safety of the car. If this was what it was like to be a celebrity, she didn't like it.

Ahead of her was Lauryn's car, parked right where it was supposed to be. Relief flooded her, and she raced ahead to get inside.

Randolph jumped out and opened the door for her. She bolted inside and pulled the door shut behind her.

"Everything all right, miss?" He asked when he got inside.

"Yes," she answered shakily, watching out the window for someone to jump out of the shadows.

"Where to?"

"Back to the apartment," she said.

The car began moving, and Andi relaxed back against the seat. She would be glad when this whole thing blew over.

* * *

What's Lauryn doing home this time of day? Andi thought warily as she stood outside the apartment.

The slightly open door of the apartment had caught her off guard. Lauryn and Jace always locked the door behind them when they came inside. And Jace was out of town, so it had to be Lauryn.

"Who's playing hooky?" Andi teased as she pushed open the door. But then she stopped dead in her tracks. The apartment was in shambles.

Fear struck her like a freight train. Was someone still in the apartment?

With caution, she slowly backed out through the door until she was in the hallway, then she raced to the elevator.

She pushed the button at least thirty times before the door finally opened. Rushing inside, she watched the hallway as the doors eased shut. They'd been robbed, and Lauryn's beautiful apartment had been destroyed.

When she got to the lobby, Andi raced to the security guard and told him what she'd discovered. While he called his superior, Andi called Lauryn to give her the bad news.

* * *

"It's going to be hard to go to sleep," Lauryn said, pulling her cardigan closer around her. "I wish Jace could get home tonight."

"I can't help but feel responsible for this," Andi told her glumly, looking around the room that they had tried their best to put back together.

"Andi, that's crazy! The officer said there have been a number of break-ins lately in the neighborhood. And don't forget, the security tape did show a couple of suspicious visitors about the time you were gone. I'm just glad you weren't here when they broke in. Who knows what would have happened."

Andi shivered. "I just feel so bad that so many of your things got broken."

Lauryn shrugged. "It can all be replaced. And what they did take wasn't even worth anything really. It's so weird. Why wouldn't they take the flat screen or the computer or my jewelry? Of course, I haven't been through everything. Maybe there's something I haven't noticed yet."

"I'm so sorry," Andi said. "This is just so creepy."

They both sat and looked around at the apartment. They'd been able to clean up most of the mess and put things back in order, but things that had been damaged were gone, leaving gaping reminders of what had happened.

Andi's cell phone buzzed, making her jump.

"What's wrong?" Lauryn asked.

Placing her hand on her racing heart, Andi looked at the call coming in. "It's Kirk," she said. "Let's hope this isn't something bad."

"How are you doing?" Kirk asked. "Any leads on the break-in?"

"Not yet. It's a little unnerving knowing someone was in here earlier. The building security is going to keep a close watch on us tonight, though."

"Good," Kirk said. "Hopefully that will help you sleep better tonight. I thought I'd call with some good news."

"Really? I was afraid to answer your call."

Kirk laughed. "I just found out the Kardashian sisters are in New York."

Andi wasn't sure how to respond. What did that have to do with her?

"I guarantee that the paparazzi will be following them around while they are in town, which will take the heat off you. Not that you aren't important, but . . ."

"But I'm definitely not as, mmm, interesting as the Kardashians are. That's great news! I'm so glad you called to tell me."

"I thought you might appreciate it. Try and get some sleep, and call me tomorrow when you have some time."

Thanking the heavens for her wonderful manager and friend, Andi told Lauryn the good news.

"Thank goodness!" she exclaimed. "The next step would be a wig and a fat suit, so you can go outside."

The image made Andi laugh.

Lauryn covered her mouth as a yawn caught up with her. "That sleep aid is kicking in. I guess I'm going to try to get some sleep. You going to be okay tonight?"

"Yeah, I think so."

"I'm glad you're here with me. With Jace gone there's no way I would dare stay here tonight."

"I'll keep the door open so I can hear you just in case you need anything," Andi told her.

They hugged good night, and Andi went into her room. The lamp beside her bed had been broken, and the corner of the nightstand had chipped off when the nightstand had been tipped over.

Since she had nothing of real value there, she hadn't had much to lose. Her heart ached for her friend, though. Tomorrow they would have a better idea of how much had been taken or damaged.

Brushing her teeth and pulling her hair back into a ponytail, Andi was ready to go to bed. She decided to take a minute and read her scriptures, hoping it would bring some peace.

Where were her scriptures?

She'd kept them in the top drawer of the dresser along with the—

It was missing. The Butterfly Box had been stolen! Along with her scriptures.

"Lauryn!" she cried.

* * *

"How do we tell the others," Andi said somberly the next morning as she and Lauryn finished documenting each missing or damaged item.

"I don't know, but we have to tell them."

"We need to call the St. George Police Department and tell Detective Hutchinson. This only adds to the evidence that this is related to what's been going on in Ava's case." Andi handed Lauryn the notebook. "Chloe is going to have a meltdown. She's already a basket case. This might just push her over the edge."

"Jace feels the same way. Whoever is behind this is seriously disturbed. I mean, it's been fourteen years since Ava died. Really, what is going on?"

Andi's phone vibrated. She glanced down and noticed Drake's name and number on the caller ID.

She wasn't up to the bad news, but she knew she had to answer.

She took the call in her bedroom.

"How are you, Andi?" Drake asked when she picked up the phone.

"I'm okay," she told him.

"You don't sound very convincing."

"It's been an interesting week," she said vaguely.

"I can imagine." He paused for a moment. "Maybe this will help lift your spirits. I heard from the board this morning, and they are willing to stand by you and keep their offer."

"They are? That's great news. Thank you, Drake. I'm so happy."

"I remembered you saying you wanted to see that new Harvey Goldstein play that opened up on Broadway. I got a pair of tickets for tomorrow night. Would you like to go to dinner and a play to celebrate and make it official?"

"How thoughtful of you. That sounds wonderful. I need to double-check my schedule, but I should be free. I am a little worried about showing my face in public, though. The story is all over the Internet."

"I understand. I can arrange to have us use a side entrance; that way we won't attract any attention."

"You can do that?"

"Of course. I'll pick you up for dinner at six. Curtain time is at eight."

"I'm looking forward to it."

She hung up the phone and paused for a moment to think about the conversation. Was it wrong to go out to dinner and a show with him? She had no physical attraction to Drake. They had a strict business relationship.

She just wanted to make sure everything was done appropriately, especially after being front-page news.

"Good news?" Lauryn asked when Andi came out of the bedroom.

"That was Drake Hampton, the resort guy. He said the board decided they want to keep me as their spokesperson."

"That's great, Andi. I hope you said yes."

"It's not official; Kirk still has to work out the contract details, but I really want to do it. Drake wants to take me out to dinner and a show tomorrow night to celebrate."

"Wonderful!"

"I feel kind of weird about it. It's a business arrangement, but it feels like a date."

Lauryn got up from her chair and went to the fridge. "A lot of business is conducted this way. Which show is he taking you to?"

"The new Harvey Goldstein show, *Love Me Crazy.*"

"How did he get tickets to that? It's the hottest show in town. It just opened last weekend."

"Guess he's connected. I don't know. So you don't think it would be inappropriate to go with him?"

"Not at all."

Lauryn's assurance helped Andi's concerns fade away. She just hoped she could stay under the radar and avoid the media frenzy while she was out and about.

Chapter 31

Cooper had offered to come to the apartment to stay with Andi while Lauryn went to work, but Andi assured him she was fine. She felt safe enough and would stay busy with a conference call with Kirk and her publisher. And afterward, Kirk wanted to talk about the contract with Paradise Bay Resort and Spa.

While waiting for the call, she Googled the name of the resort, hoping there was some information about it. Drake had told her they wanted her pictures to add to all the promotional material before they went online, so she just looked at pictures of Nassau and some of the other hotels and spas and got pumped up about going to the Bahamas.

Lauryn's travel agent had sent some information about traveling to Greece and some possible itineraries for them. Using Lauryn's frequent flier miles, the agent found several flight options for them. All they had to do now was decide which one worked best for the three of them.

Her phone buzzed, indicating she had a text. It was Lauryn telling her to expect a delivery. She wanted to give Andi a heads-up so she didn't get frightened when someone came to the door.

Andi listened for the door while she continued surfing the web. On a whim, she went to Jocelyn's Grandma's Berries website. The berry-farm business had exploded recently, and Jocelyn and Jack had their hands full. Not only could customers pick their own berries, but Jocelyn had a selection of berry products available, ranging from berry jams and jellies to chocolate-dipped confections.

A knock came at the door, and Andi stood up, glancing at the mirror in the living room as she walked by. She grimaced. It had been ages since she'd had a hair appointment. She was in desperate need of a trim and a color job.

Stopping to look through the peephole, she saw a delivery guy standing with a large bouquet of roses.

She hurried and opened the door.

"Flower delivery," the guy said, his eyes barely peeking over the large bouquet.

"Wow, those are gorgeous," she said as the soft fragrance seeped into the room.

"It's heavy. Would you like me to bring it in for you?"

"I think I can manage," she answered, not comfortable letting a stranger in the house.

She reached for the bouquet, and the delivery guy lowered the flowers to expose his face.

She drew in a sharp breath then blinked several times to make sure she was seeing clearly. "Michael!" she exclaimed. "Oh, my gosh! Is it really you? What are you doing here?" She held her hand over her mouth, completely shocked at the sight of him.

He laughed then said, "Any chance I could put this down? My arms are about to fall off."

"Of course, I'm sorry. Here," she led him inside. "There," she pointed, "just put them on the table."

Her heart thumped wildly in her chest. Was he really here? It was like a dream.

He placed the flowers on the table then turned. For a split second, they looked at each other. And then, without wasting any more time, they fell into each other's arms.

"I have missed you so badly," he said, squeezing her so hard he lifted her off her feet.

"I never thought I'd see you again," she answered.

"I had to see you." He lowered her to the floor. "I was going crazy."

"But the show," she said. "The contract. Aren't you going to get in a lot of trouble?"

"Not if we don't get caught. Silas told me to go and do what I needed to do. He just didn't want to know anything about it."

"I can't believe you're here." A catch in her throat belied her emotions. She'd tried so hard to bury her feelings since she left Michael, but being in his arms brought them all rushing back to the surface.

"You don't know how long I've thought of doing this. I just had to finish the show so I could finally get my life back."

After a moment they both stepped back, taking another long look at each other, then Michael led her to the couch, where they sat down and continued facing each other. Michael kept hold of one of her hands in his.

"Speaking of the show, how did it go after I left?" she asked bravely, not sure whether she wanted to hear the answer.

Michael closed his eyes and groaned. "I can't tell you how it ended, but let's just say you'll be happy with the finale."

She tried to gather her wits to form a response but instead found herself lost in his eyes. The sound of his voice brought a feeling of belonging with it. There was an undeniable connection between them.

"Andi?"

"I'm sorry," she looked down at their hands, "I think I'm still in shock having you here."

"After you left, I hoped I would develop feelings for one of the other girls. I was determined to. I tried everything I could think of—"

"Everything?" she asked.

He smiled. "Well, almost everything."

Her brow furrowed. "Almost everything?"

Placing his palm on her cheek, he said, "I didn't spend the night with any of the girls, if that's what you're wondering."

"You didn't?"

"No. Of course, the show will probably edit the footage to make it look like something went on, but I want you to know, directly from me, I didn't ask any of the final three to stay the night with me. There was no point."

She didn't know what to read into his comment, but she was tremendously relieved that he'd chosen not to sleep with any of the girls.

"Andi, we have to talk," he said. "I don't know what your feelings toward me are, but there is something very special about you . . . about us, and I think we should explore it."

She nodded hesitantly and took a deep breath, praying she wasn't simply letting her emotions guide her actions. "I still stand by what I told you earlier—about my religion. But at the same time, I've never felt a connection like this with anyone. So I guess, for now, I agree."

He nodded and looked up at her. "That's fair, I guess." He smiled and added, "It's interesting to see you here, away from the island."

She suddenly became very aware of her appearance. Trying to smooth her ponytail with one hand and her T-shirt with the other, she said, "I wasn't going out today, so I didn't bother getting cleaned up."

"What are you talking about? You look amazing. In fact, I think you're most beautiful when you're just yourself—no makeup, hair loose, barefoot on the beach."

"I could get used to that," she said, feeling a bubble of happiness well up in her chest.

"So tell me, what have you been up to since you left?"

She told him about the progress of her book, her new job as spokesperson for Paradise Bay Resort and Spa, her plans to go to Greece soon, and, of course, her trip to Africa in the spring.

His expression fell.

"What?" she asked.

He shrugged a little sheepishly. "I guess I wanted to find you sad and lost without me. Instead, you probably don't even have time to see me."

"Believe me, I have time."

"Look at all you've accomplished and are involved in. You are such an incredible woman," he said. "I'm so amazed by you."

She rolled her eyes.

"It's true. I talked to my parents about you. They both had you pegged as the one I would fall for and choose in the end. You were the one they wanted me to choose."

"They did? Have they already watched the show?"

He sighed. "No, and I'm not supposed to say anything because this is definitely a secret until the show airs, but . . ." He paused as if weighing his decision of whether to tell her or not. "Both of my parents worked on the staff at the plantation."

Her mouth dropped open.

He laughed. "It's true. They wanted to interact with the girls to get to know them. It was my idea, and Silas bought into it to add a twist to the show. I know how some people put on a good front when they need to, but behind closed doors they're totally different people. None of the girls knew until the first half of the final episode, when they met them for the first time as my parents."

"That's awesome! Was it a shock to any of them?" She laughed, thinking of all the catty, horrible things some of the girls had said and the unflattering behavior of some of the others. Then she stopped short. Had she done anything to be ashamed of?

"My parents only had good things to say about you, in case you're wondering. My dad especially."

"So, wait then, which one was your—"

Michael smiled.

"Kana! The gardener. He's your dad!"

Michael nodded.

She clapped her hands together and laughed. "I would have lost my mind without Kana—I mean, your dad—there. He seemed to show up just when I needed him. He always had something wise and helpful to say. Michael, he's a wonderful man. He seemed so sweet and humble. It's hard to believe he's also an important businessman."

"He doesn't really have the heart for running a business. He always told me to remember where our family came from and that we are blessed because of the hard work and sacrifices of our ancestors. He also always said it was disrespectful to them if we didn't keep up that legacy of hard work."

"Hence your being the yard guy at the bed-and-breakfast."

"Exactly. He believes a person is never too good to dig in and get their hands dirty. My mom's the same way. In fact, she was telling me that her ancestors were among those who walked across the plains to Salt Lake City."

"You mean pioneers?"

"Yes, pioneers. She has some journals and family histories about some of their experiences."

Andi was taken aback by this revelation. She knew Michael's mother had a connection to the Church but didn't realize how deep it went.

"I've thought a lot about you and your beliefs since you left. Many of my friends who have married are now all divorced. My mother says that your church believes in families and marriage."

"We do. Very, very much. We believe families will be together forever."

He nodded. "Despite the fact that my mom had some negative experiences with the Mormon Church, I think she believed in some of your church's teachings. She always taught me about families being together. I believe it too."

"Divorce still happens to people in our church, but the fact that we think in terms of eternity instead of just our life on earth gives us a different view of marriage and family. We definitely understand that it is worth fighting for and preserving."

"I have a couple of friends whose wives never even changed their names on their driver's licenses, just in case the marriage didn't work out. Another one is waiting to have kids until he's convinced he and his wife will stay together. I want more than that. I'm not willing to settle for less."

"You don't have to. That's exactly how I feel."

He studied her face for a moment. "I like that. Now that I think about it, my mom has taught me a lot of things from your church that I didn't realize until we talked about you. Like your Word of Wisdom."

"The Word of Wisdom? Is that why you were so nice to me about not wanting wine on our date?"

"I didn't realize it at the time, but yes, it was. I occasionally have a glass of wine with a meal, but as a whole, our family doesn't drink. I do drink coffee. I'm not saying we live the Word of Wisdom, but my mother referred to it many times growing up. I thought it was something like the food pyramid in school or something. I didn't know it was a Church teaching."

Andi shook her head. "I'm so confused. Forgive me for asking, but if your mother believes in the Church's teachings, why doesn't she go to church? Just because of some negative experiences with other members?"

He furrowed his brow. "It went a little deeper than that. I still don't know all the details—it's painful for her to talk about—but she and my father, who was not a member, got into trouble and ended up getting married because she became pregnant with my oldest sister. This did not go over well at all with my grandparents. In fact, they were so ashamed of her that they practically disowned her. Some of the people in town said horrible things to her, members of your Church, and it broke her heart. She left, married my father, and has never been back since." He sighed then added, "She told me she believes in the teachings but not in the Church."

"That's sad."

"Yes. I've only met my grandparents once. They passed away before I could ever see them again—and before they or my mother could make peace and forgive each other."

"That is so sad. Your poor mom. I bet that's been hard on her."

He nodded but offered a slight smile. "There is a little bit of a happy ending, though—she's reconnected with her siblings and they've gotten very close."

"That would be hard, especially thirty-five or forty years ago."

"She's finally found peace, but it took her a long time to get it. I guess it is hard to receive forgiveness in your church?"

"Hard? I guess it depends on what the person has done and how much they want to repent."

"It took my mother a long time. I've made a lot of mistakes. It would probably take me longer and may even be impossible," he said, glancing away for a moment. "And maybe you wouldn't even consider being with someone like me."

A stab of pain went through Andi's heart. She knew that not only would God forgive him, but that she could love and accept him for who he was now.

"No," she said. "It may take some work and time, but repentance—forgiveness—is very possible."

He pulled in a deep breath and released it, nodding slowly as her words sunk in.

"I really wish I'd known all of this earlier in my life. I wouldn't have done a lot of the stupid things I did. I was really confused when I was younger. I thought my grandparents never came to visit us because we lived so far away. I was about sixteen when my mom finally told me what happened to her and why she left her family and the Church. My sister was getting married and wanted to invite my grandparents to her wedding. Things have gotten a lot better since all of that happened, though."

"Which one was your mother on the show?" Andi asked, suddenly realizing she didn't know.

"She worked at one of the events, helping with the food."

Andi thought for a minute. "Wait, was she the woman who talked to me about eating because she liked how I was snarfing down all the pineapple and shrimp?"

"That would be my mother. That's one of the things that's annoyed her about a lot of the girls I've dated. She likes a girl who will eat a decent meal, someone healthy and strong."

"She probably wouldn't appreciate that I had an eating disorder for many years."

"She was concerned when she read it on your bio, but after she met you, she said she changed her mind. She likes that you have overcome it and that you've done what it takes to get yourself healthy again. She read all the bios on all the girls. Having to overcome challenges herself, she appreciates that you did, too. Both of my parents mentioned that there was something different about you, something genuine." He shrugged. "They liked a few of the other girls, too. Not all of them, though."

"Does that mean they got to tell you their opinions?"

"Absolutely. That was the whole point. Their input means so much to me now. There was a time I didn't listen to them, and I made a huge mess of my life. They keep me grounded and focused on what's most important." He grinned and rolled his eyes. "Of course, Silas made sure there was plenty of drama in the show and suggested I keep a few girls around purely for the sake of keeping the drama alive."

"I guess that's the reality of *reality* shows."

"That the shows are manipulated and edited to keep viewers interested?"

She nodded.

"I'm afraid so. I tried to keep it real, but I felt like I was an actor at times." He rolled his eyes. "I can't go into it now, but you'll see it for yourself. You are going to watch the show, aren't you?"

"Yes, but I'm nervous. I have a hard time watching myself on film."

He seemed surprised by her revelation. "You've done so much in front of the camera."

"True, but I have had some horrible experiences on live television that have left me scarred for life."

"You mean the time you fell off the bench when you were promoting your fitness machine on QVC?"

She groaned and covered her face with her hands, but he reclaimed her hand quickly. "You saw that?"

"I thought it made you even more lovable and sweet." He stroked her cheek with his finger.

"Have you seen how many hits it got on YouTube? Of course, sales skyrocketed after it happened. I guess the public is okay with a few flaws. You wouldn't believe how many requests for appearances I got after that."

"See, there you go being wonderful again," he said. "That's why I had to come and find you. I had to see if what I felt on the island is real. Haven't you wondered too? Haven't you thought about me?"

She closed her eyes and nodded. "That's part of the reason I'm here in New York. To get my mind off of you."

"Did it work?"

"Well, not anymore."

He burst out laughing then he pulled her into a hug and kissed her forehead.

"I couldn't forget about you either. But there has to be more to a relationship than just attraction and having so much in common." She knew she had to admit to it because anything else would be a straight-up lie.

"Because that's not enough?"

"It's huge, it is, but what I believe is who I am. I can't separate it. It's a lifestyle, not just something I do for a couple of hours on Sunday."

"Andi, I almost feel like I've been raised Mormon. I'm familiar with so much of it—I just didn't realize it."

"That's wonderful, Michael. It is. But when I get married, it's going to be forever, which means it has to happen in the temple."

"And only members can go inside?"

She nodded. "And not all members can go there—just those who are worthy to go in."

He pulled a face. "So it's not enough just to get baptized. I have to become an elite member?"

She laughed. "No. It's not like that. Any member who lives the teachings of the Church is worthy to go there. You know—obey the Word of Wisdom, pay tithing, go to church, stuff like that."

"Oh, okay. Well, I'm not opposed to finding out more about what the Church teaches. I believe there has to be a better way to live, you know? That's a start, isn't it?"

His expression was serious, his eyes sincere. He was stealing her heart, piece by piece.

"Yes, that is a start."

He hugged her again and held her close. "I've dreamed about this for weeks. Holding you again. Being with you and feeling that special something you have. Talking about things that matter to both of us. Getting to know you better."

"How are we going to do this? We can't be seen, can we?"

"Silas said as long as he doesn't know what I'm up to, he doesn't care. We just have to be careful. This is a big city—I bet it's easy to blend in, even with the paparazzi lurking around. I've never been here before. There's so much I want to see."

"I'd love to show you around. I'd like to get to know you better, without Silas around."

His phone vibrated on the coffee table where he had put it. He glanced over.

"Who is it?"

"Silas."

They looked at each other and burst out laughing.

"I'm sure he knows you're here," she said.

"Most likely. I'll call him back."

She thought for another moment. "And Lauryn knows you're here."

"I contacted her to ask her to help me find you."

"How did you get—"

"It was in your paperwork. You had to provide some contact information."

She remembered putting Lauryn's number down as an alternate contact source.

"Ah, very clever of you."

"I was desperate. I wanted to find you. I wanted to tell you that I was sorry you got sent home and that you had that horrible experience with the plane, especially after what happened on the zipline. I knew it had to have been terrifying."

"It was. But it helped me grow, and I learned a lot through it all."

"I'm glad you feel that way about it. And now you have all these wonderful things going on in your life."

"Some of them are wonderful, some of them scary."

"Scary?" His forehead wrinkled.

"Yeah, but you didn't come to hear about that."

"If it involves you, I want to know."

She found herself telling him about the freaky things that had happened recently, briefly describing the current threats and close calls her friends had had.

"And then to come back to the apartment and find that someone had broken in and stolen the Butterfly Box. Well, it's just so bizarre. Whoever is behind this is really serious about hurting one of us, or all of us."

"I'm not going to leave you alone until we find out who is behind this," he said, his eyes dark. "You're sure the authorities are working on it?" He held her hand even tighter.

"Yes, they are. And they have a few leads, but they keep running into dead ends. They are hopeful, though. I guess they've discovered some new information in Ava's case, at least, that might be helpful. We're going to have a big conference call soon to talk about it."

"Until then, I'll be your bodyguard. I won't let anyone hurt you."

The feeling of gratitude, security, and joy melted together, forcing her to exercise control of her emotions. She'd never met anyone as wonderful as Michael. She began to pray that the Lord would guide them and bless him to be open to the Spirit and to the gospel. For both his sake and hers.

Chapter 32

"I JUST FEEL SO GUILTY that the box got stolen," Andi said glumly.

"It's not your fault," Lauryn reassured her for the umpteenth time. "Someone got past security, and that's all it took."

"I wonder if we'll ever get it back." Andi thought of all the treasures inside as well as the memories and its priceless sentimental value. "I know Emma told me she didn't blame me, but she has this tone to her voice that tells me she does."

"Ignore the tone," Lauryn said. "She's just upset it happened—she's not upset at you."

"I hope so. I feel terrible about it."

"The police are doing all they can. Maybe they'll figure out who took it—that would help the detectives in St. George."

"That would be nice. It has to be connected somehow." Andi had racked her brain a million times trying to figure out what was going on, but whoever was terrorizing them had left no traces of their identity.

"So you and Michael are going out again?" Lauryn asked casually. She slid off her heels and propped her feet on the coffee table.

"Yes, as long as we're careful about it. I think he must have scoured the Internet looking for things to do in New York off the beaten path—to avoid the paparazzi. We've done things and seen things I didn't even know were here."

"That's sweet. I really like him," Lauryn said. "He couldn't be more handsome or thoughtful. It's going to be hard for you when he leaves, isn't it?"

"I'm trying not to think about it." Andi needed to take a calming breath. Then she burst out, "Lauryn, what am I going to do? I think I'm falling in love with him."

"Whoa," Lauryn sat up. "Andi, that's big stuff. I mean, he's awesome, he really is, but he's not—"

Andi put her hands over her ears and squeezed her eyes shut. "I know. I know."

But her efforts to block Lauryn's words didn't erase the reality of the situation. She had to face it.

"Sweetie, I'm sorry. I know you're well aware of that fact."

"I am. Painfully. Granted, he says he's interested in investigating the Church, but I don't want him doing it just for me, you know?"

Lauryn nodded.

"But his mom has taught him a lot about the gospel without him even realizing it. It's not that big of a stretch for him."

Lauryn nodded again.

"Still, the more I see him and the closer I get to him, the harder it will be if he doesn't end up accepting the gospel."

Lauryn opened her mouth to speak then closed it again.

"On the other hand, he's had all these high-profile relationships with these celebrities and was a big Hollywood-scene partier. I don't know if I could live with that. What do I do?"

"Have you prayed about it?"

"Of course. All the time. Even when we're on dates, I'll pray so I can see something in him, some reason why I shouldn't be with him."

"Are you praying for God to make everything right, or are you praying that you'll understand His will and plan for you?"

Andi blew out a long breath. "Mostly for Him to make it right, I guess."

"As wonderful as Michael is, you need to find out if you're even supposed to be with him. Sometimes something is good, but that doesn't mean it's *good* for us. Kind of like cheesecake."

The words took some time to sink in, but their truth was evident.

"If it is right, you'll be able to handle Michael's past. You will be able to keep from judging him and accept him for who he is, in spite of what he's done in the past."

"You're right." She shut her eyes and thought about it. She had faith that she could put his past behind them and that they could move forward together.

"I have to ask, though—what about Cooper?" Lauryn asked.

Andi groaned and buried her face in her hands. "I'm a horrible person. I know I'm hurting him. I don't want to. I don't mean to, but I am."

"I've run out of excuses to give him."

"I need to just come clean with him. I'm just so torn. I want Michael, but he's not a member; Cooper is a member, but I'm just not in love with him." She looked at Lauryn. "What do I do?"

"Be honest with Cooper. And with yourself. This is a decision only you can make, but if I were you, I'd spend a lot of time on my knees."

"I fell asleep on my knees last night," Andi told her. "I've never had my legs fall asleep from the knees down before."

"You'll make the right decision."

"I sure hope so. I need the Butterfly Box," Andi said with a whimper.

"We don't need the box," Lauryn said with determination. "We can all still fast and pray together. I'll text everyone and tell them. Tomorrow is Sunday; we can do it then."

"Thank you." Andi knew that her prayers had been selfish. She'd wanted to make things happen her way—and that wasn't how it worked. Now she needed to pray for the strength that if Michael wasn't right for her, she'd be able to walk away.

* * *

"Detective Hutchinson, how are you?"

"I called to tell you we've had a breakthrough in the case. We've been able to identify a number where some of the threatening texts might have originated."

Andi gasped. "You have? Who is it?"

"We haven't identified the owner of the cell phone account because it's listed as a company phone, but you might find this interesting: the number is a St. George one."

"Really? Someone from St. George is sending those texts?"

"Apparently so. Have you girls tried to narrow down any people who would know all of you from the time Ava was alive?"

"Yes, all we can come up with are family, Church, and school members. After high school, we all went different directions and don't really have any common friends."

"I've checked out all the individuals you listed who might be possible suspects, and they all check out, except one, who is already in jail."

"Joey Donovich."

"Right, but he's in on drug-related charges, and he's been incarcerated for five years. Unless he's got help on the outside, it's not him."

Andi remembered how much she'd liked Joey in high school. He was in drama and had a beautiful singing voice. He had liked Ava all through high school, and she was cold and sometimes mean to him. Still, he didn't seem the type who would murder someone.

"Thanks for your help, detective. We'll keep working on names and let you know."

"I have a feeling something is going to break open," the detective said. "If all of this is connected, then he'll most likely make contact again soon. If I were you girls, I wouldn't go anywhere unaccompanied."

Andi swallowed hard. "We won't," she choked out.

* * *

Under cover of sunglasses and hats, Michael and Andi ate lunch at Carnegie Deli that afternoon then rode the subway to Canal Street. He'd heard so much about it, he wanted to see what it was all about—and Andi figured that although it was a hot destination for tourists, they'd be able to blend in with the crowd sure to be there. Of course, Kirk had been right about the paparazzi swarming the Kardashian sisters. One of the girls had just broken off a relationship with some NFL football star, and the news was flooding the tabloids and Internet. She had no idea how celebrities put up with all the attention.

They browsed through the long row of narrow shops for more than an hour, admiring the craftsmanship of the knock-off brands, even making a few purchases. Andi spotted some Chanel sunglasses she liked, and Michael noticed a Dolce and Gabbana belt.

"You like purse, lady? You want purse? I have Gucci, Prada, Coachy handbag."

Andi laughed at the way the woman said the designer names so quickly, adding the *y* to Coach.

"No, thank you."

"Only thirty-five dollar."

"That's okay, thank you."

"Okay, I do thirty. You like this one?" The elderly Asian woman held up a gorgeous bronze-brown-toned purse with large polished buckles and other embellishments on it.

Dang, I do like it, Andi thought with a suppressed smile. She knew not to take the first offer, and she shook her head and acted like she was ready to leave.

"You buy sunglasses, I give you purse for twenty-five."

She caught Michael's eye and the smile on his lips. "How much for the sunglasses?"

"Fifteen. I give you both for forty. Good deal."

"I don't have forty. Sorry."

"How much you got, lady?"

"Thirty."

"No good." The woman hung up the purse.

Darn. She wanted that purse. She looked at Michael, and he winked with understanding. He cleared his throat and said, "Will you give it to her for thirty-five?"

The woman thought for a split second then said, "Okay. Deal."

Michael counted out the cash and handed it to her. She stuffed it into the pocket of her apron then put the purse in a black plastic bag.

"Wait!" Andi said. "Did you put the designer name on it?"

The woman huffed and shook her head then reached into her pocket and pulled out a metal plaque. She slid the prongs into the faux leather and fastened the name securely.

Without saying anything else, she handed the bag to Andi and walked away.

"Are you getting the belt?" Andi asked Michael.

"Nah, I want to keep looking."

"Here, let me give you back the money you paid her," Andi said, fishing for her wallet.

"Absolutely not."

"Hey, I didn't mean for you to buy it."

She pulled the purse from the bag so she could look at it again. "Oh no!"

"What?"

"It says *Parda*!"

Michael burst out laughing.

"Darn it! What a waste of money. Except I do really like the purse."

She opened her wallet to give him the cash for the purchase.

"I don't want your money," he said with a laugh. "It's not every day that I buy my girl a Parda handbag."

Andi laughed. The more she thought about it, the funnier it got. They both found themselves giggling as they continued to walk through the throngs of people packed along the street.

As they waited on the street corner for the light to change so they could cross, Andi's phone vibrated.

It was Drake.

She groaned inwardly. She wasn't going to answer. He'd been way too intense with her during their last phone call, so much so that she called

Kirk and left him a message telling him about her concerns. She wanted to talk to him about taking over the contact with Drake and the company so that their relationship could remain professional. Besides, she knew he was still counting on her to go to *Love Me Crazy* with him—something she wasn't exactly looking forward to.

The phone indicated that he left a message. She was curious to know what he said in the message, so she quickly activated her voice mail and listened.

> *Andi, hi, this is Drake. I must apologize for my behavior earlier. I have been under a lot of stress lately, and I fear I might have taken that out on you. Please accept my apologies. I have decided to go out of town for a few days. We might have to move your photo shoot a couple of days back. Let me know what your schedule is like next week. I'm traveling to the resort site in Nassau to see how progress is coming along. The spa is near completion, and I will take some pictures so I can show you when I return. In the meantime, I'm going to have to cancel our date for dinner and the show. However, would you still be interested in the tickets for the show tonight and dinner reservations? Everything is already paid for. I have even arranged for my driver to pick you up and remain with you the entire evening.*
>
> *I'm at the airport now and am getting ready to board. I will be out of touch until I arrive in Nassau. Please take a friend and enjoy your evening. The driver is planning on picking you up at five thirty for dinner, but if you need to change the time, I will give you the number.*
>
> *Have a wonderful time tonight. It will be unforgettable, I promise. We'll talk soon.*

"Everything okay?" Michael asked.

"Yeah, I think so." She felt immensely relieved about the canceled date. As they walked toward the subway entrance, she asked, "Did you have anything special planned for tonight?"

"I thought we could go out to dinner then walk around Times Square. That's about the only thing we haven't done yet. Why?"

"How would you like to go out to dinner and to the hottest new Broadway show in town?"

His forehead crinkled as he thought for a moment, then his jaw dropped. After a moment, he said, "Wait a minute, you're not talking about *Love Me Crazy,* are you? I've tried to get tickets to that ever since you told me you wanted to see it."

"The guy from Paradise Bay Resort and Spa just left a message. He had tickets for tonight but decided to go out of town. He offered them to me along with dinner and his personal driver."

"Personal driver?"

"Yes. Not that I mind walking or riding the subway."

A big grin appeared on his face. "Should we do it?"

"You're kidding, right?"

His expression grew thoughtful again, then he burst with excitement, saying, "Of course we should do it!" He scooped her into a hug and swung her around, nearly wiping out a couple of mean-looking linebacker-sized men wearing black leather jackets and black sunglasses in ninety degree weather.

"Sorry," Michael said to them.

The men looked like they wanted to rip our Michael's heart, but he didn't give them a chance. He grabbed Andi's hand and pulled her down the stairs leading to the subway. Luckily the men didn't follow.

Andi texted Kirk and told him the update on Drake and that he had made a nice gesture to apologize for his earlier behavior. She explained that he had gone to Nassau to check on the resort and that she would call him later. Right now, she had an amazing evening with Michael ahead.

* * *

"Hey," Cooper said when Andi answered her phone. "How are you? I got worried when you didn't respond to my text earlier."

"Hi," Andi said. "I'm sorry. I have been so swamped today."

"I just wondered if you were busy again tonight."

"Actually, yes. I am." She didn't know how to tell him or what to say. She had to have a talk with him and tell him what was going on. She owed him that.

"Oh," he said, not masking his disappointment.

"I'm sorry. I have plans tonight."

"That's too bad. I was hoping to take you to the Comedy Club. One of my favorites is performing tonight."

The awkwardness of the situation held her tongue. She didn't want to make him feel bad because she had another date. Besides, she wasn't sure she was ready to tell him Michael was in town.

"No problem," he said. "I understand. I'll call you tomorrow. Have a fun night."

He hung up before she had a chance to say good-bye. The last thing she wanted to do was hurt him, but she knew she was.

"Everything okay?" Lauryn asked when she got off the phone.

"That was Cooper. He's upset."

"When are you going to tell him what's going on?"

"Tomorrow. I promise. I care too much about him to not be up front with him."

Lauryn agreed. "I don't know if he told you, but his last girlfriend dumped him without any warning. I know he likes you a lot, but I also wonder if he's just also enjoying having a girlfriend. He's the kind of guy who loves being in a relationship. He really loves showering attention on a girl."

"I've noticed." Andi didn't say that as much as she loved all the attention, at times it felt, well, suffocating. "I've never been so pampered and fussed over in my life."

"Honestly, it would drive me a little crazy," Lauryn said.

Andi's mouth dropped open.

"It would. I am all for being treated like a queen, but Cooper almost smothers girls with all of his attention. The right girl will love it."

She was relieved to hear Lauryn say that. "I want to love it, but I feel the same. It's just a little too much for me."

Lauryn frowned. "I understand. I just hate to see him hurt again. He's so hard to work with when he's sad. But he does some of his best work when he's like this. Maybe this will help him with his new line."

Andi laughed. "Hey, whatever I can do to help." Andi looked in the mirror, trying to decide if she should change her diamond stud earrings to a dangling rhinestone pair.

"So, are you excited?" Lauryn asked. She held Andi's bolero jacket that matched the kelly-green cocktail dress she was wearing.

Andi decided to leave in the earrings she was already wearing and slid her arms into the sleeves of the jacket.

"I feel like Cinderella on my way to the ball. Without ugly stepsisters of course. Or glass slippers. Or . . . okay, never mind. Totally not Cinderella, but I do feel like a princess."

"You guys lucked out getting to go to that show. Tickets on eBay are going for five hundred dollars a pair."

Andi looked in the mirror, loving her reflection. The gorgeous chiffon cocktail dress was one of Lauryn's new creations and reminiscent of 1960s Hollywood glamour. They'd pinned Andi's long, blonde-highlighted hair up into a messy bun on the side and curled loose tendrils of hair down the sides of her face and neck.

"This dress is amazing. How lucky am I to have you for a friend? I just wish I could show it off. Drake texted and told me he arranged for us to go in the back way, and we have box seats, so we should be able to avoid the media."

"He's really connected. I hope to be so important someday."

"You don't think he's in the mafia, do you?" Andi asked, quizzically raising an eyebrow.

Lauryn's phone buzzed. "I doubt it. Was he wearing a pinkie ring when you met?"

Andi laughed. "I don't think so."

While Lauryn checked her phone, Andi spritzed her hair one more time with hair spray.

Lauryn stood, frozen, staring at the phone in her hand.

"What's up?" Andi asked, unscrewing the wand from her lip gloss.

Lauryn didn't answer.

"Lauryn?" Andi turned, noticing that her friend's face had washed pale. "What's wrong? What is it?"

Lauryn offered her phone to Andi.

Another one bites the dust, the text message said.

"What? I don't get it. Who sent this?"

"I don't know that number."

"What does it mean? We need to call and find out who sent this."

Andi brought up the number and pushed the call button.

"It's ringing," she said. She hadn't even thought about what she would say when the person answered, but she didn't care. She was getting sick of the games and the harassment. It was time for this to end.

The ringing continued, with no person or voice mail picking up.

"Nothing," she said, closing the phone and giving it back to Lauryn. "We need to report this to Detective Hutchins in St. George. You never know."

"I don't want you to go tonight," Lauryn said, her expression still pale and fearful.

"I couldn't be safer tonight," Andi reassured her. "Michael will be with me the entire time. Well, unless I use the ladies' room, but I will have him wait outside the door. I promise. Really, you don't need to worry. He would risk his life to protect me. But what about you? You're the one home alone, with Jace still gone. We should have someone come and be with you."

She shook her head. "I'll be fine. Roger is next door. He used to play for the Giants. I saw him earlier, and he and his wife are going to be home all night. They're really upset about the break-in and are starting a neighborhood watch program in the building. Believe me, I'm safe."

A buzz from the intercom let them know Michael had arrived and was on his way up.

"I hate to leave you," Andi said.

"I'll be fine. Go have fun."

"Okay," she said reluctantly. "Thanks for letting me use the dress." She gave her friend a hug. "Be safe while I'm gone."

"I will. Oh, I forgot to tell you. I finally heard back from Emma. She said that she would love to fast. They ended up having to bottle-feed Demetria, so she can join us. She also sent me a text about some pictures you sent her."

"Of the front of your store?" Andi decided to add a pack of gum and some tissues to her clutch purse.

"Yes, and another one. I'll forward them to you. I didn't understand what she was saying about them."

A knock on the door stopped the conversation. Andi and Lauryn looked at each other with excitement.

"You stand there. I'll open it," Lauryn said.

Andi felt ridiculous but couldn't help wanting to see Michael's reaction. She felt absolutely incredible with her hair done and wearing Lauryn's dress.

"Good evening, Lauryn. How are you?" Michael gave Lauryn a kiss on the cheek after she welcomed him inside. He stepped back and gasped. "Andi," he whispered. He paused for a moment then walked toward her, an approving smile on his face. "Oh, wow. Andi, you look amazing."

"Thank you," she said, accepting his hug and kiss on each cheek. "You look pretty amazing yourself."

His suit was black with a dark gray pinstripe in it, and his tie was . . . kelly-green paisley.

"Wait a minute." She held him at arm's length. "How did you come up with such a great tie to match?" She glanced over at her friend, her eyebrow raised accusingly. "You two were in cahoots over this, weren't you?"

"Guilty," Lauryn said. "He's actually doing me a favor. This tie is from my new men's line, and Michael was nice enough to test-drive it for me. Of course, it doesn't hurt that he looks like a male model, either."

Andi smiled. "He does, doesn't he? Too bad we can't let anyone else see us."

"Actually, that's not altogether true," Michael said.

"It's not? Our contract strictly states—"

"Silas called. He has an idea."

Andi groaned. "I'm afraid to ask."

"I know. I was surprised when he called and told me what he was thinking, but if you're game, I am."

Andi closed her eyes, mentally preparing herself. "Okay, I'm ready."

"Ever since our story hit the front page, there has been a flood of response to the network and the website for the show. In fact, if you look online at the most searched stories, we're number one."

Andi and Lauryn looked at each other, both of them wide-eyed, their mouths hanging open. Then Andi started to laugh. "You mean we beat the Kardashians?"

"You know what they say—no publicity is bad publicity," Lauryn said. "I guess that's true."

"Exactly," Michael said. "Silas has decided he wants us to go out. In fact, he wants to make sure we get seen, so he's contacted a couple of newspapers to alert them."

"He's turning this into a publicity stunt. I don't know how I feel about this." Andi tried to consider all the possible implications, adding, "And I don't know if Drake will like it." She worried that she'd already tested the limits of that situation, and she didn't want to risk losing the job.

"My guess is that they will feel the same. The publicity could potentially help them," Lauryn said.

"You think?" Andi felt like she needed to call Kirk and see what he thought. At least with his approval, she wouldn't be blindsiding him if the plan went bad.

"If you're worried about it, let's not do it," Michael said. "Really, there is no pressure."

"But the media already knows we'll be there?"

"Silas can call and let them know plans have changed."

Why she would want to help Silas, she didn't know, but she figured that if Kirk thought it was okay, she would do it.

"Okay, let me call my manager and make sure he's okay with it. If he says yes, then I'm fine with it."

She went into the bedroom and shut the door to make the call.

"Hey, Kirk, I have a question for you." She explained the situation to him. "I had to ask you since Drake has gone to Nassau to check on the resort and is out of touch."

"I'll be honest," Kirk said. "I didn't think he was really all that upset about you being in the tabloid. You know what they say—no publicity is bad publicity."

Andi laughed. "That's what Lauryn said."

"I can see why Silas wants you two to be discovered. It's going to cause a frenzy of interest in the show. He's smart to turn it into some free advertising. Of course, you'll have the spotlight again. Still, it will help boost ratings."

"So you think I should do it?"

"I know you don't want all that attention again, but with the show behind you, I don't see any harm, really. Just ignore all the headlines and speculation when they hit the newsstands. I'll handle the media. By the way, did you say Drake went to the resort?"

"Yes, he wants to check on the progress for himself. He said the spa is nearly done and the hotel is close. I'm dying to see pictures."

"I'll check around and see what I can find online then forward it to you. I have a friend down there who works in real estate. I'll bet he can give me some information and maybe even pictures."

"That would be great. I'm getting so excited."

"Have fun tonight, Andi. Don't worry about the press. You've been in this business long enough to know how it works."

"I know. I've tried really hard to avoid scandals, though."

"As your manager, I've appreciated that. But I'm telling you, it's all free publicity for you, for Paradise Bay Resort and Spa, and for the *Looking for Mrs. Right* show. It's your choice, but free press is hard to pass up."

Andi groaned, knowing he was right. "All right. Thanks, Kirk. I'd better run. We have a driver waiting for us."

They said good-bye, and she rejoined Michael and Lauryn in the living room.

"Well?" Michael asked.

"He said not to worry about it. In fact, he said the exact thing about publicity that you did, Lauryn."

"It's true," Lauryn said. "When Laszlo Molnar tried to destroy my first show, it actually ended up helping me and hurting him. You two go have fun."

"Thanks for you help," Andi said, giving her friend a hug.

"I'll be with you. It will be okay; we'll face them together," Michael assured her.

She didn't doubt it for a second. She felt safe and secure with him.

Michael offered her his elbow, and Andi looped her arm through his. It felt wonderful being with him, and she was glad they didn't have to hide or worry about being recognized. And since it was almost the last evening they would have together for a while, she was happy they could enjoy it.

Chapter 33

THE DRIVER OF THE TOWN car didn't speak English well, but they managed to learn that he was going to take them to dinner and wait for them then take them to the show.

While they traveled through the cab- and pedestrian-packed streets of New York, Michael and Andi held hands and talked, learning more about each other's families and backgrounds. She loved learning about his life on the island and how different their upbringings were.

Michael's phone vibrated, and he checked to see who the caller was.

"Andi, I'm so sorry, but do you mind if I take this call quickly? It's my friend in Africa."

"No, please, go right ahead."

While Michael visited with his friend, she decided to check her messages. She was annoyed with all the junk e-mail she was getting and needed to figure out how to change her settings to screen out some of the garbage.

Lauryn had forwarded Emma's messages, and she opened them remembering that Lauryn had said that Emma's text hadn't made sense.

"Hey, check out the pictures you sent. The guy in the background is the same in both."

She clicked on the first picture, and her phone started to download it. She frowned as she waited. She hadn't noticed a guy in the background before.

While the picture was downloading, the driver pulled up to the curb in the back of a high-rise building. Andi peered out the window and saw that they were in an alleyway that was dark and strewn with garbage.

Michael noticed they'd arrived as well and ended his call. His expression reflected the same confusion as Andi felt.

"Where are we?" he asked.

"Drake said he would bring us in through the back entrance," she said slowly. "I guess this is it."

"This is supposed to be a nice restaurant?" Michael asked.

"Yes. He only does fancy and expensive."

The driver got out and opened their door.

"You're sure this is the right place?" Michael asked him as he stepped out of the car then turned to assist Andi.

"Yes," the man said with a thick Indian accent. "It is correct."

"So, where will you be waiting to take us to the show?"

The man's forehead wrinkled with confusion.

"You know, after dinner? Do we just come here?"

"Come here? Yes, this is the place." He seemed nervous and kept looking at his watch. Andi wondered if Drake had given him a tight schedule for the evening. If they didn't finish dinner in time, they might not make it to the show.

Michael handed the man a ten-dollar bill then took Andi's hand.

The man bowed and said, "Oh, sir, one more thing. You are to go to the thirty-fourth floor."

"Thank you," Michael said.

They walked to the back door, which, to Andi's surprise, actually opened. The place looked devoid of the activity one would expect of a busy restaurant.

Once inside, they both commented on the dark, dirty surroundings and wondered if they really were in the right place.

"I'm going to ask him again," Michael said, holding Andi's hand firmly. "I don't think he totally understood what we were asking."

Michael opened the back door and looked both directions. "He's gone."

"Maybe he thought we'd be awhile and went to get some food for himself," she offered.

"He's probably smart if this is any indication of the restaurant we're going to."

"Drake wouldn't send us to a dump, I promise. Come on, let's find the elevator." Andi was trying her best to stay upbeat and positive. She wanted this night to be memorable.

"Tell me more about Drake. What do you know about him?" Michael asked as they followed a dimly lit hallway lined with unmarked doors on either side.

They were about to turn around when Andi spied a sign that pointed the directions of the exit and elevator.

"You sure you don't want to go that way?" Michael pointed to the exit.

Andi laughed. "If this place is bad, we'll leave. I promise."

They pushed the call button and heard the elevator engage.

"I don't even have any idea where we are. Were you paying attention to where he brought us?"

"No," she said. "I think we're downtown, but I'm not really sure. I wish Drake was available in case we need to call him."

"If we need to leave, we can just take a taxi somewhere else to eat. It'll be okay." He slipped his arm around her waist and kept her close to his side.

The bell dinged, and the elevator doors opened. Andi was glad the car was well lit and clean. She felt her hopes lift.

As the elevator began the climb to the thirty-fourth floor, she remembered the picture that had been downloading on her phone. She pushed the screen on her phone to bring it up. She couldn't see anyone in the background, but then again, the picture was small. Touching the screen several more times enlarged the photo, and she was able to scan around the picture until she saw a man standing behind a tree. He wasn't looking her way, but his profile was clear.

"That is so weird," she said.

"What's weird?"

"The guy in this picture looks a lot like Drake." She showed Michael then decided to bring up the other photo. Her phone quickly loaded the picture, and again she enlarged it and scanned around until she found another image of a man.

"Does that look like the same person to you?" she asked. She wasn't one hundred percent sure, but she could see why Emma thought it was.

"I can't say for sure, but yeah, I think it is. Were these taken at the same place?"

"No," she answered, "not the same day or place."

"Probably not the same person, then." Michael looked closer then shook his head.

"I just can't tell. I wish the light was better. The guy in the first picture totally looks like Drake, though." She couldn't understand why he would be in the background, however.

"Interesting. Were you in an area of the city he would go?"

She thought about it and figured that, yes, it was possible. Drake was fashionably dressed when she had seen him, so it would make sense for him to be in the garment district. Still, why wouldn't he say something, unless he hadn't seen her?

"I'll have to ask him," she said, wishing the uneasy feeling she was having would go away.

Her phone vibrated with an incoming call and startled her. She nearly dropped her phone.

It was Kirk.

"Hello?" she said, glad he was calling. She wanted to tell him about the bizarre night so far.

He spoke, but his voice was garbled and then the connection was lost.

"No service?" Michael asked.

She shook her head. She'd have to call him back when they got to the restaurant.

The elevator slowed as they approached the floor.

She reached for Michael's hand and held on tightly.

"Don't worry. One way or another we are going to have a nice dinner tonight," he said with a wink.

"Good, because I purposely didn't eat much today, and I'm starving."

The elevator landed on the floor and remained there for a moment. Finally the doors opened.

The hallway was as dimly lit as the one on the ground floor. By the looks of it, the place was abandoned. There was no carpeting on the floor, and lumber, tools, Sheetrock, and other construction items littered the hallway.

"Okay, that's it. We're leaving." Michael pushed the button for the doors to close. "I'd rather have a hot dog on the street than stay in this creepy place another minute."

"Good! I agree. Let's get out of here."

They waited for the doors to shut.

"I knew this couldn't be the right place," Andi said. "This is just an old, abandoned apartment building."

"Why don't you text your friend Drake and tell him to call when he lands. Maybe he can explain this."

He pushed the button again, but the doors remained open. There didn't seem to be a response from any of the buttons.

"How comfortable are those high heels?" Michael asked, looking down at Andi's feet.

"Thirty-four flights?" She pulled a face. "At least it's down."

"That's my girl."

He led her from the elevator and navigated the construction-strewn obstacle course of a hallway to the doorway marked Stairs.

Michael reached for the knob and turned it. It was locked.

Andi's heartbeat escalated. "Michael?"

"Yeah, that's weird. Who locks the door to a stairwell?"

"Let's try the elevator again," Andi suggested.

They sidestepped around the debris and returned to the elevator.

"Wait," Andi said before stepping inside. "Before I lose service, I want to call Kirk and Lauryn just to let them know what's going on."

"Good idea," Michael said.

She dialed Kirk's number, but her call went straight to voice mail. "Shoot!" she said then left him a message. However, after she hung up she realized that he had probably left a message for her when his call didn't go through.

Sure enough, when she checked there was a new message. In fact, there were two.

"Andi, I don't want you to panic," his message started, "but I just found out something very disturbing. There is no record at all of any construction of Paradise Bay Resort and Spa. In fact, there has been a hold on all new construction while the planning commission rezones some of the commercial land in Nassau. I don't know what to make of it, but according to my friend, Paradise Bay Resort and Spa doesn't exist. I'm going to do some more digging, but in the meantime, I'd like you to let me take care of all interaction with Drake and his so-called company. I don't want you to get involved any further until I get to the bottom of this."

Her shocked expression clearly alarmed Michael. "What's wrong?" he asked, moving closer to her.

"Listen to this," she said, replaying the message for him.

He listened, his own expression shifting from confusion to concern.

"I don't understand," she said when he handed her phone back to her. "What's going on? What is this?"

"Don't worry. We're getting out of here." He began to push buttons and tried to access the emergency equipment in the elevator, none of which was operating.

Andi accessed her second message, and when she heard Drake's voice, she grabbed Michael's arm and said, "Listen to this!"

She hit the speakerphone button.

"Welcome, Andi. For starters, I want you to know that I've waited nineteen years for this day. I've failed to deal with you and the others up until now, but this time I will be successful. I'm sure you've missed your dear friend, Ava. Soon, you'll be able to see her. All of you will."

Andi's stomach lurched, and she felt nauseated. "Oh my gosh!" she cried. "Michael, we are in major trouble." She pulled in a sob as tears filled her eyes and spilled onto her cheeks. Another wave of nausea hit her, and the contents of her stomach threatened to surge to the surface. She lunged for a bucket nearby and threw up several times.

"My gosh, Andi, what's going on? Are you okay?" He flew to her side, holding her arm as she panted and began to sob. "Andi, tell me what's happening. Who's Ava?"

There was a dirt-stained cloth next to the bucket, which she used to wipe her nose and mouth.

"Oh, Michael." She fell against him and buried her head.

"You're shaking like a leaf, Andi. What did he mean by that message? Tell me what's going on?"

"Ava's . . . my friend . . ."

"Okay."

"She's dead." Andi broke down and sobbed even harder. Her mind whirled. What did Drake have to do with this? She didn't understand.

"Andi, you have to get ahold of yourself. You have to tell me what this is about."

She nodded, wiping at her cheeks and nose. "This is bad, Michael. This is so bad. I'm scared."

"Take a deep breath and talk to me. I'm not going to let anything happen to you."

She did as he said and managed to stop crying. Somehow Drake was going to do something to all of them. But how? And who was he? And why did he want them dead? Had he been the one responsible for Ava's so-called accident?

She began to explain as quickly as possible about Ava's death and the suspicious circumstances surrounding it. She also gave him more detail about the strange messages and occurrences each of them had experienced.

"The zipline, that emergency landing," she said, "I don't think those were accidents. The face in those pictures on my phone, that's him. All this time he's been setting me up."

"Wait a minute." Michael held his head. "You're saying he killed Ava and now he's after you and your friends?"

"Yes. I don't know how or why, but it's Drake. But I don't even know who Drake is. Why does he want to hurt us? I don't understand."

"I don't either, but right now that's the least of our troubles. We need to get out of here. Fast."

"The elevator isn't working."

"He's rigged it somehow, but I think I can get that door to the stairwell open." He jumped to his feet and scavenged through the mass of equipment and tools until he found what he was looking for.

Wielding a hammer, Michael rushed to the door and began slamming the doorknob with the hammer. With each blow the doorknob got looser and looser. Andi's hopes that they would escape soared. What if Michael hadn't been here with her? What if she had gone on this date with Drake by herself?

The thought turned her stomach again, and she leaned against the wall to take some steadying breaths.

After several more powerful strikes with the hammer, the doorknob crashed to the floor and bounced several times, landing in a pile of scrap Sheetrock.

Michael gave the door a shove, but it didn't budge. He hit it again, this time ramming his shoulder into it full force. Nothing.

"It must be bolted on the inside. Call 911," he said.

He began hitting the door with the hammer, and Andi felt herself sliding down the wall. They had to get out.

Andi pushed the numbers, but the call didn't go through. Again, no service. She needed to get near a window. Testing the doors in the hallway, she found them locked, one after another.

The rhythmic pounding of the hammer on the steel door echoed through the building. Where was Drake? What was his plan for them?

Only two doors left.

Grabbing the knob, she gave a turn. To her surprise, the knob rotated.

Fear struck her like a blow from the hammer. What was behind the door? Drake had thought through every detail—he hadn't left the room unlocked for no reason. "Michael," she said in a whisper.

He didn't stop.

"Michael!"

He quit swinging and looked at her as sweat trickled down the sides of his face.

"It's unlocked."

The realization hit him. "Wait. Don't go in without me."

Holding the hammer overhead, ready to swing, he joined her by the door. Then, nodding for her to stand back, he kicked the door open.

The room was dark except for a half dozen or so spotlights shining on the wall, illuminating a collage of pictures inside each ring of light. The windows in the room were boarded or bricked in, and the walls had been painted black.

After glancing around for another minute until he was satisfied it was safe to enter, Michael tried to flip on the light switch, but found none. Andi walked up to the first mass of pictures covering about a four-foot square.

"It's Ava," Andi said, looking at the first grouping of snapshots. Some of the photos showed Ava posing, but most of the others were candid, taken when she wasn't aware a camera was on her. Andi had never seen the pictures before.

She shuddered violently as her gaze shifted to the shelf on the wall, which contained a single black silk rose.

"Who's this?" Michael asked, moving to the next set of pictures.

Andi studied the girl in the candid shots for a moment. She too had a black rose on her shelf. "It's Amber Jeffries. She died earlier this summer."

Some of the pictures were of Amber through her bedroom window. Andi shuddered again. There were pictures of Amber when she was older, with her husband and children. She blinked back the tears that filled her eyes. Drake—or whoever he was—had killed someone's mother and wife.

They moved to the next set of pictures.

"Jennifer Robbins! She died years ago in a . . ." Andi felt sick to her stomach again. Jennifer had been a cheerleader with Ava. "She died in a car crash that was listed as an accident. Michael." She turned to Michael, swallowing the bile that stung her throat. "Drake is responsible for their deaths." She shivered and turned to the doorway. "He wants to kill me. I've dragged you into something horrible."

"Shh," Michael said, pulling her close. "We're going to get out of this."

"Let me try my phone again. Have you tried yours?"

"I don't get service," he said. "I'll bet anything he's using a cell-phone blocker to scramble the signals."

"A what?"

"It's a device that sends out radio waves—schools and hospitals use them. It's illegal, but I doubt Drake is too worried about that."

"What do we do?"

"I don't know, but this guy has been thinking about this for a long time."

"Yeah. Apparently since high school," she said in a strangled voice.

Michael's eyes grew wide then, and he tightened his hold on her.

"What's wrong?" she asked.

He tried to stop her, but she turned and saw what he was looking at.

"Oh my gosh!" Her knees buckled, and he held her tightly so she wouldn't collapse on the ground.

There on the wall was a collage of pictures of Andi, some of them as current as the *Looking for Mrs. Right* show. The snapshots taken were pictures that only someone involved in the show would be able to get.

"He had a crew member involved in this," Michael said. "There's no other way those pictures could have been taken."

"That means everything that happened on the show wasn't an accident. He was trying to kill me." Andi buried her head in Michael's shoulder. She didn't understand any of this. Who would do something so twisted and horrible?

"I'm assuming the rest of the pictures are your friends?" Michael said, assisting her to the next grouping, where she found Lauryn's pictures. Tears streamed down her face as she thought of the danger her friends were in. Seeing their smiling faces in the pictures, unaware that any minute they could be attacked, was more than she could bear.

"We have to stop him," Andi said. "This can't happen." Lauryn's, Emma's, Chloe's, and Jocelyn's pictures each reflected vibrant, incredible women. They weren't just her friends—they were her sisters. She would not let anything happen to them.

"He's probably here, Andi, waiting for us to make a move." Michael kept his arms protectively around her. "Do you know what this Drake person's connection to you and your friends is? Anyone in high school who was angry with you?"

"No! None at all. I don't remember having any enemies in school. I don't know, Michael. I don't know."

"It doesn't really matter right now. We just need to get out of here. If I keep trying, I think I can get the door open."

Without looking back, Andi left the room, taking Michael with her. Her survival instincts were starting to kick in. Anger was replacing fear.

Michael slammed into the door, the hammer leaving a dent with each blow, but the door remained strong.

Andi looked around for an object she could use to help. She had to do something to get them out of there faster.

None of the other tools was of any use—screwdrivers, wrenches, measuring tapes, paintbrushes—nothing would do any damage to the door.

Leaning against the wall, Andi stared across the hall at the room that housed the death shrines. Thankfully, no black roses lay upon the shelves in front of her friend's pictures—yet.

He—Drake, or whoever he was—had left that door open on purpose. He'd wanted her to find it. To see what he was doing.

She suddenly realized that there was one last door she hadn't tried, and she was leaning on the wall right next to it.

If she could find a window, maybe she could get the attention of someone in the next building. She had to try. All the other windows were bricked up.

She grabbed the handle, holding her breath as she turned the knob.

As she twisted the handle, she gasped, and Michael whipped around to see if she was okay.

"The last door," she said after opening it a crack. "It's unlocked."

Chapter 34

Michael put his finger up to his lips and tiptoed toward her as he cocked the hammer in his hand.

She stepped back out of the way, her heart beating wildly in her chest. Just as he was about ready to kick the door in, the lights flickered then went black.

"Michael," Andi whispered, barely squeaking out his name.

"I'm right here," he said. His hand connected with her arm as he moved to her side.

"I'm afraid to go in," she whispered. Whoever was responsible for all of this was surely waiting for her, for them, inside that room.

"We don't have to go in. I can use my phone for light and keep working on the door," he offered.

"Do you think you'll ever get through it?"

"I think so. Eventually." Then he sighed. "Maybe. It's like it's welded shut."

In the dark silence, even their whispers sounded like cannons.

"I hate just sitting here, Michael. What should we do?"

"We can look inside that room, or we can wait until he comes to us."

"No, I refuse to sit and do nothing," she told him in a strained whisper.

"All right, then," he said, letting go of her arm. "Let's do it."

She dug deep for courage to confront whatever, or whoever, was in that room. If they didn't do something, they could be stuck in this building until one of them . . .

She shuddered, thinking about what could happen and wondering why Drake would do this to her and Michael. How did all of this tie in with the past?

They held on to each other as the silence crowded in on them.

"We have to do this," Michael said, so softly she almost couldn't hear him.

"I know."

"Whatever happens, I want you to know I'm falling in love with you. I will do whatever it takes to protect you."

"Oh, Michael," she said with a whimper. "I feel the same way. We have to be okay. This can't be the end."

"It won't be." He kissed her. "Are you ready?"

"Yes." Her voice shook as she answered through her silent tears.

He shined the light of his phone on the door and stood back about two feet. Then, drawing in a sharp, deep breath, he reared back and slammed his foot into the door, sending it crashing open and against the inside wall.

Silence followed as they both froze to see what would happen next. Everything remained still.

They peered through the doorway, and Andi said, "Oh no," and started to cry harder.

There, in the middle of the floor with a spotlight beaming down on it from the ceiling was the Butterfly Box.

"Is that the box that got stolen?"

"Yes."

"Stay here," Michael said.

He took two cautious steps into the room and shined his cell phone light all around. Andi followed the light and saw that the room appeared empty. Again, the window was boarded up and the walls were painted black. Andi looked at the boards, desperately searching for a sudden flash of inspiration on how to escape. But there was none. Even if they took the effort to pry the boards away from the windows, they were too high up for anyone to notice.

She looked at the box illuminated by the light, feeling violated and vulnerable. He'd broken into Lauryn's apartment and taken the box. He'd lured Andi and Michael here to this trap to terrorize them, and she didn't dare even think what else he had in mind. She wasn't sure exactly who Drake was, but she knew he wasn't messing around. This was serious, and terrifying.

The light on Michael's phone began to dim. It was losing power.

Andi quickly opened her phone to give him light.

He took one more step into the room then stopped.

Andi's breath caught in her throat.

"I have an idea," he said. "Why didn't I think of this before?"

"What?" she asked, praying he'd thought up some way to save them.

He looked around to see if they were alone. Andi was sure there were hidden cameras watching their every move, so she quickly stepped back toward the doorway so he could whisper to her.

"The escape hatch in the elevator," he said softly. "We can get out through there."

That's right, she realized with a sudden start. She'd seen people use those in movies. It sounded dangerous and frightening, but staying here doing nothing was worse.

She nodded her agreement.

He reached for her hand and took a step toward the open elevator doors.

"Wait," Andi said. "I want the box."

"I'll get it," he said without hesitation.

She nodded as more tears threatened. How could she have done this without him?

Feeling panic and fear in her heart as she watched him walk slowly into the room, Andi wrung her hands and prayed for his safety.

He was almost to the box when a sudden click and a hiss sounded in the darkness. Michael froze.

He looked down. The trip wire, barely visible in the darkness, glistened like a glass web from a deadly spider.

Without waiting to see what was going to happen, Michael grabbed the Butterfly Box and flew from the room. He grabbed Andi's hand as he came through the doorway.

At that exact moment, a loud pop sounded. Then, with a deafening blast, a plume of fire exploded in the room.

Andi screamed, and Michael pulled her toward the elevator.

Forcing herself to calm down, Andi held the box and shone the light of her phone up on the ceiling of the elevator while Michael checked for the escape hatch. When he found the panel that moved, he climbed onto the bars that ran around the inside perimeter of the elevator car. Bracing himself against the corner of the car, he pushed the panel open with both hands.

Andi glanced back in terror as the roar of flames and dancing light illuminated the hallway. Smoke from the fire began to fill the air, the acrid fumes burning her nose and throat.

He ducked his head inside the hole and used the light from his phone to scan their options.

"We can get out!" he yelled, his voice muffled through the ceiling.

He came back inside and hopped down from the bars. "There's a doorway to the roof up there. We can get out," he said urgently. "I'll help you up first."

She nodded, fighting the paralyzing effect of the fear consuming her. It was this or stay and die.

With his help, she hoisted herself up onto the bars, wishing she weren't in heels and a cocktail dress. Michael held her legs firmly in place while she stood to get to the ceiling exit. Once she had her torso through the hole, she found some metal bars to hold on to while she pulled her body up. Trembling but fueled by adrenaline, she grabbed on to the thick steel cables of the elevator and stood to give Michael room to pull himself through.

"Here," he said, shoving the Butterfly Box through the hole. She scooped it up and held it under one arm while keeping her other hand firmly wrapped around the elevator cable.

A moment later Michael's head appeared, and then he lifted himself up through the hole and climbed on top of the elevator and stood with her.

There was a seven-foot difference between the top of the elevator and the bottom of the door leading to the roof, with a small ledge inside the elevator shaft.

"I need to get up on that ledge," Michael said, coughing as curls of smoke drifted after them from below.

He tried several times, but the ledge was so narrow he couldn't get the right leverage to get up onto it. Andi was terrified he was going to fall through the space between the elevator and the shaft and plummet to his death.

"You're going to have to do it," he said after a few more tries, sweat beading on his forehead in the growing heat. "Stand on my shoulders."

Her first thought was to tell him he was crazy, but she knew it was their only option.

Swallowing hard and trying not to cry, Andi kicked off her high heels. Michael knelt down on one knee, and she swung one leg over and sat on his shoulders. Still holding the cable, he slowly stood, making a great effort to keep his balance.

He turned to the doorway, and Andi first tried to get to the doorknob and turn it from her seated position, but she couldn't reach it. Holding on to the ledge, she focused on the door and the small crack of light that shone around the door frame. Freedom was on the other side.

She got one foot onto Michael's shoulder then carefully got the other one up and slowly straightened her legs. Walking her hands up the door, she stood completely erect and found the doorknob.

When she turned the knob, the locked clicked and the door opened about an inch. There was a chain-link lock at the top of the door. She would have to stand on the ledge.

"You can do it," Michael encouraged with another fit of coughing. Smoke was coming up through the hatch more heavily now. He needed to shut it, but it was out of reach while he held her.

Using the doorknob to steady herself, Andi put her right foot on the five-inch ledge and then her left. Michael held her feet steady while she reached up and unlocked the chain latch. The door to the rooftop flew open.

She fell through the door, nearly landing on the ground, and hurried to turn around to help Michael.

He quickly slammed the hatch shut to prevent more smoke from coming through then handed the Butterfly Box up to her.

Andi shoved it off to the side with her foot so she could kneel down and help him.

"I think I can do it," Michael said. "Just grab one of my arms with both of yours so I can get one of my feet on the ledge."

Andi put her left foot against the outside wall and braced her thigh against the door frame, then reached down and grabbed Michael's arm. His other hand held the ledge for support.

"Ready?" he asked.

"Yes."

No sooner had she answered than a loud clank echoed through the elevator shaft and the cable and wheels began to turn. The elevator was going down.

"Hurry!" Andi screamed.

Michael swung his leg up and hooked his foot onto the ledge just as the elevator dropped downward, leaving him hanging.

Andi hung on to him, ignoring the pain tearing at her arms as her muscles strained to hold him.

"My foot's slipping," he cried.

"No!" she screamed as she dug deep and pulled with every ounce of strength she possessed.

She managed to get his shoulders and arms through the doorway, then she reached down and grabbed his belt and pulled while he scrambled the rest of the way through.

They both collapsed as he made it safely onto the rooftop. They were scraped and bleeding but safe for the moment. Andi and Michael both gulped in lungfuls of fresh air, trying to rid themselves of the choking smoke. He reached down and took one of her hands in his, holding it tightly to his chest as they lay where they had fallen, still unable to believe what had just happened.

"My phone!" Andi cried suddenly. "Maybe I have service now."

She flipped open her phone and saw that she did have service, but her power was almost gone.

She quickly dialed 911.

"This is 911, what is your emergency?"

" My phone is about to die. Please listen."

"Ma'am, can you give me your—"

"You have to listen! My friend and I are trapped on the roof of a high-rise in lower Manhattan. The top floor is on fire. We were trapped here by a man named Drake—"

She looked at the dead phone in her hand. *"No!"* she screamed and began to sob.

"They'll find us!" Michael grabbed her hands and looked her straight in the eye. "You told them enough. They'll find us. We need to get off this roof, though."

He helped her to her feet, and they ran to the edge of the building. There was another building connected to the one they were standing on, but it was a twelve-foot drop to the top of that roof. They raced to the other sides, only to find a sheer drop to the ground below.

"We have to jump," Michael said firmly.

"What?"

"Look." Michael pointed at the doorway they'd escaped from. Black smoke was beginning to pour out of it. "We have no choice."

"I can't."

"Andi, I know you can. I'll go first, then I'll try to help you from down there. It's all in the landing, remember? Here," he said. "I'll take this." He took the Butterfly Box from her. "We're almost home free."

She nodded quickly, tears streaming down her face. "Be careful."

They kissed briefly, then he turned, climbed onto the ledge, and pushed off.

Andi leaned over and watched him sail through the air, landing hard on the rooftop below. His left leg buckled on impact, and he fell over and rolled several times then lay motionless in a crumpled heap. The Butterfly Box rolled and skidded till it finally stopped about twenty feet away.

"Michael!" she screamed. "Michael."

Fear clutched her heart. She had to help him.

"Oh my gosh!" she whimpered as she forced herself up onto the ledge. She looked over the side and let out a cry. "Father help me. Help us. Be with Michael. Please let him be okay. Help me make it."

She paused to take another breath before she dropped—just as the door to the roof of the other building opened.

And out walked Drake Hampton.

Chapter 35

JUST THE SIGHT OF HIM fueled a bright-burning anger inside her, turning her fears to fury.

She expected to be afraid of him, but she wasn't. She felt a need to mangle him.

He began to laugh when he saw her and started walking her direction, stopping momentarily at Michael's body and giving it a shove with his foot to turn him over.

"Who are you?" Andi yelled. "Why are you doing this to us?"

He walked closer to the wall upon which Andi was perched and looked up, laughing again. "You know, I don't remember you being stupid in school. I seem to remember you making the honor roll."

Searching her memory, Andi tried to figure out who Drake really was, but nothing clicked.

The smoke blowing from behind her stung her eyes as she stared at him, and she found she didn't know which was worse, the raging inferno behind her or the psychopath below.

He held up his arms. "Here, I'll try to catch you." His mocking laugh assured her he had no regard for her whatsoever.

A couple of loud pops from the fire behind her drew her attention briefly. Flames leapt from the doorway that was quickly disappearing in the inferno, and suddenly there was a deafening explosion that rocked the building.

With a lurch, Andi tumbled off the ledge.

She landed on her feet but quickly collapsed to the ground and rolled from her backside to her shoulders, up over her head, and onto her stomach.

The impact knocked the wind out of her, which panicked her far more the screaming pain in her knees, back, and neck.

She began to see black spots before her eyes as her body grew limp from a lack of oxygen.

Like she was at the end of a tunnel, Drake's laugh echoed distantly in her ears as she felt herself slipping.

Slowly, her muscles relaxed enough for her to catch her breath, and she shut her eyes to focus on getting air into her lungs. A sharp pain in her head hit with lightning speed, expanding until she thought her skull would crack. Then it quickly subsided.

Gasping for as much air as she could, she lay there, wondering what was next. Surely Drake would have to realize he'd gone too far and come to his senses.

But she was wrong.

His foot slammed into her ribs full force, and she felt several of them cracking beneath the blow. She doubled over and felt her eyes bulge from the pain and pressure.

"How do you like that?" he snarled. "The pain you feel is nothing, *nothing,* like the pain you and your friends caused me." He added another savage kick and screamed, "You think I'm a monster? Well, you created this monster! I did nothing to you, *nothing*. But you and your friends managed to destroy my life."

He kicked her again.

"And now you get to know how it feels. You and all your friends who played a part," he kicked her again, "in what happened."

Sobs were caught in Andi's throat. The excruciating pain had caused her to go numb, and she felt like her spirit was separating from her body somehow. Yet she was completely conscious of what was happening.

With astonishing clarity, she thought about what he was saying and began to put the pieces together. The picture of a boy—a misfit, an outcast—began to form. A boy who kept to himself and was a target for bullies. His face appeared in her mind, and she suddenly matched it with Drake's voice—but not his appearance.

The two faces swam before her in the fog of pain and fear: the boy—Herbie Finke—and the man who stood before her now, who called himself Drake Hampton. They didn't look anything alike—Herbie had had a full head of bushy red hair; even his features had been different—and yet . . .

He must have seen the realization on her face because he said, "That's right, Andi. I don't look like the same Herbie you remember, do I? Well, that's your fault, isn't it?"

Her mind spun as she recalled dozens of instances where she remembered seeing the boy Herbie getting beat up by cruel boys at school, being scolded by teachers for not getting his schoolwork done—and being teased by her friends. Not being mean-spirited, she had never taken it too far. In fact, she'd always felt sorry for Herbie. Ava had been the worst. And Amber. They'd seemed to get some delight out of tormenting him.

Andi had never actually done anything directly to Herbie, but she'd never stopped any of her friends from being mean to him. She'd never stood up for him.

She was jarred back to the present by Herbie screaming at her, telling her all of the despicable things that had happened to him in school—the cruelty, the pain, the humiliation. His tirade continued, and he began talking about his home and the abuse he'd suffered.

Andi lay still, wanting to hold her ribs so that it wouldn't hurt so much to breathe, but she didn't want to draw Herbie's attention.

". . . and she just let him beat the crap out of me, time after time. Over and over." Herbie was sobbing as he babbled. "After he finished with me, he'd beat her. Night after night after night." He stopped walking, breaking down into hysteric sobs. After a moment, he stopped. "That last night was different," he whispered then laughed sardonically. "I had come home crying again because of you and your friends. He hated it when I cried, and when he was drunk it was worse. This time he was drunk enough to smash his own son's face against the banister." His voice became more high-pitched, and Andi listened in mute horror as he continued. "He broke my jaw, my nose, and both my cheekbones. When I saw myself in the mirror afterward, I passed out."

Drake's voice broke, and he let out an anguished noise halfway between a laugh and a sob. "But there was one good thing about him being drunk—he didn't have much of a sense of balance. My mom always said drinking would kill him. I guess it did."

Terrified that when he stopped talking he would come after her, Andi prayed for God to deliver her. She prayed help would arrive in time.

"Seeing him fall down those stairs after I pushed him, lying at the bottom, broken, bleeding . . . dead, felt good. Yeah." He drew out the word. "It felt real good. I took care of the problem, and no one ever found out. Not even my mother. Not even you and your horrible friends—until now."

He walked to her side and bent down so he could speak directly in her ear, his breath hot on her cheek as Andi's mind reeled. "I was in the hospital for weeks after that—my face was totally destroyed, and the reconstructive surgery was more painful than you can imagine. When I was released, my mother moved us away. But I never forgot about you and your friends. About the role you played." She heard his teeth grinding together as he sucked in a breath. "If it hadn't been for you, he might have left me alone that night. The bullying I went through after all the surgeries was even worse than what I'd experienced from your little friends. But you set it all in motion."

Andi was finding it hard to breathe. It all made sense. The flash of familiarity she'd had when she first met Drake. The threats and attacks against her friends. "Herbie, I'm so sorry for what happened to you—but it was your father who injured you. And it was awful that the kids used to bully you, but look at yourself! You can't do this!" she cried desperately, knowing that he could snap at any moment. She had to keep him talking. Herbie had already killed several people. It wouldn't be a problem for him to kill her now.

"Oh, I can do this. I can do anything I want. I've enjoyed having fun with you and your friends. You probably didn't realize I was there with you in Hawaii."

"What?" His comment didn't make sense to her.

"Yes. The centipede, the zipline, the airplane . . . all me. Silas never suspected, either. I was right there the entire time. Watching. Waiting."

She thought for a moment. "Who—"

"Remember Tom?" He smiled. "You had no idea, did you? I thought I had you when that strap broke."

Andi heard the wail of sirens in the distance.

Herbie swore. Then he turned on Andi. "You!" Instead of kicking her, he shoved her body with his foot to flip her onto her back.

A moment later his knee was digging into her stomach, and his hands were around her throat. "It's time to finish what I started in Hawaii."

Terror paralyzed her. She couldn't move.

Suddenly a pair of hands came from behind Herbie and yanked him off of Andi. *Michael!*

Andi barely had strength to raise her head, but when she did, she saw Herbie and Michael roll across the rooftop.

Somehow Herbie ended up on top and began pummeling Michael with his fists. Michael's leg was twisted at a horrible angle, and one of his arms was pinned behind his back.

Blood spurted from Michael's nose as Herbie smashed his fist into Michael's face.

He was going to kill him.

Andi pushed herself up and scanned around for something to use as a weapon. Even with sirens coming, she couldn't waste a second. The next blow could end Michael's life.

She dragged herself to the only object available, the Butterfly Box. Making as little movement as possible, she half crawled, half dragged herself up behind Herbie. Then, stifling the scream that rose to her throat as the pain from her broken ribs threatened to engulf her, she rose up and lifted the solid wood box overhead to bring it crashing down on his head just as he turned and looked at her with fiery red vengeance in his eyes.

Like a felled pine, he toppled to the side, landing with a thud on the ground, his forehead gashed and bleeding, pieces of the Butterfly Box and its contents scattered everywhere.

Andi turned to Michael. His eyes were shut; he lay motionless.

"Michael, no. Please," she cried, holding her ribs with one hand and using her other hand to scoot closer to him. She laid her ear on his chest to find a heartbeat, but another explosion from the fire filled the air with noise and smoke.

They had to move, or they would be consumed by the raging fire that was growing in size and fury by the second.

Using what energy she had left, she grabbed Michael and pulled him onto her legs then tried to drag him away from the oncoming flames, but she didn't have any strength left.

"Help!" she cried, her voice getting swallowed up by the roar of the fire. She tried to move him again but began coughing from the smoke and collapsed. The only thing she had enough energy left to do was close her eyes.

* * *

Andi looked out the hospital window at the blustery day. Clouds had descended on the city, and it had been raining nonstop. She was aware she'd been here for some time—she'd been out for most of it—but this morning she'd awakened to the dark clouds and unbearable pain over her entire body.

With several broken ribs, it hurt to breathe or move; her ankle was fractured, her hip and shoulder were banged up, and her back was bruised all up and down her spine.

A tap on the door made her turn her head, forcing her to let out a cry of pain. The muscles up the back of her neck were sore too. "Come in," she croaked out.

To her pleasant surprise, Lauryn poked her head inside the room. Then, to her further delight, Chloe walked in, and right behind her were Cooper and Jace.

Lauryn had a giant bouquet of flowers, and Chloe had balloons.

"Hey, Andi, you up for visitors?" Lauryn asked, setting the flowers on a shelf.

"Chloe! I didn't expect to see you." Andi held her ribs as she spoke.

"Oh, sweetie," Chloe said, her voice catching in her throat. She gave Andi a careful hug. "Look at you."

"I look like I'm dressed up for Halloween," Andi tried to joke. "What are you doing here?"

"Well, I was going to come so we could go to Greece, so I just figured I'd come anyway."

"Boy, I've really messed that up."

"Are you kidding?" Chloe remarked. "Don't even think about that right now. The good news is it's all over."

"Yeah," Lauryn said. "Finally."

Andi nodded, not trusting herself to speak. She'd been an emotional wreck since she woke up, remembering everything that had happened and everything she'd learned about Herbie.

"Andi," Cooper said, seeming to sense her unease.

"Hi, Cooper." He gave her a kiss on the cheek and a gentle hug.

"You doing okay?"

"I'm okay. I'm still shook up, but I'm okay."

"I can't believe what happened to you and Michael. That must have been terrifying."

She nodded.

"Hey, Cooper," she said softly. "I'm really sorry about everything. I never meant to hurt you. I was just trying to sort out my feelings. He showed up unexpectedly and—"

"Shh," Cooper said. "It's okay. We can talk later. It's all good." He nodded toward Chloe. "You know what I mean?"

She raised her eyebrows, and he nodded. If any girl could appreciate the kind of guy Cooper was, it would be Chloe.

"Thank you for everything." She gave him another hug, and he stepped back to let Jace take a turn.

"Wow, Andi, that guy really did a number on you, didn't he?" Jace said. "You have kind of a Quasimodo vibe going. I like it."

The comment was so out of the blue and unexpected that it caught Andi off guard. Her laughter turned to groans because it hurt so badly. "Don't make me laugh," she told him. "It's too painful."

"Sorry," Jace said. "Good thing you're in such good shape and you're healthy. No way you could've survived it otherwise." Jace gave her a squeeze.

Andi just nodded. It was probably true, but she wasn't really up to talking about the incident at the moment. She'd been trying to process all of it and still couldn't wrap her head around what had happened. The fire department and paramedics had arrived on the scene and rescued them from the inferno, but Herbie had succumbed to smoke inhalation shortly after arriving in the emergency room and died. His troubled, sad life was over. He could never hurt them again. They would never know the details about what he'd done to Ava's car to cause the accident that killed her, but the police had gathered enough information after searching his apartment to know without a doubt that Herbie had tampered with the brakes, causing her to lose control and crash. Chloe had nearly suffered the same fate but had been fortunate enough to survive the ordeal. She would always struggle with lasting complications from her injuries but knew they served as a reminder that she had been watched over and protected that day.

She couldn't dwell on that now. Michael was still in intensive care with internal bleeding and head trauma, not to mention a complex fracture of the tibia in his left leg. Because of the nature of the break, he needed to have surgery to pin it back together. He was in critical condition, and Andi couldn't bear the thought of what might happen. His parents were on their way and would be arriving anytime.

Andi noticed Lauryn give some sort of signal to Jace with her eyes, and Jace immediately piped up. "Cooper, I've heard the food here is great, and I haven't had any lunch. You want to join me?"

"Oh, no, thanks. I—ow!" He rubbed his side where Jace elbowed him. "Sure. I'm in the mood for something. Girls?"

Andi didn't answer. Lauryn and Chloe declined.

After the two men left, Andi chuckled. "That was subtle."

"I know," Lauryn said. "I'm sorry. I wanted them to give us some time alone. As hard as this is, we need to talk about it."

Andi shut her eyes.

"I don't think you know this," Lauryn said, "but Drake—I mean, Herbie—called me about an hour after you left for your date."

"He what?" This was the first she'd heard of that.

"Yeah. He called and said he wanted to buy you a gift to help celebrate signing the contract with the resort and he needed my help. I was supposed to meet him at the subway stop at Times Square, underground by the Q train. He said something about going to Tiffany's."

"And you went?" Andi was sick to think he had been after both of them at the same time.

"Of course I did," Lauryn said.

"Did you meet up with him?" Andi asked.

"Well, I waited and waited and was starting to get worried and annoyed when I got a text from him. He told me that he had been delayed and he would just take a taxi and meet me at Tiffany's, so I got in line with the crowd to get on the train. The platform was packed, and as the train approached, the people in the back started pushing forward." Lauryn put her hand on her chest and took in several steadying breaths. Recounting the event obviously brought up the feelings of fear and panic she must have felt.

Chloe reached over and patted Lauryn on the shoulder. "It's okay, sweetie."

Lauryn gave her a weak smile and rested her hand on top of Chloe's, which had remained on Lauryn's shoulder.

"The train came screaming into the tunnel, and all of a sudden I felt two hands on my back. I turned to tell whoever it was to step back, but before I knew it, they gave me a shove and I stumbled forward, heading straight for the tracks.

"Lauryn," Andi cried in alarm, "are you serious?"

"It happened so fast I couldn't even react. I knew what was happening—I saw train tracks and the headlight of the train and heard the screeching of brakes—but I couldn't do anything about it."

"What happened?" Andi asked, knowing that it had to be something good because Lauryn was standing there with them.

"These two kids—huge, mean-looking, totally-had-to-be gang members—reacted immediately and grabbed me before I fell off the platform. Basically they saved my life. They were heroes."

Andi was speechless.

"I will never forget what they did," Lauryn said. "The whole platform erupted in applause."

"What about the person who pushed you?" Andi asked.

"No one saw it happen. Or, if they did, they aren't admitting it. But I know what happened. I know I was pushed. It had to be Herbie."

"I agree," Andi concurred. "You should have seen the pictures, the little death shrines he had for each of us and for Ava and Amber. It was so disturbing and creepy. He's been planning this and stalking us—"

"But why did *he* do all of this?" Lauryn asked.

"I know why," Andi said.

Chloe and Lauryn looked at her with surprise.

Andi told them what she knew, finding it difficult to tell the story but knowing that she had to. When she was finished, she added, "The police thought his father had fallen down the stairs because he was so drunk. And with the condition Herbie was in when they found him, they just rushed him to the hospital. Herbie got away with it. He had taken care of the problem; he'd gotten control of his situation."

Chloe shook her head. "It's just so awful—all of it. But even after what he tried to do to us, I still feel a little sorry for him, you know? It wasn't right of Ava or Amber or anyone to torment him like they did."

"Ava was mean to him," Andi agreed. "She was mean to a lot of people, and you're right—that is terrible."

"She was worse when she was with Amber," Lauryn said. "It would be hard to be on the receiving end of their teasing. It was cruel. Especially to someone who had such a horrible childhood. I never teased him, though."

"Neither did I," Andi said. "But I never tried to stop it, either."

Chloe's expression fell. "I didn't either."

"That doesn't give him a right to kill us!" Lauryn exclaimed.

"In his mind, though, it did—after everything that happened," Andi said. "He'd gotten away with his father's murder and then Ava's. I'm sure he felt confident he was ahead of the law."

A knock on the door stopped the conversation.

"Come in," Andi said.

Cooper poked his head inside. "Michael's parents are here."

Chapter 36

"His parents are here?" Andi swallowed. She'd almost gotten their son killed. How could she face them?

"Jace and I are going to give him a priesthood blessing now. We thought you might want to join us. I'll meet you there—I have to make a quick phone call." With a quick wave, Cooper was gone.

Lauryn and Chloe stood on either side of Andi and assisted her as best they could. Andi was incredibly grateful they were with her right now.

Before they left the room, she had a thought. "Did anyone ask Joss or Emma if they were okay?"

"I did," Chloe said. "I got in touch with both of them that day to warn them. Emma and Nickolas had taken the baby to visit relatives in another city, and Jocelyn and Jack had been staying at her grandmother's house because they were fixing up Jack's house to sell."

"Good," Andi said and breathed easier. "They both texted me, but I told them I'd call later when I was up to talking."

They left the room and walked slowly to the elevator to go up to the ICU. Andi felt her heart begin to race. She would forever be afraid of riding in elevators, but she had to get to Michael, and taking the stairs would be way too painful.

Closing her eyes and keeping her breathing steady, she tried to concentrate on happy thoughts and on the blessings she had: her life, love from family and friends, and the gospel. Most of all, she concentrated on her gratitude to her Heavenly Father for all He had done to help her and her friends in the past few days.

This train of thought made her realize something. "Hey, did Cooper say they were giving Michael a blessing?"

"That's what he said," Lauryn answered. "Why?"

"He's not LDS. Neither are his parents, technically."

"Technically?" Chloe asked, hiking her purse up on her shoulder with one hand while keeping a firm grip on Andi's elbow with the other.

"His mom grew up a member, but she left the Church in her late teens." She didn't get into the details. It wasn't the time or place.

They arrived outside the doors of the ICU, and Lauryn picked up the phone to talk to the nurse.

The door buzzed, and they walked inside.

A somber tone greeted them. The lights were low, and the beeps and whirs of machines filled the large space where a half dozen beds were strategically placed around the room. Fortunately Michael was the only patient at the moment, which made it possible for all of them to visit him together.

Andi felt like she was seeing a dear friend when she laid eyes on Michael's father, Kana. His warm smile and his gentle hug told her more than words ever could.

"It is very good to see you," he said. "I am so sorry about all you've been through." His kind eyes reminded her of what Michael had told her his father had said during the show.

"Mrs. Makua." Andi only remembered seeing Michael's mother the one time, so she didn't feel quite as comfortable with her.

"Andi." Mrs. Makua shook her head. "You poor, sweet girl. What you've been through."

"It definitely seems like something you see on the news or in a movie," Andi told her. "Not reality. I feel horrible that Michael got dragged into it."

Mrs. Makua laid her hand on Andi's cheek. "He is a strong boy and a fighter."

"I'm only here because of him," Andi told her, feeling tears threaten.

"Please, call me Evelyn." The two women hugged, then the group stood in a half circle around Michael's bed.

It was difficult to look at him. Andi couldn't bear the sight of all of his bandages and bruises. It was all her fault for dragging him into the situation. He had been willing to give his life for her, and she loved him deeply for the man he was and the great sacrifice he had made for her.

Tears filled her eyes, and she tried hard to not let them fall, but they spilled onto her cheeks. Would he wake up so she could tell him how sorry she was and how much she loved him?

"I would like you to give him one of your blessings," Kana said, turning to Jace and Cooper.

Jace nodded. "Mrs. Makua, is that all right with you?"

"I haven't decided," she said hesitantly.

"You have told me about this priesthood our entire marriage. Your father gave you blessings, one that saved your life," Kana rebuffed her. "Why would you deny your son this power?"

Evelyn bit her bottom lip, which had started to tremble. Her expression grew pained and emotional.

"Our son would want this," Kana said. "These men only hold back because of their respect for you. But he needs this." Kana paused and swallowed. "He needs this."

Tears trailed down Evelyn's cheeks. She closed her eyes and nodded.

Kana went to his wife and gave her a hug and a kiss on the cheek. They pressed their foreheads together, sharing a moment of closeness.

"Cooper, if you will anoint, I will pronounce the blessing," Jace instructed.

The blessing proceeded, and as the two men laid their hands upon Michael's head, a calming spirit rested on those around the bed.

Andi closed her eyes and listened not only to the healing words and promises Jace was pronouncing upon Michael, but also to the whisperings of the Spirit that gave her the strong impression that God loved her and was aware of everyone present.

Not only did Jace call down the power of heaven to heal Michael, but he also asked a blessing on his parents, that they would allow him to follow what he knew was right and true concerning the gospel. He added that Michael's mother had prepared the way for him to receive the gospel and that it was time for her to return to the fold as well.

The boldness of the prayer and the strength in Jace's voice sent a shiver up Andi's spine. She peeked over at Michael's mother, who had tears streaming down her face, causing Andi to choke up too. She looked at Michael, so still on the bed, and yearned to see his smiling face, hear his laughter, and feel his gentle touch. Her heart had become attached to his—she was lost in love. What they had experienced together sealed the bond they would forever share. She would not, could not, ever give up her conviction to her beliefs, but how could she give up Michael?

After the blessing, Kana and Evelyn hugged, and so did Jace and Lauryn. Then, to Andi's surprise, so did Chloe and Cooper. She didn't want to bring attention to it, but she had to admit that the two of them looked pretty cute together.

She turned her attention to Michael and reached for his hand, wishing there was some response, but his fingers remained limp and lifeless.

"We chose you, you know," Kana said. "It was difficult watching you leave the show."

"It was hard for me to leave," she agreed.

"We were very concerned when your plane went down. You have been through a lot. You're like a cat with nine lives."

Andi laughed. "I hope I have a few lives left."

"So do we. Our Michael cares a great deal about you."

"I know." Andi nodded and swallowed, a knot forming in her throat. "I care about him also."

"But?" Kana asked.

Andi looked at him with surprise. She hadn't eluded to the fact that there was a problem.

"You are strong in your faith. You would not marry outside it?"

"No," Andi said without hesitation. "I know it probably doesn't make sense to you."

"My wife loves her children very much and supports them in everything they do. I know that more than anything she wants them to be happy and to always be part of their lives. If your religion is important to Michael, she will not stand in his way. Or mine."

"Yours?" What was he talking about?

"I have been reading your Book of Mormon, and I have many questions about it. I would like to find out the answers to my questions. I have never had religion in my life, but many of the things in this book make sense to me."

Andi smiled. "That's really wonderful. I'd be happy to sit down and talk with you to see if I can answer your questions. I'd also be happy to get you in touch with the missionaries."

"This priesthood blessing today," he asked. "Do blessings like this happen often?"

"Whenever they are needed. Some blessings are just from a father to a family member. My dad used to give me a blessing before the first day of school every year. It always helped me not be nervous."

Kana's gaze shifted as he thought about her words. "This is good. I like these blessings. I would give good blessings."

Andi laughed, and out of the corner of her eye, she saw Evelyn crack a smile. "I think you would too."

"Hmm, I think I will speak with my wife. Maybe you can stay here with Michael until we return?"

"I would love to."

There was already a chair near Michael's bed, so she sat down in it and picked up Michael's hand, studying his face.

As the others quietly left the room, she closed her eyes and prayed with every ounce of faith she had that he would recover completely and quickly. She loved him, and he loved her. There had to be a way to make it all work out.

* * *

Andi sat in the quiet of the waiting room, leaning forward, her head resting heavily in her hands.

After waiting around the hospital for several hours, Lauryn, Jace, Cooper, and Chloe had left. They all needed food and fresh air. Andi had been released an hour ago from the hospital but didn't want to leave. She was hungry, and her head felt thick and foggy, but she needed to be close to Michael. Just in case.

Michael's parents were in the room with him. His mother hadn't said much to her after the blessing. In fact, she had turned a completely cold shoulder to her. Andi was afraid that Kana was pushing the issue of religion with her and that Andi was getting the blame for being the reason the whole "Mormon" thing was happening.

She shook her head sadly. She'd never pushed the Church on them. All she'd ever done was stand up for her beliefs. Michael and Kana had made their own choices to learn more about the gospel. Evelyn probably didn't see it that way.

Her phone buzzed, waking her from her thoughts. It was a text from Lauryn.

"How is Michael? You want some company?"

Andi texted back. "No change yet. Would love some, if you're not busy."

"We're on our way up, then."

Andi smiled. Lauryn was so busy and had a business to run, yet she would put everything on hold for her friends. And to have Chloe here with them was also a bonus. Their trip to Greece would happen someday soon. She would make sure of it.

Growls from her stomach told her she needed to eat. Her body was still weak and fragile, but she knew she was healing and getting her strength back. It was important that she eat, though.

While she waited for her friends to join her, she went to the vending machine and looked at her choices. Nothing sounded good, but her stomach needed something. She chose a granola bar and some peanut M&Ms. She could get something substantial later.

Munching on the granola bar as she walked back, she thought about everything that had happened over the last few days. It seemed like something out of a Steven King novel. She was sure she'd need therapy for it. But there was a huge relief in knowing that Herbie had been caught and that their nightmares were over. The mystery surrounding Ava's death would finally be solved, and they wouldn't have to live their lives watching over their shoulders.

Shoving the last bite of granola bar in her mouth, she turned the corner to the waiting room and gasped, choking on the oatmeal crumbles in her mouth.

"Oh!" she gasped in a fit of coughing. "Ow. Gosh!" She doubled over, holding her ribs, and coughed hard to clear her throat. There in front of her were Lauryn and Jace, and Chloe and Cooper. But next to them were Jocelyn and Jack, and Emma, Nickolas, and their adorable baby, Demetria.

She stood, rooted to the spot, covering her mouth with her hand as she dissolved into tears.

Her girlfriends surrounded her, holding her, hugging her, and lifting her. She couldn't believe they would come so far to be with her.

"H-how? Wh-when?" she stuttered. "I don't believe this."

Jocelyn gave her an extra hug. "We almost lost you. We wanted to be with you."

Andi turned to Emma, who looked like her wonderful, beautiful self. "Emma. You came all the way from Greece?"

"Nickolas had some business here in the States, so he figured why not come now?"

"I need to see your baby," Andi said. "I can't believe you're a mom."

Emma escorted her over to Nickolas, who held the wide-eyed, angelic Demetria in his arms. "Nickolas, thank you for bringing them. Oh, Emma." She wiped at her cheeks. "She is so precious and so gorgeous."

Emma nodded then slipped her arm around her husband's waist. "I know."

Andi stroked Demetria's soft cheek and the baby smiled. "Look at all that black, curly hair. She is amazing."

"We were very worried about you," Nickolas said. "I thought Emma was going to go into the cockpit and tell the pilot to fly faster, she was so anxious to get here."

"I wanted to. It took forever," Emma said. "Slowest plane ride of my life."

Andi's ribs were screaming at her for moving too much, and she couldn't help grimacing as she swallowed hard and held her sides.

"Do you need to sit?" Lauryn asked her, quickly coming to her aid.

"Yes, I think so." Andi let her friends guide her to the waiting-room chairs.

"You sure you don't need to be in a hospital bed?" Jocelyn asked.

"Do I look that bad?" Andi groaned as she rested back in her chair.

"For someone who's been through so much, I think you look amazing," Jack said.

"Thanks, Jack. And thanks for coming. This is so incredible to see all of you." Andi looked around at her friends, the people who meant the world to her. She felt extremely blessed.

"So, how's Michael?" Chloe asked.

Andi noticed that Chloe and Cooper sat especially close to each other. She again kept the observation to herself, but she hoped that something would happen between them. She loved Cooper, but she wasn't *in love* with him. He would be so happy with someone like Chloe. And Chloe deserved someone who would treasure and adore her like Cooper would.

Andi shrugged, turning her mind back to Chloe's question. "His parents are in with him now. They've been in there for a couple of hours."

"Why aren't you in with them?" Lauryn asked.

"His mom doesn't seem to want me around. I think she's upset about the blessing. I don't know what to do. She blames all of this on me. And she should." A sudden gush of tears erupted. "Because it is all my fault."

"Oh, honey, no," Chloe said, coming to her side and giving her a hug.

"Andi, you can't do that. You can't blame yourself for what happened or the fact that Michael was involved."

"It's hard not to. If he dies—"

Just then the door to the ICU opened, and out walked Michael's parents. Kana had his arms around his wife's shoulders. He was crying, and she was sobbing.

"No," Andi said, shaking her head.

Chloe tightened her hold on Andi, who felt herself slipping.

Evelyn could barely walk she was crying so hard. Kana continued to assist her as they made their way to the group, where Andi could barely manage to breathe.

"He's," Evelyn said, through racks of sobs, "he's . . ."

Finally, Kana spoke. "He's awake."

Andi literally broke down, becoming a puddle of tears in her chair. Lauryn held her on one side and Chloe on the other. Little Demetria seemed to pick up on all the crying, and she too began to cry.

Then, unexpectedly, Evelyn held her arms out toward Andi.

Lauryn and Chloe helped her to her feet and took her the few steps to where Michael's mother waited to embrace her.

"He's awake," she said as she hugged Andi. "He's awake."

Andi didn't know what to say. It was a miracle. There was no doubt in her mind.

Kana patted Andi's shoulder. "The first thing out of his mouth was your name."

Shutting her eyes, Andi thanked God for sparing his life.

"He wants to see you," Evelyn said, pulling back from Andi and looking at her face.

Chapter 37

"Are you sure that's okay?" Andi asked.

Evelyn nodded. "Of course, my dear. He needs to see you."

Lauryn quickly handed several tissues to Andi. She took them and shared one with Evelyn. The two women wiped the tears from their eyes, laughing at the extreme emotion that overwhelmed them both.

"I think I need to sit down," Evelyn said, and Jace jumped to his feet with Cooper right behind. Together they helped Michael's mother to a seat. "Honey, will you help her to the ICU?" she asked, turning to Kana.

Kana wrapped one arm around Andi and supported her as she walked.

"We've seen a miracle," he said quietly to her.

"I know," she answered, still amazed.

He gave her a squeeze and held the door for her. "You go ahead," he said. "You two need this time together."

Andi hugged him as best she could then shuffled through the doorway. She slowly crept toward his bed, where he lay still, his eyes closed.

Her heart filled to overflowing at seeing him there, knowing that he'd finally broken free from death's grip.

In silence she approached his bedside and stood next to the bed, afraid to talk or touch him for fear of startling him.

Then, steeling herself and determined to stay strong, she slowly lowered herself to the chair next to the bed and rested her hand on the mattress for support.

The movement caused Michael to stir, and his eyes slowly opened. Dazed and still in a fog, he turned slightly, a smile playing at the corners of his mouth.

"Andi," he said, wiggling his fingers as if reaching for her.

"I'm here," she said, taking his hand in hers.

"I love you," he said, his voice barely audible.

"I love you too," she answered.

Chapter 38

"DID I DREAM ALL OF this, or did it really happen?" Michael asked.

"I'm afraid it's not a dream," she told him softly.

"Are you okay? Did he hurt you?"

"I'm okay. You're the one who got hurt."

"I'm fine." He shut his eyes. "When I woke up, it was the first thought that flashed through my mind—whether or not you were safe, that is. I couldn't bear the thought of him hurting you."

"I felt the same way about you."

He didn't speak for a few moments. Then he turned his head slightly and opened his eyes. "We need to be together," he said.

"I know."

"Forever."

"Okay," she said, wondering how much of this was the medicine talking.

"There's only one way." His words were slurred together a little, and she moved closer to him, not wanting to miss a single syllable.

"Andi?"

"I'm here."

"We have to go to the temple."

"Michael." She patted the hand she was holding gently, unable to believe what she was hearing.

"Promise me," he said, slipping away to sleep.

"Okay." Obviously he was in limbo somewhere between sleep and consciousness now.

"Andi," he said as forcefully as he could. "Promise."

"I promise, Michael."

* * *

"Shh! It's starting!" Chloe announced. She grabbed Cooper's hand and pulled him onto Lauryn's couch beside her. "Joss, Em, are you watching?"

Over the computer, both girls announced they were there and tuned in. The final episode of *Finding Mrs. Right* was about to air.

Jace and Lauryn shared the large beanbag on the floor while Michael and Andi sat on the love seat directly facing the television.

As the show's opening scenes played across the scene, the group cheered at the clips of Michael carrying Andi on the sand and of them snorkeling in the ocean together.

Michael had his arm around Andi's shoulders and gave her a squeeze. "Silas said I'm still getting hate mail from women all over the country because I didn't keep you on the show."

"Won't they be surprised when we announce our engagement tomorrow!" Andi had never exercised so much patience in her life. The show's producers, mostly Silas, insisted that they keep their relationship on the down low until after the finale. A few of the tabloids actually speculated that Michael was seeing someone from the show and not the woman he was left with at the final lei ceremony.

They had remained indoors for most of the eight weeks during the run of the show, but around week five, Michael was ready to go ballistic. Instead of doing something crazy, he did something wonderful. He bought tickets for Andi and himself, and they flew to Paris for a week, where they could go outdoors and not be recognized.

It took all the willpower they possessed to come back to New York, but Andi had book-tour obligations and needed to carry on as if Michael weren't a part of her life. She was renting the spare room at Lauryn and Jace's apartment for the time being, and Michael had sublet an apartment for six months. He wasn't about to leave Andi after all they'd been through.

Luckily, Cooper knew a wonderful psychiatrist who specialized in posttraumatic stress disorder, and both Andi and Michael attended sessions together. The ordeal had been harrowing and traumatizing, but together they were healing and growing closer to each other day by day.

"How in the world could you even stand that woman?" Jace asked Michael. "I don't care how pretty she is . . . she's a snake."

"Jace!" Lauryn exclaimed.

"Actually, Lauryn, she is. I was scared of her most of the time," Michael confessed. "She was out to win and wasn't about to let anything stand in her way."

"Wait. What are you guys saying?" Emma asked from the computer.

"We can't hear," Jocelyn added. "Talk louder."

Chloe hurried and filled them in during the commercial, and Cooper went to the kitchen to get another piece of pizza for both of them.

Andi caught Lauryn's eye, and they both smiled. Chloe had been flying to New York every other weekend, and Cooper had flown to southern Utah on the opposite weekends. There was no question: the two were a perfect fit and things were moving fast for them.

"Can I get you anything?" Michael whispered in Andi's ear.

"I couldn't be better," she said.

"You said that right," he teased.

She turned to him and gave him a quick kiss. "Thanks for not getting all kissy and intimate with those women. I don't think I could have watched it if you had."

"I made Silas crazy because he kept wanting me to 'take it to the next level' with some of them, but I couldn't. Believe me, I kissed Kimmie once . . . actually, she kissed me, and that's all that happened. I could hardly stand it. That's why I ended up keeping her around to the end." They spoke softly because the others didn't know the outcome. Andi made him tell her because she couldn't stand it any longer.

"Silas made a deal with you?"

"Exactly. He told me that I had to keep Kimmie around for the finale because if I wasn't going to give them any steamy scenes, they'd have to spend more time in editing to make it look like we were getting cozy and intimate. But believe me, we weren't. There was no one but you. I tried to like the other girls, but I just couldn't do it. That's how I knew."

"Knew what?"

"That you were the one for me and it was time to make changes in my life. I knew I wanted to be with you, have a family with you, and spend eternity with you."

She shut her eyes and rested her head against his shoulder. Was it possible that he could be any more amazing? She doubted it.

"Hey, are you two watching the show or what?" Emma said from the computer, which Lauryn had moved to the coffee table.

Andi laughed. "Yes, we are watching. It's kind of anticlimactic since I know the ending, though." She kissed Michael on the cheek, and he shrugged.

"I guess we all know that, but don't say anything about the show. We want to be surprised."

"You're gonna love this," Michael said.

The finale showed Michael with the last three girls: MJ, Tara, and Kimmie.

"I approve of MJ and Tara," Andi said. "They were neat girls."

"MJ was really cool. Tara was a little shy and reserved for me. Nice girl, though."

As the show progressed, Tara left after Michael took her to visit her family in Vale, Colorado. She was emotional and devastated, and Andi didn't blame her. Michael probably broke every girl's heart on the show.

MJ's hometown date was next. She was from Nashville, Tennessee, and her family was as country as corn bread. They even had a hoedown in Michael's honor. Andi couldn't stop laughing at the sight of him trying to square dance with MJ, but when it came to throwing horseshoes, he ticked all of MJ's brothers off by beating them on his first try.

Kimmie was from Boston and took Michael to a Red Sox game followed by a tour of the Freedom Trail.

"I'd never been to Boston, so that was pretty cool. I wanted to shove Kimmie into the harbor a time or two, but other than that, it was a good date," Michael shared with them.

Finally, the moment of truth arrived.

With MJ and Kimmie dressed in gorgeous evening gowns, Kimmie's by the famous designer Francisco, and MJ's (according to Lauryn) off the rack at Macy's, Michael was ready to make his choice.

The girls were standing on a perch with a dramatic drop to the ocean behind them. Flowers and palms were all they needed for the perfect setting.

Wearing a gorgeous black suit with a crisp white shirt and mango-colored tie, Michael walked out from the trees and joined the girls.

Kimmie lifted her chin and gave him an "I got this in the bag" smile.

"I can't stand her!" Emma cried over the computer.

"Our feelings exactly," Lauryn told her.

"Why did you keep her on so long?" Emma demanded.

"Ratings," Michael said. "That's all it was."

"What a bunch of hooey!" Cooper announced. "You've shattered my image of reality shows forever."

The commercial ended, and it was time for the dramatic conclusion.

Michael listened as each girl explained why she was the perfect woman for him and why he should choose her to be his Mrs. Right.

They all listened closely as Kimmie said, "I knew from the first time I met you that we were right for each other. If you choose me, your life will be—"

"Miserable," Michael said.

Everyone burst out laughing.

"Wait, what did she say?" Chloe cried.

"She said that my life would be filled with love and laughter," Michael said.

"Shh, here we go," Chloe said anxiously.

Andi couldn't help anticipating what was about to happen next. Michael didn't tell her how he ended it.

"MJ, Kimmie, you are both amazing. I have enjoyed our time together. MJ," he walked up to her and took her hands in his. "Will you come with me?"

Michael walked with her to a secluded spot where the final lei hung from a beautiful glass stand.

"You are one of the most accomplished, self-assured women I know. I admire you so much. However, I'm not in love with you. I'm sorry."

MJ started to sniff and get teary eyed. She nodded and wiped at her tears. Then she started to shake her head and laugh a little. "Let me be the first to wish you good luck," she said. "You're gonna need it."

The group burst out laughing, and Cooper literally fell onto the floor laughing so hard. "I love her!" he exclaimed as tears leaked onto his cheeks. "That is television history!"

Michael hugged her good-bye and then walked toward his other choice.

"Look at Kimmie's face!" Cooper yelled. "She knows she's got it."

"So she thinks," Chloe said.

"I can't even look at that woman!" Emma said over the computer.

"Here we go. Everyone quiet," Cooper said.

Michael held her hands in his as he spoke to her. "Kimmie, you are passionate—"

"Intense," Michael corrected.

"You are beautiful—"

"Full of Botox and silicone," he elaborated in person.

"And you know exactly what you want in life."

"And a bulldozer," he finished.

Kimmie smiled and nodded like she was agreeing.

"That woman!" Emma screamed.

Chloe shushed her.

"I came on this show looking for Mrs. Right. You're not her."

The room erupted.

Andi felt sorry for the girl, even though she deserved what she got.

Jace and Cooper high-fived, and Emma and Jocelyn were freaking out in Greece and Milford Falls.

"Dude, that is awesome!" Cooper said to Michael.

"Wait, she's going to talk," Lauryn said, pointing at the television.

"At this point, I'm afraid she's going to slug me in the gut," Michael said. "The woman has shoulders like a linebacker."

"You're sending me home?" she asked for clarification, her head cocked to the side, one eyebrow lifting in disbelief.

He nodded. "I am."

She looked at him, her eyes narrowing, her chin dipping low.

"You'd better get out of there," Jace said to Michael.

Michael took one last look at Kimmie, then, without warning, he took off like a shot, running for the cliff, peeling off his suit-coat jacket and ripping off his tie. Then he hopped from foot to foot as he tore off his shoes.

In the background, Kimmie could be heard crying and saying how she'd been humiliated and that he didn't deserve her anyway.

Just before leaping, Michael held up both hands in a "hang loose" signal to the camera then made a perfect swan dive into the ocean below.

Everyone in the room burst into applause.

Andi threw her arms around Michael and hugged him tightly.

"That was incredible!" she said. "So worth waiting for."

"I thought you'd like it," he replied. "I did it for you."

"I love you," she said.

"I love you too."

Epilogue

ANDI STOOD ON THE DECK of the cottage, overlooking the turquoise blue water of the Pacific Ocean. The wind tugged at a few strands of hair and swirled the scent of exotic flowers around her.

Married! She couldn't believe that after a full year of waiting, she and Michael were finally married. They'd been sealed in the Kona Hawaii Temple that morning, with friends and family surrounding them. Her father and Michael's father had sat as witnesses of the ordinance. On either side of them had been her mother and Michael's mother. Her friends and their husbands had attended. If heaven were anything like that moment inside the temple, then she was going to do whatever it took to get there.

The entire wedding party had flown on a chartered jet to Kauai, where a large celebration in honor of their marriage took place.

When she first went on the *Finding Mrs. Right* show, if someone would have asked Andi if she ever thought Michael would join the Church and they would be married in the temple, she would have laughed. Never in her wildest imagination did she think something like this could have happened.

But here they were, sealed together for eternity.

"Hey, there you are." Michael came out onto the deck and stood next to her. "Everything okay?"

"Couldn't be better. Can it always be like this?" she asked thoughtfully.

"Like what?"

"Like paradise? Like heaven?"

"I think we can keep it pretty close," he answered. "I doubt it will be perfect, but as long as we're together, good or bad, it will be heaven."

"Are you excited for the reception tonight?"

"Not as excited as my mom," he said, giving her a kiss on her temple. "And yours. Those two haven't stopped talking since they got together."

"Who would have guessed my mom's college roommate was your mom's best friend growing up." Andi turned toward him, and Michael pulled her close. "Such a small world."

"And here we are, back where it all started."

"It's been quite a journey, hasn't it?" She rested her head on his chest.

"And it's just beginning."

"Speaking of journeys," she said, looking into his face, "how did you ever pull off a honeymoon to Africa without me knowing it?"

"It wasn't easy, but I felt I needed to make up for the fact that you had to miss the expedition in the spring," he said. "Luckily I had all your friends in on it. They helped keep my cover."

"What? Am I the only one who didn't know?"

"Pretty much."

She slapped him playfully on the shoulder. "I'm going to have to keep a close eye on you."

"Promise?" he said, kissing her forehead.

"Hey, did you hear Emma's news?"

"That she and Nickolas are expecting again? Yeah, Nickolas told me. I'm so happy for them."

"Her and Lauryn's babies are due about a month apart." She was so happy for her friends. Lauryn had been trying for so long to get pregnant, and, ironically, just when they had finished the adoption paperwork, they were finally able to conceive.

"Your friends are great," he said.

"Thanks. I completely agree—they are amazing. And how cute are Chloe's little girls? Those dresses Cooper designed for them for the reception are so adorable."

"He's going to love being a daddy, won't he?"

"It's nice to see them so happy." She thought about Chloe and Cooper and the little girls. They'd taken their relationship slow but were talking about marriage as soon as Chloe could get her ties with Roger completely severed.

"Oh, and I was talking to Jack. He said he and Jocelyn are serious about coming with us to Zambia when we go in the spring. They want to go soon, since I guess they plan on starting a family."

Andi sighed contentedly. "That would be the best trip, having them along." She snuggled back to her husband's arms and knew that this was pure bliss. Things wouldn't always be this ideal, but for now she would enjoy the happiness she and each of her friends had at the moment.

"It was nice of Kirk and his wife to come."

"Yeah, he's such a good manager and friend. It's because of him that my book has been on the *New York Times* best-seller list for five months. He's become a marketing maniac. Going to Africa will actually seem like a vacation from all the book tours and appearances. It will be nice to think about helping others and forget about myself for a while."

A knock came at their door.

Michael checked his clock. "We don't have to be down for pictures for an hour. I wonder who that could be."

He went to the door and opened it to find one of the employees holding a beautifully wrapped box.

"Thank you," Michael said, taking the box.

"I was told to tell you to open it now," the boy said.

Michael laughed. "Oh? Well, thank you. We'll do that."

Michael shut the door and brought the package to Andi. "We're supposed to—"

"I heard. Who's it from?"

"It doesn't say," Michael answered, finding no note on the gift.

"There's only one way to find out." They sat down on the bed and put the present between them. Andi tore off the paper then opened the lid. She let out a little gasp when she saw what was inside.

Filled with joy, she lifted a wooden box with a jade butterfly inlay on the lid out of the container.

"It's almost identical," she whispered. She carefully opened the lid and found an envelope addressed to her.

A new box for a new beginning. A reminder of the past, a symbol of the future. The Butterfly Girls, always and forever.

Andi looked up at Michael and smiled.

"There's one more gift to go along with this," he said.

Andi ran her fingers along the delicate butterfly, admiring the beauty and craftsmanship of the box while he got up from the bed and got something out of a drawer. He came back with a small black box wrapped with a gold ribbon.

"What is this?"

"Just open it, you'll see."

She pulled off the ribbon and opened the lid. There on a black velvet bed lay a golden butterfly pendant with six small diamonds on the body of the butterfly.

"Michael, it's just beautiful. Thank you!" She circled her arms around his neck and gave him a brief kiss then a hug. "I love it. I almost feel guilty. The other girls—"

"Also got one."

"What?"

"I got one for each of your friends. Six diamonds for the six Butterfly Girls. I included Ava."

She laughed and shook her head. "How in the world did I ever get so lucky to find you?"

"Luck had nothing to do with it," he said. "Come to think of it, we need to thank Silas."

"Silas! Please tell me you're kidding."

"It was his show that brought us together."

Andi groaned. "It's true. I can't believe it, but you're right."

"I found my Mrs. Right after all."

"And just think, the world has to suffer while Kimmie looks for her Mr. Right."

"Silas will do just about anything for ratings. He'll be at the reception, you know."

"I know. I need to thank him for helping us find each other."

"I think there was some divine help up there. And I'm thinking Ava had something to do with it too." He chuckled. "She didn't have to make it quite so dramatic, though."

Andi giggled then laughed out loud. "If Ava had anything to do with this, it wouldn't be anything less than dramatic."

About the Author

In the fourth grade, Michele Ashman Bell was considered a daydreamer by her teacher and was told on her report card that "she has a vivid imagination and would probably do well with creative writing." Her imagination, combined with a passion for reading, has enabled Michele to live up to her teacher's prediction. She loves writing books, especially those that inspire and edify while entertaining.

Michele grew up in St. George, Utah, where she met her husband at Dixie College before they both served missions—his to Pennsylvania and hers to Frankfurt, Germany, and San Jose, California. Seven months after they returned they were married, and are now the proud parents of four children: Weston, Kendyl, Andrea, and Rachel.

A favorite pastime of Michele's is supporting her children in all of their activities, traveling both in and outside the United States with her husband and family, and doing research for her books. She also recently became scuba certified. Aside from being a busy wife and mother, Michele is an aerobics instructor at the Life Centre Athletic Club near her home, and she currently teaches in the Relief Society and is the activity day leader.

Michele is the best-selling author of several books and a Christmas booklet and has also written children's stories for the Friend magazine.

If you would like to be updated on Michele's newest releases or correspond with her, please send an e-mail to info@covenant-lds.com. You may also write to her in care of Covenant Communications, P.O. Box 416, American Fork, UT 84003-0416.